Dear Readers,

Okay, I'll admit it—authors have favorite books. I know, I know, books are like children, and we don't always want to admit to liking one better than another, but it's true. The Goddess Summoning books are my favorite children.

As with my bestselling young adult series, the House of Night, my Goddess Summoning books celebrate the independence, intelligence, and unique beauty of modern women. My heroes all have one thing in common: they appreciate powerful women and are wise enough to value brains as well as beauty. Aren't respect and appreciation excellent aphrodisiacs?

Delving into mythology and reworking ancient myths is fun! In Goddess of the Sea, *I retell the story of the mermaid Undine, who switches places with a female U.S. Air Force sergeant who needs to do some escaping of her own. In* Goddess of Spring, *I turn my attention to the Persephone/Hades myth and send a modern woman to Hell. Who knew Hell and its brooding god could be hot in so many wonderful, seductive ways?*

From there we took a lovely vacation in Las Vegas with the divine twins, Apollo and Artemis, in Goddess of Light. *And then we come to what is my favorite of all fairy tales, "Beauty and the Beast." In* Goddess of the Rose, *I created my own version of this beloved tale, building a magical realm from whence dreams originate—good and bad—and bringing to life a beast who absolutely took my breath away.*

From fairy tale let's move to comedy and hotness in Goddess of Love. *It is perhaps the funniest and steamiest of all the Goddess Summoning books. After all, Venus herself is my heroine! Finally, we move to an epic story that has intrigued me for a long time, the Trojan War, and Achilles, a hero who I think has deserved his own happily ever after for a couple thousand years. Check out how I manage it in* Warrior Rising.

I hope you enjoy my worlds, and my wish for you is that you discover a spark of goddess magic of your own!

P. C. Cast

Praise for *Goddess of Love*

"Sexy, charming and fun, *Goddess of Love* is the fantasy romance of the year! You will fall in love with this book. (I did!)"

—**Susan Grant**, *New York Times* **bestselling author**

"Ms. Cast has taken mythology, Cinderella, a bit of Shakespeare and a dash of Shaw and mixed them with her own style of comedy for a winning read that is [as] heartwarming as it is funny." —*Huntress Book Reviews*

"As always with Ms. Cast's Goddess saga, the blending of mythology and the modern world feels smooth and effortless . . . Delightful."

—*Midwest Book Review*

"Touching, clever and an excellent heiress to the Goddess Summoning series." —**SmartBitchesTrashyBooks.com**

Warrior Rising

"A riveting page-turner . . . [*Warrior Rising*] is a shining example of just why this author is on the top of many readers' favorites lists. Simply put, it's a Perfect 10 for this reader." —*Romance Reviews Today*

"An amusingly tongue-in-cheek take on the Trojan War featuring a modern-day heroine . . . Funny, irreverent and clever . . . You can't go wrong."

—*The Romance Reader*

Goddess of the Rose

"P. C. Cast [is] well-known for her blending of mythological tales and romance . . . [A] beautiful adult fairy tale . . . Readers will be enchanted."

—*The Best Reviews*

"Outstanding . . . magic, myth and romance with a decidedly modern twist. Her imagination and storytelling abilities are true gifts to the genre."

—*Romantic Times*

Goddess of Light

"A charmer . . . Cast continues her unique brand of delightfully mixing a modern-day romance with a mythological legend . . . Creative."

—*Midwest Book Review*

"Pure enjoyment . . . Anything can [happen] when gods and mortals mix."

—*Rendezvous*

"A fanciful mix of mythology and romance with a dash of humor for good measure . . . Engages and entertains . . . Lovely."   —*Romance Reviews Today*

Goddess of Spring

"One of the top romantic-fantasy mythologists today."

—*Midwest Book Review*

"As always, there's a dash of humor and lots of meltingly hot sex."

—*Affaire de Coeur*

"Enchanting . . . Lovely."   —*The Romance Readers Connection*

"A veritable feast for readers who just can't get enough fantasy dished up with their romance. Mythology has never been so fun!"

—*Romance Reviews Today*

Goddess of the Sea

"Captivating—poignant, funny, erotic! Lovely characters, wonderful romance, constant action and a truly whimsical fantasy . . . Delightful. A great read."   —*The Best Reviews*

"A fun combination of myth, girl power and sweet romance [with] a bit of suspense. A must-read . . . A romance that celebrates the magic of being a woman."   —*Affaire de Coeur*

Goddess

OF

Legend

P. C. Cast

B

BERKLEY SENSATION, NEW YORK

THE BERKLEY PUBLISHING GROUP
Published by the Penguin Group
Penguin Group (USA) Inc.
375 Hudson Street, New York, New York 10014, USA
Penguin Group (Canada), 90 Eglinton Avenue East, Suite 700, Toronto, Ontario M4P 2Y3, Canada
(a division of Pearson Penguin Canada Inc.)
Penguin Books Ltd., 80 Strand, London WC2R 0RL, England
Penguin Group Ireland, 25 St. Stephen's Green, Dublin 2, Ireland (a division of Penguin Books Ltd.)
Penguin Group (Australia), 250 Camberwell Road, Camberwell, Victoria 3124, Australia
(a division of Pearson Australia Group Pty. Ltd.)
Penguin Books India Pvt. Ltd., 11 Community Centre, Panchsheel Park, New Delhi—110 017, India
Penguin Group (NZ), 67 Apollo Drive, Rosedale, North Shore 0632, New Zealand
(a division of Pearson New Zealand Ltd.)
Penguin Books (South Africa) (Pty.) Ltd., 24 Sturdee Avenue, Rosebank, Johannesburg 2196,
South Africa

Penguin Books Ltd., Registered Offices: 80 Strand, London WC2R 0RL, England

This book is an original publication of The Berkley Publishing Group.

PRINTING HISTORY
Berkley Sensation trade paperback edition / December 2010

Library of Congress Cataloging-in-Publication Data

Cast, P. C.
    Goddess of legend / P.C. Cast.—Berkley Sensation trade pbk. ed.
        p.   cm.
    ISBN 978–0–425–22816–6
    1. Time travel—Fiction.   2. Seduction—Fiction.   3. Lancelot (Legendary character)—Fiction.
4. Arthur, King—Fiction.   I. Title.
    PS3603.A869G634 2010
    813'.6—dc22

                                                                    2010035188

PRINTED IN THE UNITED STATES OF AMERICA

10   9   8   7   6   5   4   3   2   1

To Trish Jensen—
the best pinch hitter I know.
You can be on my team anytime, Fluffy!

ACKNOWLEDGMENTS

Thank you to my wonderful editor, Wendy McCurdy, for being sure this book was born.

As always, I appreciate my friend and agent, Meredith Bernstein. You know this book (and LOTS of other books) wouldn't have happened without you.

And a special acknowledgment to my fabulous author friend Trish Jensen. You're wonderful, baby! Fans o' mine, please check her out at www.trishjensen.com.

PROLOGUE

"THEY will believe I entrapped you." Coventina, the great water goddess, turned her head, unable to look at him.

"I am not entrapped, my love. I am simply resting from the darkness of this world," Merlin said. He touched her smooth cheek so that she had to turn back and meet his gaze. "And since when have we cared what others say, Viviane?"

His use of the nickname he called her at their most intimate moments couldn't even make her smile. "It is a curse to have the ability to see into the future," she said.

"In many ways, love."

"Yes. But have you always seen this for you? For me? For us? Why let me love you, knowing what you have known?"

"'Tis a man in the far future, a healer named Phil, who proclaims love is what it is. It has no future or past, but simply the present."

"This healer does not impress me," Viviane said. "We have a past, and we could also have a future. See it. Believe in it."

"I cannot see our future, my love. It pains me too much when I am not allowed to alter what I see." His sigh was deep. "The future of Arthur and Camelot pierced me enough that more wounds feel unbearable."

She gazed at his wonderfully familiar face and saw the goodness, strength and kindness that had first drawn her to him. But she also saw something else—his visage was shadowed by a weariness that made him appear a decade older than he had just months ago.

If only there was a way she could take some of the burden from him. She'd known loving a mortal would be difficult and that she would, eventually, have to lose him, but Merlin was a powerful Druid, and the goddess had hoped that his magical powers, so utterly tied to the earth, would give him the strength to live as her consort far longer than an ordinary mortal would have the ability to live.

It was ironic that it had not been the stress of loving a goddess that had been Merlin's undoing. Instead it had been the encroaching darkness that seemed eerily drawn to his human charge, Arthur Pendragon, the boy grown to man who was like a son to him, that had caused the Druid to want to escape the world badly enough that he had bespelled himself and would soon fade to nothingness in the self-made prison of this deceptively beautiful crystal cave.

That damned Arthur! Why had he not listened to Merlin and chosen a wife other than young, beautiful and utterly vapid Guinevere?

As if reading her mind, Merlin said, "My love, please do not blame Arthur. It isn't his fault, not entirely. Nor is it Guinevere's fault. None of us can choose where we love." Merlin leaned back against the fur pallet he'd arranged for himself in one smooth corner of the crystal cave. "I know I'm being a coward, but I have seen what will happen to him—to all of them. I have also seen that I cannot change it. It is . . ." He paused, looking close to tears. "It is as if Arthur is embracing his destruction. I have done everything in my power to help him. I have fought with him, counseled him, begged him, cajoled him—nothing works. In every scenario of the future I see, the light and goodness that is Arthur is utterly destroyed by the darkness of jealousy and greed, lust and anger."

Viviane felt a flutter of panic as he closed his eyes. How was she going to go on forever with him here—not alive and not dead—simply unchanged, sleeping in this coldly beautiful tomb, where she was unable to speak with him, or touch him, or hold him?

"But, Merlin, there must be a way to influence these events. There must be a way to save this one man." *And in doing so,* she added silently to herself, *I would save you, too.*

Merlin shook his head. "It is beyond my power. It is beyond your power."

"It cannot be beyond my power!" the goddess cried in frustration.

"Viviane, my only love, you know that even the gods are not allowed to tamper with the balance of light and dark. The choice between the two is a mortal one, and darkness is reigning in Camelot."

"Of course I know that! But I am an immortal. I wield the very essence of life. I must be able to save your son for you."

"I fear his fate is sealed. He will die brokenhearted. Betrayed by love, he will go willingly to his death. Now, please, my goddess, my love, allow me to sleep."

Viviane dropped to her knees beside his pallet and pressed her cheek against his thigh. He stroked her golden hair with a hand that was increasingly weak.

"I am so weary . . ." he whispered.

As his eyes fluttered shut again, perhaps for the last time, Viviane sat up, her heart pounding with the beginnings of hope.

"Wait! Merlin, you said there is nothing in this time or reality that makes Arthur change his mind. But could something, or perhaps some*one*, from another time or another reality affect a change? Have you looked into that possible future and divined failure, too?"

His blue eyes opened and met hers. "I did not look into a future touched by another time or reality. You know I cannot manipulate time or realities." Merlin's voice was soft, almost inaudible.

"You cannot, but I can!" Viviane shook his shoulders. "You must look, my love, and give that future a chance!"

"I cannot," he whispered. "The spell is set. Besides, you cannot simply cast a net out into the waters of time or the waves of reality. There must be a plan . . . a reason . . . a unique soul . . ."

"But I can try! I will look into the future and see if—"

"They do not even know us in the future." With a spurt of anger Merlin briefly sounded like himself again. "You are nothing more than a vague legend. I am an absent mentor, often blamed for the entire debacle."

Viviane was horrified. How could people forget her? She was goddess of the ancient world's waterways. Forget her? She thought not. If she had a plan, a great one, as befitted one such as herself, not only would she save her beloved, she would be certain that her name, her legacy would live on forever. Oh, and she supposed if she saved that dumb, damn Arthur, that would be okay, too.

How could the futures blame Merlin for a king's poor choices? This must also be rectified. And she was just the goddess to do it, by damn. "I will find a way, my love. I will."

Merlin let out a puff of laughter. "Oh, Viviane, what I love so much about you. Your passion. Your desire to make things right. Your devotion to me. How is it possible that a simple magician had the fortune to be loved by one such as you?"

She stroked his arm. "There is nothing simple about you, my dearest. But this I know. There is good. Goodness shines from you, as if the sun has kissed your radiance. Perhaps that goodness is why we find ourselves in this predicament. But I will find a way. This, I promise you."

Merlin shrugged and lay back again, breathing out the energy that had animated him. "Even should you find someone who might help you, you cannot simply displace a life. You know that. Souls cannot be yanked about without any care for lives lost and futures broken. Balance and reason must be maintained."

Viviane leaned forward and took Merlin in her arms. "But if, by some wondrous twist of fate, I do succeed, will you swear to come back to me?"

He looked long into her eyes and Viviane watched compassion and love war with weariness and heartache. Finally he raised one hand and began swirling it in the air.

> *I leave a part of me*
> *tied, Arthur, to thee.*
> *My future to thine,*
> *our fates here combine.*
> *Survive and you shall give*
> *me reason, once again, to live.*

The power that had been building around Merlin's hand was visible, a shining glow in the air. With a gesture more resigned than hopeful, he threw the glistening power out at the walls of his entombing crystal. They shivered as they absorbed the spell.

"There. It is done. Save Arthur and you save me." Merlin bent and kissed his goddess, sharing his last waking breath with her.

Weeping, Viviane pulled away from her lover, who was now silent, completely under the spell of eternal sleep that hid him from the misery of this life so thoroughly that he had even managed to escape the Underworld, where memory would torment his soul.

Slowly, the goddess stood and covered him lovingly with a thick pelt. She kissed him once on his cool forehead and then turned and resolutely walked from the entombing crystal cave. *Forget me? Blame Merlin? I think not. Arthur, gird those damn loins.*

VIVIANE wrapped herself in fog as she emerged from the cave that overlooked her mystical lake. On a wave of magic, her power carried her across the water to the lush green island the curtain of mist parted to reveal. She walked quickly to the graceful stone tower that was the only structure on the little isle the locals had long ago named Shalott. Surrounded by rowan trees and shrouded in her magic, she hardly needed the concealment of the mist, but the goddess automatically called it to her. For what she was about to do, she wanted there to be no chance of prying eyes.

She didn't enter the cream-colored tower as she usually did, but instead paced back and forth along the gentle bank, letting her white samite robe trail through the wildflowers that carpeted this special island. Power swirled around her, causing the birds, newly awakened by dawn, to squawk in alarm and leave their perches in the rowan grove. She breathed in the scent of musky moss, the pungent odor of wild thyme that surrounded her as she disturbed the softness of it beneath her feet.

How could she have allowed this to happen? She'd recognized that Merlin had been damaged by the world from the moment she'd met him. He was a powerful Druid, yet he was filled with unusual gentleness and such a tender heart that even the wild creatures of the forest could be lured to eat from his hand. Viviane smiled through her tears. He'd lured her, drawn her from her lonely isle in the middle of her mystical lake. She'd willingly become his lover. As a goddess, she couldn't conceive of not being able to heal that which the world had broken inside him.

"I could have healed him, had it not been for that wretched Arthur!" she cried. Her angry words made the usually placid waters of the lake begin to roil, and their cool blue depths darkened ominously as the morning light became veiled. Viviane frowned, lifted her hand and, bringing her temper under control, flicked her fingers out at the lake and commanded, "Darkness, be gone! Whether my anger is stirred or not, you are not welcome in my realm!"

Instantly the waters obeyed her. They quieted and the darkness that had begun to stain them dissipated like dew in the noonday sun. Viviane stared out at the familiar waters, disturbed more than she liked to admit by the swiftness with which the depths had reacted to her temper. Darkness had actually touched her lake—that was alarming.

"Balance of light and dark? Bah!" Viviane hurled the word into the mist, but this time the reaction to her outburst was under her control, and the water-thickened air around her swirled and shimmered in reflection of the goddess's power. "There is no balance when one mortal can draw so much darkness that my realm is even tainted."

I should be honest with myself, she thought as she began to pace back and forth along the moss-lined bank. *It isn't as simple as focusing my anger on the king of the Britons. Guinevere plays a role in this tragedy. As does the all-too-perfect knight, Lancelot.* The goddess grimaced.

Merlin hadn't shared many of Camelot's secrets with her. He'd said she was his escape, his respite from pain, and so he didn't wish to speak of those dark things, but the Lady of the Lake had eyes and ears everywhere there was water, and she had certainly seen and heard enough to know that Merlin's direful predictions were going to come true.

"And that truth broke your heart, my love," she whispered to the mist.

No! She wouldn't allow it. She was a goddess. She had powers mortals couldn't begin to comprehend, not even a mortal as spectacular as her Merlin.

Viviane stopped pacing and stared out at the familiar waters of her home. "I need someone not of this time—not of this place. Someone who has a unique way of seeing people and situations, who embraces light instead of darkness and who will also not be awed by the beauty of Camelot, nor too dazzled to consider . . ." Consider what? What was it she needed to do to change the future enough to save Arthur from his tragic fate and thus free her lover?

Her lover . . . Viviane felt her shoulders slump and she pressed her face in her hands and wept bitterly. She missed him already and had to struggle with herself not to rush back to the crystal cave and sit beside his still form. Her breath caught on a sob. She was a goddess, but she was also a woman, and a brokenhearted one at the loss of her Merlin. Even her realm—that which had given her such thorough pleasure for eons—seemed somehow less now. Nothing meant as much without—

Viviane's head came up. "That's it! Arthur may lose everything, but if he still has his love, his Guinevere, then his heart will not be broken and his fate will change." Excitedly, the goddess began to pace again. "That is what I must do. I must find a woman—a spectacular woman from another time, another place, and bring her here to seduce Lancelot from Guinevere so that Guinevere returns to Arthur and is balm to his wounded soul!" All would be well. Merlin would awake and, she decided, would make love to her as he'd never done before. Oh, how she already missed the lovemaking. A magician in truth Merlin was, in more ways than any of those dolts at Camelot could possible imagine.

Resolutely Viviane moved to the edge of the water, so that her bare feet were caressed by the kiss of the waves meeting the bank. She raised her arms and the mist automatically thickened, swirling magically around her as if anticipating the spell.

> From the depths I call my power,
> lake, sea, rain, mist, dew—hear me at this hour.
> My will is to find a unique soul;
> an outlander is my goal.

The goddess paused, remembering Merlin's warning that a life cannot be displaced from its own fate. She considered ignoring her lover's words and dealing with the consequences later. But no. The drawing spell must be perfect. She would get only one chance. Already events were spiraling out of control in Camelot—soon it would be too late to affect the future, if it wasn't already.

No! She wouldn't think like that. She was a goddess, and through the magic of her watery realm, she would change Arthur's fate and save her lover.

Viviane refocused, pulling her power from the depths of the lake that spread like waved glass at her feet.

> Bring me a mortal
> through my divine portal.
> Her fate must mean she is free,
> her life thread broken so she may come to me.

The goddess closed her eyes, concentrating so hard that beads of sweat broke out over her smooth brow.

> *Her eyes should be able to see*
> *her heart's desire—love it should be.*
> *Her mind sharp and true,*
> *willing to see the world anew.*
> *Encroaching darkness she'll cure;*
> *life and love are her allure.*
> *It is her soul my thread will find,*
> *with water and sight I bind.*
> *Lake, sea, rain, mist, dew—search and discover*
> *the mortal through which Arthur's heart will recover!*

Tossing the ball of light that had been building between her hands as she created the spell, Viviane threw her arms wide and hurled her will, her power, her divine magic out and into the lake. Instantly the waters changed color from a deep, sapphire blue to a silver so bright that had a mortal been unlucky enough to glimpse the transformation, he would have been forever blinded by its brilliance.

> *She must be beautiful, she must be bright.*
> *She must instantly recognize our plight.*
> *She must be happy, she must be smart.*
> *And 'twould help a great deal if she's a bit of a tart.*
> *Now go! Do my will!*
> *My command you must fulfill!*

The glowing surface of the lake swirled around Viviane, and then tendrils of light began to lift. Fingers of radiance snaked over the water, thin and searching.

"*Go!*" the Goddess impatiently shouted her command, and the threads of light lifted, lifted, lifted . . . and then shot off into the morning sky to disappear from this reality to times unseen—places unknown.

Viviane stared into the sky long after her magic had dispersed. And then, with a sigh, she walked forward, letting the comforting water enfold her while she floated down to her palace made of pearl that rested deep beneath the waves. Now she must wait and hope that the drawing spell lured the perfect mortal fish into her divine net.

If only I can discover the right woman, the goddess mused as she entered her palace and impatiently brushed away the naiad hand-maidens who surrounded her, singing their desire to serve her every need. *And isn't that always the way of the world—the right woman is often the only thing that can dislodge those gods-be-damned Fates . . .*

CHAPTER ONE

I SABEL decided the morning couldn't be more perfect. Well, possibly better if she was sore from a great night of sex, but that wasn't in the cards. Not today, probably not tomorrow. Probably not in this decade. Nonetheless, a beautiful day.

She finished adjusting the tripod that held her favorite camera and then straightened, drawing in a deep breath of the sweet Oklahoma air. She didn't peer through the camera lens as would most photographers. Of course she would eventually, but Isabel trusted her naked eye more than any lens, no matter how clear or magnified or uber-telephoto. So she studied the landscape before her as she sipped from her thermos of Vienna roast coffee.

She caught a glimpse of herself in the silver of her thermos. Distorted as it was, she could tell she was smiling. And her lips, which every lover seemed to comment on, looked like big clown lips. Men seemed to love them. She was always trying to suck them in. She didn't believe for a second that Angelina's were for real. Unfortunately, she knew too well that hers were.

"'When the young dawn, with fingertips of rose lit up the world,'" she murmured, surprising herself with the Homeric quote. "Appropriate, though . . ." Isabel sighed with pleasure. The light here was absolutely exquisite! Oklahoma's Tallgrass Prairie had been the right choice to begin her new photography collection, *American Heartscapes*. It was early spring, but the ridge in front of her was already covered with knee-high grasses, waving oceanlike in the morning breeze. The air had the scent of impending rain, but there were so many more scents that filled her. The grasses, the lake, the occasional odor of a skunk. Nature. What a high.

The sky was an explosion of pastels washed against a backdrop of cumulus clouds that puffed high into the stratosphere—mute testimony to today's weather forecast of midday thunderstorms. Isabel hardly gave the impending storm a thought—she'd be gone before the first raindrop fell. But even if the weather chased her away, she didn't mind. On the ridge before her, under the frothy cotton candy sky, was a sight Isabel knew would make the perfect cover photo for her collection. The landscape was dotted with bison. Isabel's eyes glistened as she gazed at them, framing pictures— creating art in her mind's eye. The huge beasts looked timeless in the changing light of dawn, especially since they were positioned so that there were no telephone poles or modern houses or even visible roads anywhere around them. It was just the beasts, the land and the amazing sky.

Isabel took another sip of her coffee before she put the cup down and began focusing her camera and setting up the first shots. As she worked, a sense of peace filled her, and Isabel's skin tingled with happiness.

"And you thought you'd lost it," she spoke aloud to herself softly, letting her voice fill the empty space around her. "Well, not lost it," she muttered as she sighted through the telephoto lens and focused on a huge bison bull backlit by the rosebud-hued sky. "Just lost the peace in it."

Ironic, really, that the collection of photographs *USA Today* had called *Peace?* had made her lose her perspective on the subject.

"Afghanistan will do that." Isabel clicked off several frames of the bison.

In retrospect she should have known the assignment was going to be a tough one. But she'd gotten cocky. Hell, she'd been a photo-journalist—a successful, award-winning photojournalist—for twenty years now. She wasn't a dewy-eyed twenty-something anymore. She was a fearless forty-two, which was part of her problem. Over-confidence in her ability had blinded her to the realities of what really *seeing* would do to her.

Of course, it wasn't like she hadn't been to war zones before— Bosnia, the Falklands and South Africa had all come before her lens. But something had been different in Afghanistan. *I'd been different. Somehow I'd lost perspective and darkness and chaos slithered in,* Isabel admitted to herself as she changed the angle of the tripod and shot several frames rapidly, catching a young calf frolicking around its grazing mother.

It had started with the soldier, Curtis Johnson. He'd had kind brown eyes set in a face that was young and more cute than hand-some. He couldn't have been older than twenty-five, and he'd flirted outrageously with her as he escorted her to the jeep she'd be riding in—the one smack in the middle of the convoy of supplies they were taking from the U.S. airbase to one of the small native settle-ments just a few miles down the potholed road.

Actually, Curtis had been so cute and clever that she'd been daydreaming about loosening up her rule on not having a fling when she was on assignment. She'd been counting the years between them and had decided that, what the hell, if sexy young Curtis didn't care that she was almost twenty years his senior, then why the hell should she care?

And that was when the roadside bomb detonated. Isabel had switched to photographer autopilot, and in the middle of the smoke and fire, darkness and horror, she'd captured some of the most pro-found images of her career—images that had included Curtis John-son, whose strong right leg and well-muscled right arm had been blown completely off. She'd never meant to capture him. She hadn't even realized he'd been part of the blast. She'd meant only to do what was instinctive; capture the truth. And then the truth bombed her in the face, and she nearly fell apart.

Curtis's eyes had still been kind, even as they'd clouded with shock. Before he'd lost consciousness, he'd been worried about her—been warning her to get down . . . get under cover . . . Then he'd bled out on the cracked desert sand and died in her arms. All hell broke loose around her, and all she remembered after that was screaming to keep her camera. She absolutely had to have the pictures of Curtis in life. For his family. For her.

Isabel shivered and realized she'd stopped taking pictures and was standing beside her tripod. She lifted a hand to the chill on her cheeks. They were wet.

"Focus on what you're doing!" Isabel told herself. "This is your chance to regain your center—your normalcy." *And to get over your grief.*

She did the buck-up thing her father had always taught her, got rid of the tears and the memories and focused on her job.

Shaking her head, she returned to the frame of her camera, her smile feeling sarcastic. Her gang of best friends would agree that an Isabel Cantelli norm wasn't anywhere near most people's norm. She could almost hear her gang chastising her. Meredith would shrug and say the Isabel norm usually worked for her—it had certainly made her successful. Robin would shake her head and say Isabel needed to find a full-time man, not just a string of attractive lovers. Kim would dissect Isabel's psyche and eventually agree with Robin that more permanence in her life would help ground her, and Teresa would chime in that whatever made Isabel happy was what she should go for.

Until a month ago and that trip to Afghanistan, Isabel would have laughed, rolled her eyes, poured herself more champagne and said her nomadic life, free of entangling man strings, was exactly what made her happy.

Then Curtis Johnson had happened to her, and Isabel's view of the world had changed, and in this new, tainted viewpoint she'd realized that she'd been fooling herself for quite a while. Or maybe it was more accurate to say that she'd been searching for herself for quite a while, because somewhere in the middle of her successful career and her group of intelligent, articulate friends and her life that was at once exciting and comfortable, she'd lost herself.

Which is why she was here, on Oklahoma's Tallgrass Prairie. She was doing the only thing she knew to reground herself—she was viewing life through her camera and searching for her true north again so she could find a way to navigate through the changing landscape of her life. Her plan had seemed to be working, until she'd allowed her mind to wander and her eyes to see the past. And the past had good and bad memories, times of joy and ridiculous fear. If there was an emotion she'd ever not experienced, she wasn't sure what it would be. She needed something to shock her into enjoyment again. If she could only figure out what it would be. But this, this natural Oklahoma beauty was working right now.

"So focus!" Isabel reminded herself, and was pleased to fall fairly easily back into the zone of framing the lovely land before her.

The next time she moved her tripod, she caught sight of the morning light glistening off the surface of what she realized was water winding through a gully to her right. Intrigued as always by varieties in landscape, she headed in that direction, loving the surprising glimpse of sandy bank and a clear, bubbling stream hidden within the section of cross timbers.

Getting closer to the water, Isabel noticed a single ray of young sunlight had penetrated the green shadows of the trees, so that a small section of the stream was being illuminated, as if by a silver spotlight. That spotlight drew her like a magnet.

She let her instincts guide her, and moved quietly and quickly down the bank, leaving the tripod temporarily behind. As she settled on the sandy ground, kneeling so that she was just above the water, Isabel focused and began clicking picture after picture, changing the angle and distance from the water as she worked. Mesmerized by the unique quality of the light, she let the magic of the lens wash away the sadness thinking of Afghanistan and the fallen soldier had caused. She'd changed position and was lying prone on her stomach, elbows planted in the sand, when the brush on the opposite side of the bank rustled, and accompanied by a massive snapping of twigs, a bison lumbered into view.

Hardly daring to breathe, Isabel kept snapping pictures as the huge beast went to the water. He snorted once at her, probably sensing the scent of an intruder, but then ignored her completely, lowered his black muzzle and drank noisily.

She wondered how she smelled to him. He'd swung his head around until he'd spotted her. She never felt fear, so she didn't believe that's what caught his attention. Did she just smell human? She wasn't wearing perfume, she was lying so still, there was no way he heard her.

What had made him look directly toward her? And why had his eyes seem so ancient and wise? When he backed away from the lake, he shook his head up and down, gave her one more unfathomable look, and then turned and loped away with an agility she'd never have believed of such a huge, amazing beast.

A thrill went through Isabel. She clicked back to glance through the pictures she'd captured of him. The bison had stepped directly into the shaft of light. Morning dew speckled the big bull's coat so that through Isabel's lens he appeared to be swathed in diamonds and mist. And he'd nodded at her. As if he were approving the photo shoot. And as he turned and left, her first thought was that every single human male in existence would give anything for that package he was carrying.

Isabel sat up and laughed aloud with delight, relieved beyond measure that the beauty and peace of this ancient land had begun to do exactly what she'd hoped when she'd discussed this book idea with her agent—it had begun to sooth her soul and help reground her creativity in something more bearable than death and destruction.

Impulsively Isabel kicked off her hiking boots and pulled off her socks. She rolled up her jeans and, still holding her camera, stepped carefully into the crystalline water. Isabel sucked air and gasped at the initial chill, but after a few slow steps, her feet got used to the temperature of the stream, and she made her way to the shaft of sunlight that had so recently framed the bison. When she got to the light, Isabel turned her face up, bathing in the morning's radiance while the cool water washed over her feet and ankles.

There was something about this place that touched her. Maybe it was just the drastic contrast between the calm freedom of the prairie—green, lush and clean—and the war-ravaged Middle East, where everything her eyes had focused on had been dry and burned and in a nightmare of conflict. She breathed deeply—inhaling and exhaling, imagining with every breath she was getting rid of all the negatives within herself and letting the water wash away the remnants of death and war that had clung to her for the past month. Without pausing to wonder why or second-guess whether she was making a fool of herself, Isabel spoke her inner most thoughts aloud to the listening stream and the shaft of light.

"This is just what I need. A new perspective, a new vision. To cleanse myself. That bull was telling me something. He was telling me to go for it. I just wish I knew what 'it' was. Tell me, Lady of the Lake," she said, grinning. "Mrs. Tiger taught us all about you in eighth grade. What is my destiny?"

Isabel knew it was just her imagination, but it seemed the silver light intensified in response to her words, and she could swear she felt a thrill of *something*. Laughing with pleasure, she threw her arms wide and kicked up water so that drops of liquid turned crystal by the sunlight rained around her, baptizing her in brilliance.

VIVIANE couldn't stay away from her oracle. She knew it was too soon for the tendrils of her magic to have found anyone, but she was filled with frustrated energy. So while her naiads milled nervously around her, the goddess sat in front of her oracle, a crystal basin filled with hundreds of pearls, and fretted.

When a pearl began to glow, she practically pounced on it. Plucking it from the others in the dark, silent batch, she held it up and gazed into its milky depths. The vision cleared to show an old woman sitting beside a large lake, spitting what looked like sun-flower seeds into the surf.

"Younger!" Viviane said in disgust, severing the thread and sending it away from the crone. She tossed the pearl back into the basin and began to pace.

The next pearl that lit up showed a child playing beside the ocean. Viviane almost screamed in exasperation. "Not that young!" she admonished her oracle.

The next two visions were utterly unsuitable. Neither were too young or too old, they were just too ordinary. At the end of her already thinly stretched patience, Viviane plucked one long silver strand of silk from the thick fall of hair that hung veil-like around her body. Holding it over the pearl-filled basin, she twirled it in a deceptively lazy circle.

> *Not too young, old or plain—*
> *with those there is no gain.*
> *Find the perfect woman is my command;*
> *beauty, grace and spirit is what I demand!*

The goddess released the strand of her hair, and as the gossamer length floated down into the pearl pool, she completed the spell:

> *From my own body I lend my oracle power:*
> *find the right soul within this very hour!*

There was a flash of silver and the strand of the goddess's hair exploded, raining sparks of liquid light, which dissolved into the pearls. Invigorated anew, silver threads rushed out from the realm of the goddess and, following seaways and lakes, rivers and streams, they searched through time and realities until one small, glowing thread shot down a tiny waterway in a faraway place called Oklahoma, in the distant, modern mortal world where, in a flash of morning light, it captured the sound of a woman's joyous laughter as she recommitted herself to the bright possibilities in life.

Viviane heard the enticing sound and plucked the glowing pearl. Holding her breath, the goddess peered within the milky depth that cleared to reveal a full-bodied blonde, oddly attired, who was dancing within a cascade of a splashing stream. Viviane's heartbeat increased with excitement.

"Show me her face!" the goddess commanded.

Her oracle tightened on the woman's face. Well, she was certainly attractive. Viviane squinted and focused on her. Not young, but not too old, or at least she didn't appear to be. And there was a definite benefit to a little age and experience. The woman laughed again, and Viviane unexpectedly found her own lips tilting up in response. The sound was musical and it changed the woman from attractive to alluring.

"Yes," Viviane murmured. "I believe she will do quite nicely." The goddess lifted her arms, causing power to swirl around her.

> *I claim this mortal as fate decrees in her world she dies.*
> *When her life there ends, it will be to me her soul has ties.*
> *My love's sleeping wishes I follow most truly*
> *so that he might escape the despair that binds him so cruelly.*
> *I take nothing that is not already decreed lost;*
> *my purpose is clear—no matter the cost.*
> *Arthur's dour fate shall not come to be*
> *and then my love will return to me!*

Then the great water goddess known as Coventina, Merlin's Viviane, hurled a blazing sphere of divine power through her oracle and out . . . out . . . into another time, another place, altering forever fate's plans for Isabel Cantelli.

CHAPTER TWO

H INDSIGHT, Isabel Cantelli decided in hindsight, sucked. She came to this conclusion after steering to avoid a chipmunk and having her SUV spin out of control.

She probably shouldn't have been digging for her dropped cell while she was happily singing "Camelot" and driving sixty on a dirt road. She probably should have let that little dude fend for himself instead of trying to be a hero saving him. Hindsight wasn't fifty-fifty. It was, at the moment, zero-one hundred.

But shoulda, coulda, woulda wasn't going to help her now. She and her Nissan were flying into Grand Lake at an alarming speed.

Isabel braced herself for the swan dive they were about to accomplish, which she doubted would be graceful. The lake, which she'd found magical just minutes ago, was about to kick her in the ass.

So many thoughts raced through her mind. Strangely enough, none of the ones she expected when she knew she was about to die. Her life didn't flash before her eyes; the life she hadn't lived yet did.

Terror, fear of the pain of dying, that all flashed. But the sadness of what she hadn't yet achieved was occupying her brain.

Her car hit the lake with what felt like a nuclear blast. And the air bag had exploded on her, practically trapping her in her seat. When it finally deflated, she tried to unbuckle her seat belt, but for some reason, it wouldn't let go. Since her window had been down, the car was filling up with water and sinking fast.

Unless a miracle showed up, there was no way she would survive. She was on her way to dying, and it was terrifying. Her heart beat desperately, and she knew that wasn't going to last long. She apologized to her heart for letting it down. She apologized to her liver for not mistreating it as much as she could have over the years. What a wasted chance. But even though she thought of friends and family, Isabel's life never passed before her eyes, like so many assure people it will when dying.

Her focus, as her chest squeezed painfully, was all of the things she hadn't accomplished yet. How could she have forgotten how much more she wanted out of life? The big one was that she'd never found love. Lust, sure. Attraction, sure. But not that elusive thing called true love. To look at a man and know, absolutely, they were meant for each other.

There were many others on her list, but she sure would have liked to experience the feeling of being desperately in love.

Woulda. Coulda. Shoulda.

And then, suddenly, she felt alive again. And she knew, just knew, that somehow, someway, she was being given a second chance.

CHAPTER THREE

"WOULD be best if you'd awake, Isabel."

"Just one more hour," Isabel murmured.

"I understand the need to nap. You've had a long journey," Viviane said, giving Isabel a shake. *You are my hope.* "We must needs to begin this mission right away. I need my Merlin."

When her new hope just moaned, turned over and said, "Coffee," Viviane felt exasperation roil inside of her. "Awake your sorry . . . person, now! But not for me you would not be here lazing and making demands. Double-cream chocolate cappuccino, yes?"

Her hope roused instantly, brushing the lush golden hair from her face. "Oh, yes, please. Where am I? Did you save me? I thank you so much. There were so many shoulda—"

"—woulda, couldas, yes, I'm well aware." Viviane snapped her fingers and a large silver stein of coffee appeared out of the mist. "Drink first. Then we shall talk."

The beautiful woman stared at her but took the stein from her hand and sipped. "I can't thank you enough," she said, then peered down into the cup. "This is the best coffee I've ever had. How did you—"

"I learned quickly how to brew while visiting your time."

"My time?"

"As I said, we have much to discuss."

Isabel knew that she was either in heaven, because the coffee said so, or she was in hell, because the woman in front of her was so ethereally beautiful, she had to be the devil in disguise.

Then again, she wasn't much into heaven and hell, but she knew a damn good cup of coffee when she tasted one. And it was waking her up fast, which was a good sign that it wasn't decaf.

She looked around. She was sitting by a lake, but it definitely wasn't Grand Lake. The flora and fauna were all out of whack. The misty fog that hovered over the water was shimmery, unlike anything she'd ever experienced there. Not to mention there wasn't an electric pole or sign of civilization in sight.

And then she noticed her attire. Most definitely not what she'd almost died in. She was dressed in a jade green gown, long-sleeved, yet the sleeves stopped short of her shoulders and flared out at the wrists. The bodice was square and offered a view of cleavage she was most definitely not used to displaying. It was a beautiful gown to be sure, in fact it would make a thumbs-up on any red carpet, but it wasn't hers.

"What is going on here?" she asked. "Where am I, how'd I get here, and who in hell are you?"

The woman smiled, again snapped her fingers, and while Isabel ogled, her silver mug refilled itself with the wonderful smelling coffee.

"I assure you, we, you, are not in hell."

"Then where am I? You? Us? And why haven't I ever photographed you, because you have to be the most excruciatingly beautiful woman I've ever seen. And I've seen them all." She sipped again, the delicious brew in her silver . . . chalice? "What's the deal?"

"I've chosen you, Isabel, for a very special, very important mission."

"I'd be flattered if I weren't so spooked. And I'd run screaming if you didn't conjure one helluva great cup of coffee."

"Are you hungry as well? The Fates tell me you are partial to pastries. Some things called beignets."

The woman went to do that snap thing again, but Isabel stopped her. "Much as I appreciate that, before you do that out-of-thin-air thing again, may I ask a few questions?"

"You deserve to have all of your questions answered."

Isabel took that as a yes. "Were you the one who saved me?"

"Yes."

"How? As soon as I hit the water and couldn't get free, I knew I was in trouble." She held up her hand and wiggled her fingers, wiggled the toes encased in silver slippers. "All better, just like that. I was a goner for sure. And then I got this feeling of, I don't know, a second chance."

"Goner? You were, I think I'd say, a finder. And yes, this is another chance to fulfill some desires."

"Well, that clears things up." Isabel glanced around at the lush greenery, at the dense forest beyond this rocky beach. "We're not in Oklahoma anymore, are we, Toto?"

"Toto?"

"I'm sorry. I didn't mean that as a slight. You seem to know my name and other kinds of creepy things about me. May I ask what your name is?"

"I'm known as Coventina. But you may call me—"

"As in the Lady of the Lake Coventina? As in the mythical Goddess of Water?"

The woman shined with a triumphant smile. "So you *have* heard of me in your times! Merlin assured me I'm but a long-lost myth."

Isabel sat stunned. The shimmer that surrounded the Lady, her long, golden hair, the blue eyes that seemed to reflect the purity of the lake behind them. "You're kidding, right? Am I being punked?" She glanced around. "Where are the cameras? You've done a great job of hiding them, because I can spot and smell one from a mile away."

"I assure you, I am indeed Coventina. And none of those camera things exist, not in my knowledge."

"I'd love that beignet now. And may I have them drizzled with—"

"—dark chocolate. Of course." That snap thing again, and then Isabel was staring at a feast. The beignets, yes, just the way she wanted them, but also fried ham, over-easy fried eggs and potatoes with onions, peppers and bits of bacon, just how she cooked them herself. This was too good. Too perfect. Too crazy.

Then again, she was too hungry to actually be rude enough to decline.

"Do you mind if I'm freaked out?" Isabel said after licking her fingers? She started to get to her feet. That's when she noticed that, with a wave of the woman's hand, her slippers became glued to the earth beneath her. She tried to free herself from them, but they were definitely superglued to her skin as well.

"Please hear me out," said the woman who, if the tales were true, didn't really need to ask.

Isabel sat back down. "You'll excuse me if I'm just a little . . . dumbfounded?"

"I understand."

"You saved me from Grand Lake."

"Yes."

"Why?"

"Because I have need of you. And I have hopes that this will all turn out so that one of your—how did you put it?—shouldas will also come true for you."

"I'm alive. I'm not just in another world?"

"Oh, I am afraid you are definitely in another world. But it's *of* this world, Isabel. Just not of your time."

"Where am I?"

"If you've been taught about me, you've been taught about Camelot?"

Isabel again just stared at her. "Surely you jest."

Coventina laughed, a sound that was so lyrical that even the lake seemed to respond to it. The lake bubbled here and there as if something beneath couldn't help but enjoy the joke with her. "I enjoy a good jest, as do many of the men and women of the castle. But I assure you, beyond this forest is the castle of Camelot."

"You mean like King Arthur and Lancelot and Guinevere and Mer— Oh. He really *is* your Merlin."

"Or was," Coventina said, and her eyes immediately turned from a stunning blue to a stormy gray. "But he has forsaken this world, too devastated by the destiny he fears is in Arthur's future." The Lady grasped Isabel's hand. "I must bring him back. I must. I fear that eternity will be an eternal misery without him."

"Why me?" Isabel asked, even as she tried not to show watery eyes. She was so not a crybaby, unless it was over the tragedy of a sweet and heroic man in Afghanistan or the birth of a kitten.

Coventina squeezed Isabel's hand even more, although strangely it didn't hurt, but felt like energy being exchanged between them. "Because you were the woman I was looking for. I asked the gods for one who was beautiful, smart and, I'm sorry to say, about to die. And what was a must for me was a woman who had an, as you put it, 'shoulda.' One who mourned in her last moments that she'd never found true love."

"What makes you think I'll find it here, Cov—"

"Call me Viviane. Merlin is the only one who ever has, but I'd like if you would as well. Because I believe you will be the one who brings him back to me."

"Okay. What makes you think I'll find it here, Viviane? And how do I bring Merlin back?"

"I cannot be certain. But if I do not try, I have not done enough to win back the man I love. And this isn't acceptable to my heart, or my waters. I fear what will happen if my unhappiness roils the waters that sustain me."

Isabel glanced over at the lake to see it suddenly making waves when moments ago it had been calm, clear and as blue as Viviane's eyes. Now it was uneasy, gray, unhappy. And it churned in her memory of Grand Lake, which had seemed angry at her just at the moment that she and her car had taken a decidedly ungraceful dive into its unsettled depths.

She looked back to the woman, wondering just when she'd wake up from this dream. Until she did, she'd try to help. "My camera equipment?" she asked.

Viviane shook her head. "There's nothing like that in this time. This place."

"Okay," Isabel said, but mourned that she couldn't capture the beauty all around her, the beauty of this woman . . . who'd make her rich were she to sell the Lady's pictures to *People* magazine . . . the amazing truth of Camelot. "Who, pray tell, am I supposed to fall for? Or who do you hope might fall for me? What if I accidentally fall for, say, the court jester?"

Again that musical laughter filled the air, and it seemed that the birds in the trees joined in. "Hester the Jester? I pray you have better taste than that."

Isabel grinned. "Then who, my lady?"

"Why, Lancelot, of course."

"You're kidding, right? If I remember correctly, Gwen almost burned at the stake for getting involved with him. I didn't almost drown to live to see fire in my future."

"But you shan't. You are Lady Isabel, come to Camelot as Countess from Dumont to discuss the sharing of land for mutual benefit of all of Briton."

"So I'm just dropping in? Uninvited?"

Viviane hesitated a moment, then pulled a necklace from what must have been a pocket in her gown. It was a stunning piece, what at first appeared to be a sapphire to Isabel. But as she fingered it, she realized it was more a heart-shaped droplet, made of some kind of glass, with a blue liquid inside. It was amazing and would have brought a pretty penny at Sotheby's.

"Oh, Viv, I may call you Viv?"

The Lady sniffed. "No, you may not."

Isabel shrugged. "I just figured that Viviane's a mouthful, but fair enough. This is so lovely! What is it?"

The Lady put it around Isabel's neck, and it fell right above her heart and barely confined boobs. "This piece is somewhat magical, Isabel. Upon seeing it, those who would be suspicious of your arrival and your motives will no longer. Inside are my tears, dropped when I had no choice but to allow Merlin to leave me.

"It does contain abilities, but I'll not let you know what they are. For there is a price to pay for any use of it. Be wise with it and it will be your ally. Use the powers foolishly, and you will pay the price."

"Do you have any rules written down? A cheat sheet? Like could I use it to suddenly make plumbing and real toilets available?"

Viviane laughed as it seemed so did the lake. "You could indeed. And then you might find yourself not being able to use the facilities."

"Yipes."

"Yes, please see what I mean. There is a price whenever you choose to invoke the power of my tears. If you must needs use it, remember there is a cost. And one more thing, Isabel. Never allow anyone to take it from you." Viviane seemed deep in thought for a moment, then spoke:

> *The heart and tears shall not leave Isabel*
> *Without the thief suffering a horrid spell.*
> *Only Isabel may off it take*
> *After these words she has spake:*
> *"Lady of the Lake, this must be done*
> *For love and life for all to have won."*

Viviane threw her arms wide, and clouds that had been gathering broke apart and rained all over the lake, all over them. Isabel wasn't into getting showered on as a rule unless she was actually in a shower, but for some reason the drops felt warm and comforting when she was feeling a little scared and definitely out of her element.

Was this a death dream? Is that how it happened? She was singing the signature song to *Camelot* when she'd taken a header. She'd been thinking of the Lady of the Lake when she'd been struggling in the water.

Seems she'd taken way too many mythology classes in college.

Well, if it was a death dream, it was a pretty damn cool one. Where else would she want to land than at Camelot? Except for the plumbing thing. But hey, they managed; she'd managed the conditions in Afghanistan; she could find a way to live without her Kohler deluxe shower. But . . . "For how long, Viviane?"

"Until we've both accomplished our goals."

"Just to be clear, am I dead at the end of this picture? Not that I'm complaining, mind you, since you saved me and everything, but do I die when Mission Impossible is over?"

"I assure you that once you've achieved this Mission Impossible— as you call it, but I will not—your fate will be in your hands."

"So if I decide I really don't want to die?"

"Your fate will be yours to decide."

"If I decide I want to return to plumbing and electricity? And my photography?"

"Your fate will be in your hands, Isabel."

"All righty, then," Isabel said, testing the necklace, and sure enough it wasn't letting go. "Is there any place I can write a Post-it on those words I need to spake?"

"You will remember them should you need them."

"Another question. If I need help or advice, may I come visit you?"

"Always."

"How will I find you?"

"Just ask in your mind, Isabel. I will answer."

"Okay, just so I'm sure about my assignment. Try to seduce Lance away from Gwen so Arthur and Gwen stick to the happily-ever-after plan. And this will help the king to save Camelot?"

Viviane laughed, and the clouds and rain instantly disappeared. Isabel envied that power, wishing she'd known how to do that with a couple of boyfriends. "Yes, that's the plan. But plans sometimes go awry."

"Oh, goody."

"You have the necklace. Use it judiciously, and you will—how do you say it in your time?—kick aces?"

"Close enough, if you're a betting woman."

"I'm betting on you, Isabel. I'm betting on love for you. The one you 'shoulda' had in your time.

Isabel was kind of regretting the last thoughts of shouldas at this point. Maybe she should have been concentrating on the *shouldn't haves*. "How am I supposed to find the castle again?"

The Lady dipped her hand into the water and threw a handful into the air. They looked like drops of silver mercury as they hung for a while, and then one by one dropped back into the lake.

Viviane pointed behind Isabel. "Your horse awaits."

Isabel looked around and there stood the most beautiful white Arabian horse, standing, snorting, impatient. Isabel tilted her head and looked down below. Definitely a female, as nothing dangled.

"Okay, Viviane, let's get something straight," she said. "First, I'm a good rider. In fact, my favorite is bareback. But I know a side-saddle when I see it, and there's not a chance in hell I know how to handle a horse that big sidesaddle."

The Lady laughed again, then dipped her fingers into the lake and tossed drops of it onto Isabel's face, then did the same to the horse's, who took it much better than Isabel did.

"And now you know, Izzy, how to ride sidesaddle. And you and Samara will be fast friends. Now ride to Camelot. You are needed. And I grow impatient for my Merlin."

"How come you get to call me Izzy, and I'm not allowed to call you Viv?"

The Lady stood. "Who is the goddess here, Izzy?"

"Okay, good point."

CHAPTER FOUR

Izzy? Only her best friends and her father ever called her Izzy. But she supposed arguing with a goddess who'd just saved her life wasn't necessarily in her best interests. As Isabel and Samara picked their way through the forest that would bring them to Camelot, Isabel pondered on just how deep a dream this was.

After all, as Viviane had predicted, she and Samara became fast friends, and Isabel rode sidesaddle as if she'd been doing it all of her life. How could that be?

Or was this truly an afterworld that no one still alive could even imagine? Was this how the universe worked? It dropped you off into a different place and time? Already she'd had to stop Samara twice to take care of business in the middle of woods, wondering if baring her butt was illegal in Camelot.

Strangely enough, every time she needed to stop, she'd find something akin to toilet paper waiting for her. She kept whispering, "Thank you, Viviane." And she could swear that the trees whispered back, "No problem."

And Samara was something else. The first time Isabel stopped, she'd roped the reins around a tree. Samara snorted in what was apparent disgust. When Isabel returned, Samara nearly sent Isabel flying several yards away. Isabel picked up that cue fast, and at the second stop, she left Sam alone. No messing with Sam's trust or freedom. Isabel was rewarded by that trust when Sam leaned down to help her up into the saddle easily. After the first time, when she'd had to look around for a stump to step on, and Sam had kept kicking it over.

The turrets of the castle loomed ever closer, and Isabel found herself clutching the necklace so often it felt like it was even getting impatient with her.

Viviane was on her side, but she wasn't by her side, which would have made her much happier.

"Looks like it's you and me, Sam." Other than her first misstep, it was amazing the bond they'd found together almost instantly. She didn't need to kick, she didn't need to slap the reins. Just a word and Samara understood her.

"So, whatcha think, Sam? Are we going to accomplish our mission?"

Samara snorted and nodded her head. But then she suddenly stopped and her ears perked. A crackling in the leaves from their left had Isabel's heart racing. Lions and tigers and bears, oh my.

Isabel held on to the necklace and called out, "Who goes there?" Which was about the dumbest thing she could possibly say, especially if she was talking to a people-eating critter, but it just sort of came out.

A man appeared from around the side of an enormous oak. He bowed deeply, then straightened. "Relax, my dearest countess, 'tis just I, come to give you formal escort to the castle."

Isabel's heart dropped right to her vagina and started throbbing there. Now *this* was a beautiful man. His hair was dark but cut quite short. His lips whispered sex, his smile screamed it. His eyes were as deep mossy green as the lush forest around them. He had a goatee, which she normally hated, but on him it worked.

He was wearing what appeared to be some sort of flexible chain mail over his chest that fell almost to his knees, he held a hunter's bow in his left hand and had a quiver strapped across his chest, the arrows apparent behind his really broad shoulders. Underneath the armor he sported a pair of tight black leggings.

The man stepped closer, his gaze dipping to her necklace, then back to her face. "'Tis unseemly to be traveling this forest alone. Where are your men? Where are your traveling trunks?"

Good question, for which she didn't have a good answer, until she touched her neckpiece. "Oh, yes, well, they are a beat or ten behind me. I was feeling a bit restless at the plodding pace of the wagon and sporting a need for a bit of privacy. But they should be catching up shortly. Shouldn't they?" she asked the trees. The trees above shivered, and she took that as a yes. After all, Viviane wouldn't have sent her to this place without more than one gown, would she? And of course it would seem unimaginable for a woman to be traveling alone.

"I'm honored that you feel safety in the forests of Camelot, Countess, but even here there is danger."

The only danger she felt at the moment was her attraction to this man. To change the subject, fast, she said, "I'm afraid, sir, that I'm at a disadvantage. You appear to know of me, you appear to have had advance warning of my pending arrival, but I know naught of you." Isabel felt a giggle bubble in her chest and was certain its source was Viviane's. It suddenly occurred to her that she was speaking and understanding Old English just fine. What a really cool dream this was turning out to be.

"Having a fair idea of your impending arrival time, I've had my men watching out for your entourage so that you would have proper escort to Camelot. Imagine my concern when news was brought to me that you appeared to be alone. And that none of your men had ridden ahead to announce you. I worried dearly that some mishap had befallen your detail."

Imagine mine, too, Isabel thought. And she wondered just how alone she'd been when she'd had to stop to empty her bladder. She felt her cheeks heat up at the idea.

"My sincerest gratitude for your concern and care."

"My sincerest gratitude for your gracious acceptance to visit us at Camelot."

"Then, I suppose, we're all happy campers! Once again, sir, I have yet to know to whom I speak. Are you, perchance"—*let us pray*—"Sir Lancelot?" Even as she asked, she was fairly certain she couldn't be that lucky. This man was older by a decade or more than the young knight she'd read about. He was seasoned just right, with laugh lines around his eyes and brackets around his mouth that bespoke of harder, longer living. And there was a wisdom and even hint of weariness in his eyes.

His laughter was again deep and deadly. "All beautiful women want Lancelot. I apologize for not being him."

"No apology necessary. But who then, are you?"

He bowed again. "My name is Arthur."

"No way."

"Way."

He's the king, Izzy.

And that means what?

That means get your aces off your horse and curtsy.

Lady, you have kind of left out a lot.

Isabel dismounted, most definitely not gracefully, then took Arthur's hand and did her best to bend into a curtsy. Since she hadn't curtsied since a tenth grade play—of all things, *Camelot*—she was a little rusty.

"King Arthur, my apologies for not recognizing you before now."

She went to bring his hand to her lips, because she was pretty certain she was supposed to kiss his ring or something, but then she began to wobble, not being all that versed lately in bowing to someone without wanting to kick him in the gonads.

He grabbed her by her waist and pulled her up, his smile so full of enjoyment she wanted to kiss every part of him but his ring.

"Countess, the ride has obviously been a long one and your legs are trying. Betwixt us, that ring kissing thing has always annoyed me."

His hands didn't leave her waist, his eyes never stopped smiling into hers. She seriously waited for him to burst into song. "Richard Harris has nothing on you," she blurted. It was a mistake. She knew it instantly as her necklace kicked her in the chest.

He stepped back, and his eyes clouded. "You are in league with Sir Richard?"

She definitely missed King Arthur's hands on her waist. "Sir Richard? Of Fremont?"

"I assure you, no, I am not. I was remembering my own Richard, who was once one of my men. Richard of Fremont is nothing more than a swine."

She had no clue where any of that information came from, but she was so relieved to see the suspicion leave his eyes. "King Arthur," she said, bending low again, "I would be ever so grateful for your personal escort to Camelot."

"And so you shall have it, Countess. And alas, look who have finally caught up with you."

Isabel turned, and sure enough there were two men on bays, riding each side of a wagon with another man driving it, and two identical dapples lugging it, appearing totally disgruntled. As well they should have been, considering the pile of luggage they were . . . well . . . lugging.

Isabel ogled. The three men were almost identical to three of her friends back home in Oklahoma. It took everything she had in her not to run to them and hug them.

But wait. *Lady, did you kill my friends?* Isabel furiously asked, albeit silently.

And the response was instant, again, silently relayed to her.

The countess, Isabel, must needs her friends. These only be visuals the lake to you lends. You know which traits each of these tends. Because, Isabel, you'll need them, so deal with it.

Isabel took a moment, shaking her head. *That didn't rhyme.*

So sue me.

She turned back to the King. "King Arthur, these are my men. Tom, Dick and Harry. But they're not the usual Tom, Dick and Harry. They're *my* Tom, Dick and Harry." It never occurred to her how funny that sounded until this very moment. She whirled back to her friends before she burst out laughing. "Please, men, this is King Arthur. Give him the total respect due him."

Tom and Dick jumped from their bays, and Harry put some kind of stop on the cart thing and hopped down, a smile wide on his face. They all bent to one knee and bowed their heads. "At your service, sir," they said in unison.

"Please rise," said Arthur. "There are no formalities here."

"Seriously," said Isabel to Tom. "I couldn't get you to bow when I beat you at quarters in college."

"M'lady, you'd unfairly plied me with Budwei—er, ale that night."

That was true. Isabel had gotten him snockered on purpose. After all, the fraternity/sorority championship was on the line. "Excuses," she said with an airy wave. "'Tis the last refuge of the weak."

"College? Quarters?"

Isabel received another thump on her chest. At this point she'd have a bruise the size of a baseball. "My apologies, King Arthur. Games we play back in Dumont. I feel that happy friends are productive friends."

The king gifted her with another winning smile. "We appear to have much in common. I too enjoy sporting with my men."

Isabel frowned. "To leave the women doing the laundry, cooking, cleaning? What enjoyment do you provide your female help, sir? When do they get a freaking break?" Isabel braced herself for another thump from her necklace, but it never came. Apparently Viviane was on her side on this one. What do you know? A feminist goddess.

Arthur seemed at a loss for words. "I'd not thought of this. Perhaps the queen can answer this. The women seem not to be incontent, but, Countess, I will inquire and, should there be a problem, shall attempt to address this as soon as possible. Mayhap, with your suggestions? These quarter things, for example."

"Whoa, let's take this slowly, Arthur. Quarters is a skill. But should you allow, I might possibly come up with something."

"I will be open to any suggestions, Countess. Now, shall we proceed to Camelot?"

"Let's roll," Isabel said. She turned back to her crew and winked. Tom, Dick and Harry all stepped forward to assist her back onto Samara. The king waved them all away. "This will be my pleasure, Countess. On our travel, may we discuss the college thing?"

When Arthur's men had materialized with his own steed, a dapple gray, he'd given them orders to stand forward and behind her own men. And then she and this king had spent the rest of the ride side by side, joking.

Isabel liked him. *Way* too much.

Not my fault, Lady.

Try harder, Isabel.

CHAPTER FIVE

O KAY, Camelot was magnificent. Isabel would have given anything to have her camera equipment with her. It was so unfair not to be able to capture the beauty of it all.

There was an actual moat that they all traversed over a bridge, a wooden bridge. They then entered a keep that was so buzzing with activity that Isabel was almost afraid. So many men working as if they were in football practice, so many women running back and forth chasing after children.

The castle itself was breathtaking. Isabel had assumed it would be made of stone, but strangely, it seemed mostly to be made of wood. And yet so many chimneys had smoke chugging from them. And she had the feeling there wasn't a single smoke alarm in the place.

What really shocked Isabel, though, was the way all of the people greeted their king. They bowed, of course, as he entered the keep, but they smiled, too. These people really liked their leader. Isabel could relate. Unfortunately.

The great hall was also abuzz with activity. But it seemed to come to a screeching halt when the king escorted her in and loudly announced her arrival. Even the animals running around—there had to be at least thirty dogs of all varieties—froze. Then the bowing and curtsying began.

"Please tell them to rise, sir," she whispered to Arthur. "They're acting like I'm freaking royalty."

Arthur's eyes widened for a second. "Countess, you *are* royalty."

Oops. "Perhaps, but I'm not so big on the bowing and scraping thing. It makes me uncomfortable. I much more prefer an equality of sorts."

He smiled again, which was really mean because his smile was lethal. "We have much in common, m'lady."

"Isabel."

"Isabel it is, then. And I am Arthur. Please, I beg you to leave off the king part."

"Deal!" she said.

"Rise, all! The lady prefers you not . . ."

"Grovel?" Isabel provided.

". . . feel the need to lower yourselves upon her entrance," King Arthur finished.

Isabel felt the need to bow a little herself. Then she stood and said, "Okay, now we're even. No more of that, all right? It's a pain for all of us. By the way, hi! Good to be here," she said, waving in what she hoped wasn't a Queen Elizabeth–type way.

Everyone, even the dogs, stared at her like she was a little, or maybe a lot, addled. But then they smiled. And several waved back.

There were what she thought were things called rushes on the floor, and the hall smelled a little smarmy. Part sweat, part pee, part burning wood, part indescribable. Yet as she and Arthur walked farther into the great room, a kind of nice smell kept wafting up.

"Thyme?" she asked.

The king looked at her. "My guess, Isabel, is betwixt the noon hour and evening meal."

"I was talking about . . . never mind. May I retire to my quarters to prepare for supper?"

"Most assuredly, Countess. Your trunks will be delivered as soon as one of your Toms, Dicks or Harrys manage to get them up there." The humor was back in his eyes, and Isabel was once again bamboozled.

She pulled herself together to ask one more thing. "Sir, my men. They mean a great deal to me. Their accommodations?"

"They'll be given the best the great hall of Camelot has to offer, Isabel."

Once again, she melted. The way her name came off his tongue really screwed with her hormones. "Does this mean they'll stay downstairs, then?"

"Do you want them up closer to you, Isabel?"

"Is that possible? I don't want to upset anyone, but I truly want them near me."

"Very unusual, but it shall be done." The king took a long look at her, then bowed. "I only wish to make you happy."

Happy would be kissing him senseless.

Her necklace again thumped her. *Stick to the plan, Izzy.*

Then stop putting gorgeous, sexy kings in my face, Viviane.

ISABEL'S room was the epitome of medieval luxury accommodations. The walls were made of rustic wood, which smelled of cedar, but probably weren't. The bedsheets were rose and forest green. She had her own special room, if you could call it that, with a piss pot in just about every corner. And in front of the fireplace was a huge tub.

There was a cheerful fire crackling in the huge fireplace, which bathed the room in a rosy glow. All in all, considering the time period, this was presidential-suite material.

Her trunks had been delivered to her room, and Viviane had thought of everything. Except floss. And a toothbrush. And Listerine.

Not happy with the lack of dental care here, Viviane.

Patience has never been a virtue bestowed upon you, has it, dear?

Not when it comes to my teeth.

Help will arrive shortly. And wear the very pale red gown tonight that I believe in your time you call pink. Lancelot is apparently partial to that shade.

Pink. Probably Isabel's least favorite color. Not only did it wash out any color from her face, it reminded her of the time when she'd been forced to play the cotton candy in her fourth grade play, *A Day at the Fair.* She'd really wanted to be the corn dog.

Isabel jumped when there was a knock at her door. "Yes?"

"M'lady, 'tis Mary. I shall be your chambermaid during your visit."

"Well, by all means, Mary, come on in."

"Me arms be full, m'lady."

Isabel turned from her trunks and went to the door. "Full of—"

She stopped as she stared down at the loaded tray in the young girl's hands. There were several twigs that appeared shredded on one side. A small bowl with what looked like salt. A pitcher of water and another small bowl of greens which smelled like mint.

This is what I'm supposed to use on my teeth?

You will find it suffices for teeth devices.

"What, no wine?" Isabel asked, motioning Mary in.

The girl tried to curtsy, which made everything on the tray wobble precariously. "On its way, m'la—"

"My name is Isabel, Mary. If I may call you Mary, please call me Isabel."

"Oh, no, m'lady! I could not possibly."

"Oh, yes, Mary, you could. In fact I insist."

"Please, Countess, I cannot."

Isabel smiled down at the girl, who couldn't be older than thirteen. Mary had long, bright red hair that would have made Ronald McDonald jealous. She had freckles racing all over her nose and cheeks. But Isabel couldn't figure out the color of her eyes because Mary was intent on staring at the floor.

"Fine, then. I won't ever ask you to do something that makes you uncomfortable. Countess will work for me if it works for you."

"Yes, mum. Countess, mum."

"Then we're all set. Please, bring on the goodies."

Mary stumbled through the room into the dressing area, set everything down just so, then turned with her empty tray. "Shall I order water for a bath, m'lady?"

"That sounds heavenly."

Finally Mary raised her eyes to meet Isabel's. They were the exact sapphire color of the necklace of tears.

Isabel grinned. It was an omen. "I think you and I are going to get along just fine, Mary."

"I believe so as well, m'la—Countess."

"I would love a bath. But before that, could you please help me find the pink gown among this mess?"

"Pink?"

"Pale red?" Isabel tried.

Mary gnawed at her bottom lip, obviously still not understanding.

"You know the color that your cheeks turn, when you're flattered by a boy? Or embarrassed by something you think you've done?"

"Oh! Oh, yes. Although, mum, in my instances, that would be a deep red." She glanced down and then up again, a twinkle in her eyes. "I must admit it does not go well with my hair."

"I doubt that, Mary. My guess is that your blush turns many young men's heads."

Mary blushed.

And boy, was she right. Almost fire-engine red on those cheeks.

"That's so kind of you to say, Countess." Mary headed straight for the third trunk and pulled out a beautiful gown. "That's more rose than pink, Mary."

"This is not your . . . pink?"

Is this your idea of pink, Viviane?

So a shade here and there. Stop quibbling.

"I think this will compliment your fair skin, Lady. Any shade lighter and 'twould not do your beauty justice."

Now that's what Isabel liked. A chambermaid with excellent taste. "Yes, you and I are going to get along really well, Mary."

"I am assured we are, m'lady."

Isabel didn't even need to ask who, or what, assured Mary as Isabel again touched her necklace. "Bring on the wine and the bath."

"Done."

"How are you with hair, Mary?"

"Do you need me to be good with hair, Countess?"

"I really do."

"Then, yes, m'lady, I am very good with hair."

As primitive as this all was, Isabel felt amazingly pampered. The gallons of bath water carted to her room had been too hot at first, but Mary had sprinkled lavender and rosemary in the tub. It was wonderfully soothing. Afterward Mary made good on her promise, roping Isabel's hair and then wrapping it into something of a bun, but with a twist, then a long, elaborate ponytail.

Mary had also added a brass broach to the left side of Isabel's waist. By the time Tom and Dick escorted her down to the dining area, she felt almost queenlike. Time to meet the real queen. Wonderful.

Isabel met both Lancelot and Guinevere at supper that night. Gwen, as King Arthur called her, was as nice as nice could be. She was a beautiful young thing; young being the operative word. Her hair was auburn, pulled back in an elaborate bun, a circlet of tiny gems gracing her disgustingly devoid-of-a-single-wrinkle forehead.

Isabel wanted to ask what face cream she used, until it occurred to her that Gwen was still nearly a child. Isabel wasn't allowed to date at her age, much less marry and cheat on her husband. If Gwen hadn't been so sweetly gracious, Isabel would have loved to hate her. The queen had the scent of rose petals emanating from her, which was a welcome smell compared to the sweat and animal odors that invaded even this dining room.

Of course, there were sweaty men and dogs hanging around

here, too, so no big surprise there. Isabel wished she'd paid more attention to the ingredients in Oust to see if she could replicate the product here.

Gwen's dress was a shimmery silver, with an elaborate chain belted around her disgustingly tiny waist. Isabel guessed that belt wouldn't fit around half the beefy men's arms who were standing at the huge rectangular dining room table.

"'Tis an honor to have you grace our hall, Countess," Guinevere said. "We have been anticipating your arrival with much gladness. My husband informs me that this will mean a great and mutually beneficial treaty between our two lands."

Oh, great, so Gwen wasn't a twit. She kept her pulse on politics, too. Was there *nothing* Isabel could find to dislike about her? Other than the fact that Gwen had the luxury of sleeping every night beside the one man who so far floated Isabel's longship?

She felt a thump on her chest.

Could you stop doing that?

Pull it together, dear. Bow to the queen and leave the lust for later.

Isabel attempted another deep curtsy, which would have failed miserably if Tom and Dick hadn't held on. She really needed to practice this bowing thing. "I'm honored to have been invited to Camelot, Your Highness. Your hospitality is much appreciated."

Gwen laughed softly, which was also disgustingly perfect. "Please, Arthur and I do not ken to the formalities. Unless you want that I should bow to you as well when we meet."

Horror of horrors. Isabel had a flashback of being in the Far East with the "you bow, I bow, you bow, I bow, who gets to bow last" thing. "That works perfectly for me," Isabel said, then nearly groaned at the shocked look on the faces around her. "What I mean, your Highness, is that we should give our knees a break."

Gwen actually grinned. "Methinks it is an excellent suggestion. Perhaps all of that bowing is also to blame for so many back ailments among our men?"

"Methinks, you might be correct," Isabel said. "Perhaps a good chiropra—"

Thump.

Isabel worked hard not to react to the bang to her chest. "What I meant to say, is that my man, Dick, here, is a wonder with back problems." Very true. He was her chiropractor in the normal world and a miracle worker, considering how much she had to contort her body to get the right shots. "Perhaps he could work some magic on your ailing men."

Many men standing by the table rubbed their backs and finally smiled their half-toothless smiles at Dick. Even a few of the serving maids took a second glance.

Dick kicked Isabel in the leg while smiling wildly. Then he bowed again and said, "At your service, Your Highness. And might I add that Tom, here, is a specialist with teeth? Should you have anyone in the castle who must needs tooth attention, he would be more than willing to offer assistance."

Tom turned green at all of the toothless smiles that suddenly swung his way. "Always at your service, Your Highness," he said, reaching his leg around to kick Dick.

Tom had been Isabel's dentist forever and friend for at least half of that. He gave her a "what have you gotten me into?" look, and she gave him a shrug. After all, she hadn't mentioned it.

Just then Harry came limping in from the great hall, his hair still wet from having to make himself presentable and his gait still showing he was hurting from the kick to his gonads. It obviously hurt, badly.

"And this is Harry," Isabel announced, "my other man. He is the one incredibly good with animals. He's been my ve—"

Thump

"Ouch!"

Everyone stared at her.

"My animal master and devoted . . . friend, for many moons. As have Tom and Dick. In Dumont, we are all friends, working together."

There was a silence while Harry attempted to bow to Arthur and Gwen, which looked painful to everyone. To a male, every single one of them in the dining room winced.

But then they followed their king's lead, holding up their steins.

"I am assuming you took one for the Gipper, master Harry," Arthur said. "He has always been a bit overly accurate with his legs."

"Oh, wait a minute," Isabel said, "you have a horse named Gipper?"

Gwen spoke up first. "I'm afraid Gipper is mine. And my apologies, sir, for his . . . exuberance. Sir Ronald of Reagan gifted him to me at our matrimonial ceremony. He is a beautiful stud but can be much of a handful. But not as taxing as most."

Harry bowed again, then headed straight to Isabel. "He's not going to be studding anytime soon. The sonofabitch nearly blew off my balls," he whispered.

"Please don't tell me . . ."

"No little Gippers showing up soon. Actually ever. And it felt good."

At the supper table, Arthur spent a few minutes introducing his men as well.

James was his first man, whatever that was. But he was bigger than any professional wrestler, so Isabel was guessing he was also a bodyguard of sorts.

Tristan, his second man, who was only slightly smaller than James and who she recognized from the woods, bowed his head. Isabel waved at him, hoping he hadn't seen her bare butt while she'd stopped to pee. Unfortunately, Tristan grinned at her, which gave her the feeling that at least he had.

And on and on with other men who meant something to Arthur or Gwen. It was a big freaking table.

And then, finally, she was introduced to Lancelot. He stood and bowed more deeply than all of the other men. He was her target, apparently, but not a single one of her hormones charged to life.

Lancelot, a darling blusher, was as shy as shy could be. To be certain, he was a striking young man, having light brown hair with sun-streaked golden threads that Isabel would love to challenge her hairdresser, Pelo, to try to duplicate. When he finally managed to meet her gaze, she figured he had hazel eyes, which were looking more green than brown at the moment because of the forest green tunic he was wearing. He stumbled his way through the greeting, which was rather sweet. But not the least bit sexy, unlike the hearty laughter with which King Arthur had greeted her. Damn, damn and triple damn, not a single sex gene in Isabel's body fired up.

The rest of the King's men were a little grumpy during supper, and she was figuring that it was because she'd asked for her men to be invited.

Isabel was in a bit of a pickle. Her attraction to Lancelot amounted to less than zero. Less than the pickled eel placed in front of her at supper. Less than Hester the court jester's jokes, which were sadly lame.

As was he, in an endearing way. He had to be seventy if he was a day, and the blue and purple silklike robes didn't do much for his pasty skin. But Hester tried so hard to entertain the crowd that Isabel decided he was a cool enough fellow, anyway.

Arthur winked at her, and then so did Hester before he bowed and took his leave. "What fun, yes?" Isabel said. Pretty much no one agreed with her. Except for Arthur, who couldn't stop grinning.

A ton of food was delivered to the table. Almost all of it meat. Even though she was not a vegetarian—not completely, but for the most part—she was totally grossed out. Especially with the meat. Boar, rabbit, squirrel and, oh man, more pickled eel. The best she found were cabbage and beets. Not her favorite veggies.

Isabel had never been a liquor person, but tonight she was drinking like a sailor, hoping alcohol would help in her mission. Both to eat the eel without throwing up and to try to seduce the child knight who was just as inedible.

You're kidding, right, Lady? This is an impossible task.

You must needs try, Izzy. Think of Merlin.

So far, just not working. He was cute enough, if you liked boys. Which she had, when she'd been a girl. But as handsome as he was, he was young. Way too young.

The sad thing was, he had no interest in Isabel, either. He had eyes for only Gwen. Which was apparent to everyone in the room except for King Arthur, who was so busy talking about this important meeting with other knights of the realm that he seemed oblivious to the looks exchanged between Gwen and the cute boy.

Seemed that everyone at the table watched and scowled, but felt nothing could be done to stop it as long as the king said nothing. Either the king had forbidden all to even *think* about the possibility, or he'd made certain no one voiced it.

She felt so bad about it all, but then again she had other things to mourn over.

Like the eel.

Like her total disinterest in Lancelot.

Like Lancelot's total disinterest in her.

Like Guinevere's total interest in Lancelot.

She was in magical hell.

Isabel could not fix all things at once, but there were a couple over which she had some control. She politely requested that a servant remove the eel, the boar, the rabbit and the squirrel, and then politely excused herself to go fashion a barf bag.

CHAPTER SIX

OKAY, so she was a little tipsy. But not so much that she didn't notice that Gwen and Lancelot had excused themselves almost at the same time. They didn't even try to pretend. It broke Isabel's heart for Arthur. He had to know. And yet he didn't seem to know. Or care.

"Would you enjoy a tour of the castle, Countess?" Arthur asked her, as the evening meal had thankfully concluded.

Thank God for Mary, who had met her in the garderobe, carrying a bowl of mint. Otherwise she'd be afraid that her breath would topple trees.

"I would love it, sir." What she wanted was a tour of his body, but the castle would have to do for now.

"The gardens," he said. "They mean much to Gwen. For a reason I cannot fathom, she tends to them almost daily, even though we have many, many gardeners to do such things."

"We all have our favorite hobbies."

"And what would be yours, Countess?"

Photography immediately came to mind, but she doubted she could explain that one. Sex was also high on her list, or it had been back in the day. Or forward in the day. She'd love to experiment here, but unfortunately not with Lance, but with the king. "I very much enjoy exercise. Sporting, as it were."

The surprise on his face was so adorable, she wanted to kiss those raised eyebrows. "Sporting? Such as exercising the horses?"

"Well, yes, but much more than that. For example, I love jogging."

"Jogging? What is this jogging?"

"Steady running for long distances."

He laughed. "And you accomplish this in gowns?"

Now here was an opening she'd been waiting for. "Actually in Dumont the women who enjoy such exercise wear smaller versions of men's leggings."

"Pardon?"

"We believe women have as much right to exercise their passions as men. Can you possibly imagine women who love to run, doing so in gowns? Preposterous. So in Dumont, when women have the need or desire to stretch and strengthen their muscles, they wear what we call sporting gear."

Arthur stroked his beard and she had the feeling he was trying to keep himself from laughing. "And what, pray tell, do you . . . they wear upon their upper halves?"

She figured a sports bra was probably going a little too far. "We wear things called T-shirts. A sort of oversized tunic, made of soft fabric for comfort."

Arthur shook his head. "Apparently my men left much out in their reports from Dumont."

"Setting aside the fact that you sent men to spy on me, let me ask you this: What kind of hobbies or pleasures do you afford your female servants?"

"Hobbies? Pleasures?"

"You allow Gwen to indulge in her pleasures."

"Of course. She is my queen and my wife."

"And yet all of your servants are not permitted to indulge in things that make them happy? You truly believe that because of their station they may not participate in activities they might truly enjoy?"

"My people are not unhappy. Are they? Have you heard grumblings?"

"No, sir, I have not. But would any voice them in front of me?"

His worried frown saddened her. "Do they appear unhappy to you?"

"Again, no. In fact they appear very loyal to their king. But consider the possibilities of allowing them just, say, a small portion of a day to follow their own dreams. To play with their own favored hobbies. How much happier they might be to go about the routine tasks they are required to do day in and day out when they know they have that small portion of time to just play. You may even find that their hobbies reap rewards that you and Camelot have never envisioned."

Arthur sat down with a thump, seeming deep in thought. "You give me much to ponder."

Isabel took his hand. "Ponder this. A happy castle staff makes for a happy Camelot. You and Gwen and your highest men enjoy the fruits of the servants' labors. How about allowing the servants to enjoy some of those fruits for themselves? Why are you, Gwen and I allowed to follow our hearts, and those who work for us not permitted to follow theirs?"

He puffed up like a blowfish. "I do not disallow my staff from pursuing their own desires! Have you not seen the many children about?"

Isabel wanted to laugh but controlled herself. "Lovemaking and childmaking is going to happen no matter what else is happening. I'm talking about other pleasures."

"What other pleasures are there?"

"Oh, please. Lovemaking is certainly a big one. But there are others. Gwen loves to garden. My chambermaid loves to dress hair. I love to run. I love to draw. The possibilities are endless. We could conduct a poll and find what really makes them happy. And then allow them the opportunity to pursue those dreams."

"A poll?"

"A chance for them to speak up about what they enjoy. And possibly allow them to voice what they don't."

The beard scrubbing was gone. He'd moved on to standing and rubbing his temples. This was a natural progression in Isabel's life, so she wasn't exactly surprised. Next he'd be begging for a drink. She'd bet money on it.

"You are an unusual woman, Isabel," he finally said. Then he stepped to his left and knocked on a bell. Within seconds Tim appeared. "Wine, please, Timothy. And two goblets."

She needed more wine like she needed more eel. But what the hell? "I promise that you are not the first to tell me this. About being unusual, I mean."

"But I swear 'tis in a very intriguing way."

"Right, one that drives men to drink."

"One that drives men to ponder as they enjoy an evening libation."

Isabel tried hard to resist, for Viviane's sake. "Should you not be sharing this with the queen?"

"Gwen enjoys evenings to . . . pursue those"—he waved his hands vaguely—"things women like to do."

I'll bet. Isabel rather liked mornings for those types of pursuits but decided not to mention that.

"She's very sweet," she said instead, fingering her necklace. "You must love her very much."

His hesitation was palpable as his eyes seemed fixated on her chest. "As I'm bound to do. She is my wife."

He sat down, then immediately stood again and started pacing. Then he suddenly stopped and turned to Isabel, his green eyes searching. "Have you loved, Countess?"

"You're asking why?"

"You have never married."

"I haven't? I mean, of course I haven't. But Arthur, you seem to know much about me." A whole helluva lot more than she knew about her countess self, as a matter of fact. Until just now, she'd had no idea whether she'd ever been married or not.

Apparently not.

Good God, Viviane, I am no freaking virgin.

'Tis true, Isabel, do you not consider that win-win?

He thinks I am at this stage.

Then consider yourself a hussy, and stop worrying about age.

"How is it that you've come by all of this information about me?"

He looked adorably confused. "I'm not certain. It must have been details my men gathered whilst they were checking upon Dumont."

"Why would you have private investigators checking on me?"

Chagrin looked cute on him, too. "My apologies, Countess. But I would be amiss should I not have knowledge prior to your arrival."

They were temporarily interrupted by Tim, who arrived with a tray loaded with two goblets. He offered the tray first to her and then Arthur, bowed as they thanked him and silently took his leave, his face betraying no sign of suspicion at what had to be an unusual situation. Isabel wasn't a connoisseur, but she was pretty sure the liquid in her goblet was either brandy or cognac or the medieval equivalent. It certainly didn't look or smell like wine.

Arthur swirled his drink before taking a sip. "How could a man not take control of your heart?"

"I haven't said that my heart has never been engaged, sir." In fact it felt quite a little too engaged at the moment, and she'd known this man for less than twenty-four hours. "I've just not met one who has made me want to be taking those vows," she said, smiling. "I take them too seriously to say them without meaning them."

As soon as the words were out, she wanted to kick herself. The pained expression on his face nearly sliced up her heart. "But," she added quickly, "I feel certain I'll know him and that elusive thing called love when I see him."

He looked down. "That makes sense to me. You are, what do they say? Particular?"

"You could say that. Why, Arthur, are you asking me these questions?"

He looked down at her necklace then up, and those gorgeous eyes drilled into her. "Because, madam, I have wanted to kiss you from the moment we met. And I know this is so wrong. My wife's lips should be the only ones that touch mine. And yet, yours beckon me."

He turned his back to her. "That was so inappropriate. Please, forget I even uttered such nonsense. I do not understand why I cannot seem to control my tongue around you."

She had a good feeling she knew why. There was a price to pay for the power of the necklace. And apparently she was not the only one who might have to pay it.

Oh, great, Lady, I want it, too. What do I do?

Well, crap. This is not going as I'd foreseen.

I will do what I can to resist.

The Lady seemed to ponder for a while, but it was probably less than a nanosecond because Arthur hadn't moved, as if the Goddess had frozen him in time as she thought things through.

It seems, Isabel, there's a fork in this road, one that carries a heavy load. This way or that, which will it be? When Merlin's happiness is what matters to me.

But—

Wait a moment, I'm not done, Isabel, as your happiness and Arthur's matter as well. I fear in my selfishness I've not thought this through. I now believe you do what you must do; that fork in the road I spoke of afore, I feel you must choose the one that matters more. 'Tis Arthur's happiness that is paramount to my man; choose your path, Isabel, and do what you can.

Well, that cleared things up. Not. So the goddess was leaving it up to her? What if she screwed it up and everyone lost? She'd feel just horrible. Or maybe if she really screwed it up, she wouldn't feel anything because she'd be dead at the bottom of Grand Lake.

Isabel had never shied from responsibility before. But this was kind of a heavy load for which she wasn't certain she was prepared.

She squared her shoulders and walked up behind Arthur,

touching his shoulder. Finally he stirred and turned back to her, the regret in his eyes clear.

She smiled gently. "Please, don't apologize, Arthur. I would be lying if I didn't find your admission both flattering and exciting. I felt exactly the same when you materialized from behind that tree."

"You are being kind."

Isabel laughed. "That's a word that doesn't often show up in a sentence about me. But no, sir, kindness has nothing to do with it. You were truthful to me, and I owe you at least the same."

"Then may I? Just this once?" he asked.

"But your love of your wife, Arthur? Is this not a betrayal to her?"

He snorted. "Betrayal. That is a word I have come to know well."

"Meaning?"

"I may seem the fool, Isabel, but I assure you, I am not. I am not blind to what is going on around me. Perhaps I am all well too aware."

Since she'd just arrived, there would be no way for her to actually know about Gwen and Lancelot, unless she'd been listening to the servants' gossip. And she wasn't about to get that darling Mary in trouble for something Mary didn't do. So she feigned ignorance. "I know naught of what's troubling you, Arthur, so I have no words to comfort you."

His chuckle was tinged with bitterness. "I have said more to a woman who is a virtual stranger to me than I've e'er said to my most trusted men."

Isabel stepped back to the bench and sat, then patted the place beside her. "Please, join me. I might have a theory on the matter." She took a healthy glug of her drink, and surprisingly it was rather good.

"By all means," he said, taking a seat beside her. "Please, let me hear this theory of yours."

Isabel toyed with her necklace, making certain his attention was drawn there for a moment or two, hoping the power of the teardrop would work here. "I believe, sir, that it is sometimes much easier to unburden one's troubles to the ear of someone who isn't so intimately involved in the situation. A nonpartisan view, as it were."

"Nonpartisan?"

"One who has little if any stake in the matter. One who has not chosen sides." Which was a bit of a lie, because if Isabel was going to choose which fork in that road to take, she had a lot at stake in this matter. Not to mention, as nice as Gwen was, Isabel was firmly in Arthur's court, so to speak.

The early summer night was warm and mixed with the fragrance of lilacs and oil from the two tall lamps set on either side of the mossy path that led into the gardens. The moon was lovely in the clear night sky but not much help as it was only at about its quarter stage. Night critters filled the air with chirps and chitters that sounded comforting somehow.

Arthur didn't seem to be taking in the atmosphere as he was still staring from her face to her necklace and back again. "And you would be this . . . nonpartisan person?"

"Should you want me to be." Oh, great, she'd just signed up to be his sounding board. His psychologist. Freud would be spinning right about now. However, maybe what he spilled would revolt her so much that she'd stop obsessing over his big, swarthy hands. His lips. His eyes.

"How do I go about this?" he asked, looking lost.

"However you would like. Wherever and whenever."

He stood again and paced. Oh, man, nice butt, thighs and shoulders. His men obviously weren't the only ones who worked out hard while he sat on his throne.

Finally he stopped and faced her. "I had this idea. I thought it was one that would benefit all; those in Camelot and those in all of the surrounding lands. To bring all of the knights of all of the realms together to meet, to discuss how we might find a way to create treaties that would benefit us all and allow us to live prosperously, peacefully and happily."

"Sounds like a great plan to me." Impossible, probably, but hey, maybe someday.

He threw his free arm wide. "And to me as well. I was hoping— perhaps in my arrogance—that this might define my legacy as king."

"There is nothing arrogant about wanting to leave a mark on the world, sir. Is it not what we all hope to accomplish during our time on this earth? To leave it better because of our actions?"

His hand went to his hip. "I most certainly want to kiss you, Countess."

Oh, me, too. Come on, come on, spill something that will disgust me.

She smiled. "Your tale is in its beginnings. Please, go on. We'll discuss that other part once you've unburdened what brings that sadness to your eyes."

He returned to the bench and sat down, taking a long sip from his cup before setting it down. Then he took her hand, running his thumb over her palm.

Isabel should have objected, should have pulled away, but it felt really gentle and she had the willpower of a moth to one of those lanterns.

He kind of shook his head. "The responses from the knights were positive. We are to meet here in the next sennight. I asked you to arrive early because our lands border one another, and I wanted us to have discussions over farming before all arrived. And," he added, looking her in the eyes, "because perhaps the knights would not . . ."

"Accept a woman at the negotiating table?"

He nodded. "I am so sorry."

"Not a problem. We'll deal with that later. So what's so sad about this great response to your offer of negotiations? I don't get it."

"This is where Lancelot comes in."

CHAPTER SEVEN

ISABEL finished off her cognac and also set the glass down before saying, "Lancelot? He sat at our table tonight. Correct? He seemed like a nice enough child."

"Ha!" Arthur barked. "Yes, indeed, he's a nice enough child. He is also the most skilled fighter I have e'er known. All he needed was guidance. I believed. In my dealings with him, I felt like he was the son I had always wanted, the son I never . . . was able to mold. I asked him to come to Camelot to be part of the men who would secure us."

"He has obviously accepted."

"He has." Arthur shut his eyes, then opened then again. Looking clearly and deeply into hers. "He has also secured the love of my wife. He has assured to help defend and secure Camelot. He swore his fealty. However, it has become painfully obvious that his loyalties have . . . shifted."

"Has he, then, betrayed you? Is he now a threat to Camelot?" This feigning ignorance was getting tough. "And if so, why do you still invite him to your table?"

"A threat to Camelot, no. I have no doubt that he would be the first into battle, should it, heaven forbid, ever come to that. And I am certain he never meant to betray me."

"But he has."

Arthur looked down at the ground, almost as if he couldn't face her as he whispered, "I feel, to my soul, that he wishes to be true to me. But I am certain, in my heart, that he . . . has fallen in love with Gwen."

"Uh-oh. And Gwen?"

"I believe she returns his love."

"Has she said as much?"

"No, no, of course not."

"Have you asked?"

"I have not been able to bring myself to confront her. If the truth is spoken, the consequences are grave. A queen's unfaithfulness to her husband and king is considered treason, and is punishable by death."

"Wow. Does she happen to be aware of that little bylaw?"

Arthur opened his mouth to answer, but then a rustling in the garden behind them stopped him short. He put a finger to his lips, then mouthed, "Stay here." He then stood and silently treaded farther down the garden path.

Isabel watched him go, her heart drumming as he disappeared into the shadows. If there was someone spying on them and they had overheard, the consequences would be huge. Too huge for Isabel to want to contemplate. She grasped her teardrop necklace, wondering if this was one of those times where she should put the powers it held into play.

But she thought of Viviane's warning. There were repercussions for its use, and she didn't even want to think of just what those might be. If she banished the intruder, what would she, or they, face as punishment?

Fear not, Isabel, this one's on me. Arthur must needs to bare his sorrow to thee.

Oh, thank you, thank you, Viviane! You are a peach!

She heard a soft chuckle in her head. Then a thought occurred to her.

Hey, wait a minute. Are you watching and listening like, all *the time? I mean, I haven't decided my path, but should it take me . . . a little or a lot closer to Arthur . . .*

Isabel, I am a Goddess. I have seen and heard it all, but I give my word not to witness, should the clothing start to fall.

"That's a relief," Isabel murmured.

"What is, m'lady?" Arthur asked.

Isabel nearly jumped a foot. He'd returned as silently as he'd left. "Oh!"

He smiled down at her. "My apologies. I ne'er meant to startle you."

"I . . . I was just worried for your safety. You are unarmed."

"'Twas just but a rabbit. No need for concern."

Isabel had to wonder what it had been before Viviane intervened.

Arthur sat again, but then looked at her and stroked her cheek with his knuckles. She barely stifled a moan of pleasure.

"I am sorry to have unburdened my private troubles upon you, Isabel."

"Believe me, your concerns and heartache are safe with me. I feel honored you felt you could trust them to me. Although I must admit that I am so sorry that such an honorable man is having to deal with all of this."

"Not dealing well, I fear."

"Talk to her, Arthur. Tell her how you feel. Allow her at least to give an explanation. Perhaps there is nothing to your suspicions. Or perhaps this will jolt her into realizing the seriousness of her actions, and promise to stop this thing before anything horrible happens to any of you."

He nodded. "You are very wise, Countess Isabel. And I thank you for your ear and your thoughts."

"You are very welcome, Arthur. I do hope that things work out for all of us . . . I mean, you."

"You have had a long, tiring day, and I have kept you far too late into the night. Perhaps you would like to retire to your chamber?"

"I'm far from tired, Arthur, but if you would like to hit the hay, I understand."

He shook his head, chuckling. "Betimes I feel that we speak different languages. I assure you that the beds in the upper chambers are made of down and very comfortable. At least I hope you find yourself comfortable."

Images of them testing the comfort of the bed together bloomed bright in her mind. And by the glitter in his eyes, she had the feeling they were pretty much on the same page, fantasy-wise.

Isabel cleared her throat. "And are you ready to retire, sir king?"

"I feel as if I could talk to you the entire night, Isabel. Why is that, do you think?"

Now how did she answer that? *Because we wanted to jump each other from the moment our eyes met?* She opted for a more demure response. "I believe, sir, that we have much in common. Many would envy our stations in life, but truly, it is often lonely at the top." Oh, Lord, did she just say that? "What I mean is, we understand one another."

"You are a good woman, Countess."

"Besides," she said, trying to bring back a little levity, "on the ride to Camelot you laughed at all of my knock-knock jokes."

He had the most heart-thumping grin. "I ne'er heard such things afore. I must say that I would most enjoy to travel to Dumont some day. It must be a happy place."

How the hell would she know? "Laughter is the best medicine," she said, then nearly groaned. Platitudes were pouring out of her mouth at an alarming rate. Some shrink she'd make. "You and the queen are welcome at my castle anytime."

His eyes clouded, which reminded her of what they'd just been discussing.

She grabbed his hand. "My apologies, Arthur. You and your men are also welcome anytime. You can do the bachelor thing."

"The ba—"

"Never mind. What I mean to say is that my doors are always open to you." Did she have doors to open?

She swallowed another groan. *Shoot me now before I choke on my own slippered foot.*

"I thank you for the offer of hospitality. And shall most definitely take you up on your kind invitation one day."

They stared at each other for several heartbeats. During those silent seconds, Isabel knew exactly which road she was going to travel. Heaven help her.

She let go of his hand—albeit reluctantly. "Now before we retire, you have yet to answer my question, Arthur."

CHAPTER EIGHT

"M<small>Y</small> apologies, "MIsabel. I have forgotten the question."
So had she.

*And I quote. "Wow. Does she happen to be aware of that little bylaw?"
Thanks, Viviane!*

"I believe I asked if Gwen is guilty of this indiscretion, is she aware of the consequences of her actions?"

"What saddens me is that she is. And she is willing to risk this. As is Lancelot."

"Doesn't seem like true love to me if Lancelot is willing to put Gwen in that kind of danger."

"I believe they cannot help how they feel. I am understanding it more and more with every moment I am in your company. There is a phrase my mother told to me as a kidling. 'The heart wants what it wants.' I can no more direct the wants of Gwen's heart as I can explain how I managed to remove Excalibur. As I cannot explain this . . . feeling for you."

Isabel wasn't just flattered, she was on fire. Or, at least, her hormones were. But even as she knew the path she'd chosen, she had to play devil's advocate. Because adultery went against her fast-and-loose moral code. "Arthur, is it possible that this is a retaliation of sorts? Are you playing tit for tat? To hurt her as she's hurt you?"

"I know not of the tit-for-tat thing, but I understand retaliation. Should that have been the case, I would have chosen to take up with any number of women long afore now. 'Tis not in my nature to even events this way."

Isabel knew this. She didn't know how, but she did. Arthur wouldn't jump into the sheets, or in this case bed furs, with another just to get back at his cheating wife. He could even have gone further, were he a vengeful jerk. He could have exposed Gwen at any moment, have her judged, found guilty and killed. Instead, he continued to protect her, no matter how much it hurt him, day in and out.

"You still love her very much," Isabel said softly.

"That I do. But not as afore. Not in the same way. 'Tis not easy to look at your wife, play the dutiful and loving husband, when you know that she yearns for another."

Isabel suddenly realized that she was totally sober, even after the delicious cognac. Her earlier overindulgence was gone, her mind clear. Which should have made her earlier clouded judgment return to practical reality. And yet she still wanted that one kiss, and she wasn't drunkenly falling in temporary love.

Permanent lust was already a given.

She was falling, hard, but with a completely clear understanding of what this all meant. Well, shit. She had to fall back in time centuries to find the one? Fate wasn't necessarily cruel, but it had a really warped sense of humor.

"Is there no such thing as divorce in Camelot?"

"Divorce?"

"Dissolution of marriage? Annulment? Bye-bye?"

"Between a king and his queen?"

"Sure! I mean, certainly. In Dumont we allow for bad marriages to be annulled. So that the partners are free to remarry."

"Without cause? Does not one partner have to admit to wrong-doing?"

She wasn't certain how to word it, but then just went for the big one. "It's called irreconcilable differences. No one is to blame, it just . . . is. The marriage is no longer palatable to either partner."

He seemed to ponder that for quite a while. "I have not heard of this. When there are grievances within the bonds, I am of course faced with the task of assigning blame. The aggrieved man will then—"

"Hold it. Don't tell me it's always the man who has been aggrieved."

"Should the woman lie with another, there is cause—"

"What if it's the man who's been cheating?"

His laughter almost echoed off the walls of the castle. "Isabel, I know not the laws in Dumont, but in all other lands of Briton, men are—"

"Held to a different standard. Of course."

He frowned at her. "I am confounded by your sudden aggravation."

"I'm sorry, Arthur. I just find the double standard upsetting. But I should not be surprised. And I should not be taking my irritation out on you. It is what it is."

"Nonetheless, I apologize for upsetting you at all."

Isabel, stop. Make his day. You are one who may teach him another way.

"No, you have been nothing but gracious. It's my fault for feeling so strongly about something that you cannot understand."

He shook his head, chuckling. "But I wish to take up this topic again at a later date. You intrigue me, Isabel. I look forward to many more conversations with you."

"And I, you." She didn't know what drove her to say it, but she added, "Arthur, before we do something that we both might regret, it's time to talk to Gwen. Tell her your feelings."

"She knows naught of my awareness."

Isabel shrugged. "So tell her you know. Ask her to choose. After all, the heart wants what it wants."

"At this moment, I do not know which answer I would prefer, Isabel."

She curtsied, a little better than before. "I look forward to those future conversations, Arthur." And, man, she looked forward to a kiss. And more. But not tonight. His attraction to her was heady, but she wasn't about to kiss a married man if he was only kissing her, or more, to show his wife that he, too, was capable of cheating in the marriage.

Arthur bowed, then straightened and looked her in the eyes. "I wanted you tonight. But I understand your reluctance. And accept your decision."

"I appreciate that, sir. My honest advice? Talk to Gwen."

"I admit to not wanting to hear her answers."

"Man up, King Arthur."

CHAPTER NINE

ARTHUR entered his bedchamber, and Gwen was already there, waiting for him.

Her dressing gown was open, her auburn hair falling down over her shoulders.

There was a time when the sight of her would have him hard and ready to pick her up and take her straight to the bed furs. The truth was, even with what he had known, he most likely would still have taken her. So it surprised him that for once the sight of her beautiful young body did not make his member hard as a bed post. In fact, his member couldn't have lifted a flea from a dog at the moment.

When had he stopped wanting his wife? When had he stopped desperately loving her? It was not before his suspicions had been confirmed. He had tried to bring her back to him with lovemaking and romantic gestures.

But her response to his love gestures were obvious. She no longer desired him as afore. What was shocking to him was that at this moment, he no longer desired her. The blue eyes and blond hair of a woman with a smart mouth and smart ideas kept running through his mind. He could not get Isabel out of his head.

Gwen headed to him. She smelled of sex already, and he wanted to back away and beg her to bathe. "Where have you been, Arthur?" she asked.

"I was debating with the countess," he said, figuring that was no lie. "We had so much to discuss about our lands."

'Twas true in a sense. He was so very intrigued with her thoughts on matters of laws and realms. He was eager to travel to Dumont at his earliest opportunity to see in practice many of the ways she had mentioned of how she ran her realm.

The lie was that he had wanted to be with the countess, in so many ways. In all of the ways he used to want his wife after a long day. Was not voicing this thought a lie of sorts? 'Twas another question he was eager to bring up to the countess the next time they had the chance to discuss such intriguing matters. He could not wait to delve further into her thoughts. And truth be told, delve into her in other ways, as well.

Arthur began to undress, and Gwen came up behind him. "Shall we call for bath water?" she asked.

Her touch used to bring him so much pleasure. At this moment he would have loved to throw her hand from his body. He thought of Isabel's words and his decision came to him in one blinding flash of clarity. This charade was over. "Gwen, I know."

"I do not ken. What do you know?"

He turned to face her. "About you and Lance."

Her mouth dropped open. "Arthur, please, of what do you speak?"

He stared down at the woman he had once loved with all of his being. "Denying it is sad and futile. His sex scent is on you even now. You would actually invite me to bathe with you? Where is your allegiance, Gwen? Where is your love? Please, if you have even a glimmer of feelings for me left in you, do not lie to me, wife."

Her silver blue eyes filled with tears. "Oh, Arthur, I am so very sorry."

"Sorry that I learned of it?"

"I swear that I never meant for this to happen."

In his mind and heart he truly believed her. Gwen was one of the most caring, loving women he had ever met. She would not, ever, hurt a person, a flower, an animal on purpose. He loved her. He just no longer was in love with her. That passion had slowly withered as first his suspicions and then his absolute knowledge had taken root to choke it. It was the saddest part to this debacle.

"I will end this all. This I promise."

He shook his head. "The heart cannot stop what it wants. You can no more end this than you can trample on your adored peonies."

"I do love you, Arthur," she said, wringing her nightgown.

"And I love you, Gwen. But please do not pretend to want me when you want another. I will protect you with my life. But I will not pretend in our bed. And I cannot abide that you keep up the pretense. 'Tis not fair to me, nor to Lance." He sighed. "I do, indeed, want a bath. But not one we share. Before I arrived here, I made preparations. My bath is being filled across the hall. Where I shall also be sleeping."

"Arthur!"

"You, my darling wife, have made the bed you will now lie in. My only request, nay, demand, is absolute discretion. I cannot protect you if you do not protect yourself."

"And . . . and, what of Lancelot?"

Even his trusted knight's name from her lips was a dagger to his heart. Gwen's infidelity had been nigh to unbearable. But learning with whom she was sharing a bed had nearly killed him. "I brought Lance here, Gwen. I took him under my wing, made him one of my most treasured soldiers. He was as a son to me. His betrayal is as hard to bear."

"You will be banishing him, then?" There was nary a hint of pleading in her eyes, just a sad awareness that this would be the obvious solution, the obvious conclusion.

"Nay."

Her head jerked back in surprise. "I am sorry? Do I hear you correctly?"

"You have heard correctly. I have need of him, for the continued prosperity and safety of Camelot. I cannot yet bring myself to forgive, but I do understand. Do not forget that I was also once where he is. I would have done anything for you."

"It cuts deeply that you speak in the past tense, although I realize that it is my own wrongdoing that has brought this on."

"I make this demand of him as well as you, Guinevere. Complete discretion, for both your sakes. For if you are caught, I can no longer protect either of you. Is this clear?"

She laid a hand on his chest. "This promise I make you, in full faith. We will stop this . . . thing between us. Lancelot loves you as much as I. We, neither of us, would ever want to bring shame or dishonor upon you."

His bark of laughter startled her. "I am afraid, sweet Gwen, that the bailey's gate is wide open and the steeds have long past left the castle."

"I'm sorry?"

"Too late."

CHAPTER TEN

I SABEL couldn't sleep. The bed was more than comfortable, although she had a feeling PETA would not approve of the fur blanketing it. She'd flopped from one side to the other, from her back to her tummy, but no position seemed to allow her mind to stop whirling and fall into slumber, peaceful or not. Oh, for some sleep meds right about now.

Her door opened silently, only the light from the hallway lanterns slicing across the room alerting her. She sat up, alarmed, but then recognized Mary, the young girl's arms filled with a couple of new logs for the fire.

"Oh, you startled me!"

Mary froze. "Countess, my apologies," she said with a small curtsy. "I thought you would be deeply asleep by this hour."

"The question is, why aren't you?" Isabel asked. "You are way too young to be working such long hours."

As Mary carefully laid the logs on the dying embers and waved to flame the fire, she said, "'Tis my pleasure to serve you, Countess."

She stood and turned, an impish smile on her face. "And truth be told, when you have no need of me, I slip in a nap or two during the day. I receive plenty of sleep."

"I'm glad to hear that, but answer me this, Mary. What do you really do for pleasure?"

"M'lady? I'm not sure I understand your question."

"You and your friends. What do you do? Do you play games? Play sports?"

"There's not much time for such things."

"So many chores, so little time, eh?"

"Something like that, yes, mum."

"We'll see about that," Isabel murmured.

"Pardon?"

"Nothing, nothing, Mary." Isabel threw her covers aside and stood. "Listen, I just cannot sleep. Maybe a short walk would do me good. Is there a way to the south gardens without going down and through the great hall?"

"Yes, there be, Countess, but the back staircase is for servants, not for the likes of royalty."

"Tonight, I am a servant, then. Please help me find my long cloak, and show me the way."

MARY led Isabel to the gardens she had shared with Arthur several hours earlier. Luckily, they encountered no one along the way. The castle seemed to be sound asleep.

Isabel thanked Mary profusely and tried to tip her with one of the hundreds of coins she'd discovered in a pouch in one of her trunks. Mary stared at it in horror and backed away. "No, Countess, I cannot. If this be found, I may be accused of theft."

"How, when I will readily tell one and all that it was a gift from me for your excellent service?"

"I am not permitted to accept such gifts."

Wow, tell that to the service personnel on cruise ships. They whistled in the air while holding their palms out at every opportunity.

Isabel vowed to herself that she'd find a way to repay Mary for her help and kindness in ways that would not get the girl in trouble.

"Apparently another faux pas on my part. I apologize if I've offended you, Mary."

"Fo paw?"

"Never mind, another word apparently exclusive to my land. Please, go to bed, and thank you for helping me."

Mary curtsied, which was beginning to get on Isabel's nerves. But she bit her tongue and wished Mary a good night. "I will find my way back, Mary. I have no need for help until the morning bath."

"Thank you, mum. And I do so hope you find the peace you are searching for."

Isabel wished for the same thing but was afraid peace eluded her at the moment.

"I see that neither of us are finding that peace tonight."

Isabel practically jumped to the turrets. She twisted around to find the source of her torment leaning against an apricot tree. "Arthur, good gods, you just scared the living . . . daylights out of me."

He bowed slightly. "My apologies, Isabel. 'Twas not my intention."

Her eyes narrowed. "Are you following me?"

He pushed off from the tree with his shoulder then stepped forward, that catlike silence of his movements almost eerie. "I believe you have followed me, as I have been wandering the gardens for some time."

"I had no idea," she said, affronted. "I just could not find sleep." Then she thought of something. "This is not Mary's fault! I demanded that she help me find my way back here in a way that would not bring us through the great hall."

"On my oath, I will assure Mary is rewarded, not punished, for her actions. In truth, she has demonstrated more loyalty to her king than I have witnessed from many others in a very long time."

He stepped around that magical bench and took Isabel's hand.

"Please join me and tell me why it is that you cannot sleep, Countess Isabel."

"I am afraid I don't know."

"Are the accommodations less than satisfactory? I will have anything done to make you more comfortable."

More comfortable would mean having him sharing her bed. His warmth, his hard body, his scent. Which, come to think of it, was vastly different than earlier. He had obviously bathed and washed his hair. She couldn't identify the spicy scent, but it was delicious.

She sat down on the bench, acutely aware that she was wearing only a nightdress and a cloak. How she wished she'd found some jeans and T-shirts stuffed in those trunks.

He stood in front of her, not joining her, just shaking his head. "I told her, Isabel."

She stared into the troubled green eyes of her dream man, her heart aching. "Guinevere?"

"Yes."

"And you told her what? Your bowling score? Your credit rating? How to work a Clapper?"

Arthur grinned and sat down. "You have a way of making me smile, Countess, even during a sad time."

"Well, that's dandy, but what are you talking about?"

"I told her that I was aware of this thing betwixt and between her and Sir Lancelot."

"Oh boy. Why?"

"Why? You advised me to talk to her."

Oh freaking boy. "I meant that as a sort of get-back-together type of thing. Or at least I thought I did."

Didn't I, Lady?

Did you, Isabel? 'Twould seem that only time will tell.

Breaking up their marriage was not my intent; I'll feel like shit if this is why I've been sent.

I sent you here to make happy both Arthur and Merlin. To satisfy them both is no such sin.

Once again Arthur began pacing in front of her, something

she'd already noticed was a habit he had when he was deep in thought. Or possibly looking deeply into his own soul.

"From the moment I set eyes on Gwen, I have ne'er felt lust for another. Not even after I had learned the truth. Ne'er."

He stopped pacing and faced her directly. "And then our meeting in the forest. And I found myself suddenly wanting a woman who was not my wife."

"I'm so sorry."

He laughed once again. "You apologize for this? You are apologizing for being beautiful? For being . . . you?"

"I have no desire to be part of the crash and burn of a marriage."

"Crash and burn? Has it not already crashed and burned?"

"You tell me, Arthur."

He had that come-and-get-me smile on his face. Isabel was certain he didn't realize that was what he was transmitting, but it was still like a huge Jump Me sign to her. "You opened my eyes tonight, Countess. You are so lovely and blunt, and that mouth of yours spouts fierceness, and yet your actions show compassion."

Well, that was as clear as quantum physics. "Thank you. I think. And how did this little chat with Guinevere go?"

His hands waved in the air. "She did not deny. She did not beg for mercy for herself, but for Lancelot. She hoped that his punishment would merely be banishment."

"I'm so sorry."

Once again his deep grass green eyes lifted to hers. "And your thoughts?"

Therapist, she decided, was not her forte. Especially when she wanted this man. And she was so wanting to jog down that one path that led straight to her own selfish desires.

"Please tell me you are not going to out them."

"Out them?"

"Gwen and Lancelot. Hurt them. Have them punished?"

"Never. However, much is out of my hands. I can protect both only so far."

"So then let's protect them."

"My pardon, Isabel?"

"You love them both, yes?"

"Most assuredly. Not as afore, but still, they mean much to me."

"You have decided, in your soul, that you do not want to punish them, correct?"

"I have."

"Then we need to come up with a plan. A battle plan, as it were."

His laughter was rich, and once again it reached down into her body. "You are a constant amazement, Countess."

"Hey, what the hell, let's get this done. We might all come out of this with what we want."

"What I want right now is to feel your lips."

"Keep your eye on the prize, Arthur."

"You have said this afore on our ride to Camelot. However, the prize, as you call it, has changed."

"You want to keep Camelot and all of your people safe. That has never changed."

"I cannot deny that. I can, however, change what this prize I want most desperately might be."

"THE plan, Arthur. We must work on the plan," Isabel said, while Arthur was unforgivably debating another plan. Although the servants had doused the garden lanterns for the night, he'd lit them again when he'd come out to ponder the future. It was all a jumble of what he had always envisioned, expected and desired. So much of it all had gone awry. When had he lost control? For some time he had wanted to keep it all together, running smoothly. And then the gods had made a mockery of his dreams and desires.

Or had they?

Isabel sat staring at him intently, her blond hair shimmering from the lantern lights, her eyes so large and inquisitive.

"I love her. I know that I do. But what does it say about me that I am not stopping what I see happening and that I have this attraction to another woman? How is it possible that I felt a desire for you on first sight?"

Wow, this honesty thing that the Lady's necklace brought about was a lot more powerful than she'd thought.

"Perhaps, just perhaps, that you fell for a beautiful woman who was just a teeny bit too young for you?"

He again shook his head. "Which makes me an old fool?"

"Arthur, you are neither old, nor a fool. Gwen is a lovely young woman. And I do believe she loves you as well. I see it when she looks at you. She respects and admires you, and is proud to be your queen."

"Do you see love or desire when she gazes upon me?"

"I haven't been around long enough to discern such a thing."

That was the biggest bunch of bullshit she'd had to gag out. All she'd noticed was lust and desire when the queen had kept sneaking peeks at Lancelot.

"Bullshit. Apologies for that word and for using it in your presence. I made it up at one point when I felt I was being deceived. You are not giving me truth."

She stared at him for a second, then broke out laughing. "You, sir, are quite honest."

"You, madam, are skirting the issue that you've promised to help me work out."

Isabel wished she could have gone back and majored in psychology. But she had nothing but basic logic to go on now. And the Lady, who she hoped would kick her in the chest if she went wrong.

"May I be blunt?"

"Blunt?"

"Truthful to the point that it might cause you pain."

"Then be blunt, Countess."

"I think you love Gwen enough to allow her happiness. I think you shield her from gossip because you want her to go about this tryst if it allows her to find her joy. I think you don't banish Lancelot because you know that the two find joy together. Would you like me to go on and have you banish me?"

"I would fight my own men to keep you here, Countess."

"Ask yourself, why do you permit this?"

"Happiness is a fleeting thing, do you not think? Am I the arbiter of happiness? The crown does not grant me the right to determine who should and should not find theirs, wherever it leads." He once again cocked his head sideways. "The truth is, I honestly know not. Strange as it seems, I want Gwen to be happy."

"You're a good-hearted man, Arthur."

"With many, many flaws it appears."

"Such as?"

"Poor judgment, perhaps?"

Isabel stood. "Are you saying poor judgment would be wanting to kiss me?"

"No, madam, that would most likely be one of my best judgments."

"No offense, but do you consider yourself good at this?"

His eyes glittered and he shrugged. "'Tis a mystery. Mayhap I am mistaken and overly boastful in that skill. How shall I ever know?"

"Sir, I'm well schooled in certain arts. Perhaps I can determine if this is a deadly fault of yours?"

Isabel waited for the thump, but it never came.

He went still. "Madam, I would most certainly accept your honest opinion."

They looked at each other for a long time before he finally lowered his head. Their mouths met tentatively at first, but the fire lit up fast. Before she could even think, his one hand thrust itself through her hair and his other went to the small of her back, pulling her closer. He broke the kiss long enough to stare into her eyes and whisper, "I must do better."

If he did any better, Isabel was going to get seared. His mouth came down on hers again, and he played so many million tricks on her lips that she needed him to hold her up. He tasted like sex, he played her mouth like sex, he nipped her lips lightly like pure sex.

By the time he was done with her mouth, the rest of her body was churning.

Arthur broke the kiss and cupped her face, which left the rest of her body in peril of dropping straight to the ground. Her knees certainly weren't helping to hold her up. She began to sink, but he quickly grabbed her around the waist and pulled her back up. "That bad?" he asked.

She knew her eyes and brain were both glazed. Her vocal chords were also in peril.

Isabel cleared her throat. "Sir, where I come from," she whispered, "we grade our students from A to F, A being awesome, F meaning failure. B, C, and D fall in between."

"And where do I fall, Isabel?" he asked, still grilling her with those mossy green eyes.

"Not only would you make the dean's list, you'd probably make valedictorian."

He shook his head. "I'm sorry? Betimes our languages do not match."

"My apologies, sir. What I'm saying is you get an A-plus."

He smiled. "And this is good?"

"Valedictorian material, Arthur."

"What is higher than this valedictorian? I would very much like to achieve it."

"I'd very much like for you to try."

"You are very beautiful, Isabel. Your hair is as soft as is your skin, and you smell so sweet."

"You're talking way too much, Arthur, when in truth, I'd prefer you just shut up and kiss me again."

But instead of covering her lips with his, his head raised and he almost slapped a hand over her mouth. "Shhh, lady. Something is amiss," he whispered.

Not the rabbit again. Or maybe it would be better if it were another rabbit.

Before she knew what was happening, Arthur had shoved her behind his back as he faced the darkness of the shrubbery down the garden path.

"Present yourself!" he demanded. "Are you friend or foe?"

A voice beyond the light of the lanterns replied, "'Tis only, I, my king. 'Tis James."

James, Isabel remembered, was the huge burly guy who was the king's first man. She didn't know whether to run and hide, or pretend to be a fence post. Arthur didn't give her a choice. He held on to her so tightly that she couldn't have moved if she wanted to.

"Come, James. Tell me why you are up and about. And why you have come looking for me."

James came rumbling in, and yet strangely he walked as softly as a ballerina. He, too, had learned how to walk softly but carry big—really big—bulk. He reminded Isabel of Shrek, and yet when she peeked out beside Arthur's side, his expression turned from worried to kind.

"M'lady Countess," he said, bowing.

"How's it going, James?" she said, for some reason liking him, once again thinking Arthur had surrounded himself with kick-ass people.

"I am afraid I must needs have a word with the king, Countess Isabel. A private word."

"What you have to say to me you may say in front of the countess, James. I trust her with news. As I trust you with my life."

Well, that was really sweet. But out of the blue. She couldn't be certain she'd trust Arthur with all of her news after such a little time, and a lot of lust. She finally disengaged from Arthur and moved to his side. "I am certain what James has to say is no business of mine. Please, let me leave you two to privacy."

Arthur grabbed her hand, holding tight, but not to the point of pain. "No, madam, whate'er the news, I know it be safe with you."

James had huge brown eyes and hair that appeared not to have been combed since he'd been a child. To anyone who didn't know him well, which she didn't, he appeared menacing. But as he glanced back and forth between them, Isabel could tell he was not mean. Just very fierce looking. Which probably was what had earned him this gig.

"I'm leaving," Isabel said, and once again tried to disengage.

"Please do not," Arthur said, holding tight to her hand. "What news, James?"

James hesitated, but then shrugged his huge shoulders. "Mordred has arrived, sir."

ARTHUR was not certain whether to celebrate or worry over the news. "In the middle of the night?"

"'Tis, as you are well aware, his usual practice."

"Mordred?" Isabel asked.

Arthur hung on to her hand even tighter, just hoping he was not hurting her. But his need of her burned more now than ever afore. "Have you given him accommodations?" he asked James.

"I knew not where to put him. I knew not whether he was welcome."

"You know that I cannot turn him away. But of course make him welcome."

"He is demanding help for his horse, who he assures me has come up lame from the travel through the forest."

"Wake up Harry," Isabel said. "He will tend to the horse. But for goodness sake, someone tell me who Mordred is."

James went instantly mute and looked away.

For a reason Arthur could not fathom, he could not lie to this woman. "He is my son."

Isabel stared at him, then back to James, whose head was low but who nodded in agreement.

"I *so* should have paid more attention in Mythology."

"My pardon, madam?" James said.

"Since this news seem happy for neither of you, I'm assuming Mordred's arrival is not a cause for celebration? The truth, Arthur."

"Mordred loves me not," Arthur said. "He feels I've wronged him."

"Have you?"

"He has not!" James boomed. "He has done everything for that ungrateful little—"

"James!"

"My pardon, sir."

"Finish your thought please, James," Isabel said.

"Do not," said Arthur.

James pressed his lips together. Obviously king trumped countess. Since he was Arthur's man, she would have expected nothing less.

What am I missing here, Goddess?

The blood between Arthur and Mordred is shared, but Mordred's intentions should have everyone scared. He's a child born of young love and lust, yet his mother understood Arthur must do what he must. The child, however, never forgave; his hatred has driven him to make Arthur his slave.

Isabel tasted blood. *Little fucking bastard.*

Bastard indeed, but here is the thing: Mordred will not rest until he is king.

Isabel digested this for a moment, not able to even meet Arthur's eyes. "Fine," she finally said to Arthur and James. "How about I go wake Harry so he may care for Mordred's horse?"

"No!" they both yelled at once. Arthur tried to grab her, but she was already slipping away back into the castle. He should have held tight to her hand.

"What now, sir?"

"She will confront Mordred. 'Tis in her nature, James. She is the type to want to know everything. She is, what one would call . . ." A word would not come to him.

Nosy? Protective? Caring?

Arthur knew not where these thoughts were coming from, but they all seemed to be accurate. Although he had no idea what the word nosy meant.

Arthur, if you do not protect Isabel, Merlin cannot live.

Merlin? What know you of Merlin? And who are you, speaking in my head?

Figure it out. Just go protect Isabel. If you haven't noticed, she is able to raise hell.

"Do I not know that," Arthur muttered.

"My pardon?" James said.

Arthur shook his head. He was either addled or . . . no, there was no other choice. He was addled.

"Confronting him will put her in danger," James said.

"It will, we must put a stop to this. She knows the back staircase, James," Arthur said. "I shall try to stop her there, you go and guard the stables."

James actually smiled. "We will catch her, my lord. But I must say, I enjoy the thought of the countess taking on the lad."

"Oh, I do not. She knows not who she faces."

"Methinks the lady has mettle."

"Perhaps too much for her own welfare. Mordred's dislike of women is well documented."

"She cares about you, m'lord, which is more than I am able to say—"

"Do not finish that thought, James. Please just help me find her."

"Yes, m'lord."

"You to the stables, I will try to find her at the back of the castle afore she makes a run."

Arthur ran, even knowing he had witnessed another smile upon his man's face. What flummoxed him was that he felt a grin forming on his own, even as he attempted to head off disaster. Isabel against Mordred. He could not even conceive of which of the two might win such a battle. Well, yes, he might. Were it a battle of words and wit, his coins would be placed on Isabel. However, Mordred relied on neither, instead preferring to use much nastier weapons.

The thought of Mordred harming Isabel had him taking the steps two at a time. No! If Mordred even attempted to lay a hand to Isabel, he would take down the lad himself, blood or not.

JAMES caught Isabel and Harry as they were halfway to the stables. He held out his arms and prided himself on being able to step side to side to effectively block their paths.

Harry adjusted the green and white nightcap on his head and growled, "I have a patient that needs attending."

"I understand," James said, then caught the countess around the waist when she tried to slip around to his right side. He held her sideways and had a rather fun and easy time deflecting her attempted blows to his body. Although he had to admit that he could understand the master's attraction to her passion.

"Let Isabel go," Harry demanded as she squirmed in James's arms. "She is a countess!"

"I apologize, Countess," James said, knowing he could be in deep trouble for even touching her. But he had one loyalty, and that was to his king. "Please allow me to explain a thing or two afore you head in there with heads blazing."

The countess stopped wiggling in his arms, even though he kept a gentle hold.

"I promise not to try to run ahead of you, James, should what you tell me be important and relevant."

James had a deep desire to twirl her once afore setting her on her feet but decided the king would not take kindly to that playfulness. He set her upright upon her feet, and then bowed. "My apologies. But truly, there are things you must needs be made aware of afore you rush in there, m'lady."

Isabel kind of wished James had twirled her around once or twice before setting her down. Could have been kind of a Six Flags ride in Camelot. But she needed to understand. So she got over it. "Tell me, James."

Harry harrumphed and she amended it to, "Tell *us*, James."

"This . . . how do you call it? This *thing* 'twixt Mordred and the king has been a long time brewing. For reasons I may not speak of, they have bad blood betwixt them. It is a constant source of misery for my king."

Isabel felt the fire starting to stir in her belly. Pretty soon it was going to be steaming out of either her nose or mouth. Or both. "And why does this make you try to stop me from going in and kicking the little shit in his—"

"What the lady means," said Harry, slapping a hand over her mouth, "is that we do not understand why we are appeasing this young man."

The big man shook his shaggy head. "Mayhap because the king

loves the boy, no matter what agony the child brings him, no matter what pleasure Mordred takes in making my king suffer for young sins."

Isabel grabbed Harry's hand from her lips and glanced over at him. "Do you see why I never wanted to procreate now?"

"I'm beginning to understand the concept," Harry said out of the side of his mouth. "But I still think you'd have made a great mother."

"You are asking me to act with due diligence?" she asked of James.

"That I am, Countess. Please allow the king to handle this situation. Perhaps 'tis time for you to retire to your chamber for the evening?"

Isabel nodded. "Perhaps. But not a chance in hell, as we say in Dumont. I insist that my man Harry and you, James, escort me to the stables."

"I fear trouble brewing," James said to Harry.

"You have no idea," Harry said, before oomphing at Isabel's elbow to his belly. "But let us go."

"Then so we shall."

Isabel, still reeling from the knowledge that Arthur had a son, and that his son was a total jerk, felt a little impatient. She lifted her skirts and yelled, "Catch me if you can!" and made a run for it.

They both ran after her; however, neither was as fast.

James and Harry did not catch the countess until she was facing Mordred in the stables. And she was already speaking her piece. She held out her arms to hold them from stepping forward.

"What brings you here, sir?" she asked Mordred. "What business do you have in Camelot?"

"Who are you to even presume to ask my intentions?"

Isabel studied him. There was no doubt he was Arthur's son. They looked alike in so many ways, including the deep green eyes. The difference being Arthur's eyes were so filled with kindness and laughter, whereas Mordred's emanated venom. "I am Isabel, Countess of Dumont. And a friend of the king. Apparently, you are not. So I ask again, what brings you here?"

Mordred made a mockery of a bow. "How do you do? However,

Countess, my business here is none of yours. Has my father stooped so low as to have need of a mere woman to come riding to his defense?"

"A *mere* woman? Listen, you little shit—"

"No, you listen, Countess," he spat out. "I am heir to this kingdom, and have every reason and right to travel to Camelot to oversee my future holdings."

"The king is quite healthy. I believe he will remain so for many years to come. So don't count your cows before they . . . breed."

Wow, that was lame, but the best she could come up with on the spur of the moment.

Mordred's eyes went wide for a moment, and then he broke out in nasty laughter. "If you have not been fully informed, *mistress*, my father already has a wife. One quite younger than you. I see his interest, as you are fetching; however, you will never take her place as queen. Unless you plot to murder her."

James and Harry each grabbed one of her arms, apparently hoping to ward off her jumping forward and scratching the bastard's eyes out. There was no need. She had no intention of launching herself at the boy.

She knew her breasts were heaving with fury, especially when Mordred's eyes leveled on them and couldn't seem to let go. Then she realized his gaze was fixed on her necklace.

She took a calming breath. "Please tell me again why you have come to Camelot."

"I have learned there will be a very important knights-of-the-realm gathering here shortly. I need to be sitting at that table." Mordred blinked several times, obviously a little confused about why he'd given up that piece of information.

"Were you invited to this meeting?" Isabel asked. "Are you a knight?"

"Of course I was not," Mordred said, finally breaking his gaze from her necklace. "My *father* didn't deem me high enough in the order to invite me. He is a pig."

This time James and Harry had to hold her back. She most definitely wanted to scratch his face, no matter what it did to her nails.

"How dare you? Your father loves you. Why is it that you find pleasure in bringing him pain?"

Mordred stepped closer and closer to Isabel, swapping his crop on his thigh. "You know nothing, lady. Including how a proper woman dresses. Are you his tart this evening? Are you going to give birth to his next bastard child?"

"What are you going to do, Mordred?" Isabel asked. "Whip an unarmed woman?"

James tried to step between them. "She is a countess, Mordred. Back away."

Mordred sneered. "She is a slut, as is my father's wife."

"Back off, James," Isabel said.

"I cannot, Countess. The king has asked me to protect you."

"Back off. This little snot has just smeared the queen's name."

"M'lady!"

"Back off. I demand it."

James backed away, although Isabel guessed he was worrying about his future. Not a problem; she'd make certain he was rewarded for his actions.

Mordred grinned and moved even closer.

Thank the gods for Tae Kwon Do. Isabel kicked the damn crop out of his hand, turned and jumped, kicking him in the belly, and had him on the ground, his hands bound with reins, within seconds. "Sorry, son, time to answer to your dad," she whispered into his ear. "He would never have let me get ahead of him. You, on the other hand, are just slow and stupid."

"You will pay for this," Mordred said.

"I'm sure I will. Your father loves you so much he will be very angry with me. Tough fucking shit. It felt too good, you little worm."

"Bitch," he spat out.

Her knee dug farther into his back. "Excuse me? I'm sorry, I believe you meant to say, 'My apologies, Countess.'"

"Apologize to the countess, son."

Isabel's head jerked up, and sure enough, there was Arthur, appearing pained and amused at one and the same time.

She attempted to rise gracefully, but that wasn't about to happen. Harry took her hand and helped her up. "I am very sorry, Arthur, but he kind of pissed me off."

Arthur moved forward and brushed hay from her clothing. "'Tis a talent of his." Then he helped his son to his feet. "Welcome home, Mordred!"

"SHOULD you care about me at all, *father*, you will have that woman brought before the King's Court."

Arthur sat on his throne, his head being held up by a forefinger. "Because she bested you when you attempted to whip her? I think not."

"You disagree that she deserves a beating?"

Arthur stared at Mordred, wondering how he had gone so terribly wrong as a father. "No woman deserves a beating, Mordred. Never. They are to be cherished."

Mordred laughed. "As you cherished my mother?"

"Your mother said nothing to me, son. No matter what your aunt might have told you, I knew naught of your existence until I asked of her well-being. I know it was too long, Mordred, but she never, ever told me. It never occurred to me. That is my fault, I admit. But once I learned of her death and your birth, I tried, son, I truly tried."

"So you have said." Mordred stood and paced, and Arthur almost laughed at how much this resembled his own actions.

But Mordred's anger still hung to him as dung to a bull. And smelled as poorly. "So you will choose the bitch over your own son?"

Arthur rose quickly, attempting to quell his fierce anger. "First, my son, there is no choice. Countess Isabel bested you this eve, and that is between the two of you. However, should you attempt revenge, I will most definitely come to her defense, for she has done nothing against you. In fact, her man tended to your horse. This after you planned an assault on his lady. Should you even attempt to show vengeance, I must act."

"So, one more time, you choose a woman over your son."

"I choose caring over spite. I wish one day you will understand the same."

"When, Father, did you choose your bastard son over your kingdom?"

When, son, did your mother choose not to inform me that she was carrying my child?

Once again, Arthur had no idea where this thought had appeared from. But he had to admit it was a fairly good one. "Your mother chose not to inform me she had my babe inside her. I was given no choice in the matter."

"You lie."

Arthur hung his head and rubbed his temples. "You, of course, will never believe me. However, the truth is when I learned of you, when I learned that your mother had died during your birth, I attempted to lay claim to you and bring you back to Camelot. Your aunt wouldn't allow it, as she blamed me for her sister's death."

Mordred stopped pacing. "I do not believe that."

"As I said you would not."

Arthur rose and began pacing as well. Mordred continued his. They kept passing one another. The rushes beneath their feet were taking quite a beating.

"We, Father, are at an impasse," Mordred finally said.

"'Twould seem so, my son. You may join my men, or you may join those who would take me down. 'Tis your choice."

"I am honest when I am loyal to Richard of Fremont."

That bit harshly at Arthur's heart, but he nodded. "Then, my son, you are a guest in my home. But you are a man who wishes to do harm to Camelot. Thus, you are considered an enemy. You have stated your intentions. I cannot tell you how deeply this cuts."

"As much as I was cut when you denied me?"

"I have *ne'er* denied you. 'Twas your aunt who—"

"Enough!"

"Fine, believe what you must. But know this, son: Should you harm a man, woman, child or animal whilst I give you comfort in my realm, I will show you no mercy. You will see the same penance as any other."

"I take note that a woman was sent to do your work this eve."

Arthur grinned. "No, I did try to stop her. But she was angry, and I did not get there in time. Regardless, son, that bruise upon your eye tells me that she won that small battle."

"For which she'll pay."

Arthur wanted to grab his son and shake him. Instead, he took deep breaths and said, "Touch her, and you will certainly suffer."

Mordred's laughter was almost sad. "And once again you choose another over your own son."

"No, son, I choose allegiance over treason. And I choose happiness over hatred. Your chosen path on both is a sad one."

Arthur turned to leave the room, feeling a disgust and sadness he had ne'er felt before.

"You owe me, old man!" his son called out to him as he closed the door.

Okay, there was still sadness, but disgust was fairly taking over. And a bit of fear.

The safety of his people was paramount. And it alarmed him that Mordred would perhaps attack them first. And the first, most assuredly, would be the woman who had humiliated Mordred this night. Even as Arthur stole one bit of a smile at her cheek, he knew he needed to round up Tom, Dick and Harry to formulate a safety plan. Isabel's safety was a priority.

It had to be private, however, because should Isabel learn of it, he'd sustain more than a black eye.

Truth be told, 'twas a good bet that should he ever want to produce another child, Isabel would make that impossible. She was a bit cranky that way.

CHAPTER ELEVEN

THE next morning Isabel was luxuriating in her bath filled with freshly picked lilacs and spices when there was a soft knock on the door.

"I have told you, Mary, you do not need to knock," she called.

"'Tis not Mary, Countess. 'Tis Guinevere."

Isabel splashed all over the place, grabbing for a towel and her robe. "One moment, your Highness!"

She set world speed records jumping out of the tub, drying herself and donning her robe. "Please come in," she said.

Gwen entered, looking so damn ethereal and sweet that Isabel felt like James on a bad day. If James could have a good day. Which she doubted.

The queen was wearing a turquoise gown. Very simple in its design, but managing to fit her like it was made for her body. Which, when Isabel thought about it, it was. Oh, to have that good a seamstress.

Then again, either the color wasn't good for Gwen, or Gwen's color wasn't right. Her smile was kind, but she appeared a little pasty, and her amazing eyes weren't glittering like they had even just the night before.

Uh-oh. Arthur had not disclosed all of the details of his talk with his wife, but Isabel had a sinking feeling her name had come up in the conversation. And this wasn't good.

She did the curtsy thing, which was again awkward. "To what do I owe this visit?" she asked, dread nearly dropping her. After all, she'd had heart-melting kisses with Gwen's husband just hours ago. Was the queen here to have Isabel executed as a . . . a . . . hussy? Was that a crime? Isabel's nerves were dancing, and it wasn't the mambo. It was the uh-oh.

Gwen floated into the room and sat in one of the two chairs. "I apologize for disrupting your bath, Countess."

"No problem. The water was getting cool on me," Isabel said, drying her hair with her towel and hoping like hell that she didn't have beard burns all over her face. "What's up?"

"Other than the beard scratches all over your face, Countess?"

She was definitely in the uh-oh dance.

And she was not a liar. So she was in a shit load of trouble.

Please, Goddess, help me through this.

I picked you, Isabel, since your truth was a plus, but right now I find it a bit of a minus. I care not one, Tom, Dick or Harry, but one of the three made your face scary.

Her face was scary? Really, scratchy she could live with. Scary felt a little too Halloweenish for her taste. But everything right now felt cartoonish.

"I will not lie. I shared kisses last eve. However, with whom I shared those kisses is my knowledge, and mine alone. Forgive me if I don't feel the need to share."

"And so it shall stay."

"Forgive my impertinence, Queen Guinevere, but your cheeks and chin also show signs of action."

Gwen's hands went to her face. "It would seem that we are both guilty of play, then."

"I won't tell on you, if you do not tell on me."

"Many thanks, Isabel."

"Right back atcha." Isabel laid down her towel. "Now to what do I owe this morning call?"

"So many things, Countess."

Everything in the world went through Isabel's mind. Gwen had learned that she'd kissed her husband? Maybe she'd learned that Isabel had kicked her stepson's ass? Isabel had had Mary pick flowers from Gwen's garden for her bath? "Please inform me."

"I have need of your counsel," the queen said.

Okay, that hadn't been on her list. And it sounded less painful than torture and death. "My counsel?"

"Yes. My husband informs me that you are distraught that the women here have no reprieve from their daily chores. That you believe they should have, as he said, some 'playtime.'"

Could have knocked Isabel over with a puff of air. "I most likely was out of line, Your Highness. I should not have said any such thing. I was just tossing out ideas as we spoke."

"I am quite entranced with the notion, truth be told."

So far, no torture and death in her future. At least she hoped not. She tried to connect with the Lady of the Lake, but the Lady wasn't talking. Apparently Isabel was on her own on this one.

Great.

"How may I help you, Queen Guinevere?"

"Please, I am Gwen," the queen said. "And allow me to call you Isabel. I do so hate formalities."

Isabel nodded. "As do I. But I'm afraid I might have spoken in haste. It isn't my place to tell you how to handle your staff."

Gwen, amazingly enough, appeared disappointed. "Are you saying you did not mean what you had suggested?"

Isabel dragged the other chair over to Gwen. "Oh, I meant it. Think about this, Queen Guinevere." She shook her head. "Gwen. The women who work at Camelot do only that. They work. The men work, for a certainty, but they also engage in play sport. The women should be allowed at least a small amount of that time themselves."

Gwen nodded, although her expression definitely showed confusion. "I do understand what you propose, but truth be told, I have ne'er heard a word of complaint."

"Oh, please, do you really believe the servants of Camelot are going to air their grievances to you?"

At that moment Mary burst into the room. "Ready to have your hair do—" She stopped short. "My apologies. I will return later."

"No, Mary," Isabel said. "I would very much love for you to take care of my hair right now."

"But the queen—"

"Will not mind," Isabel said. "Is that not right, Gwen?"

"Of course not. Come in and do your work, Mary."

"Yes, my queen."

"Her talent, not her work," Isabel said.

"My pardon?"

"The thing is, Gwen, that working on hair is not labor to Mary. She enjoys it. And she's very good at it."

"Thank you, m'lady," Mary said, her eyes still glued to the ground.

"I know, Gwen, that I am being so intrusive. However, the point being that you are not using your men and women in the most productive way. Mary, here, should be working with hair. She's brilliant. For example, she could spruce up many of the men's hair. Have you not noticed many are, shall we say, in need of de-shagging?"

"De . . . ?"

"They need haircuts."

"They do?"

"You have not noticed?"

"In truth, no. Another apparent fault of mine."

"It's not a fault. Just, apparently that you only have eyes for"— Isabel stopped herself just in time—"the things that matter to you. And I believe you have always felt that Arthur's men are his men, and not necessarily your concern."

"What do you recommend?"

"They need to clean up their act. For example, Arthur's first man, James, is quite a handsome brute. However, his hair is a mess."

Mary nearly choked.

Gwen took a hard look at Mary, nodding. "Oh, yes, you are *that* Mary. The one who turns James all amelt when he speaks of you."

Isabel was obviously missing something. "I apologize, Mary. I didn't expect for you to take on a horrid task with hair. I honestly just wanted to fight for your happiness."

Gwen tried to hide a smile but did a lousy job.

"What am I missing?"

"Oh, lady," Mary said, hands all aflutter. "My thanks. I do so enjoy working with hair. However, I will perform any tasks my king and queen ask of me. With pleasure, of course. May we, perhaps, brush your hair alone, Countess?"

Isabel looked back and forth between the queen and the servant. "Okay, what's the deal?"

Gwen spoke up first, her eyes still full of mirth. "Forgive me, but I believe this is the Mary who has captured James's heart. Am I correct, Mary?"

The poor girl looked like she was going to faint.

"Wait a minute," Isabel said, trying to give Mary a moment to catch her breath. "As in James, the sweetest brute alive who is Arthur's first man?"

"I knew he was smitten with a Mary," Gwen said. "I have heard Arthur jest about this. But I am so sorry to say I did not know which Mary."

"How many Marys do you have?" Isabel asked.

"I honestly do not know. We have so many Marys and Liliths and any number of names. I believe, however, that we have but one Prudence. I know not what her mother was thinking upon her birth."

Isabel looked back at Mary's flaming face. "Are you the Mary James has set his heart on?"

Mary shifted her feet and looked like she wanted to flee. "Yes, mum."

Gwen let out a small laugh. "James, in love."

"What is so funny?" Isabel asked. "James would be lucky to have Mary."

"No, no, 'tis not the match that is mirthful. 'Tis just the idea of James besotted that is something that has me—"

"Happy for them?" Isabel said.

"Yes, of course, happy for them."

Mary kind of curtsied again. "Thank you, my lady."

"Isabel."

"Yes, my lady. I am well aware of your name."

"Which you still refuse to utter."

"Yes, mum."

"Mary . . . and you *do* recognize that I use your first name?"

"Yes, mum."

"You're only thirteen."

"They are waiting until she becomes fourteen, Isabel," Gwen said. "'Tis the time we have decided upon."

"You have decided for them? As if they have no choice in the matter? Then again, at fourteen I was still working the monkey bars on the playground. I still thought boys had cooties."

Both of them looked at Isabel like she was batty. She even heard Viviane sigh in her head.

Okay, once again she was blowing it. Even if it felt kind of skanky, Isabel understood that in this time, age was a different matter. So she focused on another problem. "Then, Mary, why have you not done something to fix his hair?"

GWEN continued to giggle, even as she had sadness wrapped around her heart. 'Twas so apparent why Arthur had pressed her to visit the countess and listen to her views. He had become enamored with the woman.

In truth Gwen could not blame him. Isabel was a lovely woman and one who had opinions she openly voiced. Arthur much appreciated listening to the opinions of others. 'Twas one of his most appealing qualities. One she had always admired.

Gwen loved Arthur. She had loved him from the moment they

had met. And yet it had taken Lancelot to make her realize that love and admiration were not equal to love and need.

Needing Lancelot, loving him, was a power like no other. Much as she loved and admired her husband, her need for Lancelot rode over everything, truly marring her good sense and tremendous responsibility. Not to mention those vows she had spoken. Those sacred vows.

"Gwen?"

Gwen shook her head and brought herself back to the moment. "Oh, I deeply apologize. I wandered deep in thought."

Isabel's eyes searched her face. "You seem to be troubled." She fingered the beautiful necklace around her neck, and Gwen could not seem to stop herself from saying, "I am, Countess. But it has naught to do with why I have sought your advice."

"Still, I am here to listen, should you want to voice what seems to be bothering you."

Gwen, eyes fixated on the necklace, said. "We . . . we have much to discuss about the workings of Camelot."

Mary attempted to bow out, but Isabel refused to allow her leave. "Please brush my hair, Mary. And then braid it as before. Plus, I would like your thoughts upon matters."

Mary glanced nervously at Gwen, apparently fearing punishment at the mere idea that her thoughts should be voiced or desired. In truth, Gwen herself was rather shocked at the concept. Servants being asked their opinions? 'Twas such a foreign concept. However, she could not, in truth, find a single reason to demand otherwise. She nodded her agreement to both the countess and Mary.

As Mary began to use the unusual brush Isabel owned, Gwen turned her attention back to her own beliefs. That Isabel would allow a servant to stay as they spoke about intimate details was not so unusual. Yet loyal servants were much like a comfortable piece of furniture. To be appreciated, but silent. And deaf.

"No wonder Arthur is so taken with you," she blurted.

Both Isabel and Mary went still.

"I understand, Isabel."

"I do not know what you believe you understand," Isabel said, although the color rising on her cheeks was a bit of a tell.

"I believe you understand very well. You were the one to talk Arthur into"—Gwen glanced at Mary, no longer seeing her as a silent piece of furniture, but as a young girl who soaked up knowledge as she attempted to grow into womanhood—"discussing matters with me he has obviously been avoiding for some time."

Isabel wrapped her dressing robe closer around her body. "Honesty is always best."

"Honesty betimes stabs, do you agree?"

"It often does," Isabel said, nodding. "But secrets often stab much deeper."

Gwen felt herself blush, but she could not bring herself to look away from Isabel's probing, yet somehow sympathetic eyes. "I do understand that, this morn. Yester morn I may have had a very different answer."

Isabel reached out and laid a hand over hers. "I am so sorry if I have turned Camelot upside down. It was not my intent. My only suggestion to Arthur was to be as honest with you as he would have you be with him."

Mary cleared her throat. "Pardon my interruption, your hair is done, mum. Unless you require further assistance, I will very happily take my leave."

Isabel sat back with a chuckle. "You are a good soul, Mary. I believe that many of your fellow workers would want to stay and listen to as much as possible."

Mary's freckles bloomed red. "I could not say, mum."

Isabel stood. "Well, I was hoping you'd help me get into one of those gown contraptions, but I suppose I can find one I will be able to lace up myself."

Mary lit up. "I know just the one, m'lady. 'Tis one of my favorites." She almost skipped to the wardrobe and, after shuffling around, brought out and laid a teal-colored gown on Isabel's bed. Although Isabel doubted the word teal had even been invented yet, just like pink.

Mary beamed even brighter as she turned in triumph. "I know not from whence this color comes, but with your hair and fair skin, I feel it will look beauteous on you, m'lady. And 'tis also easy for you to lace up yourself."

Gwen hid a grin. "You very much wish to escape Isabel's chamber, do you not, Mary?"

"Oh, yes, me queen. Overly much."

Isabel frowned. "Have I upset you, Mary?"

"No, Countess, no!" Mary said, wringing her hands. "You have been nothing but kind to me. I would wish for all guests to be such."

"But you do not want to stay to help us in the discussion of how to make the working women find a bit of joy?"

Mary pursed her lips. "Have you, perhaps, moved further in your discussions than secrets and such? I truly do not want to be part of that. 'Tis not my place."

Gwen stood and locked eyes with Isabel. "We have, Mary. That is a discussion for another time. I now have need to listen to Countess Isabel's discussion of joy for the women of Camelot. And the countess, it appears, would very much appreciate what you would have to opine in the matter."

"Countess?" Mary whispered.

"Very much, Mary. As a matter of fact, I fear we cannot do this without your counsel and help."

Mary looked back and forth worriedly, but then smiled. "I am honored. But first, Countess, serious discussion demands serious dress. Please allow me to help you."

The thought of dressing, or worse, undressing in front of a queen was a little discomforting. Isabel glanced around the room, but there wasn't a single private space in sight.

Her necklace warmed.

In this day, Isabel, nudity is quite common. Be not shy in the presence of other women.

So I should feel comfortable removing my clothes and letting others see me out of my robes?

Yes.

Forget it. I don't want to be naked in front of a queen whose body is . . . oh, hell, sacred.

Just dress yourself, Isabel, and stop whining; you have more important issues you need to be mining.

Isabel sucked in a breath and removed her robe, tossing it onto her bed.

She pulled the gown over her head as fast as she could, covering her butt, her breasts and her "stuff" as fast as possible. But it wasn't cooperating as much as she'd like. This was the most embarrassing moment of her life. Well, this life. She had a more embarrassing story in her older, or newer, life. That streaking incident in '85, for example. And the first time she allowed Jimmy Zwersky to partially undress her in fifth grade so they could compare.

Gwen laughed. "You are a shy woman, Isabel."

Isabel turned, even as she was still struggling to get the dress over her head, so her voice was muffled. "I prefer to dress alone."

"Would you prefer I leave, Isabel?"

"No, I'm good now," Isabel said as she finally got the freaking gown down over her body. God damn, she did *not* want to talk to the perfect Gwen about body issues. It was pretty obvious that the queen had none to worry about.

"May we please continue to discuss other matters?" Isabel asked, as Mary began working on the damn lacing process.

"Most assuredly, Countess," Gwen said. "You seem to feel discomfort in your gowns."

Isabel gritted her teeth. "In my land we allow women to wear much more comfortable clothing."

"Truly? Such as?"

"Well, because we enjoy gaming, we allow our women to wear pants, such as men do. We do not force ourselves to wear gowns at all waking hours."

"You wear men's breeches?"

"Yes and no. They are made for women. For the comfort and sporting fun of women. They are not so tight. But they allow the freedom to engage in events that they could not possibly do in gowns."

Gwen smiled and clapped. "So intriguing! I must learn more of this women sporting idea. And these 'pants,' did you say?"

"Show me the women who make the clothing, and I will be happy to guide them on how to create them. I realize many will not be comfortable in even trying them on, but they may warm to the idea once they have a chance to try them."

"Yes, yes! And guide us in the sporting?"

"Here's how we do it, Gwen. We allow all women at least an hour to play in whatever sport they choose to engage in on any particular day. They may wear those pants or breeches things for that playtime. They are given a time out from the backbreaking work they engage in for the rest of the day. If they are shy, as I am, they wear smocks or aprons or whatever they like overtop their shirts and tights."

Gwen's eyes were lit up like silver stars. "And the men make no objections?"

"First off, Your Highness, the men not only do not object, they must be ordered away from the ladies' playground, as they tend to ogle. Second, when the women are happier at the end of the day, it follows that so are the men, if you understand my meaning."

Gwen laughed. "I understand. And do so recognize the sheer genius of the plan. We must needs implement this at Camelot."

"I am so glad you see how this benefits your female staff. May we take up this conversation later? I have a morning breakfast meeting to attend."

"With Arthur?" Gwen asked.

Isabel nodded. "And others. It is nothing intimate, Gwen. It is a strategy meeting."

"'Twas once upon a time that I was welcomed at such meetings," Gwen said.

"Then, for goodness sake, we will go together. No one forbade you, correct?"

Gwen hesitated. "But I was not invited to the meeting."

"I believe your thoughts on the matters facing us all are most definitely important. I invite you."

Gwen smiled. "I most assuredly recognize why Arthur appreciates you, Countess."

Mary finished lacing Isabel's dress, then turned to them. "My queen, Countess, may I ask you to keep a secret for me?"

"Of course," they both said.

"I would very much appreciate that the news of James and me not get out to others in the castle. Not just yet."

"Your secret's safe with us, is it not, Gwen?"

"'Tis. But, Mary, why?" Gwen asked.

Mary blushed again. "There be many other girls who have set their sights on him, and I prefer not to upset them until we announce the news to all."

The idea that the human equivalent of bigfoot would be such a catch kind of boggled Isabel's mind. But she nodded. "Is this why you have kept him so . . . shaggy, Mary?"

Mary giggled. "When you see him shorn and well dressed, you will understand."

Not in a million years. Well, maybe, under all of that fur he was something of a handsome giant. And he had a gentle touch for someone who had been trained to fight and kill. "How soon do you turn fourteen, Mary?" Isabel asked.

"In two sennights, m'lady. We plan to marry days following."

"Don't you have to post banns, or some such thing?"

"Banns?"

Probably a little before the banns time. History was getting muddled in Isabel's mind.

The thought of a girl of just barely fourteen entering into marriage really gave Isabel the willies. But she understood. Sort of. She glanced at Gwen. "This is cause for celebration, right? I mean, James is Arthur's most trusted man."

Gwen hesitated, but then looked cheerful. "Yes, it indeed should be a day of celebration! What shall we do?"

"How about we put the other servants to good use? Part of their playtime can be helping create decorations. It will be fun."

"No, I cannot even ask for this," Mary said.

"Who asked you to ask, Mary?" Isabel said. "It is what people do for their friends."

Mary, who had been fussing with Isabel's gown and hair, stood up straight, bringing her to about five feet tall. Which made her about a foot and a half shorter than her future husband. Her blue eyes welled up with tears. "Friends?" she asked in a shaky voice.

"Yes, friends," Isabel said, then raised her brows at Gwen for confirmation.

"Yes, Mary. Friends," Gwen agreed.

ISABEL and Gwen headed down the steps together, but Isabel stopped her halfway down. "We need to have a bridal shower for Mary."

"A bridal shower? What would this be?"

"You know, where you celebrate the upcoming marriage of the bride."

"I have ne'er heard of such."

"Trust me, it will be fun. Kind of like a slumber party for the girls to share in the joy of Mary's upcoming wedding."

"Slumber party?"

This language barrier was getting on Isabel's nerves. "Trust me, it will be fun."

Gwen squeezed Isabel's arm. "Then we shall have it. Is there planning involved?"

"Of course. But it must be kept secret from all the men, and from Mary. It will be a surprise. But we will have to engage the help of some of the servants."

"I know just the ones to ask to help in this adventure. I so look forward to it."

Isabel swallowed, then said, "Do you mind if I create the menu, Gwen? I mean, I am not dissing your cooks, but truly, if I see one more pickled eel placed before me, I most definitely will lose my cookies."

"Lose your—"

"Have need to run so that I might empty the contents of my stomach."

Gwen laughed. "Oh, I see. Eel does not appeal to you."

"I honestly cannot believe that eel appeals to anyone."

"Truth to tell, I am not fond of it myself, but 'tis a favorite of many of the men. Arthur is not one. He prefers greens and the cheeses made from goat milk."

Of course he does. One more reason to fall for him. If Isabel was ever going to find a reason to reject him, she had to find *something* that disgusted her.

And if she were ever to find a reason to be disgusted by Gwen, she needed to find a flaw. Other than the fact that she thought Gwen was an idiot to desire Lancelot over Arthur, she couldn't think of a thing. Although that was a biggee.

Yet she found herself really enjoying Gwen. The woman was open to new ideas, was even excited about them. Gwen was way ahead of her time. She would be thrilled living in Isabel's lifetime.

The fact that she was an adulteress was kind of a minus, though. Then again, the fact that King Arthur had somewhat accepted it was a bit of a plus.

Not the Lady of the Lake's plan, however.

Plans do change, Isabel. Go with yours, I trust you well.

Isabel couldn't even begin to express the joy she felt at Viviane's leap of faith, no matter how misplaced it might be. She had trouble believing in herself. But with Viv's confidence—

Viviane, you twerp.

—Viviane's help, she just might pull it off.

"May we discuss a few matters?" she asked Gwen.

"We may discuss anything."

"First, what do you think of Mordred?"

"He is a young beast. He has caused nothing but heartache for Arthur. I try not to hate, but my feelings for him come very close."

"Oh, we so agree on that one. How is it possible that a man as kind as Arthur had a child such as he?"

"Arthur knew not of him until it was too late to change the boy's hatred."

"Why doesn't Arthur just ban him, then?"

Gwen stopped her and looked into her eyes. "The young man is his son. You have not known Arthur long, but you should already know the answer."

"Right, I get it. But the boy needs to be . . . I don't know . . . have his ass kicked."

Gwen laughed. "Indeed. I have heard you did a good job last eve."

"News travels fast," Isabel said.

"I do have my sources, Isabel. May I have my turn at this question and answer?"

"Of course."

"Do you realize that my husband is enamored with you?"

Isabel froze. "I realize that your husband loves you."

Gwen smiled and nodded. "He does. He has a large heart. But he was very plain when speaking of our situation. He no longer cares as he once did."

"Do you?"

"I love him very much."

"Wrong answer."

"I still care very much."

"But you are in love with another."

Gwen decided to stare up at the ceiling. "I care about another."

"Wrong answer."

"I share deep feelings with another."

"There you go! Right answer. Truth, Gwen. It makes so much more sense."

"Then tell me true, Isabel. Are you wanting my husband?"

Truth sucked sometimes. "Not at the expense of hurting your marriage."

"'Twas not my question."

"Fine. If he wasn't married, yes, I would attempt to pursue him. But he's married."

"To a woman who is craving another."

"Which, to tell you the truth, I find dumbfounding. But then, I don't blame you for being attracted to Lancelot." *Stupid as all hell, but who was she to judge?*

Gwen took her arm and led her farther down the stairs. "We are in a . . . what are we in, Countess?"

"A pickle?"

Gwen laughed. "We share a common language, and yet we do not. But, yes, we are in somewhat of a pickle."

"I must tell you that I will enjoy any vegetable that is pickled. But please, no more—"

"Eel," they both said at once.

"I will see what I can do with the people in the cooking rooms," Gwen said.

"I have a suggestion."

"Then I must hear it."

"Trevor should be made top chef. When I couldn't stomach last night's meal, he fed me foods that kept me from starving."

"Then you are in luck, as Trevor is in charge of the morning meal."

"Please, no eel omelet."

Gwen laughed. "Learn to just say no. And, by the by, Trevor is also not a lover of eel."

"Thank heavens." They hit the bottom of the staircase and headed to the formal dining room, where the meeting was to take place. "Okay, Gwen, here we go."

"Yes, Isabel, here we go. Would have been better had we tipped a bit of wine first."

"Wow, really early for that, Gwen. But okay, let's do it," Isabel said as she and Gwen veered from the hall and into the kitchen.

CHAPTER TWELVE

Isabel knew instantly that inviting Gwen to the meeting had been a bad idea. The look on Arthur's face told her so.

But she was rather puzzled why, since she'd had the impression that he'd always kept his queen involved in the politics of his kingdom. Gwen seemed so in tune with the intricacies of Camelot. It was something Isabel had rather admired last evening, when Gwen had seemed right up to date.

Gwen, too, obviously recognized that her husband had not expected her to join this party. Once she graciously greeted all at the table, including Lancelot, she took her leave.

All the men had stood and bowed, but holy cow!

Isabel felt at a loss. She was the only woman among a dozen burly and apparently a bit unhappy men, and she'd have liked Gwen to be there so she didn't feel so out of her element. So alone.

How strange that she'd so quickly bonded with the woman who she had been asked to betray in one way and ended up betraying in another. What the hell was wrong with her? Suddenly she felt like shit and wanted to run. Only Arthur's eyes meeting hers kept her from tearing away from the room.

You are not alone, Isabel, I am here, and it is at a time like this that you must keep your neckpiece near. I recognize your confusion and understand your fear; my deepest apologies that you question all you hold dear. Should you wish to withdraw from this pact we have made, I will undo this scheme, which I have laid.

Isabel touched her necklace and smiled at the men. "Please, sirs, take your seats. It seems to me we have much to discuss. And I don't know about you, but I'm starving. So let us break fast and stuff ourselves with food and ideas."

The necklace warmed comfortably against her chest.

"She does not speak as we do," one giant said.

"Because she comes from a very different region," Arthur said, coming to seat her. "'Tis why we need her. Her views are refreshing."

As he helped seat her, he whispered, "May we speak privately after this meeting?"

"You betcha," she said, "as long as there are none of these men following along."

His low chuckle drummed right through her. He straightened and moved back to his own chair, his hands moving in a "sit, sit" motion to the rest of the men. Then he clapped. "Trevor! We are ravenous."

"Oh, thank the gods," Isabel murmured. No way was Trevor going to feed her pickled eel. When she and Gwen had visited the kitchen, Isabel and Trevor had made a no-eel deal.

"DID the meeting go well in your mind?" Isabel asked Arthur as they strolled through the bailey. Even now, warriors were hard at work, exercising their swording skills with one another. The clanging of steel on steel—at least she believed it was steel, but who the hell knew?—rang out through the air.

"You won over every one of my men with your unique thoughts and ideas, Countess. I particularly enjoyed your suggestion of an occasional fair held at our borders, so that we may continue to enjoy harmony betwixt our people."

"Hey, a party is a party. Especially at peak harvest time."

"And you want to call this Thanks and Giving?"

"Well, we can call it whatever you would like, Arthur."

"I enjoy the Thanks and Giving notion."

"Tell me this, Arthur. Why was Mordred not at the table this morning?"

"Because until he swears complete fealty to the kingdom of Camelot and disavows his allegiance with Richard of Fremont, he is disallowed at all brainstorming meetings."

That stopped her short. "He is in league with that pig?"

"So my sources say."

Isabel felt outrage bubble up. "How dare he come here, acting as if he's just waiting for you to hand over the throne?"

"There are many words and actions Mordred has sprung upon me and all of Camelot that make no sense."

"And yet you permit it. You invite him into your castle."

"He is my son, Isabel. What would you have me do?"

"Giving him a good spanking would probably be at the top of my list."

"A spanking?"

"A good whack or ten to his backside."

"You mean whipping?"

"With spanking, you do not use a whip, you take him over your knee and spank with your hand."

Arthur barked out a laugh. "'Twould seem he is a bit too old to lay him over my knee. But the image amuses me."

"His actions gall me."

"May we speak of more pleasant things? I do not wish to spend what time we have together on troublesome issues that I have brought on myself."

She was about to argue that he hadn't brought on this particularly bad-tasting piece of trouble, but stopped herself. "Yes, of course. It is too nice a day to waste."

Arthur steered her toward the stables. "Would you care for a ride, Isabel?"

"Oh, I would love it." She jabbed a thumb over her shoulder. "Are they going to keep us company?"

Arthur glanced back at the men following close behind them. "Break off, sirs. I will meet up with you again shortly."

As they entered the stable, it was obvious right off the bat that Harry was not a happy camper. "If you have come for a ride, I'm afraid Samara cannot be ridden, Izzy. She has been hurt."

"Hurt how?" Isabel asked.

"Her leg has been lamed."

"How?"

"I can only say that foul play may have been involved. I can't see how she could possibly have caused this injury on her own."

"That little sonofabitch!" Isabel said. She turned on Arthur. "That beloved son of yours is a mean, nasty little prick."

Arthur grabbed her shoulders. "Hold off, Isabel. We do not know that this was the machinations of Mordred."

She felt her eyes welling but did nothing to wipe away the tears. "Who else would want to harm Samara? You know the answer, Arthur. You just don't want to see it."

"How would he even know which horse is yours, Isabel?"

Harry cleared his throat and shuffled his feet.

"Harry?" Isabel said, looking over at him.

"Well, when he came to stable his horse, I overheard a conversation between him and one of the lads. Mordred commented on Samara's beauty and apparent fine lineage and asked the boy if the king was considering breeding her. The lad told him that Samara belonged to the countess, not the king. And then Mordred said that perhaps he would discuss the possibility of a pairing between his steed and her mare."

Before Isabel could indulge in another tirade, Arthur said, "I will have my men investigate, Isabel, I promise you this. And no matter where it leads, the person responsible will be held accountable, should it be a stable boy or even Mordred."

She wrenched herself from his hold and ran to Samara's stall.

"Oh, my poor baby," she said, opening the stall door and wrapping her arms around the horse's neck. "I am so sorry."

Samara nickered softly against her neck.

"Who did this to you, do you know?" she asked, stepping back and tickling Samara's muzzle.

Samara nodded her head.

Isabel glanced down at Samara's foreleg, which was wrapped in what looked like cotton cloth. Apparently that was about the only thing available in these times.

"Dick will be coming to massage her leg," Harry said from behind her.

She whirled to see both Harry and Arthur standing outside the stall. "She knows who did this," Isabel said. "We can bring Mordred down here and see how she reacts."

"Isabel, you are not thinking clearly," Harry said. "Samara is ornery with most of the stable boys. It even took me at least fifteen minutes to settle her down enough to allow me to examine her. And you well know that animals love me."

She turned back to Samara, scratching her neck. "We will find who did this to you, I promise. Okay?"

Samara nodded her head again, then pressed her muzzle against Isabel's chest in what one could loosely interpret as a "woe is me" gesture.

"Isabel, if you'd still like to take that ride, you are welcome to any number of my horses."

Isabel wasn't so sure that she could ride any other horse beside Samara sidesaddle. She'd hate to embarrass herself if the magic did not extend beyond her own horse. She shook her head as she left the stall and closed it. "I fear I've lost the desire for a ride."

"A stroll, perhaps?"

As much as she craved time with Arthur, she just felt heartsick over what had happened to Samara. "I'm so sorry, but I don't think I would be the best of company, Arthur."

"I am guessing that even when you are not at your best, you are still the most worthy companion I could wish to be around."

She smiled. "Okay, perhaps a short stroll."

"Excellent." He turned to Harry. "Sir, I wish for you to instruct the stable lads that Samara should be guarded at all times. If needs be, have one set up a bed of sorts in front of her stall so that none can disturb her again."

"Sir, I'm sorry, but I do not feel all that comfortable giving orders to your servants. I have no authority here."

"You have authority in the name of the king, Harry. I bestow it upon you."

Harry bowed slightly. "As you wish."

Arthur held out his arm and Isabel took it, loving the feel of his well-muscled bicep beneath her fingers.

"I just cannot understand, Arthur, the abuse of innocent animals."

"Nor, I, m'lady, nor I. As you may have noticed, I have a love of dogs."

"No, really? I could not tell, being too busy trying to keep from tripping over them all."

Arthur smiled and squeezed her hand. "There, now that's better. Now tell me, what is this Izzy thing?"

THE two ended up at the east gardens, which were just as beautiful as the others, but in a totally different way. There was a large pond here, teaming with bright, beautiful fish. And as far as Isabel could tell by the scents, this garden was made up mostly of fragrant herbs. It made sense, as the cookhouse was nearby, and beyond that were rows upon rows of plants, which she guessed would be producing fruits and vegetables very soon. And beyond that was an orchard in full bloom with the promise of apples and maybe apricots and cherries and peaches. She wasn't certain just what types of fruit trees they had in this time. But all of the different fragrances were intoxicating.

"Camelot is lovely, Arthur. Truly."

"My thanks, Countess. Although I cannot take credit for much of this. 'Tis the artistry of my people, and of course—" He stopped short and swallowed hard.

"And of course, Gwen," Isabel finished for him. "You should not feel reluctant to speak of her, Arthur. We have spent but a short time together, but I really do like her. She's a lovely lady, and I see perfectly why you fell in love with her."

He led her to a concrete bench and they sat. "So you see how I cannot bring myself to condemn her?"

"Absolutely. As we have said before, the heart wants what it wants. Sometimes it's a very fickle thing."

"It would seem that mine is just as fickle."

"As it can be for any human. Would you care to hear the story about the first boy I fell madly in love with?"

His sad eyes lit up with humor. "Oh, yes, madam, I would enjoy that very much."

"Well," she said, settling her skirts around her, "his name was Billy Thornton and we were in second grade."

"Second grade?"

"We attended school together."

"You do this in Dumont? School the young men and women together?"

"Indeed. So anyway, Billy and I sat side by side in class, at the back of the room, because we were both good students."

"You were seated by how well you did in the learning?"

"Yes. The problem children were seated right up front, so the teachers could keep a closer watch on them."

"Such different customs for two lands so close to one another."

"Yes, I suppose, but anyway, it was obvious he had a crush on me. He pulled my pigtails all the time and—"

"This was a sign of affection?"

"Yes. When we were that young the only way to express if you liked a girl was to tease and taunt. If a boy ignored you, that was a sure sign he wasn't interested at all. But if he teased, then you knew he liked you. Or at least wanted to grab your attention."

"Ha! That is so true. That at least we have in common."

"So then on Valentine's Day"—she held up a hand to stop his question—"it's a holiday we celebrate once a year, where sweethearts express their feelings for one another." She figured discussing having a Hallmark moment would be too hard to explain so said, "Mostly by writing handmade notes to one another with all kinds of sappy tidings and pictures of hearts and things like that."

He nodded. "This happens, too, at Camelot, yet we do not set aside a particular day for this."

"I know, it's possible we in Dumont overdo the holiday traditions."

He was actually grinning now, which made Isabel feel all fluttery. She loved his smile, and she loved being the one who could put one on his face when his heart was heavy.

"So on Valentine's Day, Billy slipped a note on my desk. It read, 'Please be my valentine.' I was really happy, as I had set my little girl's heart on him as well."

"I am certain that you were fetching even as a young girl. I do so wish I had also known the young lady you were then. I am certain that I would have battled with this Billy for your affections."

"I'm not certain that he would have fought that hard for me."

"Why is that?"

"Because at recess—the time we broke for the midday meal—all of the girls compared the notes we received that day. Imagine our surprise when Billy had offered the exact same Valentine note to six of us."

Arthur chuckled. "And you say he was one of the brighter boys in this classroom of yours?"

"Okay, so he was probably a bit of a knucklehead in the romance department. I think he was hedging his bets."

"And what was your reaction?"

"I was heartbroken. He was my very first crush."

"But you did not retaliate?"

"Oh, sure we did. The six of us surrounded him at lunch."

"And?"

Isabel once again didn't think she could adequately explain what a wedgie was, so she improvised. "We took turns pouring our milk over his head and in his breeches."

Arthur slapped his knee, laughing. "The ire of a mistreated woman is not to be taken lightly."

His laughter was so rich and infectious, Isabel couldn't help but join in. "Indeed. We can exact very creative revenge."

"Remind me to never incur your wrath, m'lady."

She leaned over and nudged his shoulder. "Should you do so, sir, you will most certainly know it."

"You ne'er answered my question afore. Your men call you Izzy?"

She shook her head. "First of all, they are not my men, they are my friends. They are equals in every sense. They agreed to accompany me on this journey because they wanted to ensure my safety."

"All right, yes, your friends. They call you Izzy?"

"It is a pet name they have given me since we were young. Very few are permitted to call me that."

"I see. 'Tis a privilege one must earn."

"Something like that."

"I look forward to the day I am afforded that privilege, Isabel."

"With the uncertainty that lies ahead, Arthur, who knows if that day will ever come?"

He took her hand. "I certainly hope to live to see that day."

Wow, that sounded kind of doom and gloomy. Not a place she wanted to head right now. She squeezed his hand. "So how about you tell me of your first love?"

He opened his mouth, but a sound from above stopped him and they both looked up. Gwen had been heading down the stone steps from the castle, a basket of sorts hanging from her arm. She froze.

Isabel slipped her hand out of Arthur's. They all were stunned silent for a moment before Gwen found her voice. "My . . . apologies for interrupting. I was just coming to gather some herbs. But I can return at a later time."

Isabel shot to her feet. "No, Gwen, please don't let us stop you. I was just regaling Arthur with a story from my misspent youth. I should really go . . . do something else." Well, she couldn't get much lamer than that, could she?

"I shall escort you back to your . . . something else, Countess," Arthur said.

"No, thank you. Once I figure out what that something else

might be, I'm certain I'll be able to find my own way. If you'll please excuse me." She lifted her skirts in an effort to hightail it out of there as fast as these damn slippers would let her.

ARTHUR and Gwen stared at one another before she made the first move by heading down the steps. "My apologies for the interruption, Arthur."

"'Twas nothing of great importance, Gwen. We were merely engaged in an enjoyable conversation."

"Something that seems to be sorely lacking between the two of us of late."

"Yes, well, there seems not to be much to share these past days."

She took another step forward, her expression pained. "I have given a vow to stop—"

He held up a quelling hand. "Please do not make any more vows you are unable to keep. It cheapens even further what was once good and bright."

"What is it you want from me?"

He stared at her. She was at once beautiful and fragile, a woman who begged for a man's strong arms to shield her from harm. 'Twas once such an alluring thing, as he so wanted to be her shield, her protector, her husband and her lover. His views had reversed course after meeting Isabel, who would likely jump into battle against anyone who would harm those she held dear. Isabel would not ask for assistance but would take on enemies, insisting she was quite capable of fighting her own battles.

Night and day, day and night. 'Twas not that he found fault with Gwen, for it was how she was raised. 'Twas just that Isabel's strength of a sudden he found much more admirable.

"What I want, Gwen, is your happiness. I am being truthful when I say this. Your happiness is very important to me. But no longer at the cost of mine."

"Then there is no going back?"

"I fear not, nor should there be. To attempt to reclaim the past when so much has happened between then and now is as attempting to save a snowflake on your tongue from melting. 'Tis, quite frankly, not possible. I am not and refuse to be another Billy Thornton."

"Billy Thornton? I do not recognize the name. Have I misremembered? Have we entertained him?"

"No, but he quite entertained me."

She wore a confused frown on her face, but then let it go. "So where do we go from here, Arthur? I cannot bear to disgrace you."

"As I said, Gwen, discretion. Always discretion. We keep up appearances as long as we are able. It is very important for the sake of our kingdom. And then I shall study this no-fault dissolution of marriage that they practice in Dumont. Perhaps we may adopt such a law in Camelot. 'Twould most definitely cut down on the frying pan injuries several of my men suffer many times a year."

"No-fault what?"

He waved. "A law they have in Isabel's land where neither man nor woman are held responsible for the . . . irreparable damage to the marriage. It is a way to save harm falling upon both husband and wife. They agree that they have recognized they are no longer suited."

Gwen smiled as she met him at the bench. "Please sit with me for a moment. I have discussed several ideas with Countess Isabel myself that I believe show much merit."

He nodded as he took her elbow and helped her to sit. "And here is where we will most assuredly find some common ground."

I need guidance here, Viviane. I am asking for a way to explain how I can care for two people, both and neither to blame.

What is it, Isabel, that you fear? That you have met two people who you now feel near?

I fear irreparably damaging a marriage that might be fixed, so my feelings are so terribly mixed.

The damage had been done long afore your arrival; as I see it all now, you could well be Arthur's survival.

Isabel wasn't so sure, but she took a little comfort in the reminder that the marriage had been in trouble before she showed up. Although she didn't have a single clue how she could be Arthur's savior in any way.

Just one last question, Goddess, and for this I won't rhyme: How is Merlin doing, and how are you at this time?

Good gods, she couldn't even help herself.

She heard the soft lilting sound of Viviane's laughter in her ear.

Truth be told, Isabel, he smiles when you and the king come together. I must believe that your match makes him feel so much better.

Isabel wasn't certain she could count it as a match at the moment. It was only a certain . . . attraction between them so far.

It is the only positive sign I have had from Merlin in the last days. Please, Isabel, he has need of your help.

Wow, not even close to rhyming. Viviane was not herself.

You have no idea.

There was a knock on Isabel's door and then it opened and Mary came bustling in, a tray filled with cheeses and bread on it, along with a stein of what was most likely mead. "Hello, mum," she said cheerfully. "'Tis a lovely day, is it not?"

Isabel smiled. "It is indeed. And you too are looking full in bloom. What brings such lovely radiance to your face?"

Mary laid down the tray then clapped and nearly jumped in the air. "James has agreed, Countess!"

"Agreed?" Isabel asked, reaching for a piece of goat cheese. "I thought that was already taken care of. You will be wed shortly after you strike the ripe old age of fourteen."

"No, no! He has agreed to allow me to cut his hair."

Isabel dropped the cheese and jumped up, grabbing Mary's hands. "That is *wonderful*, Mary! Truly, truly wonderful! Oh, he will look so handsome at your ceremony."

"And that is not all. It seems that the king has suggested that all of his men follow suit, so that they all appear—what was the word?—receptacle as well!"

Isabel nearly choked. Hell, most of them already looked like receptacles. "I think you mean respectable."

"Yes, that."

"Oh, Mary, that is such good news!" She raised the stein in toast, even if Mary had nothing to toast with. "Here's to a beautiful wedding." She took a sip, but a small one. She wasn't used to the strong brew and wasn't certain she'd ever get used to it.

Either it was the mead or her feeling of pride that Arthur had listened and requested that his men clean up their acts that was warming her insides. Most likely the latter. She held up the stein to Mary. "Are you permitted to drink this swi—er, mead, Mary? If so, please join me."

Mary's freckled nose wrinkled. "'Tis permitted, mum, but I care not for the taste."

"Then share some bread and cheese?"

Mary shook her head. "Thank you again, but no. I do not want to add any bulk to my body afore my wedding day."

Isabel chuckled. Every bride's nightmare. At least that was something that hadn't changed over time. She racked her brain, wanting to do something for Mary to celebrate.

Then it hit her. "Mary, do you already have the gown you are to wear on your special day?"

"No, mum, but I hope to engage the help of our seamstresses in the next couple of days. The queen has demanded that the men who I shear offer a small payment for my services. With what I save, I am hoping to be able to afford to purchase a very special dress for the occasion."

Isabel walked over to the wardrobe. "Take your pick," she said, pointing at her gowns. "Any one you want, it is yours."

"Oh, I could never!"

"Oh, but you can! I insist. It is my marriage gift to you. And you cannot refuse a marriage gift, now can you? That would just be plain rude."

Mary glanced longingly at the dresses, then turned back. "But, mum, you are so much taller than I. And so much more . . . bountiful up here," she said, cupping her own breasts.

"What are seamstresses for if not to do a little nip and tuck work to adjust gowns to fit the bride? And you can save what you earn from going into the haircutting business to help you and James save up for your own private cottage on the estate. Win-win."

Mary's eyes filled with tears, and she tried to blink them away. "Really, mum, I just don't know."

"I do. Choose. And tomorrow we'll go down or up to the sewing department, or whatever you call it, and we'll start on the alterations."

"What if I choose one you especially love?"

"Then I'll especially love seeing it on you during the best day of your life."

Mary stood mute for a moment, then flung herself into Isabel's arms. "Oh, mum, this is the nicest thing anyone has e'er done for me."

Isabel hugged her back, feeling tears attempting to spill from her own eyes. "I am so happy to do this small thing, Mary. And now let's pick out a dress."

She looked up and went still when she found Arthur lounging in the doorway, arms crossed, staring at her intently. She wondered if she was in big trouble for stepping over some kind of line until his lips lifted in a slow smile. He nodded.

She returned a shaky smile, then gave him the "shoo-shoo" gesture so he wouldn't freak Mary out. He nodded and retreated, but not before mouthing, "I shall return shortly." Whether to chew her out or kiss her, she had no idea. She didn't care. Just having him back was good enough for her.

CHAPTER THIRTEEN

TRUE to his word, Arthur returned less than an hour later. "May I enter, Countess?"

She finished brushing—or twigging—her teeth, stuffed a bunch of mint in her mouth and turned. "Yes, sir, you may."

"Has the vow-day dress been decided upon?"

"After a little argument over color, it has indeed."

"Color?" he asked, as he walked in, a flask of wine and two goblets in his hands.

"She had her heart set on the red, but I talked her into the green. The red kind of clashed with her hair. The green complimented her coloring much better."

He set the goblets down and filled them. "I believe you have a better eye for such things than most." He handed her one of the goblets.

"How long were you standing there?" Isabel asked, accepting the wine.

"Long enough to recognize why I have these feelings for you, Izzy."

She lowered her head hiding her grin. "You do know I only afford those closest to me to call me Izzy."

"I do."

"So you are assuming I have allowed you into my circle of closest friends?"

"I have high hopes, and so I am taking the chance. Have ne'er waited in my life to be invited. I have this tendency to barge in. 'Tis a terrible fault of mine."

"Yes, you brute!"

"My belief, beautiful lady, is that you can handle the brute."

The look in his eyes told her his intentions were so very not honorable. Which was as sexy as sexy could be.

She backed up. "Mary could return at any moment."

"She could," he said as he backed up and kicked the door closed and then turned the lock. "But she would have a very terrible time entering."

"I don't suppose you put the Do Not Disturb sign out there?"

"No one will disturb us. At the risk of being beheaded."

Isabel gulped. "You're teasing, yes?"

"You tell me, Isabel. Am I teasing?"

"You would never hurt anyone like that. So, yes, I know you're teasing."

He held up his goblet. "To the most unusual woman I have e'er met, Isabel. And the most full of heart and care and passion. I am so happy to have met you."

They clinked and drank, and then she answered, "And to the most compassionate and loving man I have ever met, Arthur. This journey has been strange and long, but had I not traveled it, and not met you, I feel it would have been such a loss. You really have been a new treasure to me."

They sipped again, green eyes locked on blue.

Then they sat in the respective chairs, which was probably a much better idea than throwing the goblets aside and jumping into bed. Although she wasn't quite certain at the moment why that was a better idea.

"You entrance me, Isabel," Arthur said. "Everything about you calls to me. I will not deny it. I also will make no apologies for it. This feeling is somewhat beyond my ken. I happened to be at the door from near the moment you wanted to do something special for Mary. 'Twas very special. As are you."

She sipped her wine again. "As was I with Mary's news that you had ordered your men to clean up for James and Mary's wedding. It was a wonderful thing for you to do."

"First, I did not order it, Isabel. I merely suggested. In battle, I order. At Camelot, I suggest."

She nodded. "Also that Gwen *suggested* that the men pay her for her services."

"We have always encouraged all of our people to offer services for pay." He waved a hand. "Should a person provide a special service, should he or she not be awarded for such? Seems only fair. There must be a name for such a practice, but I know not what it would be."

"In my land it is called capitalism."

"I have ne'er heard of such, but any word will do."

"Whatever. I thank you and Gwen for promoting capitalism. It honestly makes your men and women work harder at their tasks, and be rewarded."

"I would like to hear your suggestions of how to bring more of this capitalism into the workings of the castle."

"Right now?"

"No, not at this very moment. At this moment I would very much enjoy hearing more tales of you."

She shook her head. "I have blabbed on too far. You must reciprocate. Tell me something about you." She grinned. "Something you haven't told another soul."

He laughed and then took another drink of wine. "I must say that I know not much of what you say. You use words I have ne'er heard. Yet I enjoy attempting to puzzle them out by the words that surround them."

Isabel felt a buzz run down her body, and she knew it had nothing to do with the wine. "I try at times to speak as you, but forget to at times."

"Please do not try. I am much enamored by who you are and how you speak. And the workings of your mind. And your beauty. And—"

"Stop! I appreciate the flattery, Arthur, but it embarrasses me."

"And your caring heart," Arthur said, with a grin. "And I could go on, but now I will stop." He refilled both of their goblets, although she'd barely put a dent in her own to begin with. But she didn't protest. She was too freakin' happy just to be with him.

Merlin is happy, Arthur and Isabel. He is still in a deep sleep, but he smiles as well.

Arthur frowned. "Did you hear that?"

Isabel didn't know whether to say yes or no.

"Hear what?" she asked, deciding noncommittal was the way to go.

"About Merlin?"

"Merlin?"

Arthur shook his head. "It must be my mind playing tricks."

She tried to word her answer as best she could. She did not want Arthur thinking he was losing his marbles. "I think that when thoughts enter your mind, they are there for a reason. To ponder upon. At least, that's how I find those types of voices in my head."

Viviane, cut it out!

Sorry!

He sat back and said, "So tell me, Izzy, what would you like to know most about me? My first love?"

What she'd love to know most is how he looked totally naked. And whether he was as good a lover as his eyes and smile promised. But brazen hussy that she normally was, she wasn't quite ready to blurt out those questions. Yet.

"I would love to know that story, but it's not what I'd like to hear first. But I fear going too far."

"Try me," he said.

She hesitated. "I would like to know what your greatest passion is. What matters the most to you, Arthur?"

He took a few long minutes to answer, rubbing his beard. In the meantime Isabel took several sips of her wine, waiting for him to tell her all kinds of things. Like it was none of her freaking business, for one. Re-winning Gwen's affection for another. Running out of the room before answering her for another.

Finally he said, "I have many of those. May I choose more than one?"

"Of course," she said, swallowing a hiccup and fear. Fear of what, she wasn't certain, but there was definitely fear hanging around her. A more benign question would have worked better.

"I want to secure the safety and happiness for all of Camelot. But I am much concerned that this is not going to be possible."

"Why?"

"There be too many who want to bring us down. 'Tis why we are having this meeting of the knights from other realms. To unite against those dark forces."

"Dumont is not one, Arthur. I promise you."

His smile was grim. "I know that, Isabel. And I much appreciate the support you are offering."

"I have men on their way, ready to defend you."

That was a bunch of bullshit. She didn't even know if she had men. But she was depending on the Lady to help her with that one.

"Your men have come already, Isabel. They are even now settling in."

"They have?"

"You did not know?"

Get with the program, Isabel. Do you think I did not bring backup?

A little forewarning might have been nice.

You should recognize them easily, as they will look familiar to you. They are the entire football team of UO, but to make this rhyme Oklahoma U.

Holy shit, you did not take them away from—

Oh, can it, Isabel, they are mirror images as are Tom, Dick and Harry.

Isabel didn't know whether to laugh or cry. She wondered if the Sooner Schooner had carried some of them.

Yes, indeed. Now please get back to Arthur.

She swallowed. "They did, indeed, arrive ahead of schedule. My apologies if this is a burden for you."

He laughed. "No burden at all. They have been nothing but a

pleasure, according to James. They even brought something called a mas-cot."

"Oh boy. They'll have your men tailgating in no time."

She saw his confusion and quickly shook her head. "I will have to go welcome them and thank them for coming shortly. But not before I hear what more you have to say."

"To say?"

"Or maybe you don't. I thought you had more than one passion."

"Oh, yes. My passions."

Once more he grinned in a way that truly made her melt and fire up at one and the same time. Something she had never felt before. Try to figure that one out, Dr. Phil.

"Yes, passions. We definitely need to get back on track here. I passionately want to keep peace between Gwen and me."

Talk about your heart sinking straight to your toes. "I understand that, Arthur. And I believe you should. Salvaging your marriage should definitely be your first priority."

Her necklace thumped.

"You misunderstand. I passionately want Gwen to be happy. That is not with me. She is much in love with Lance. I cannot stop them nor do I want to hurt them in this. Truly, I am most concerned that I cannot protect them as well as I need to do. I care about the two very much."

"Even though they have—"

He leaned forward and put a hand to her lips. "They have followed their desires. Would I ask for a different outcome? Perhaps. But 'tis done, and cannot not be undone. Now I must secure their safety. And truth to tell, all will be well."

Isabel ran her hand through her hair. "I honestly don't understand."

"'Twould be a horrid price both would pay if they are caught. I will try to guard against this to the best of my ability."

"You are a good man, Arthur. With a big heart. We have a saying in my land. 'What happens in Dumont, stays in Dumont.'

Unless you're dumb enough to talk about it to every person you meet outside of Dumont."

"I very much enjoy the thoughts of the people of Dumont."

"As do I," she said, which was a bit of a whopper of a lie, considering, hey, she didn't know a single citizen of Dumont.

She took a last glug of her wine and stood. "Now perhaps I should go and greet my men."

He took her hand. "You have not yet heard my third passion."

"Maybe later, Arthur."

"Please, it is short."

She nodded and sat back down. In fact, she was ready to lie down. This drinking so early in the day was not good for her equilibrium. "Your third passion?"

He kept hold of her hand, running his thumb over her palm. For a moment he seemed to waver, but then he looked her straight in the eye. "To lie naked with you. To make love with you. To kiss you so passionately that 'twill make you dizzy. That is my third passion. And of the passions I have mentioned, 'twas not necessarily ordered properly. It just took me some time to build up the courage to voice this one."

Thank the gods she was sitting, because sure as hell her knees would have caved on her. And for maybe the first time in her life, she was totally speechless.

They stared at one another for so long that the sun could have set and she wouldn't have noticed.

Finally he broke the gaze and stood. "I should have not said such a thing. It was untoward." He bowed. "My deepest apologies."

Isabel grabbed his arm and pulled him closer as she stood, so they were face-to-face, body-to-body. "I bet you one of our horses that you cannot get me out of this contraption called a gown faster than Mary can."

He grinned, then cupped her face. "Oh, Countess, how you underestimate me."

CHAPTER FOURTEEN

O H, how Isabel had underestimated him. In every single way.
Arthur had her gown off in record time, kissing her senseless
the entire way.

"You're good," she said, as her gown dropped to the floor.

"I very much hope, lady, that you feel the same way in a while."

Other than the gown billowed around her ankles, she was
naked, and suddenly felt shy. She covered her breasts with her arms.

"Oh, Isabel, please, no. You are so beautiful."

Isabel had no idea how the workings of men's tunics, breeches or
other stuff worked. She was only able to shed him of his outer vest
before being at a total loss. "I'm afraid I don't know what to do."

Arthur, who'd been fixated on her body, went still and drilled
her with his gaze. "Are you telling me you are still untouched?"

She had no freaking idea how to respond. She was at a total loss
for words.

Viviane?

No answer. And it suddenly occurred to her that Viviane had promised her privacy at times like this. Great. Really fucking great.

"Does it matter?" she asked. "I just have no idea how to deal with men's clothing."

"It matters very much to me," he said, looking and sounding angry.

He pulled her gown back up over her body. His heaving breaths no longer sounding full of lust and longing. They sounded full of an attempt to resume control of his body.

"Please tell me what's so wrong, Arthur?" she asked, holding the unlaced gown around her. "What did I do?"

He picked up his vest, the only garment she'd managed to strip from his body. "I will not take away something that is the province of your future life mate."

He headed to the door, shoving his vest back on with every stomping step.

"You wait just one minute, buster! Get your ass back here and talk to me."

He turned back, just as he was about to switch the latch on the door. "What more can I say? I am not upset with you, madam, I am upset with myself. I deeply, deeply apologize for what I was about to do."

"If you hadn't noticed, I was a very willing participant."

"Which was heady indeed. Truth be told, it overruled all else."

"Then why are you taking it out on me? And why am I suddenly madam instead of Isabel, or even Izzy? You might believe you're punishing yourself, but you are punishing me more. Why?"

He deflated just a bit, which hurt Isabel's heart. Abandoning the door, he approached her. "Let me help you with the laces."

"Fine, while you do, why not help me to understand what just happened here."

"'Tis not a nice story," he said, as he began lacing her like a pro.

"As if we all don't have many of those. Spill, Arthur, please."

"'Twas a time I was a bit too full of bluster. Too filled with my newfound power and fame. I was but a lad but wanted quite desperately to be a man."

"I get that. But what does this have to do with us? With this?" she asked. "I believe the truth is in order."

He sighed. "Yes, you deserve the truth."

And a freaking good orgasm. But for now she'd settle for the truth. "Yes," she said, trying desperately not to start crying.

He nodded. "Then the truth you shall have." He gently pulled her hands from her dress, seeming to need something to do.

"Tell me, Arthur."

"Where to begin?"

"Right after successfully freeing Excalibur."

He nodded yet again. "Soon after I met a young lady enamored with me named Elizabeth. She was lovely and sweet. I was feeling bold and powerful, and felt the world was mine."

"As you should. You had done something no one else could."

He finished lacing her up, then turned and sat back in one chair. Isabel again sat in the other. "Go on," she said.

"This sweet young girl allowed me to . . . make love with her. 'Twas a hurtful experience for her, as I was very much not as worldly in some things. 'Twas my first time as well."

"You knew how to take swords out, but not quite how to put them in?" She saw his expression and chuckled. "I apologize. That joke was in very bad taste."

He cocked his head. "Unfortunately, all too true. I had terrible nightmares about what I had done. For I left without an apology. I, after all, had more important missions to accomplish. A few years passed, yet the nightmare of that day still weighed on my mind. I attempted to contact her, to ask of her well-being. But I was told she passed in childbirth."

"Holy shit! Here comes Mordred."

"I had nary a clue that the child was mine. I swear this to be true. Her sister took over care of the child and led Mordred to believe she was his true mother. She had hatred of me, though I attempted to make peace with her. But she would have none of it. I counted and knew he had to be mine. 'Twas twisted, 'twas a horrid time for all. I tried to make all right, Isabel. I truly did."

"I believe you, Arthur."

"The reasoning for this story is to tell you how much I fear ever hurting another woman in such a way again. And you, Isabel, I fear hurting most."

"I have to believe Gwen was also a virgin when you married her."

"That is true, but I was very careful, knowing this. I was very careful to make certain no harm would come to her."

"Then why did you freak out with me?"

"Freak out?"

"Why did you stop?"

He shook his head. "Do you not understand? My body was out of control. I wanted to take you. I wanted to ravish you."

"So? I wanted to be ravished."

Arthur stared at her. "I might have hurt you. I had already done that to another. I could not live with that."

"Did I appear frightened?"

"No, Isabel, but 'tis because you have no knowledge of the pain a woman endures the first time."

Like hell she didn't. Brian Gordon had been just as clumsy and clueless as Arthur. And, hell yes, it had hurt like hell. But she got over it. Rather quickly, actually.

"You could have been just as gentle with me as with Gwen."

"I could not."

"Why not?"

"Because with Gwen I was in full control of my faculties. I had learned from that first experience with Elizabeth. And Gwen was more of a piece of fragile artistry. 'Twas easy to treat her as such."

"I know I'm not a piece of fragile artistry, although the jury's still out on how offended I am. But just what is so very different here?"

"I have told you, Isabel, with you I was not in control. 'Tis a fact that I have ne'er wanted a woman as I do you. Even as a lad, and full of lustful thoughts, 'twas not as this."

Isabel wanted to scream. He was making no sense and at the same time too much. He was a gentleman and a gentle man. But her thrumming body was simply pissed off.

Then again it felt really good to hear that he had wanted her that badly. Why hadn't she just said that of course she wasn't a virgin? That she had had several lovers over the years? Good lord, at her age you'd think her vagina had closed over permanently if it had never been penetrated.

The moment had come and gone, however, and her hesitation had cost her. Big time. To blurt out now that in truth she was very familiar with what he would call bed sport would seem disingenuous. And would probably anger him because she hadn't spoken the truth to begin with.

She stood up, feeling a kind of defeat like no other. "I thank you for your honesty, Arthur. I wish only that I had done the same when you asked."

He, too, stood. "Your meaning?"

She couldn't seem to meet his eyes. "It doesn't matter now."

He reached out and took her chin, forcing her to meet his all too probing gaze. "To me it matters a great deal. In the end, Isabel, truth is all we have."

Oh, jeez, could she feel any worse? Her entire life in this land was a lie.

"May we discuss this at another time? Right now I am spent, and may I say, not in the way I had hoped. But I have much to do before the evening meal and need to get to it."

He stared at her for what seemed an eternity, then gave a short, curt nod. "Another time, then. I, too, have obligations. I have not gone through my swording and bow skills as yet today, and must needs do this, lest I become fat and lazy. This evening, perhaps?"

Her laughter shook. It would take at least a year or more of total sloth for Arthur to gain a pound or lose an ounce of muscle. His body was finely toned from shoulders to toenails. At least it felt that way. How she wished she could have explored for herself. "Perhaps. We'll see."

"I will see you at the evening repast, then?"

"You will. I never miss a meal if I can help it."

He chuckled. And then before she knew it, he cupped her head and ravished her mouth. Her hormones, which had finally started to go back into dormant mode, sprang back to life as if zapped with electricity.

Arthur kissed like no other man she knew. His lips were firm and sure, intent on molding hers to their bidding. His tongue made only an occasional appearance, to taste her mouth and touch her own tongue. He didn't try to shove it down her throat as too many men had done, didn't use it as an oral fuck, just playing and teasing and basically driving her crazy.

Long moments later he broke the kiss, but then laid his forehead against hers. "Oh, Isabel. Your taste and your scent and your feel are almost too much to bear," he whispered.

"Oh, right back atcha," she said.

"Until this evening?"

"Yes."

He stood back, albeit appearing totally reluctant to do so. His eyes swept over her, from face to feet. "Trust me, Isabel, you have no need of shyness. You are so beautiful."

He went to move past her, but she touched his arm and he turned back. "Yes?"

"So are you."

He grinned. "You are presuming. You may take back those words some day. I have many a battle scar on this body, Isabel."

Although the thought of him being hurt nearly made her shudder, she understood this was the way of this world. And then she thought of Curtis and Afghanistan, and realized brutality hadn't changed, only the nature of it. Still, she couldn't wait to explore every single one of those scars. If she ever got the chance.

She walked with him to the door, but before he opened it she stopped him again. "Arthur? The next time we have the chance to speak, I promise the truth. Because you're right. In the end it is all we have."

He smiled. "I look forward to it. You have an endlessly fascinating life, Isabel."

If he only knew.

"Until this evening, then," he said with a slight bow.

"Yes. Be careful out there. Sword play isn't for sissies."

He laughed. "I know naught what a sissy is, but I can well imagine."

They were both smiling as he swung the latch and opened the door.

Their smiles fizzled instantly.

"Mordred," Arthur said.

The smug little bastard shoved off from the wall across from Isabel's door. "Father. Countess. I feared that you would not emerge the entire day."

ARTHUR knew that Isabel's first desire was to lunge at his son and claw his eyes out. So he quickly blocked her path to thwart disaster. "Did you have issues to discuss, Mordred?" he asked. "You had but to knock."

"Oh, issues aplenty," he said. "And another to add to my list."

"Then let us do so, at some other—"

"You smug little stalking, animal-abusing, ungrateful creep," Isabel hissed, attempting to break through Arthur's barrier. With no luck, thank the gods.

"Please, Isabel," Arthur said, "allow me to handle this situation."

Her breaths were coming fast. "How do you think he knew where you were if he didn't follow you?"

Mordred's grin widened. "The countess is very astute. And lovely. You have chosen a lover well. Should you care to share her services with your son, I would not object."

Arthur felt a rage like no other. He leapt forward and grabbed Mordred's tunic with both hands, shoving him back against the wall. "You will apologize to the lady. This very moment, Mordred."

Mordred's smile had gone missing, yet the malice in his eyes still gleamed bright. 'Twas such a sad sight for Arthur. He shook his son. "Apologize. Afore I have you escorted from Camelot and ban your presence for all time."

"If what I have said is untrue—"

"'Tis untrue. Isabel and I are not lovers. I say again, Mordred. Apologize to the lady."

"Forget it," Isabel said, coming up beside them. "This kid is incapable of an honest apology."

And then she performed an act that was remarkable and shocking all at once. She twirled once and then with one leg raised, rammed it into Mordred's knee.

Mordred yelped in pain and might have collapsed, were it not for Arthur's hold on him.

"And *that* is for Samara. How does it feel? Should you ever come near my horse again, you will receive worse. Understand, you little shit?"

Arthur then witnessed something in his son's eyes directed at Isabel that had never been directed at his own father. A spark of respect.

Mordred winced as he tried to regain his footing on his own. "My apologies, Countess, if I spoke out of turn."

"I don't give a good damn about your meaningless words, Mordred," she said. "Your actions are what define you. Just shows that nurture won out over nature in this little genetic pool battle, you creep."

Even though Arthur had Mordred at least five inches above the ground, Mordred managed to ground out, "You are allowing a mere whore to berate your only son and the heir to your crown?"

"Oooh, you had me at mere whore," Isabel said, and wound up once again to attack.

"Isabel, no!" Arthur said. "Allow me to finish this."

He dropped his son back to the ground, knowing the pain it would inflict on his leg.

Mordred yelped.

The pain to his son was hurtful, but the words against Isabel hurt as much. "You will accord the countess the respect and courtesy she so rightly deserves," Arthur prompted. "She has never wronged you. It is you who appears to have wronged her, with words and deeds. Make this right, Mordred, or I shall drop you on that leg many more times. Or worse, I will allow the countess to have at you."

"I will."

"You will what?"

"I will attempt to set things right."

"Not good enough," Isabel said, the heat of her anger in her eyes still so strong, it could manage to warm the entire castle.

Arthur nearly groaned. "He has apologized, Isabel."

"To me, not to you." She glared daggers at Mordred. "Your father loves you. He has been doing his best to make up for the years he didn't even know that you were his son. And you have repaid him with nothing but hatred and retaliation in mean, evil ways."

"Isabel," Arthur began, but was apparently not allowed to finish, since she was . . .

On a tear.

Once again he knew not where that voice in his head was coming from, but it seemed appropriate, as Isabel appeared to be able to tear Mordred limb from limb.

She stepped even closer, right in Mordred's face. "He *loves* you, you little brute. He would have gladly taken you and cared for you had he known. *But he did not know!* He is paying penance for something that was not his fault. And you are adding to it, forcing guilt upon him. A burden he doesn't deserve to carry. So you either straighten up and treat your own father with the respect he deserves, or I will be certain to make your life as much of a living hell as you are making his.

"He has the resources to make it happen, but you are counting on his love to keep you cozy and safe. I also have the resources to make that happen, Mordred, but I do not give a rat's ass what happens to you, so hiding behind your father's love in my world is just not going to happen. Do not underestimate me. *Capisce?*"

"Capisce?" Mordred and Arthur said at the same time.

"Understand?" she enlightened.

Mordred nodded. "I . . . Capisce."

"Apologize."

"He needs not—"

"He absolutely does."

Mordred swallowed hard, and for the first time since e'er Arthur laid eyes upon the lad, there seemed to be no menace in his eyes. "I . . . apologize, Father."

"For?" Isabel persisted.

"For believing you had abandoned me. That you cared naught what had become of me."

"Not true, my son. Had I known . . ."

Arthur couldn't go on because he felt choked by unshed tears.

Isabel pushed off from the wall. "Then I suppose it's time that you take him to your healer. He probably needs a brace on that knee."

Arthur took Mordred's waist, then hoisted him up into his arms.

"Father! I cannot be seen carried this way."

"Do you think you will be able to navigate those long steps on your own? I assure you that I will set you down should I hear another coming along. To keep up appearances, of course, that father and son are just upon a walk, discussing father and son things."

He swiveled, his son cradled close, as he so wished he had been able to do since Mordred was a babe. "Isabel?"

She turned, just as she was about to reenter her quarters. "Yes?"

"Do you know the whereabouts of your healer, Dick? I know that mine is far off this day, visiting the outlying huts of our farmers."

"Last I heard, he was cracking the necks and backs of many of your men. He is in what I believe you call the healing quarters."

"Thank you," he said, and it held meaning much beyond just directing him to her own healer. He had high hopes that she understood just how much.

"You are welcome. And again, sorry, Mordred, though you had it coming." Then she looked again at Arthur. "Yes, I do understand."

She stared at Mordred, cradled in his father's arms. "And you, you little jackass, try to figure out who is caring for you right now. He loves you, more than you know. Without his love for you, there would be a ton of his loyal men and women who would have demolished you by now. Including me."

* * *

As they navigated the steps that would take them to the healing rooms, Mordred looked up at Arthur. "She is a fierce warrior, Countess Isabel."

Arthur nodded, trying not to show strain. After all, Mordred was no babe at this time. "That she is, most when those she holds dear are threatened or hurt. Did you harm her horse, Mordred?"

"I ne'er meant it to be a lasting injury."

"'Twas a nasty, horrid thing to do."

"Yes, I understand now." He laid his head against Arthur's face, which was such a feeling unlike any Arthur had ever felt afore with his own son.

"Are you going to banish her for attacking your son?"

Arthur stopped for a moment, then kept taking the steps. "Yes. The same day I charge you with attacking her horse."

"So you would choose her horse over me?"

"No, Mordred, I choose good over evil."

"Do you call my actions evil?"

"I am sad to say that, yes, I do. You attacked an innocent animal. To what purpose, Mordred? To what gain?"

Arthur needed to shift Mordred in his arms. "Please, son, help me understand your purpose."

"The countess threatened us, Father."

"How? She is nothing but kind."

"You are carrying me to the healer, my father."

"You provoked, harming her animal."

Mordred said nothing for moments. "I feel she is a threat to our dynasty."

'Twas the closest Arthur had ever come to wanting to toss someone down a staircase. And his son, no less. But he held on and kept moving. "Why the countess? She comes in peace. She comes to make treaties that will benefit us all. Why, Mordred, is she such a threat?"

"Because you are clouded by your feelings for her."

Arthur stopped again, this time considering stomping his own son. "You know this how?"

"By the way you reacted when I made a pass at her."

Arthur laughed. "Son, if that is your belief of a pass to a woman, I have much to teach you."

"She means more to you than Gwen."

Again, Arthur was stopped, but only in his head. "I have known her but awhile. I know not what I feel about anything. 'Tis very dangerous to judge afore an assessment has been made. It is the fatal flaw of any losing battle."

Again, silence as they descended, and Arthur felt his arms might well give up the fight all too soon. He strained to keep his son secure.

"Is all she said true?" Mordred asked, breaking the silence.

"Who? Countess Isabel?"

"Yes, is what she said the truth?"

"It is."

"Why did you never just explain this afore?"

"Son, I have told you this many times over the years. Yet you refused to believe me. How is it that hearing it from the countess finally got through to you?"

"Perhaps because she was so fierce in the telling, whilst you always just spoke quietly."

"Ahh, I must keep this in mind. To get through to you I must begin shouting."

Steps from below had Arthur placing Mordred back on his feet, so that his son would feel no shame. 'Twas the young girl, Mary, skipping up the stairway. She stopped short as she encountered them. "My pardons, my king and . . ."

"My son, Mordred."

She curtsied. "Sir."

"Are you off to Isabel's room, Mary?"

"Yes, my king. With herbs and flowers for her bath. Is that . . . acceptable to you, sirs?"

"Absolutely," Arthur said. "And should you have a chance, please pick flowers just for her pleasure."

"Yes, my king. May I . . . may I pass?"

"Of course."

Mary smiled and skipped right on by. As soon as she reached the top of the steps and turned the corner, he again heaved his son up and into his arms. "You are most assuredly a man, Mordred. You are heavy beyond measure."

They traveled several more steps before Mordred mumbled, "She was protecting you. I believe she cares for you very deeply."

Arthur did not have to ask from whence that thought appeared in his son's head.

"As do I for her, Mordred. She is a fascinating lady."

"When did you and the queen lose that love? When the countess arrived?"

Arthur nearly tripped. "As I have said, Isabel and I have not been lovers. We have just met."

"I believe this. But that was not my question."

"Mordred, you are my son. Whether you believe it or not—and at this moment you should believe as my arms may never survive this journey—there are pieces of life that are private to every individual, whether he be king or serf. This is a part of my life that I must ask you to allow me to keep private."

They were almost there, thank the gods.

"I say only this, Father, I would not place blame. The countess speaks her mind."

"You touch her horse again, Mordred, and she will speak with a knife. Or worse. And I do not believe you want to come face-to-face with worse."

CHAPTER FIFTEEN

MARY all but cartwheeled into Isabel's room not five minutes after she'd sent Arthur and Mordred on their way.

The only thing stopping her from acrobatics was the tray in her hands. More delicious-smelling herbs, flowers and those damn twiggy things she was forced to use to clean her teeth.

"Hello, Mary," she said, smiling at the young girl's exuberance.

"Good afternoon, mum!"

Mary looked around for a place to set the tray, as the table was still filled with remnants of other trays. "How about on the bed, Mary?" Isabel suggested.

Mary turned, but stopped. "I was certain I had made up your bed finely this morn."

Whoops! She and Arthur hadn't gotten very far, but far enough to dishevel the coverlet. "It was my fault, Mary. I was . . . restless."

"No worries, mum, I will tidy up."

Isabel sat her butt down beside the tray, then patted the bed on the other side of the tray. "If you can manage to sit long enough, please tell me what has you so excited."

"Gilda says she can easily fix the gown to fit me! Is that not wonderful?"

"Oh, Mary, it truly is! But I had no doubt." She grabbed Mary's hand. "You will make such a beautiful bride."

"Thanks to you, Countess."

"Hey, my gown had nothing to do with that. It is you. You are a lovely young lady, and you would shine, even in a burlap sack."

Of course, Mary looked confused. But before Isabel could attempt to explain, Mary—bless her heart—shrugged off what she failed to understand, apparently trusting that Isabel had given her a compliment.

"Leastways, mum, I have a missive as well. From the queen, no less!"

"From the queen, no less! Impressive. And what does the queen have to say to me?"

"She would like you to meet her in the loft where the seamstresses work."

"To what purpose?"

Mary giggled. "She is attempting to teach them how to make man breeches for ladies. Yet she has no stitching skills, lady. None at all."

"There is no difference other than size, Mary, but I will happily meet her, for this might be a very good day for us all. Let's go."

Isabel took Mary's hand and then led her through the door. "Show me the way."

Mary began leading her through a labyrinth of stairways and hallways. "May I ask, m'lady, what kind of play we will be engaging in wearing these garments?"

"Whatever floats our boat."

Mary giggled again as they ran up more steps. "Betimes I do not understand your meaning, Countess, but I do not question because you are so much fun."

Isabel stopped her. "You, Mary, are the little sister I wish I had."

"Oh, mum, that means more to me than I can possibly say."

"Good. Will you now finally call me Isabel?"

"No, mum."

Isabel grinned. "Yes, indeed. The stubborn little sister I always wanted." She glanced upward. "Beat you up the stairs."

"When it snows in Hades," Mary said as they raced.

MARY and Isabel were both still a little out of breath by the time they arrived in the huge seamstress room. It was truly amazing! There were at least fifty women, stitching at a pace that would make a Singer proud.

Some appeared to be working on new tunics for the men, many appeared to be sewing up pants, others working on plain muslin gowns, a few on basic aprons.

Mary grabbed Isabel's hand and dragged her to a woman who was the spitting image of Betty White. This must be Gilda, the woman who was working on Mary's wedding gown.

Isabel grinned and held out her hand. "You must be Gilda."

"That I am, mum," she said, staring at Isabel's hand as if it were a boa. She set everything aside and attempted to stand.

"No, no! Please sit," Isabel said. "I didn't mean to disrupt."

"She speaks a fair bit different from the rest of us, Mary."

Mary huffed out. "She be from a different land and 'tis how they speak in hers. But she is also a countess and deserves your respect."

Gilda grunted but went right back to stitching.

Mary stomped her foot. "She gifted me this dress."

"Let's hit the road, Jack," Isabel said, trying to walk away as fast as possible.

Mary stood her ground, grabbing Isabel's arm and holding on tight. "Would James want you to act thusly to the woman who gifted his son's future wife with something so beautiful?"

The woman stopped stitching and looked up slowly. "'Twas a very nice thing you did, m'lady. I thank you on behalf of James and Mary."

"And?" Mary prodded, still with the death grip on Isabel's arm.

"And my future daughter would be ever so proud to have you stand aside her at her vow ceremony. Even as I have told her the foolishness of the request."

"I would be proud to stand beside Mary."

Gilda looked up, her huge brown eyes full of surprise. "In truth?"

"Of course! Mary is my friend." She turned to Mary, who was nearly jumping up and down. "Don't you have closer friends you would prefer, Mary?"

Mary stopped bouncing on her toes. "I do, m'lady. Or I did. But my choice is you. If it does not upset you."

"If I agree, will you agree to call me Isabel?"

"No, mum."

Isabel laughed. "I didn't think so. Yes, I happily agree. It would be an honor beyond any requests I have ever been asked to perform."

Before they turned from Gilda's workstation, Isabel glanced down to see a slight smile on the woman's face.

They walked away, and Isabel whispered, "You have your hands full."

Mary grinned at her. "Or perhaps, it is she who will need to keep a watch."

"My money's on you, babe," Isabel said.

"Here is the queen, madam, the purpose for your visit."

"Your Highness," Isabel said, then whispered to Mary, "I wager I am able curtsy lower than you."

"Ha!"

They both dropped into low, then lower, then even lower curtsies. Mary beat her again, and Isabel fell over on her, where they laid laughing. "By the end of our bets, Mary, you will own everything I have."

"I do so want that necklace, Countess."

"I bet you do," Isabel said. "However, it's the one thing I'm unable to give up. Try again."

"Rise now," Gwen demanded.

Isabel sat up but didn't get to her feet. "In a nicer tone, Gwen, I'll consider whether or not to agree to such a rather rude demand. Until then, we are having a very good time down here."

Although Mary obviously had stopped having a good time. She attempted to stand, but Isabel held her down.

Gwen looked shocked. "'Twas not a demand, Countess, 'twas but a request."

"Sounded more like a demand, Your Highness. I'm so not into that haughty holier-than-thou thing."

The entire room went completely silent, as if sound had been sucked from it.

"I ne'er meant it as such," Gwen said.

"Then in a nicer tone," Isabel suggested, staring up at the woman who had first won Arthur's heart. And then shattered it. Isabel liked Gwen and disliked her all at once, and wasn't certain which of the pieces of this amazing puzzle fell into which category.

"I need not be nice," Gwen said, her eyes suddenly squinty.

"Not part of your job description? What, you only need to be gracious to those of your station and bitch queeny to all else?"

Isabel ignored the gasps.

She got to her feet, pulling Mary up with her. But she kept Mary behind her. "Until you learn to have fun with the people who work so hard to make your pampered life comfortable, you will never connect in an important way. These people work their asses off to make your life glorious. Treat them like shit, and you receive the love and respect of no one. You haven't earned it."

"Off with her head!" was the next thing Isabel expected out of Gwen's mouth. But the queen seemed to be speechless.

So far Isabel's head seemed to be secure.

"You are such a kind lady, Gwen. What the hell? What is wrong? I thought you asked me here to show me something really nice. What is it?"

Gwen rubbed her temples. "Yes, we are here to see . . . What are we here to see, Jenny?"

A young girl, probably a year or two older than Mary, stepped forward. "We are here to see the women's leggings, as you had requested."

"I suggested, I did not request. But I find it wonderful that you have set it in motion, Gwen."

"You have attempted to take over Camelot, Countess," Gwen said.

"Excuse me? I had nothing to do with this. We had a good chat and you thought it was an idea to pursue."

"Liar! The marriage of James and Mary was my idea. This," she said, waving around vaguely, "this was all my idea! You stole it. You stole it all from me."

"Okey-dokey, then. It's all your idea. No problem. No patents happening here."

Isabel glanced around and every single face was frozen in shock. Hers probably was as well.

"Do you know if she's had a little too much wine this morning, Mary?" She watched Mary and the girl called Jenny exchange worried glances, and then Jenny shook her head no and shrugged.

"Heretic!" Gwen yelled.

"I don't have my handy dictionary with me, Mary, but isn't that a word that means witch or something?"

"I am not sure of the word witch," Mary whispered, "but I believe it means you are of the underworld. Of the dark forces."

"So I'm guessing it isn't a compliment?"

Mary was apparently too afraid to laugh.

"Gwen, how about you and I take a walk and talk about this?" she said, figuring she'd direct Gwen straight to the first pond and dunk her face in it until the woman sobered up.

"You will walk me straight into hell! You want my husband and my crown and my throne, and I see it all now."

Isabel turned to the closest seamstress. "Please go find the king. Find my man Tom if you can. But most importantly King Arthur. He will know who else needs to be here."

The girl hesitated. "The king will not trust my request."

"Please. Tell him that Isabel requests it. It is an emergency. He will thank you. Now run behind me and out as fast as you can."

The girl glanced from her to Mary. Mary must have given her some signal, as the girl nodded and said, "Yes, m'lady."

Had to give her credit, that little girl had lightning speed.

But apparently Gwen caught it, and caught it in LSD time.

Or so Gwen appeared. "That was beautiful," she said. "All others are allowed to leave as well. They are innocent and have not tried to harm me. You have."

"Then allow them to leave. You and I can speak privately."

"No! They have work to do."

"It appears, Gwen, this is personal. Just you and me. No reason to involve anyone else."

"You stole James."

"James? You mean Mary's James? I don't even know the man, other than he's my friend's future husband and your husband's most trusted soldier."

"You would steal him from Mary as you stole Arthur from me." Gwen shuddered and then seemed to whither. She took several labored breaths before lowering her accusing arm. "I am so sorry. I do not know what is the matter." She shook her head. "Isabel, I wanted to show you the progress we have made on the breeches for women."

Okay, this wasn't crazy and this wasn't drunk. And this was so very far out of Isabel's knowledge and comfort zone.

"I have been watching, Gwen, and I'm very impressed. And I thank you for taking my suggestion and running with it."

"Your suggestion?" Gwen nearly screeched. "'Twas my idea. Mine."

At this point Isabel was hoping for medieval doctors to come in and take Gwen off to the loony bin. No such luck.

"And you will in no way be part of the ceremony between James and Mary," Gwen said. "All was my idea. And I will have it as I see fit. Or they will not have it at all."

Isabel felt slapped in the face. At this point Mary was shaking. Isabel held on to her hand. "Should you in any way harm Mary because of my words or actions, I will most definitely take her and James back to the safety of Dumont. Mary has done nothing but be my lady in waiting, or whatever you would call her, and, I would hope, friend. I will not allow you to punish her for actually having fun doing her job. And doing it well. Now you tell me, Queen Guinevere, how you want to play this."

Again, Gwen was silent for quite some time. And then she did the funniest thing. She bent over in laughter, which shocked Isabel, and probably everyone in the room.

GWEN finally reined in her mirth, but in truth, it took some time. She had just been told to go to Hades by a woman who had walked into her castle and in less than two nights had won over the hearts of more castle staff than Gwen had been able to in the years she had been queen.

The countess had been rolling on the floor with a servant, the two so happy.

Gwen had ne'er ever been close to such a relationship. Truth be told, it had ne'er even entered her mind. And right now her mind felt not so well. She could not seem to control her emotions.

"You may stop protecting Mary, Countess. I have no plans or desires to harm her well-being. This I swear. We are going to have a lovely ceremony in the great hall for Mary and James."

Isabel, who was standing as a guard against harm, seemed to settle. "We accept that promise, Your Highness."

The countess turned to Mary. "Want a two-for-one bet on the best curtsy, Mary?"

Mary's red curls went wild as she shook her head. "No, mum, I believe we have strained the queen's patience as is."

"Truth told, you have not," Gwen said. "I apologize if I sounded impatient. I was anxious, only, to show you, Countess, what we . . . what these talented seamstresses have put their hands to."

Isabel looked around. "Most appear to be making great progress."

Gwen smiled. "Yes, for the women. They should be ready by the morning fast."

It was quite satisfying to Gwen to see the look on Isabel's face. "You are attempting to take Arthur from me."

"Are you serious?" Isabel asked. "I was attempting to bring the two of you back together."

"That is true, my queen. James heard as much," Mary said.

"Liar!"

Isabel and Mary looked at each other.

"You call her a liar, you call me a liar," Isabel told her.

Gwen ignored this. "We begin my idea of playtime for all women one hour after breaking fast on the morrow."

She glanced around the room, and the workers who had stopped in midstitch for some reason immediately returned to their work in earnest.

"Oh, Gwen, thank you!" Isabel said, lunging forward and hugging her. "And I am so sorry for being snippy with you."

Gwen was taken aback, as she had ne'er seen such joy from another woman so blatantly displayed. But truth be told, she felt so very happy inside.

"So what will our first playtime involve?"

"Wow, you have caught me off guard, Gwen. I never thought you'd pull this off so fast." Isabel peered across the room, then clapped. "My apologies for disrupting you ladies, but I'd like to have a vote."

"A vote, mum?" Mary asked behind Isabel's back, as a certainty still afraid to come forward and face her queen. 'Twas a sad thought that Gwen had not treated the servants better. They had alas been tools to forward her desires and needs. She could not even begin to name many of them. Not even the young lady who fled from the room. 'Twas sad and humiliating. She was a failure as a queen. In many more ways than one.

"How many of you want to participate tomorrow morning?" Isabel asked. "Please don't raise your hand if you don't mean it.

Please only raise your hand if you are truly interested. And there is no punishment should you decline, yes, Queen Guinevere? It is not demanded of them."

"They are free to choose, Isabel."

"The queen has said so. You may choose yes or not, with no repercussions whatever you decide. Should you choose not to play, then that hour will be yours, free to do whatever. As long as you do it making yourself happy. Hell, you can get naked for your men."

Many giggled.

"What play will this be?" a lady, who did not even look up from her stitching, asked.

Gwen looked at Isabel, as she had no idea. "Countess Isabel, I am certain, must needs answer this one."

Isabel glanced around and finally said, "It all depends on the weather tomorrow."

At that very moment, the clouds opened up and a rumble of thunder shook overhead.

"Should it be inside the castle, then so be it. Have any of you heard of Duck, Duck, Goose?"

"As in the menu?" one asked.

"As in the game."

ISABEL and Gwen strolled down the stairs. "Duck, Duck, Goose?" Gwen asked, with a smile.

"You have to start small with women who have never known real play."

Gwen took a few steps before turning to her. "My deepest apologies for my surly mood back there."

Isabel nodded. "What was that all about, Gwen? I haven't known you long, but long enough to feel it was so unlike you."

"You two, you and . . ."

"Mary. Her name is Mary. And she is about to marry Arthur's first man."

Gwen blushed. "Yes, yes, Mary. You were making a mockery of the curtsy to the queen."

Isabel's head dropped back so that she had a great view of the ceiling "Oh, please, get over yourself. We were having fun. It was no slight to you. We were in a contest."

"It felt to me as a slight to my stature."

"Give me a freaking break, Gwen. Since when did you really care about that? To this date, I have seen you only as gracious to one and all. Yet today your claws came out. For no good reason."

Gwen looked down, then her knees seemed to give out. She sat down on the steps, and Isabel sat with her. "What is it, Gwen?"

"I'm jealous, Isabel."

"Of what exactly? If you mean this morning, *nothing* happened between Arthur and me."

Not exactly true, but *almost* nothing happened. Much to her disappointment.

"This morning?"

Isabel wanted to shake herself. "What I mean is that we talked. As we always do, we talked."

There, that was true enough. They'd talked. Kissed and came close to naked and hot, sweaty sex, but those points didn't need to be included.

"'Tis not what is between you and Arthur that upsets me."

Oh, excellent! Was that a green light?

"Then what?"

"I saw the funning between you and . . ."

"Mary. Her name is Mary!"

"Yes, I am so sorry, Mary. I witnessed how happy she appeared in your company, and I felt the envy claw at me."

"Why?"

"Because I ne'er had such a friendly exchange betwixt any of my servants and me."

"Hey, they're still loyal to you."

"'Tis not the same. As castle servants, loyalty is to be expected."

"I believe true loyalty ought to be earned not just expected or required."

"What have I done wrong?"

"Nothing much different than what royalty has been doing forever. Princess Di, was an exce—" Her necklace thumped. She sighed. "You view them as tools, not as people. Should you actually learn their names and anything about their loves and lives, you could do something like—gasp!—befriend them individually."

"You have been here naught but two nights, and yet you have already managed to accomplish that."

Isabel took Gwen's hand. "The men and women who serve you are loyal, Gwen. And trust me, you could be much worse. You could, for example, be Hitler."

Thump.

"But you are not. From what I've heard, all who work in the castle have much respect for you. If not for that respect, you and Lance would have been outed a long time ago."

Gwen's head snapped up. "My pardon?"

"Oh, please, Gwen, about the only ones in this castle unaware are the dogs and the chickens. And I wouldn't put half the dogs on the stand."

"What you speak is befuddling. I . . . have always taken my vows to Camelot seriously."

"To Arthur, not so much. You broke that one when you strayed on your husband. It's a credit to him that he is forbidding those who know—and trust me, everyone knows—to speak of how you've broken your vows."

Gwen stood. "That is not true."

Isabel looked up at her. "Which, that you've broken vows or that everyone knows about it?"

Gwen glared down at her. "You have, Countess, overstepped your bounds and my hospitality. I request that you and your retinue prepare to leave Camelot."

Isabel, studied her nails, which truly needed a manicure. She vaguely wondered if Mary was good at that, too. Or if Mary had a friend with the skill. "Are you having your period, Gwen? Or getting close? Because you've been acting PMS-y all day. Up-down, up-down. You can barely keep your emotions under control."

"Get out."

"Go get Arthur to tell me this, and I will most definitely grant your wish." Isabel stood up and was at least six inches taller than that ethereal queen who had turned into a dragon in a nanosecond. PMS for sure. "Until he also agrees that I should leave your kingdom, I'm not going anywhere. Mary asked me to stand beside her at her wedding, and I plan to be there, standing with her. If you and Arthur both object, I will give her my apologies."

Gwen collapsed onto the steps again, breaking into sobs. "What is wrong with me?"

Isabel's heart broke, and she sat down and cradled Gwen. "About to have that time of month?"

"Time of month?"

"I honestly do not know what you call it. In my time—"

Thump.

"—my land, I mean, it means having your period. That time of the month when you . . . bleed . . . down there."

"It is quite about that time."

"See? Hormones are a bitch."

"Who are hormones? Are they people I should know?"

"None you really want to."

Gwen hiccupped into her chest. "How could you possibly know these things?"

"Trust me, I know, Gwen. I'm famous for pounding men over their heads with copper pots at that time of month."

Gwen giggled. "Truly?"

"Truly. We need to go back to my room and have Mary bring you some tea. Possibly filled with some parsley, sage, rosemary and thyme."

Gwen looked up at her. "Truly?"

Isabel shrugged. "It worked for Simon and Garfunkel. It has to work for us."

"And then, we might just order wine."

"Hey, that might work, too."

ISABEL found herself practically dragging Gwen to her chambers. By the time they reached the room, Mary was there, sprinkling things into the tub.

Mary stood straight, glancing with fear from Gwen to Isabel. "My apologies, mum! I was merely preparing your bath. I will return when you are ready."

"We need tea, Mary," Isabel said.

"I am so very sorry, Mary," Gwen said, "for ruining a fun day. And we do not want tea, we want wine."

Isabel figured the last thing Gwen needed was wine, but try to talk to a woman going through PMS. She nodded at Mary, mouthing, "I'm sorry!"

"The dark or the white kind?" Mary asked.

"Both," Isabel said. "And please, some cheese and meats and lots and lots of bread to soak up the aftermath."

Mary curtsied, and then Isabel curtsied, and then Mary ran from the room before they got into another battle and giggling fit.

"I do not feel able to climb up on that bed, Isabel."

"How about we just plop down on the floor, Gwen? We can talk and chat like teenagers as if we're having a sleepover."

Gwen slipped to the floor without argument. "What is happening to me, Isabel?"

"Trust me, you will be feel so much better in the morning." Wait, PMS. Maybe in a couple of days without a pharmacist around to help. "Or very soon."

MARY was so busy keeping the overloaded tray in her hands steady, she nearly ran head-on into King Arthur. She stopped as fast as she was able, which made the tray that much more dangerous.

She attempted to curtsy even as she babbled out her apology.

The king helped her steady the tray, then took it from her hands. He had a smile that could fell a bull. "'Tis all right, Mary. My deepest apologies for startling you."

It took her many moments to collect her breath.

"The queen is no longer up with the seamstresses, King Arthur, if that is where you're headed."

"I was not. Was I supposed to be?"

It appeared that Lily had failed to find him. "No longer. Sir, I, sir, I, Your Highness, sir, I am so deeply sorry for my clumsiness."

He chuckled softly. "'Twas not your clumsiness at fault here, Mary. 'Twas mine." He glanced down at the tray, with the two goblets, the two wines, and the assortment of meats, cheeses and breads. "Are you headed to the Countess Isabel's quarters?"

"I am, sir."

"So she is entertaining?" he asked.

"She is, sir."

Mary had not been in the king's company for long, but she very much understood the appearance of a man hurt by news. 'Twas the same jaw-ticking, eyes-dropping look she had received the first two times she had refused James's proposals.

She weighed loyalties, and just had to believe that she was not betraying Lady Isabel. "She is entertaining the queen, m'lord."

He glanced up, the light that had extinguished from his eyes only moments ago returning. "She is with Gwen?"

"Yes, m'lord." She felt like skipping. 'Twas twice today that she had made a royal happy. 'Twas a happy day indeed. She could not wait to find a moment to tell James.

"Then by all means, Mary, allow me to carry this tray to the door for you."

"But, sir!"

"Shhh! We shall be extremely stealthy as we approach. And I will leave prior to your entrance. They shall never be aware that I was near."

"But I cannot allow you to carry this tray, my king. 'Tis my job."

"We shall keep it a state secret," he said, with a quite fetching smile. "James would ne'er forgive me for not treating his lady as the lady she is."

"I am no lady, m'lord, I am but at your service."

As they walked up the stairs and down the halls, her king said, "All who toil at Camelot are men and women, nothing less."

Mary smiled. "You and my lady Isabel would get on well. She said much the same thing just an hour ago in the sewing room about treating all in the castle with respect."

"Did she now?"

"She is amazing, m'lord. She has treated me with nothing but kindness and generosity, and if truth be told, she makes me laugh."

He nodded. "I see, so she is perfect."

"Well . . ."

"Find me a fault, Mary."

Mary hesitated. The king grinned at her. "Go ahead. Name one."

"She is a bit picky about the tools I have brought her to clean her teeth and cleanse her breath. She mumbles often about a thing called Listerine. And she wishes for a thing called floss."

Mary stopped him a few steps away from her mistress's doorway. "I have most likely spoken out of turn. I very much want the countess to believe in me."

The king nodded at her. "If the condition of her teeth is the most you have to say about the countess, do you not realize just how loyal you are to her?"

"There is nothing, sir, to report otherwise. Although I must admit, should there be something else, I believe I would not say so. And I will not apologize for this. Yet I apologize. Yet there is nothing else. But if it were so . . ."

He grinned and whispered, "I get it, Mary."

"She is standing at my side at my wedding, sir."

"And I will be standing at James's side."

Mary felt her heart jump. "This is true?"

"He asked, I accepted. Is that a problem?"

"No, sir. No, not at all. Although after the queen demanded that Isabel leave, I believed that perhaps we would need to travel to

Dumont to say our vows. James does not know this yet. But I believe his love for me is enough that we may exchange vows in any land of our choosing."

The king set down the tray. "When did the queen ask for Isabel to leave Camelot?"

Mary felt her face go from the norm to red-hot fire in a short instant. She should not have overheard that exchange between her queen and her countess on those steps. She had only followed to be certain that Isabel—oh, goodness, she was thinking of her as Isabel—had all that she needed.

She could not face the king. "I cannot say, sir."

The king took her shoulders. "When, Mary? Please tell me."

Her slippers were about the only thing she felt good about paying attention to. "I ne'er meant to hear this conversation."

"Please tell me."

"The countess and I were having fun in the sewing room. I know naught what upset the queen. But upset she was, and then the next thing I remember is that the queen was laughing and then weeping, and the countess was helping her. I was not trying to listen, I was trying to see if the countess had need of me. The queen, well, she did not seem well. My countess did not have need of me so much. The queen had need of her. They were sitting on the steps and talking. And then Isabel . . . I mean the countess . . . held her up and led her to the room. The queen, I fear was just not quite right. And my countess was trying to help."

He nodded. "Go on."

"Countess Isabel ordered tea, but the queen demanded wine. So Isabel ordered that and cheeses and meats and breads to soak them up, as she said. I do not know what is happening in there, sir, but I know that when I left them, they appeared happy enough together. I do not fear for the countess's life, or I would be the first to intrude."

"You feared for the countess earlier?"

"I did, sir."

"From Gwen? From your queen?"

"I cannot answer that question. Even Countess Isabel would ask me not to answer."

Arthur nodded. "Your lack of an answer speaks louder than any other. It also speaks to loyalty, Mary. So very important. James is a lucky man." He picked up the tray and handed it to her, holding on until she was steady, which took a moment because here was the king helping her.

"Mary," he said, looking deeply into her eyes, "I ask you not to spy, only to inform me as soon as possible if you sense anything wrong."

"Such as?" she asked, feeling a quakiness in her knees once again.

"Such as a threat from one person to another."

"The countess would ne'er harm . . ." She stopped herself. "I cannot imagine either harming the other."

"I am going to stay here in the hallway, and I am asking for a report of what you see and feel inside. I do not want details, I do not expect any wrong happening in there, but I must know before I charge in on my own."

"You would do such?"

"If Gwen is planning to harm Isabel, yes, I would."

As Mary headed to the door, it came to her thinking that the king had not worried about Countess Isabel harming the queen. Then again, it had not occurred to Mary, either. Very strange indeed that both of them were much more concerned about the welfare of the countess than the queen.

CHAPTER SIXTEEN

ARTHUR knew that waiting outside of Isabel's bedchamber was more than ridiculous. And that his fear of Gwen bringing harm to Isabel was also without merit.

Yet his need to protect overwhelmed him. The very perplexing thing that confounded him was it was not his wife he felt the need to protect.

Mary finally left the chamber, seeming almost out of breath. She ran directly to him and curtsied. "My king."

"Tell me, Mary."

"The countess has asked me to pass this missive to you, sir. The queen is not well."

"My thanks," he said, trying very hard not to rip the note from Mary's hands. He took it and opened it as slowly as desperation allowed. *Arthur, Gwen needs medical attention. Please have Gwen taken back to your bedchambers, and call for Tom.*

Arthur crushed the note in his hand and tossed it aside. "Thank you, Mary. Please go find Isabel's man, Tom," he said before storming into Isabel's quarters without knocking.

The sight afore him was truly amazing. Isabel was pumping at Gwen's chest, then stopping to give her kisses of sorts.

He had worried about Isabel?

"What are you doing?"

"I think she's gone into some kind of shock," she said, huffing afore beginning the process all over again.

Isabel was holding Gwen's nose shut, while blowing into her mouth. 'Twas shocking. "Stop!"

Isabel stopped the blowing thing and began the pumping her chest thing. "Do you want Gwen to live or not?" she asked.

"Of course."

"Then back off! I should have seen the signs. Her delusions, her mood swings. For chrissake, I thought it was PMS."

"I need to help."

"Then bring me some water."

As he poured, he watched in horror. But in that moment Gwen coughed and shook her head.

Isabel sat back on her heels and wiped her brow. Then she lifted Gwen into a sitting position and accepted the chalice of fresh water from Arthur. "Welcome back, Gwen. That was a tad worrisome. Please sip."

Gwen grabbed the base of the goblet and attempted to drain it down, but Isabel disallowed it. "No, a sip or two at a time. We will rehydrate you, but not all at once."

Arthur had never felt so helpless afore. He knew naught what had happened to his wife, he knew naught what Isabel had just done, he only knew he had been unable to do anything worth use, save pour a glass of water. He fell heavily into a chair.

If he puzzled this out, he had to conclude that his wife had a medical episode, and that the woman he ached for had just saved Gwen's life right afore his eyes. And he had stood helpless.

"Arthur."

He heard, but the beating in his ears prevented him from hearing.

"Arthur!"

He opened his eyes.

Isabel sat looking up at him. "Arthur, I know this is getting old, but would you please carry your wife to your chambers? She is good for now, but she needs Tom to check her over."

"Tom is but a tooth healer."

"To be any kind of healer in my land, you must understand all types of medicine. He is best equipped to diagnose what this is."

"Dia—"

"Figure it out. But we need to help her back to her bed. Man up, big boy. Carry your wife to your chambers."

By then there were many in the room. Isabel took control of them all. "Mary, please bring as much fresh water as you can gather to the king and queen's quarters."

"Yes, mum."

"Jenny, please bring to Tom every type of flower and or herb that the queen used in her tea or any other food today."

The girl named Jenny curtsied and disappeared.

"Mordred! Oh, good to see you up and about." She glanced down at his leg. "Appears, however, that Dick trussed your leg like a goose's, or something."

"I wish to be of service in any way I may, Countess."

She nodded. "Then how about you lead the way so that no one else impedes Gwen's transport back to her own bed?"

"My pleasure, Countess," Mordred said.

Arthur almost grinned as he saw his son appear to beam with pride at having a mission to accomplish. Arthur should have kicked his son in the ass a long time ago. With one swift and most amazing kick, Isabel had done all he had failed to do.

"Arthur!"

He shook his head, trying to rid it of all regrets. "Yes, tell me what I should do."

Isabel stared up at him, and there he felt a bond. But he had not time to reason it out now. "Is she able to travel?" he asked.

"Yes, and Mordred will forge the way."

Arthur bent to Gwen, who still appeared sickly. "Are you able to wrap your arms around my neck, Gwen?"

"Lance?" she asked in a very small voice.

Arthur almost dumped her on the spot.

But Isabel took hold of his arm. "No one but you and I heard that, Arthur. Just pick her up and carry her to your bed."

"Her bed. It is no longer mine." But he picked her up regardless. "Mordred, my son, I believe you are our escort."

"Yes, sir, although possibly a slower one than you prefer."

Arthur turned back before leaving the chamber. "I thank you for saving the queen."

Isabel smiled at him. "Never a dull moment at Camelot."

He winced as Gwen clawed at his neck. "You realize that had the positions been reversed, she might well have not worked so hard to save your life as you did hers."

"I like to think that she would."

Arthur shook his head but smiled. "When we get over this crisis, I must needs speak to you of a place I like to call la-la land."

As he carried Gwen from the room, he heard Isabel's musical laughter fill his ears.

"Mum, had it been you!" Mary said, bursting into her room. She threw herself at Isabel, nearly dropping her.

"It wasn't me, Mary. What I'd like to know is who and what it was."

Mary straightened up, scrubbing her eyes against her apron. "I do not know. But it shall not happen to you."

Mary sailed straight for the tub and began scooping up all of the herbs and flowers.

"Mary."

"I will not allow anyone to poison you, Isabel. I will not."

Isabel grinned. She'd bet good money that Mary forgot she forbade herself to call Isabel anything but countess or madam or whatever the hell.

"Mary."

"What if it were meant for you? What if I had served you something that made you ill? How would I possibly be able to do what you did to save the queen?"

She turned back to Isabel, who was still getting over the shock of whatever had happened to Gwen. Mary's apron was filled with all the herbs and flowers that she'd sprinkled just a while ago to make Isabel's bath heavenly.

"Dump them back in the tub, Mary."

"No, I will not," Mary said, her freckles looking angrier than the rest of her face. "They might well be dangerous."

"Please, Mary. I am asking, not demanding."

"And if I refuse?" Mary asked, chin raised high.

"Then I will ask you to go pick more so that I enjoy my bath."

Mary's shoulders deflated, but she turned and dumped the contents of her apron back into the tub. "But how do I protect you from poisons?"

Isabel grinned. "Want to hop in the tub before me?"

Mary giggled. "If you wish, countess."

"Want to drink the bathwater?"

Mary giggled more and couldn't seem to stop. She sank to the floor. "Only if 'twould turn me as beautiful as you . . . Isabel."

Isabel stood stunned for a moment. Which had zapped her more, Mary finally daring to call her by her first name or Mary saying such a sweet thing, she didn't know. But that verbal taser only lasted for a moment. She laughed and dropped down to the floor with a still giggling Mary. Isabel grabbed and hugged her.

Then they laughed together for a while before Isabel took Mary's shoulders and pushed her back. Then she laced her hands through Mary's hair, shoving it back as well.

"Mary, you are such a beautiful young lady. I *wish* I had been as pretty as you are when I was your age. Heck, you know what the boys called me when I was thirteen?"

Mary shook her head. "No . . . what?"

Oh, good gods, she couldn't remember. She knew they called

her something that led to a bloody nose or two, but she was spacing on her nickname.

Stick chick.

Thanks for checking in, Viviane.

You are welcome. Just a reminder.

"They called me stick chick. It hurt a lot."

"I do not even understand what that means," Mary said.

"I was tall for my age and quite skinny. So the boys teased me mercilessly. But what it really means is that nasty people say nasty things to make themselves feel better. I got over being stick chick a long time ago. If any have ever said mean things to you, I promise you they are just being petty. Their comments mean nothing and are unfounded. You are a beautiful young woman. You are marrying a man very high up in the realm of Camelot. And I guarantee he did not ask for your hand because he finds you less than beautiful. Are you not happy about that?"

Mary bowed her head. "I wish betimes that James was not so high up in the realm."

"Because?"

"Because then my friends would not have turned against me so fast."

"They've turned against you?"

Mary nodded, and a teardrop landed on her knee. "And then I was assigned to be your servant, and even more turned away."

Isabel saw the heartbreak in Mary's eyes and wondered what kind of world this girl lived in where she had to choose between friends and her man. Or between success in whatever form, rather than remaining stagnant. She supposed in her own day that sort of thing still happened. For example, a stupid, bigoted jackass of a father who would rather see his daughter dead than marry outside her race or religion. But this. This was just wrong.

"Mary, do you love James?"

"Oh, yes, I very much love him."

"Good. Then remember those friends who are happy for you after you marry. And once you do marry and your station rises, bring them with you. You forget those whose envy and jealousies colored their judgment, and do what you will. Forgive them or ignore them. But never, ever forget those friends happy for you, okay?"

"Countess Isabel, I will ne'er forget you."

"You had better not!" It was juvenile, Isabel knew, but she felt so close to Mary already, almost as if they'd known each other forever. Had it only been a couple of days?

She held up her pinky finger. "We will be pinky-finger friends for life, should you agree."

Mary stared, obviously confused. But finally it seemed to dawn on her. She held up her pinky finger, and the two hooked them together.

"Pinky finger friends for life, Mary. The most important bond."

"Friends for life," Mary said.

Isabel held back tears. Finally she stood, pulling Mary up with her. "And now, miss, please go sweetly ask others to bring me lots and lots of hot water."

Mary stared down into the tub. "Isabel, what if . . . ?"

"The queen ingested it, Mary, she didn't bathe in it."

"You are certain of this?"

"According to Jenny, who came with news, Tom is. He helped her to vomit it out of her system."

"That is unpleasant."

"Tell me about it."

"I will have hot water brought to you as soon as possible."

"Thank you, Mary."

They smiled a wonderful friendship smile before Mary turned to leave. But she surprised Isabel by turning back. "I was more than a bit proud of you today, Isabel."

Isabel, feeling so drained she bet she could sleep for a week, smiled. "Thanks, Mary. It was just training I learned in my youth."

And wished desperately that she could have used it on Curtis in Afghanistan. But there had been so much blood.

"And, Isabel?" Mary said once again.

"Yes, Mary?"

"The king was quite worried about you."

"Me?"

"'Tis not as if he was not worried for the queen. Just a thing that I recognized as he was standing outside fretting. He was asking of you."

"Thanks for letting me know. I will reassure him at supper that all is well."

AFTER her long, luxurious bath, Isabel got out, feeling somewhat refreshed, yet still drained. A day full of such promise had gone horribly wrong.

Mary, who had the uncanny ability to know exactly when Isabel would be needing her, came in to help her dress and fix her hair. Today she formed it into a simple long braid that she somehow managed to work so that the braid curled around Isabel's neck to rest against her chest.

"I picked some flowers this morn, deciding I would weave them into your hair for the afternoon and evening; however, after today . . ." She shuddered.

"Mary, we don't even know if it was any type of flower that made the queen ill. And as we have discussed, she would have had to eat or drink whatever was harmful."

"Does not hurt to be cautious a' times."

Superstitious was more likely, but Isabel didn't voice it.

"I have a message for you from your healer, Tom, mum," Mary said as she stood and admired her own handiwork. "He asks that you meet him in the queen's bedchamber."

Isabel stood. "By all means, lead the way."

CHAPTER SEVENTEEN

Turned out that the royal chamber was not all that far from her own, relatively speaking. Mary informed her that the proximity was deemed to be an honor. The more important the guest, the closer their quarters to the king and queen's.

The royal bedchamber was exactly that: royal. Tapestries covered much of the walls, the coat of arms of Camelot, she suspected, being the one hanging above the head of the bed.

The bed itself was canopy style, with hunter green silks covering it and draping down the sides. Right now the silks were pulled back and held with gold sashes so that Gwen was visible in the massive bed, appearing pale and frail.

Tom sat dozing in an oversize chair near the crackling fireplace, lending a warm, rosy glow to the room. Seeing no one else in the room to give her leave to enter, Isabel stepped quietly across the huge space and gently shook Tom.

He awoke with a start and a snort, then sat up and blinked. "Oh, Isabel. Good, it's you."

He stood up then pulled and tugged at his leggings, grimacing. "My kingdom for a nice pair of chinos and a polo," he said.

She hugged him, laughing softly. "You do look kind of ridiculous." Then she stepped back and searched his face. "Are they treating you well? I have rarely seen you except at meals."

"If this were a medieval Hilton, I'd give it five stars. Yes, they've been very accommodating to all three of us. But thank goodness the Lady was kind enough to allow us to bring a few luxuries from home."

"Really? Such as?"

"Harry found a deck of cards in his trunk. After we send the servants to bed for the night, we get together for a few rounds of poker."

"Hey, next time invite me."

He grinned. "We've been avoiding it. I think you put yourself through college stealing our money."

"Oh, bull . . . oney."

Still, they grinned at each other. She and Tom had dated a couple of times in college, until they'd decided they made much better friends. Then it became their sworn duty to find each other's soul mates, forcing each other on more blind dates than either cared to remember. Isabel won when she'd fixed Tom up with Brenda Newesome, a sweet girl she'd met when they'd both been waiting tables to help pay tuition.

It was love at first sight, and Tom and Brenda had been together ever since, with three kids—twin boys and an adorable little girl.

"Oh, Tom, I'm so sorry. Brenda and the kids. I hope they aren't going crazy with worry."

"Hey, I'm a doppelganger, remember? The Lady assured us all that life is going on as usual back home. You are the only one here for real."

Isabel wondered if anyone missed her back in Oklahoma. Were people looking for her? Had they found her body?

No, Isabel, you have not been found. Your penchant to disappear on assignment is renowned. As events in Camelot come to unfold, your story at home will to all be told.

Thank you, Viviane.

Thank you, Isabel, for the pride I feel for choosing a woman who is Arthur's ideal.

Isabel truly wanted to get away from accolades. She was happy to have helped another human in distress, but this was feeling like something she'd continue to need to live up to. She knew her own life, her own faults. Perfection wasn't even in the Isabel dictionary. In the "How Many Times Can You Possibly Fuck Up Your Life?" category in Guinness, her name could be prominently displayed. In bold.

She mentally shook herself. "How's your patient?" she asked.

"Ah, yes." They both moved to her bedside. Gwen had been changed into nightclothes at some point. Isabel found herself irrationally hoping that Tom, with the help of Gwen's maid servant or lady in waiting or whatever they were called, were the two to have disrobed and redressed her, and not Arthur.

It was a ridiculous thought since the king had obviously seen his wife naked plenty of times.

"I had the distinct pleasure of attempting to discern the contents of the queen's stomach, once she'd expelled them. What became abundantly clear was that she had recently ingested some form of wild mushroom. I learned from the cook who prepared her morning repast that the queen had recently discovered them and requested that they be served in her eggs this morning."

"Poisonous mushrooms?"

"Would be my best guess, yes."

"It would account for her hallucinations? Her irrational behavior? Her . . . heart attack?"

"As far as I can tell, considering the appalling lack of equipment, it wasn't a heart attack per se, just pure and unadulterated poisoning. You saved her life giving her CPR and keeping her alive long enough to let me help, Izzy."

Isabel smiled. "CPR. Which you taught me a long time ago."

"Who knew you were such a good student? I thought you were just amusing me when you agreed to be my test dummy."

"How did you get her to vomit?"

Tom grimaced. "The old-fashioned way. The super-model special."

"Two fingers down her throat?"

"Exactly. She wasn't exactly happy about it. Almost bit my fingers off. But if not for you, Izzy, she would not be here."

ARTHUR could not believe the jealousy that had turned his stomach over as he stood in the doorway and witnessed Isabel's familiarity with the tooth doctor. He should be worrying about his wife. He should be considering the idea of a possible murderer wishing harm to Gwen or any at Camelot. But his mind only saw the touching between Isabel and another man. He strode into the room, attempting to keep his need to rid the tooth doctor of all of his own teeth under control.

"And I bore witness to it all," he said.

They both turned.

"Arthur!" Isabel said.

"King Arthur," toothful Tom said, offering something of a clumsy bow. There must not be much formality in Dumont, because all seemed out of practice.

"I bore witness to many things today," he added. "And I know no way of repayment that will be good enough to express my gratitude."

Tom and Isabel glanced at each other, grinned, then said at the same time, "Hey, it's what we do."

They both chuckled as Arthur frowned in confusion.

Isabel smiled, then took Tom's arm in hers and bumped against him playfully. "We have been friends for many, many years, since we were both in school back in Ok—"

"Dumont," Tom interrupted.

"Yes, Dumont."

Arthur stared at their hooked arms, and Isabel detached and stepped slightly aside.

The king looked down at Gwen. "Will she recover?"

"Fully. She needs bed rest, plenty of water in small amounts. If she feels an insatiable need to keep drinking, she needs to be stopped. Small quantities in everything. She needs to be reintroduced to food gradually. Chicken or beef broth at first, maybe rice or bread pudding. Nothing greasy or heavy for quite some time. But give her a few days and she should be good as new."

"I must needs relay all of this information to her servant, Jenny."

"Already done," Tom said. "I gave her the drill. I then sent her to rest because she herself was quite shaken. But she will be here to relieve me shortly."

"So the mushrooms were the poisonous substance, as you suspected?" Arthur asked.

"I am nearly positive that must have been it. Nothing else in her routine had changed, according to Jenny."

"And Gwen brought these mushrooms to the cook herself?"

"She did. There was nothing nefarious here, King Arthur. It was just a horrible accident."

"I wonder where she came upon these mushrooms? I have seen nothing like this on the property or in the gardens. Then again, I suppose I do not monitor such details as I should."

"She found them at the farthest cottage at the southeast end of the grounds," Tom said. "At least, that's what she told me in between . . . expelling some."

Arthur's eyes first rounded, then narrowed. "I know the cottage of which you speak."

"Then I suggest you get your gardeners out there to pull and dispose of them as soon as possible. Before someone else sees them as potential delicacies and not the deadly poisons they might be."

Arthur nodded, then glanced down again at his wife. He should have felt a need to stroke her pale face, to pull a chair to her bedside and sit vigilance.

"If you would like us to leave the two of you alone, Arthur," Isabel said, "we will be happy to give you privacy."

"No need," Arthur said, as he stared at his wife. "She appears to be in much better care than I am capable of providing." He took Tom's hand and shook it. "My eternal gratitude."

Isabel was a bit shocked. She had not witnessed handshakes in the normal form since she'd been here. She'd assumed such a practice had not been invented yet. Just ring kissing and groveling and manly grunts of approval between the men.

"I cannot begin to repay you. Either of you. For saving her, I mean."

"No need, sir," Tom said. "It's—"

"—what you do," Arthur finished, a slight smile tipping up his lips. "I am very grateful that you are here to have done it."

"You're welcome."

"May I escort you out, Countess?" Arthur asked.

"You may," Tom said before Isabel could reply. "And don't forget, Izzy, we still have that bet."

"I know this is an unseemly request," Arthur said as they walked the never-ending steps down to the great hall, "but would you agree to walk with me to the cottage where I believe Gwen found her mushrooms?"

"The scene of the crime?" Isabel teased. Then seeing Arthur's confusion, she sighed. "Yes, I will be happy to help you find the poisons."

They strolled down winding mulch paths, the vegetation becoming much more dense the farther they walked. The quick flash of the earlier thunderstorm had passed, and the sun was shining once again.

Both were silent for a while before Arthur finally said, "I assume you consider me a bastard for not sitting by Gwen's side."

"It's not my place to judge, Arthur."

"Yet you have opinions on all things, Isabel, you must have one on this."

She stopped and faced him. "You truly want my opinion? No matter what?"

He actually grinned. "Yes, Countess, I really do."

"Great, then gird it up, tough man. Here's what comes to mind, just off the top of my head."

"I am girded."

"I believe we are heading to the cottage where Lance and Gwen meet. I think after their last meeting she found the mushrooms. I believe you are not sitting by her side right now because you refuse to be a hypocrite. You have made certain that she is in no danger of dying, and you have those around her making certain she is well taken care of."

"So far, you are correct."

"Don't stop me, I'm on a roll."

He continued to grin, and damn, she loved that grin. But he kept silent.

"You asked me here to not just help you, but because you wanted us to be alone in a beautiful, isolated spot. You wanted to tell me things you could not say inside the castle. In short, Arthur, you wanted to get me alone."

"May I speak now?" he asked, his eyes still glittering with humor.

"You may."

"You are correct, but you missed one important point."

"Which is?"

"Because I believe this is Gwen and Lance's trysting spot, I did not want to come here alone. I feared I might do something rash, and I wanted a voice of reason beside me to keep me from acting on impulse."

"I see." Isabel stopped him. "Arthur, you have a good six inches on me and probably at least half again my weight. What makes you think I could possibly stop you from doing anything you set your mind to?"

"Well, for one thing, I witnessed how you handled Mordred."

"Arthur, you were holding on to him at the time. Not the same thing."

"And second, your words are more powerful than any weapon. I can face a sword, but I have very little defense against your words, your thoughts."

That admission truly stunned Isabel. Would that she had that much power over any human. "You give me way too much credit, Arthur."

"We shall see when my desire to burn that cottage to the ground overwhelms me."

"Well, I have a good argument against that drastic measure right away. If you cannot contain the fire, you are in danger of destroying much more than just that structure."

"Now see, that is the cool-headed thinking that needs to be drummed into my simple and short-sighted thinking."

"Taking it out on a perfectly innocent cottage is not going to change what happened there, Arthur. The cottage did not cause the events."

He took her elbow and they continued walking. "Do you believe in fate, Isabel?"

"Yes, I do. Although I truly admit that sometimes fate takes some funny turns at times."

"How so?"

"Well, for example, I believed my purpose in coming to Camelot was one thing, but I believe fate conspired to make it something totally different."

"I still see the mutual benefit of our adjoining lands as a priority for Camelot and Dumont."

She hadn't even been thinking of that, but she didn't correct him. "I agree. And I still see it as wholly attainable."

"But now you believe fate had something more in mind?"

"I do."

"What would that be?"

"This is going to sound very conceited."

"I am listening."

"I believe I'm here to, I don't know, do whatever is in my power to help you save Camelot from those who wish to bring you down."

"That is not boastful. In truth, it touches me greatly. But my theory is slightly different."

"Okay, let's hear yours."

"I believe you were sent here to save me."

Oh boy, he kind of hit that nail on the head. Well, not exactly. The ultimate purpose as far as the Lady was concerned was to save Merlin. But that truly meant saving Arthur first. "You?" she asked carefully, though her heart began drumming.

"Yes, do you not see it? Even as I was building this dream of bringing knights to the table, my marriage was in deep trouble, and I was too exuberant about the future of Camelot, of all of Briton, to see it.

"But just as the awful stench of betrayal began to be near to unbearable, you showed up. Fate stepped in and gave you to me."

Isabel laughed. *More like Viviane.* "I am not a gift, Arthur."

"You are to me."

She had no answer to that. "How far to the cottage?" she asked instead.

"Why, Countess Isabel, I believe I have achieved what heretofore I believed to be the impossible. I have left you speechless."

She desperately searched for something to say, something witty, wise, dumb, it didn't matter. But Arthur was right. She was speechless.

A gift? No one had ever considered her a gift before. A curse, maybe.

Arthur chuckled. "Come, Isabel. 'Tis just around the bend."

They were nearing the curve in the path when Arthur raised his arm as a barrier, then put a finger to his lips. For a moment Isabel was confused, probably still dazed by Arthur's sweet admission.

But then she heard it, too. A rustling up ahead. In one swift move Arthur pulled an arrow from the quiver on his back, then raised his bow and armed it. "Stay here," he said softly.

Like a lethal panther he began silently moving forward toward whatever prey he might encounter.

Isabel's heart just about pounded out of her chest. Fear for Arthur had her nearly hyperventilating. She clasped the teardrop necklace in her hand, wondering if now would be the time to invoke its power.

No, Isabel, the time is not now. Save its power for when its power . . . packs a pow.

Wow, Viv, was really dipping low into the rhyming pool.

Arthur is a warrior second to none; allow him to protect your smart-ass buns.

Arthur took cover behind a large pin oak, then slowly peered around it, his bow still raised in the direction of the noise.

His body was taut, tense, and Isabel caught a small sampling of what it must be like to watch this man head straight into a battle, ready to take on whatever enemy he would encounter beyond.

But then, just as suddenly, his shoulders relaxed, and he lowered his bow, removing the arrow and shoving it back into the quiver.

"Lance," he called, "'tis I, Arthur."

"My lord," Lance responded, "I did not hear you approach."

Arthur looked back and waved Isabel forward. "Actually, 'tis both the Countess Isabel and I, Lance, come to search for . . ." His voice trailed off. Isabel joined him and understood why. In the clearing in front of a charming wooden cottage was Lancelot on his knees, savagely pulling mushrooms from the ground and adding them to a very large pile beside him.

The cottage itself showed signs of Gwen's touch. Flower boxes hung in places along the outer walls, filled with colorful marigolds and pansies, miniature snapdragons and petunias. Wildflowers flourished on either side of the structure. A slight flowery scent managed to hit her nose, but it was quite overwhelmed by the dank scent of vegetation from the forest and, right now, overturned earth. The clearing looked almost like a mine field.

At the sight of Isabel, Lance scrambled to his feet and bowed, but not before she caught a glimpse of his tear-stained face. "Countess," he said, then attempted to swipe at his cheeks.

Arthur again took Isabel's elbow and they moved farther into the clearing. "I am going to assume, Lance, that you have been made aware of the dangers those mushrooms present."

"They almost killed her," Lance said, his voice choky.

"But they did not, thanks to the quick wits of—"

"My healer, Tom," Isabel interrupted.

Lance glanced at the mushroom still in his hand and crushed it savagely before adding it to the pile.

"Your healer, Countess, relates a slightly different tale. I cannot express my . . . I mean we, on behalf of the king, owe you much gratitude."

"No, no you don't."

"We were scouting for the culprits ourselves, Lance," Arthur said, "but I had planned to then direct one of my gardeners to come and destroy them. It appears you have saved us that trouble."

"It is . . . it is my pleasure to do so, sir. I feared that perhaps another who stumbled upon them might make the same mistake as . . . as the queen, and heaven forbid it be one or more of the children."

"Heaven forbid, indeed. What plans do you have for that pile, once you have finished pulling all you find?"

"I plan to burn them, sir."

"Good thinking. Just be sure to keep the fire contained, Lance. We would not want it to get out of control and burn down the cottage."

Isabel hid a grin, as it was nearly the same warning she had given Arthur during their stroll here.

"I would, with your permission, Lance, take one of those back to the castle with me, to show to the cooks as warning. Preferably one still relatively intact, as the ones you have mangled look not like much of anything except crushed grayish vegetation."

Lance quickly bent and pulled another savagely from the pungent earth. Then he stepped forward and, with a quick bow, said, "Will this do for your purposes, my king?"

"It will indeed, Lance," Arthur said, taking it and placing it into the pouch at his hip. "Well, then, carry on. And I thank you for your concern for the safety of the people of Camelot."

"At your service, sir. Always."

That was, when he wasn't busy servicing Gwen, Isabel thought, then mentally kicked herself for the nasty nature of that observation.

As she, herself, was lusting after a married man, she had very little wiggle room to judge.

And Lance's passionate proclamation that he would always be at Arthur's service held a wealth of meaning, well beyond just being a good little soldier. It was obvious to Isabel that behind his boyish sincerity lay a boatload of guilt.

Isabel was dying to explore the inside of that cottage but knew that would be too cruel to Arthur, so she suppressed the request.

"Shall we return to the castle then?" she suggested. "I have need to check on Samara before the evening feast."

"Certainly." They turned to go, but then Arthur swung back. "And Lance?"

"Sir?"

"Please do not allow your anger and grief to cloud your judgment. If I managed to approach without you being aware, another might be able to do the same."

"Yes, my lord."

"You have the keenest senses I e'er have witnessed. Use them. I would not want to lose one of my very best."

"Yes, my lord."

"And do be careful about that fire."

"Yes, my lord."

He swiveled back around and held out his arm. "Shall we?"

"Let's do it," Isabel said, gladly laying a hand on his bicep.

THEY had walked for several moments afore Isabel whispered. "You are an amazing man, Arthur."

He glanced at her in surprise. "I am very happy you think so. But what provoked that observation?"

"Any other would want to throttle that boy senseless."

"Other than a short-lived sense of satisfaction and some sore knuckles, what would that accomplish?"

"Oh, I don't know. Maybe teach him the error of his ways?"

"That moat has been crossed, Isabel. There is no taking back what has already occurred, and it most certainly would not change his feelings for Gwen. I cannot beat the love for her out of him."

"That is true."

"I believe at one time, when I first began to suspect, that I had hopes that this thing betwixt the two would fizzle, as a fire doused with water. I no longer believe or hold hopes for any such thing. Truth be told, were I able to voice my feelings to Lance, I believe I would wish him well and ask him to forever treat Gwen as she deserves."

"You have an amazing capacity for forgiveness, Arthur."

He pondered that. "Perhaps not so much that as a newfound understanding of how they are feeling. It must be a heavy burden to love that deeply and not be able to express it and proclaim it to the world."

"Why can you not privately allow Lance to know how you feel? It might well lift some of that burden."

"The moment I voice or acknowledge, Isabel, no matter how kindly or understanding that discussion might be, the moment I lay voice to it, I am accusing him of treason."

"You've voiced it to Gwen. So in effect, haven't you accused her?"

"I have let her know that I'm very aware of her infidelity. She understands the implications. She also understands that at any moment I could proclaim it to all who will listen, and she will pay that steepest of prices. She will pay with her life."

"Well, that would be a ton of fun to have hanging over your head."

"She also knows that I would ne'er do such a thing to her."

"She trusts that you love her that much."

"Yea, I guess she does. She does not overestimate how much I care for her welfare. What she perhaps overestimates is that love and caring are not necessarily the same thing. No longer."

"May I ask you something?"

Arthur chuckled. "Since when have you ever asked permission?"

"Now. Because your honest answer is important to me."

The castle came into view as they rounded a bend. The scents of sweat and work animals nearly overwhelmed her. She almost wished to run back to the scent of the forest, even though it also held odors she would just as soon avoid.

"I do not believe I have ever been less than honest with you, Isabel," he said, just a little offended that she had to qualify the question. "But you have my word that my response will be an honest one."

"Why did you confide in me? Who is to say that I would not turn around and blab this to someone who would use it against you or Gwen or Lancelot?"

"I believe we have been over this."

"We have?"

"Yes, but perhaps I was too circumspect. Allow me to elaborate, with all of the candor at my disposal." He stopped her and turned her to face him, so that she might see the truth in his eyes. "From the moment I laid eyes upon you, I was taken with you. As we traveled to the castle, you were the most enjoyable companion I had e'er spoken with.

"I knew before we had reached the bailey that you . . . moved something inside me that I had ne'er before felt, not even while courting Gwen."

"Okay, we have been over this before," she said, blushing a bit. Her blue eyes shied from his own. She attempted to free herself of his grip. "Never mind."

"No, please allow me to finish." He released her and held up his hands. "I hold you not against your wishes."

She looked up at him. "You do not have to worry. In that I trust you completely."

"Yes, I must worry." He shrugged. "I wanted you. But I just felt that if you believed that I was simply some randy bastard who had no morals, who had no problems with betraying my vows, you would lose all respect for me and would reject me. I could not allow you to believe such a thing. Call it self-serving, but I not only wanted you, I wanted you to believe in me. Perhaps so that any relationship we had would be true. To each other. To accomplish that, I had to be honest about what was happening around me. So that you would not dismiss me out of hand as a cad and adulterer. I did not want you to believe it was pure lust that drove my attraction."

"You took a huge risk, Arthur."

"Perhaps. But you . . . I cannot explain it . . . You were that important. And I saw in your beautiful blue eyes that you felt at least a portion of what I was feeling. Perhaps misplaced, but I had to trust in that and take the chance. Or risk the possibility that I would ne'er have a chance at all. And I firmly believe in wanting to look back at my life at the end of my days with no regrets. Not forging ahead with my feelings for you would have been a regret I would have lived with all of my days."

Her eyes went moist, but she blinked back any tears. "Thank you," she whispered. "I am so glad for your honesty. And your hopes and desires are not just one-way, Arthur. You are so right. Had I not known about the troubles in your life, I would never have allowed my feelings for you to grow, or for you to kiss me, much less make love."

"Point of order. We have not made love."

"Not for my lack of trying."

He smiled but then had to stop himself. "I cannot in good conscience take something that you should be saving for the man who will win your heart someday."

"Oh, Arthur, you dolt. Do you not realize you have already won my heart?"

He could not help it. He cupped her face and kissed her. It was almost savage at first, but he attempted to cool his desires. Softening the kiss he coaxed her mouth open. He marveled at how their lips seemed so in line. They were meant to intertwine.

Her tongue tasted of mint and his knees nearly buckled when it traced his lips before returning to tangle with his own. 'Twas a devastating thought that this might be as close to the act of lovemaking that they would e'er get. And after the amazing sight of her naked body, 'twas near to unbearable.

She broke the kiss afore he was ready, but he accepted it as her right. Her kiss-swollen lips and dazed eyes just continued to make his body betray him all the more with desire. Yet he stepped back, bending over with hands on his thighs, attempting to retain his control. His breaths heaved in and out of his chest. Finally, he squeezed his eyes shut once, then stood. "I must needs walk this off afore we leave the forest."

"Arthur?"

"Yes?"

"I think I have something to say that might cool your ardor."

"A dunking in Lake Camelot naked in the middle of winter would not manage to cool my ardor, Countess."

"This admission may just do that."

"How is that possible?"

"Because I was not completely honest with you."

That worked. Arthur had been subjected to more lies and betrayals in the past months to last any man's lifetime. He crossed his arms over his hurting, burning, squeezing chest. "I am listening."

She obviously saw something in his face that worried her, as she began biting at her lower lip. "It's not any lie I told you, it was not dishonesty. It was more that you took me by surprise with your reaction to something and I was startled and embarrassed and—"

"Please, to the point, Isabel. I am ready for whate'er this is." He was not, not by any means. But to know what you were facing was a much better tactical battle strategy than not knowing what or who would be betraying you next.

"Please don't be angry."

"I cannot predict my emotions or reactions until I understand what I am facing."

"When we . . . When you and I . . . When we . . ."

"Please, Isabel, do not torture me any longer."

She took a deep breath. "When I could not figure out how to help you take off your clothes . . . do you remember?"

"That memory is seared in my mind, Isabel. I have thought of almost nothing else since this morn. What about it?"

"It was true that I didn't even know where to begin to help you out of your garments."

"I remember."

"It wasn't because I knew nothing of a man's clothing."

"It seemed quite apparent to me."

She waved. "Yes, yes, I was confused by how all of your clothes came together. Or came apart, as it were. But it wasn't because I had never been with a man."

"My pardon?"

"I am not a virgin, Arthur. But you made that assumption, and I was confused and embarrassed and—"

He felt his own jaw drop. "Are you saying back there," he asked, hiking his thumb over his shoulder toward the castle, "and here, in this forest, we could have been making love, but that you knew not how to undress me?"

"Something like that."

His astonishment and relief was so overwhelming that the disappointment over lost opportunities fell by the wayside. He started laughing. "This is your horrible secret?"

"Are you laughing at me?" she asked, standing tall and looking all huffy and haughty.

"No, Isabel, I am laughing at myself. How many times this day I indulged in fantasy and justification for seducing you without regard to your future. The many times I considered how to gently introduce you without harming you and to forget the guilt that might accompany me after the pleasure."

"So you are not angry?"

He could not stop himself from laughing. "I am furious."

She eyed him skeptically. "You have a funny way of showing it."

"You have no idea how many possible betrayals passed through my mind. I was, as I have heard you say, scared shitless of what you might tell me. This, Isabel, did not make my list."

"So that furious part? Is it directed at me?"

"No, it is directed at me, for not giving you a chance to explain. One rule that I teach all of my soldiers is to listen. I was not listening."

"I was not talking. I pretty much lied by omission."

He stroked his chin, the relief coursing through him almost making him weak. "Is that the extent of your exorbitant perfidy, Countess?"

She took a moment, wagging her forefingers to and fro. "Yep, I believe that's about it."

"And are you contrite?" he asked, unable to keep the smile from his face.

"I cannot tell you how much. You are not the only one who has thought of little else."

"Then this king has decided to absolve you. It shall never occur again, am I right?"

She curtsied. "My most dire wish, sir, is that it actually begins to occur."

"You will allow me to teach you how to undress me?"

"I have always been a big proponent of higher education."

He grinned, picked her up and twirled her around. "I am so in love with you, Isabel."

He set her down, dumbfounded that those words had escaped his lips. The shock on her face told him they were very premature. "I am sorry. I know not from where that came. Perhaps an abundance of exuberance."

"Perhaps from the heart?" she whispered.

"But those were not words you were prepared to hear."

"It doesn't make them any less special. In fact, more so, as they were not planned. You spoke what you were thinking."

He shook his head. "I had no right. And I know 'tis a sentiment you perhaps are not prepared to return."

"Then again," she said, running a finger from his temple to chin, "perhaps it is."

"If 'tis, may I hear the words from your lovely lips?"

"I am falling in love with you, Arthur. It seems an untenable situation, but the heart wants what it wants, right?"

"It does."

She offered him an impish grin. "Last nonvirgin to the castle has to be served all of the eel."

He watched for a moment as she lifted her skirts and then took off running.

Grinning, bursting with happiness and gratitude to the gods or to fate, he took off after her. Not very fast, however, for he was well aware of her aversion to eel.

Chapter Eighteen

THE evening meal began as a somber affair. Apparently all were worried about the health of their queen. But Arthur stood tall and announced she was quite on the way to recovery, and the mood lightened. Even Lancelot had arrived, which sort of stunned Isabel. She thought for certain the poor little puppy would be attempting to sneak into Gwen's heavily guarded quarters or be off plotting revenge against mushrooms worldwide.

As her platter was placed before her, she realized that she'd been served a ton of vegetables and duck and not one ounce of eel.

She looked over at Arthur, and his plate was piled high with the vile stuff. He grinned and winked at her, then whispered to a server. That platter of eel was replaced with a bowl of what looked to be some kind of stew.

She ducked her head and smiled, digging in to her veggies. Oh, yes, like it or not, she had fallen fast and hard. She was so in love with Arthur it almost hurt.

Arthur spoke into James's ear, who then spoke into Tom's ear, who then spoke into Isabel's ear. "He says that the bet did not include actually having to eat the eel. Does this make sense?"

She nearly had wine flying out of her nose and mouth. She caught herself and tried to pull it all together. Then she whispered into Tom's ear, "Relay to King Arthur that this is a thing called a loophole. And he is lucky to be given reprieve this time."

Tom relayed the message to James, who said, loudly, "A goose pole?"

"A loophole," Tom said to James. "A loophole! You know, when a person attempts to get away with something. By using sneaky tactics! Jeesh. And the countess has decided to give the king reprieve on this one."

Again, Isabel and Arthur's eyes met, and neither were able to contain it. They both fell into gales of laughter. Isabel covered her face with her napkin, hoping when she lowered it, everyone would have magically disappeared. No such luck.

But, instead, Arthur stood. "Sirs, the Countess Isabel and I must needs discuss possible goose poles in our potential treaties at the meeting. Please stay and enjoy the sweets."

He came around to her chair. "My apologies, Countess, I did not discuss whether you would prefer to stay for the sweets."

"Oh, no, King Arthur," she said, standing. "I am quite anxious to explore the possible repercussions of these goose poles."

ALL decorum they attempted to maintain dropped the moment they entered the solarium, two rooms away. And then Arthur took her hand and led her back out to the gardens, both finally allowing their laughter to let loose.

Isabel had to hold her tummy. "Oh, Arthur, we were so bad."

He grinned, the light from the lanterns making his eyes gleam. "Yes, but it felt so wonderful."

"We should return to the table, having resolved our disagreement over goose poles."

He laughed again. "We shall announce our mutual understanding when we break fast in the morn."

"Are we for it or against it?" she asked.

"I assume we must define what 'it' is."

Isabel almost lost it. "I guess we must."

Arthur stopped grinning, then pulled her close. "I am so happy when I am with you, Isabel. You make me feel like I can soar. From the moment we parted this afternoon, I felt lacking, your presence so missing from me."

Isabel sucked in a breath because she couldn't have said it better. It was a busy afternoon, yet empty. Without Arthur there, it just wasn't the same.

She nodded. "Yes, Arthur, I miss you when you aren't there as well."

"You fill a need inside me. I cannot describe it. I know not what our solution is that will make us all happy, I only know this: I do not believe happiness is available to me without you in my life."

"We will figure it all out, Arthur. Somehow, someway, I believe that Gwen and Lance, and you and I will end up happy. Let us trust fate again on this one."

There was a knock from inside the solarium, and they quickly stepped apart. James stood there, his eyes lowered, shuffling his humongous feet.

Arthur picked up a pebble from the rock garden and tossed it at the door. When James looked up, startled, Arthur motioned him out.

"What is it, James?"

"I have a message for the countess," he said, with a small bow in her direction.

"What is it, James?" Isabel asked.

"Mary, miss Mary, the one who—"

Isabel smiled. "I know who she is, James. She is my trusted friend."

"She, well, she asked me to tell you that she has come down with a bit of a headache, and that she will be unavailable for the rest of the evening. She sends her sincere apologies and hopes that you"—he coughed—"are able to turn down your own bed furs this night. She is most sorry, Countess."

Right. Isabel would bet that Mary had never taken a sick day or night in her life. But it was so sweet that she almost cried. "Please, James, convey my sincere hope that her head feels better in the morning."

He looked up and nodded. "Oh, yes, she will be . . . I mean, she hopes to be better by morning light."

"If there's anything I can do? Shall I visit her?"

"No, no, I believe she is already abed."

"Well, then, James, I suggest that if she is still awake that she sips a bit of tea, with a dollop of honey and perhaps just a drop or two of sweet mead."

"I will most certainly offer such." He went almost as red as Mary's hair. "I mean, I will have her mate bring it to her, should she wish."

"Thank you. Please give her my best."

"I will."

"And James?"

"Yes, mum?"

"Tell her thank you."

"I will. And I believe she will already know you would say such, Countess."

"Of course she will. She and I are pinky-finger friends."

James's chuckles followed him back into the castle. "Pinky-finger friends," he said. "I have had a good laugh over that one."

Arthur looked at her, his puzzlement all over his face.

"Want an interpretation?" Isabel asked.

"If that means that you will explain what just occurred, then indeed, I most definitely need an interpretation."

"Quick or detailed version?"

"The one that I will understand."

"Okay, here's my take. James left the dinner table and went to see Mary. Mary assessed the situation and created an excuse she could give me, wanting me to know that she would not be breezing into my chamber this evening to assist me in preparing for bed."

"Because?"

"To give me complete privacy."

"To what purpose? Did she expect a man to visit you, Isabel? Are you expecting a visitor? Who is he?"

Okay, Viviane, I'm really stunned. Are all these men quite so dumb?

He's a man newly smitten, and he is so taken his recent history has left him shaken.

His denseness, Viviane, is leaving me mute.

Oh, come on, Isabel, it really is cute.

Viviane was right. Isabel knew that all of the emotional scars could not possibly have completely healed by now. Maybe that was part of her role. To help heal him.

She looked up at him and raised her hands to attempt to smooth the distress. The muscles in his jaw were clenching, his eyes begging for answers.

"Arthur—"

"Tell me true, Isabel."

"Listen to me. Mary has become my trusted friend. She knows me better than anyone here."

"Yes?"

"Who do you think she was clearing the way for? Who do you think she felt I would want to spend time with privately?"

"Every man here would want to be with you. I could not even begin to count—"

"Arthur. Who do you believe Mary would be convinced I would wish to be alone with?"

She watched as the lightbulb finally switched on in the big dumb man's head. It was a hilarious sight to behold, but she knew laughing at this point would not be a good idea.

"Me?" he said.

"The man wins the duh prize."

"She was attempting to give you and me time alone?"

She shook her head. "As was James, dummy. They conspired to allow us to spend time together without being interrupted."

"There is no other?" he asked.

Her heart broke. She placed a hand over his. "I know you've been hurt, Arthur. But we will go nowhere while you keep suspecting that I might be the next to hurt you."

He took her hand and kissed her fingers, then placed it right back against his beating heart. "I am so sorry, Isabel. I know not how to properly ask for your forgiveness."

She could think of several ways. But first things first.

"You told me today that you confided in me because you felt you could trust me."

"'Tis true."

"And yet tonight, that trust was gone."

He frowned. Really frowned. "Not true. It was a totally different matter, Isabel. I trusted you with private matters."

"Have I broken that trust?"

"No, of course not. Still, 'tis not the same."

"Tell me, what is so different?"

"You have so many men friends. You have all of my men wanting to do anything to make you happy. You even made my son learn what loyalty means. Something I have ne'er been able to do."

"Your point?"

He looked down and then finally up. "So many men want you, Isabel. It eats at me."

I so want to kick his ass, Viviane.

I agree, Isabel, but form a better plan.

Isabel sat down. "Just what happened today in the woods, Arthur?"

"I admitted my feelings for you," he said.

"And?"

"And you also said what you felt for me."

"Was I lying?"

"It would hurt beyond imagination should that be a lie."

"Yet you still harbor doubts." Isabel stood up. "Mary was trying to give us time alone. It would have been perfect. You could have shown me how to undress you. We could have made love. But you are so sure I'm just as other women, that trust you said you felt was not entirely true, was it?"

"Please do not let us end the evening this way, Isabel. I have made so many mistakes, and I am sorry for them all. But you told me you loved me this very day, and I am not allowing you to take that back because I am a . . . dolt? Then I am a dolt. But that does not mean I do not love you as much as I do.

"I answer to my mistakes, Isabel, but my feelings for you I refuse to say are wrong. You tell me, how, if you indeed return my feelings, as you said this day, that you can turn your back on me now?"

Isabel didn't think she'd ever love another man like Arthur. Stupid as she might be, she turned to look at him.

"There are no other men, Arthur. Tom, Dick and Harry are friends. As for others here in the castle, I believe you are a bit overly concerned on that front. Not a single one of your men has made an inappropriate move or said an inappropriate word to me. Well, maybe Mordred, but we took care of that. The others in your realm? They have been nothing but complete gentlemen."

"I see the way they look at you. I hear what they say during skills practice. I nearly knocked Edward down with my sword just yesterday. Too many dream of getting close to you. I can barely hold back my anger at the thought that any might try."

"And I see castle maids nearly swoon every time you swagger into a room. I hear them giggle and comment on the fact that they work for the most handsome king in all the world. Do I accuse you of being inappropriate with any of them?"

"I would ne'er!"

"Well, I would ne'er, either!" she said.

They stood at a standoff, practically glaring at each other. She felt like she was in the medieval OK Corral.

Isabel took a deep, calming breath. "There is no other, Arthur. Not here, and not back in Ok—in Dumont. If you wish, you may interrogate Tom, Dick or Harry. They will tell you the same thing. In fact, they would all probably laugh at the notion."

He cocked his head. "Why is that? You are so beautiful and smart and funny. I would think you would have suitors lining up for a chance to court you. To ask for your hand."

Isabel laughed. "You would be wrong. I am so busy on various assignments, I have no time."

"Assignments?"

She waved. "You know, countessing things."

Finally, finally, his lips curved in a smile. "Countessing things."

"Yes, you know. 'Hey, you! You do this.' And, 'Hey, you! You do that.'"

"Ah, yes, countessing things."

"Right. Just as you are busy doing kingly things."

"Right. Where I say, 'Hey, you. You do this.' And, 'Hey, you. You do that.'"

"Exactly."

His smile bloomed into his full-blown, heart-melting grin. "I understand."

Sure he did. Even she didn't understand the babble she'd just blurted out.

He looked down. "Then why me? Why now?"

Men. Ego stroking apparently had not begun during her generation. It was an age-old tradition.

She touched his arm. "The why you is easy. Because I felt the same as you did the moment I laid eyes on you. Quite before I had any idea who you were."

"I was there, Isabel. I saw your face. You feared me."

"Because you startled me. You have a way of silently approaching that is awesome. But the moment you smiled at me, Arthur, I was toast."

"Toast."

"Smitten. Taken with you. Attracted to you."

"Oh. Appears I like this toast thing. Then I, too, was toast."

She nodded, hiding a smile. "As for why now, who knows, Arthur? As you said, fate perhaps. Would I have chosen to fall for a very married king? I don't think so. Especially one who was still grieving over . . . well, things.

"I did not choose the time, the place, the man. In fact, the last thing I was supposed to do was fall for King Arthur." Boy, that sure was true. "But I cannot help or decide what happens or why."

"Except for when you are performing the 'hey, you do this' countessing tasks."

She socked him on the arm. "Now you are making fun of me."

He rubbed his arm as if that were a fierce blow. "Teasing you, pretty lady. You are one of very few people I have e'er met who can take as well as she gives. 'Tis a quality of yours I greatly admire, and one which gives me much pleasure."

That single word hung in the air between them. Finally Isabel gave a short cough into her fist and then said, "Have I allayed your fears, King Arthur? Have I answered your questions to your satisfaction?"

"You have. And I am deeply sorry for expressing my doubts."

"Big bad kings don't have doubts. They strut around doing kingly things."

"Oh, yes, how is it possible I misremembered? Hey, you, Countess, do this."

He kissed her, pulling her flush against his hard, really hard, body.

His lips moved over her face, to kiss her temple, and then suckled the lobe of her ear. "You smell so good," he whispered. "You always smell good."

If not for his arms firmly around her, Isabel had the feeling she'd fall to the floor like a rag doll.

But finally she'd had enough of this foreplay, because need was a powerful thing.

She straightened and pulled away. "There is this game I like to play."

"Yes?"

"Yes. It's called, last one to my bedroom has to get naked first." And then she picked up her skirts, ran into the castle and up the back staircase.

* * *

ARTHUR caught her right before she hit the door to her quarters. As he had followed her, laughing the entire way, he debated which he wanted more, but it seemed to him to be a win-win, so decided a tie was in order.

He picked her up, swallowing her squeals of protest with his mouth. He carried her into the room, only to stop short. There were candles alight everywhere, and a tray with a cask of wine and two goblets sitting side by side.

"Mary," Isabel said.

"Remind me to reward Mary," he said, and laid Isabel on the bed.

He looked down upon her, the glow of the candles making pretty Isabel almost breathtaking.

"I want you," he said. "Do you feel the same?"

"Who ran up here faster?"

He decided reminding her that he could have overtaken her at any moment would not be a great idea. He dragged air into his lungs. "I am at your mercy. But please, help me to settle down."

She laughed. "No, sir. I want a lesson in how to undress a king."

"You are very much not helping, madam."

She looked into his eyes, and Arthur was lost. He feared he would lose all ability to satisfy her afore either of them were unclothed.

She rolled off the bed and rose blithely to her feet.

"Your tunic appears easy enough, sir, as I can simply pull it over your head," she said quietly. "However, you need to allow me to remove it."

He held his arms up, and she pulled it over his head and off, tossing it aside.

"And next would be what I can only consider a turtleneck, but I am certain you have another name for it."

"I am certain I do, however, for the life of me, Isabel, I could not name it if you placed a dagger to my throat."

"No chance of that."

She removed his undergarment, leaving him naked from the waist up.

"Oh, Arthur," she breathed, tracing the scars across his body.

"I am so sorry," he said.

"No! Do not apologize. The beauty of these is that you fought and won."

"Or merely survived," he breathed.

Her lips moved over his body, and he knew not how to stop her. He did not want to stop her. Yet he was dying to get his turn on hers. "You are killing me, Isabel," he said.

"So I am actually killing a king? There must be a terrible punishment for that."

"I cannot begin to tell you how severe if you do not let me touch you," Arthur managed to say.

"I am quaking in my knickers," she said. "Now, please tell me how to make you naked from the waist down."

"If I admit the secret, may I please, please touch you?"

"Yes."

"There is something called a belt. It is a manly way of saying laces of sorts."

Isabel giggled. "Found your belt, King Arthur."

"'Tis way beyond time you did, Countess."

He felt the belt give way, and his leggings loosen around his hips. Isabel slipped lower, as did the material around his legs.

She forced one leg up and his clothing off. Then drove him near to mad as she kissed her way up his naked ankle to his calf to his thigh. Her soft hand followed, but inside his thigh. She stopped afore his privates. Unfortunately.

"Take off the other half, please, Arthur."

"I am taking off everything, yet you are not allowing me to help you do the same."

"I have learned the tricks of your clothing. Once again, I wager it will take you more than mere moments to figure the workings of mine."

Arthur kicked aside his clothing and had no trouble making

Isabel naked in seconds. She did not look displeased at losing the wager as he once again picked her up and set her on the bed.

"I have needed this, needed you, from our first moment, Isabel. Had I my druthers, I would have attempted to seduce you that first moment in the woods."

"Please just allow me to explore you."

Arthur laughed, even as he pulled her up and into his arms. "How much more exploration do you want?"

"Years."

"That sounds wonderful. However, 'tis my turn."

His fingers trailed up and down, from the side of her breast to her hip and up again. "You are so soft. I wish my hands were not so rough."

"I love your hands, Arthur."

He leaned over and took her breast in his mouth, suckling and licking her oh-so-sensitive nipple. Isabel cried out, arching upward. The sensation radiated all the way down and nearly exploded between her legs.

His tongue ran slowly one more time over her breast, and then his mouth returned to hers, kissing her as his hand traveled down over her belly, and then lower. Those rough fingers explored her, spreading her lower lips apart, and gently caressing her.

"Oh, dear gods," she said as an orgasm shook through her. Her entire body shuddered. He held her close, still stroking her until he'd managed to wring every ounce of shattering ecstasy out of her.

He raised his head and smiled down at her, his green eyes heavy but sparkling. "Oh, lady, the gods created you for loving. You are so sweet and wet and beautiful in your . . . your . . ."

"Happiness," she finished for him.

She grabbed his arm, pulled him over and down onto his back. "I very much want to give you happiness," she said.

"I am already . . . oh, gods, Isabel," he said as she slipped lower and took him into her mouth. "Please, I do not want to be anywhere but inside you, part of you, when I find this . . . oh . . . this happiness. Please."

Isabel lifted her head but continued to stroke his penis. "I want your happiness any way you want it."

He choked with laughter. "Hey, you, please do this," he said, then rolled her to her back.

"Do what, my lord?" she asked.

"Spread yourself for me. Allow me entrance."

"You had but to ask."

He kneeled between her legs, again stroking her into a near frenzy. "I will not hurt you?" he asked.

"You will if you stop."

He laid overtop her and kissed her. Then slowly, way too slowly, he entered her.

She took his face in her hands. "Arthur, it feels so good. Please, it does not hurt. Do not hesitate."

His eyes squeezed shut, then he began to move inside her. Still slowly, but so steady, and Isabel realized in her fog of frenzy he was trying to prolong the exquisite agony.

But she was going to come again, and soon. She grabbed his hips, pushing against his body, needing to feel it all over again, although in a totally different way. "Please, Arthur. I need this."

The floodgates opened. He pushed into her harder and faster. She felt his body tense beneath her fingers before he looked at her and said, "I am so in love with you, Isabel." His orgasm hit the inside of her like an internal bomb. As she felt his semen hit the innermost parts of her, she, too, came.

CHAPTER NINETEEN

'TWAS almost dawn afore Arthur reluctantly left Isabel. He did so only after she had demanded he had need to go do "you, do this, and, you, do that," kingly stuff.

He was still smiling as he entered the outer quarters of the royal chambers where he had laid his head for days now.

He stopped short when he saw Gwen, perched upon his furs.

"Late night, Arthur?"

"It appears that you are feeling much better, Gwen. I am very glad."

"Where have you been?"

"Why in the world would it matter to you?"

"You are my husband. I am entitled to know where my husband has been."

He stepped farther into the room, finding himself angry that she would ruin his exhilaration over the night he'd just had. He had so hoped to climb into bed and relive the memories over and over until slumber overtook him.

"I believe that you have lost the right to even inquire, Gwen. But since you ask, I fell asleep elsewhere."

'Twas the truth. In between lovemaking, both he and Isabel had dozed, only to have one or the other awake to have the other kissing and fondling, until they would make love again.

"You were with another," Gwen said.

"Gwen, your hypocrisy astounds me."

"I am still your wife, Arthur. And still the queen."

"By my grace only, if you need that reminder."

She stood, and Arthur looked at her, trying to remember the last time he had wanted her. It was a sad fact that he could not. She was a beautiful woman to be sure, small of stature with a slight frame. She had a flirtatious smile that he one time found enchanting.

Yet right now she appeared pale, and her eyes so accusing, almost mean.

"It is your precious countess, is it not?"

"First of all, she is not mine, unfortunately, but precious works. And second, you lost all rights to ask questions of me many moons ago. Go back to your own bed, Gwen. This is mine, and I desperately want an hour of sleep afore I wake to start the day."

She stepped forward. "Arthur, I am so sorry. I made a grave error. But now I am ready and willing for the two of us to renew what we had."

"You will toss Lance aside so easily?"

"You, my husband, are my first priority."

Arthur could not believe the disgust that had him almost heaving.

"Do you not understand," he asked her, "how much Lance loves you? We found him at your trysting cabin, tearing and shredding those mushrooms that made you ill. He was torn apart. Has he been just a toy to you? Do you not care at all?"

She looked defeated. "Yea, Arthur, I care very much."

"Then why this pretense? I have already promised you I will not expose your love for him. I still care enough for you to protect you."

She shook her head. "I trusted, Arthur, that you would also stay true to me, no matter. I was always certain of your fidelity."

Arthur nearly gaped at her. "Do you hear yourself? Do you even listen to yourself? I am protecting your infidelity, even allowing it for your happiness and Lance's, and yet you accuse me of wrongdoing should I happen to . . . consider another?"

"You are my husband!" she said.

He honestly could not believe this conversation. He wished, so much, to puzzle through it with Isabel. She would have a wise answer. Or maybe, as he had come to learn, a smart-ass one. It did not matter. He just already ached for Isabel's advice, her laughter and, heaven help him, her lovemaking. Even as she had already depleted whate'er he had in him, he felt it already filling again.

"Gwen, you are making little sense. Perhaps you would be better off in your own bed."

"Come with me."

The thought of that repulsed him. "You would lie with me not long after your time with Lance?"

"I ask only that you hold me, Arthur."

"Perhaps, my wife, we have a failure of communication." He stopped, wondering where he had heard that afore. He shook his head. "Should you need holding, I will have a man bring Lance to your bed. I have no desire to do so. However, I am very happy that you are looking and feeling better."

"Your countess hurt me!" she said, as he was heading out the door.

That stopped him. "Once again, she is not my countess. How, pray tell, did she hurt you?"

"My chest and midsection hurt. I am told that she was pounding on me. I believe she should at least be punished for assaulting me."

Arthur stared, wondering who the hell this woman was. "Thank the gods Isabel pounded on you, Gwen. She did that saving your life. Were it not for her 'pounding' as you call it, we would be holding services as we dropped you into the ground."

"I am your wife," she said as she stalked from the room.

"So you have said," he retorted. "Over and over and over again. It means nothing any longer."

* * *

ISABEL was having the most glorious dream. One where Arthur slipped into bed beside her and snuggled up against her.

Then she felt a hand cover her breast and she shot straight up.

"Get your hands off me and away from me before I neuter you, you—"

"'Tis me, Isabel," she heard. "And trust that I would have to fight off that neutering thing."

She shoved her hair out of her eyes. "Arthur?"

"Yes, Countess."

The dim light from the smoldering embers in the fireplace gave her too little illumination. It sounded like Arthur, but to be certain, she asked, "What kind of kingly thing are you performing now?"

"Saying, 'Hey, you, do this. Lie back down with me without any neutering.'"

She tried to shake off the fog. "Why are you being kingly at this hour, Arthur?"

"I needed to catch you in between your countessing."

She laughed, then slipped back down into the bed. "Seriously, what are you doing back here?"

He scooped her body, his arm draped over her waist. "I had a desperate need to be with you."

"Arthur, I cannot even imagine more lovemaking. I'll be lucky if I can walk tomorrow."

"No lovemaking. I swear. I will be lucky if I can hold up a sword. Just loving. I needed the feel of you."

She heard the catch in his voice and wiggled her way around to face him. "What's wrong?"

He pushed her hair from her face, then kissed her brow. "Who is to say that something is wrong? Can a man not just want to be with the woman he loves?"

She frowned, although she doubted he'd be able to see it. "Remember that conversation we had earlier about honesty? Truth?"

She felt his chest heave slightly. "Yea, I do. You would have to invoke that at this time."

"I invoke it, King Arthur, every single time."

"And should I, perhaps, invoke an 'I care not to talk about it right now'?"

"It would be so unkingly."

His chest rumbled with laughter. "How so, Countess?"

"Because kings face troubles head-on. They do not avoid them by slipping in bed with countesses, who are busy not doing countess things."

"What were you busy doing?"

"Dreaming about kingly things."

"Good dreams?"

"You are avoiding the question, and that is so very unkingly."

"You are not naked enough, and that is so uncountessy."

She pulled away from his embrace and sat up. "Arthur. What is it?"

He sat up as well, brushing his hands through his hair. Al least she thought so. The lighting was a little iffy.

"When I returned to my bedchamber, Gwen was waiting for me."

"Oh, good! She's feeling better."

"I suppose that depends on your perspective."

"Oh, bad. That sounds bad," Isabel said, reaching over to the cup of mint by her bed and grabbing a fingerful.

"She believes I am having an affair."

Isabel sighed. "Yo, Arthur, you are in my bed."

"She wants us to reunite."

Isabel didn't know how a truly broken heart felt until that very moment. "Oh, I see." She tried to gather her senses, which had scattered to the winds. "Well, then, I guess that's that. I wish you well. Now get the hell out of my bed."

Arthur leaned over and scratched something over something and suddenly the candle beside her bed came to life.

It wasn't University of Oklahoma stadium-light illumination, but they were able to see each other.

"Please, Arthur, go back to your wife."

"Do you honestly believe I would be here if that had been my choice?"

"I'm guessing that you came to tell me the news."

"I climbed into your bed to say good-bye?"

"Well, that was kind of weird, but I can believe it. You have a sweet heart."

"Oh, Isabel, do you truly think that of me?"

"Arthur, I no longer know what to think of anything. You have been in love with Gwen for so long."

He stood up. "I came to tell you, nay, *show* you how I feel. You did not even give me the chance to finish. You wrote the ending to this story afore I could fully explain."

"Arthur."

He shook his head as he moved to the door. "No, Isabel. I came here for help and guidance and comfort. Instead you handed me judgment. I am so sick of this." He turned and looked at her. "I was here because you were my choice. There was no question or doubt. Minutes ago I would have given my life for you. I am such a fool. Not very kingly, is it?"

"Arthur."

"Sleep well, Countess."

Chapter Twenty

"WE must do something," Mary whispered to James. "There is something terribly wrong with my lady. She is teaching us this CPR thing and demanding we be allowed to have what she calls recess each day, but she is very much not herself."

"And my lord," James said. "He is working us harder than e'er, and his temper is short. We are mostly afraid to utter a word, when afore he asked us to speak up at all times. I have ne'er seen him slice through anything set before him as he does now."

"We must formulate a plan," Mary said.

"Yes. Yet I cannot think of one."

"Leave it to me, James. But I will need your assistance to put it in play."

James smiled at his bride-to-be. "I love you so much, Mary. I cannot wait to make you my bride."

She grinned back at him. "And I cannot wait to call you husband. But if our vows are to be perfect, we must needs fix this rift between the king and the countess. They are standing up for us."

"Yes."

Mary suddenly jumped up and James caught her. "What?"

"Our vows! Our vows! The king is an honorable man and the countess is such a priceless lady. Our vows!"

"I am sorry if I am not quite following your logic, Mary."

"No need. I will let you know what needs be done when I have it all in place."

"I trust that you will." He held her close, but not too hard. He had once hugged her so tightly that she had cried out. 'Twould never, ever happen again. "We will be happy together. This I do vow."

She laid her head into his neck. "We have a very long lifetime for you to continue to prove it true."

"I very much look forward to it."

As the days passed, there was progress, although, it seemed, not with Gwen. She laid abed and had continuous complaints.

But her seamstresses had finished many breeches, and Isabel had coaxed the women into taking possession and actually wearing them. At least for that hour when they were set free to play.

This morning Isabel had decided to teach them how to play a primitive form of putt-putt golf. The women were happily whacking away when Mary came running to her, tears streaming down her face.

"What is it, Mary?" she asked.

"I am afraid my vows with James are off."

"What? Why?"

Mary looked around. "May we go elsewhere? Some privacy?"

Jenny, Gwen's chambermaid, walked over and asked, "May I help?"

As diplomatically as she could, Isabel said, "Yes, please. If you would oversee the rest of recess?"

Mary sniffled. "I need Countess Isabel."

Jenny nodded. "Of course. I will be happy to take over for the rest of the hour, Countess."

"Teach them to get the freakin' stones in the holes. That's the goal. Stones in the holes."

"Yes, Countess."

She turned and focused on Mary. "Now tell me, please, what happened."

Mary swiped away the tears. "May we please go to your chambers to talk?"

"Of course."

Isabel tried questioning Mary as they ascended the stairs, but Mary kept shaking her head. Isabel figured Mary wanted complete privacy, which she understood, knowing that Mary had been shunned by many of her peers, lately.

Mary pulled her into her own room, almost shoved her farther, and then kicked the door closed.

"What happened, Mary? Let me help. Maybe you and James can talk this through. You love him. You have told me as much. He treats you like gold. What went wrong?"

Mary's tears dried up as if she were facing the sun in the Mojave. "If James and I are to exchange vows happily, Isabel, then we need those standing witness to be happy as well."

"I'm sorry? Mary, I don't understand."

Mary stuck two fingers in her mouth and let out an ear-piercing whistle. She smiled at Isabel and said, "Tom taught me that when he was doing my teeth-cleaning."

Isabel was considering how she was going to punish her friend when her door flew open and James entered, dragging a blindfolded Arthur in his wake.

"James, this has become not my favorite prank," Arthur said. "I went along, but now this might have gone a bit far."

Isabel glanced at Mary. "Traitor," she whispered.

Mary shrugged.

James pulled the blindfold from around Arthur's head. Arthur blinked and looked around. As soon as he spotted Isabel and Mary, he glared at James. "Traitor."

James shrugged.

James and Mary, looking so immensely pleased with themselves, banded together.

"You two are standing up for us during our vows in just days," James said. "And you will, and I mean will, be happy at our ceremony."

"James," Arthur began.

James held up his beefy hand. "You know, King Arthur, that I am loyal to you. I will run with you into battle, and I will protect you until my dying breath."

"And you, Countess Isabel," Mary said. "You have become a friend such as I may never know again. I would stand afore you in any situation where someone would do you harm."

"But we are tired," James said, taking up the apparent narrative, "of your surliness of late. As you have been avoiding one another as the plague the past days, we can only surmise that there are . . . are . . ."

"Issues," Mary finished. "Those which need be aired and addressed. You will," she said, pointing back and forth between the two, "fix these problems afore our marriage vows."

"Whate'er happened betwixt the two of you," James said.

"Get over it!" they yelled in unison.

With that, the two huffed their way out of the room, slamming the door shut behind them with a decided bang.

Isabel and Arthur stared at each other for several moments, and then broke out in laughter.

"I believe we have both just been spanked by our parents," Isabel gasped.

"I'm feeling decidedly unkingly," Arthur said. "Just when did I lose control?"

"No," she said, still laughing. "It shows just what a great king you are."

"Surely, you jest," he said. "My first man just berated me."

Oh, how Isabel wanted to say, "Don't call me Shirley." But somehow she was fairly certain the joke would not translate.

"Don't you realize how excellent this is?" she asked.

"Perhaps I do not recognize the underlying meaning behind two servants giving their king a dressing down, as it were."

"The underlying meaning, your Highness, is that they love you enough, they trust you enough to take such extreme measures. They know that you will not punish them, because they trust that you care."

"Ah, mayhap the difference between my people and you. James and Mary, at least, trust that I care."

Isabel stared at him while she mentally pulled the dagger out of her chest. "I never realized you had a cruel side, Arthur. It's good to know. It helps me so much in getting over you."

He strode over to her. "Isabel, I did not mean—"

"You touch me and I will take out both your knees."

"Then take them," he said, grabbing hold of her shoulders. "Go. Do it. But I am going to hold on to you until you listen to me if I have need to I will take you down with me when my legs become useless."

It was totally disgusting that his hands on her already had her body responding as if he were moving them all over her, not just holding on to her upper arms.

"I believe I have heard enough."

"No, you heard just enough to form conclusions. Incorrect conclusions, as it turns out. For a smart, compassionate woman, Isabel, I cannot understand how you would hear only part of my story and instantly believe the worst of me. Ye gods, woman, we had spent the evening together in the most intimate of ways. And yet not an hour later you shut me out. You closed your hearing and your mind. Were you already regretting what we shared?"

"No, but you said Gwen wanted . . ."

"I know what I said, Isabel. I also know what you refused to allow me to finish. Are you willing to allow me the opportunity now?"

"I'm listening. I'm not ruling out the knee-kicking thing, but I'm listening."

"That is a start," he said, letting her go. He turned and walked two steps, then spun around and stepped right back to her. "What you ne'er allowed me to finish the other night was that I turned Gwen down. I do not want her any longer. I have not for some time. When she asked if we could try to go back, I said no, Isabel. I told her that now she was betraying not just me, but now Lance, as well.

I recovered from the pain. Truth be told, I fell for another. You. But I fear Lance would not. You saw him at the cottage. He was near to mindless with grief and anger and worry.

"I returned to you, because with *you* was where I wanted to be. And I wanted to talk it out with *you*. Do you honestly believe I would climb back into your bed furs to say to you that I had decided that we had fun, but alas, I had decided to start over with Gwen? Just how cruel do you believe me to be?"

Isabel stood, stunned. "Oh. My. God. You tried. And I didn't let you. I was so afraid that it was a farewell gesture that—"

"Shhh," he said, putting a finger to her lips. "I understand your upset and confusion, Isabel. Please remember how quickly I grew angry at the thought of you with other men. Add to that that I am still married to Gwen, it is understandable why you would leap to that conclusion. Were the situation in the reverse, I fear I may have done the same."

"You are giving me an excuse, when I have none. No, you would not have done the same. You would have listened. But, Arthur, I was so afraid that what we had . . ."

"I know, love, I know," he said as he pulled her into his arms.

"Why are you so forgiving when I don't deserve it?"

He chuckled into her hair. "Perhaps because it is the kingly thing to do?"

"No, the kingly thing to do is telling people to do this, or people to do that."

"Then perhaps it is something a man does when he loves a woman."

"I'll take that one for a thousand, Alex."

He grinned, brushing her hair from her face as he kissed her temple, her forehead, her nose. "I know not what that even means, and I find I do not care. I know not who this Alex is, but I do not care. What matters most to me is that we clear this misunderstanding betwixt us."

"Oh, Arthur," she said, wrapping her arms around him, standing on tiptoe to rain kisses over his neck. "I am so very sorry."

"As am I. I am certain that there should have been a much better way to relate the events." He smiled down at her. "Okay, I fibbed. I am curious as to what you will trade for a thousand whate'ers. And who this Alex is."

"It is a game we play at home. It is a reverse thing. You, the player, will be given the answer, and then you will formulate what the question would be."

"Pardon?"

"Exactly. Although actually it would be, 'What is pardon?'"

He shook his head. "I am baffled, love."

"For example, someone would say, 'The land that King Arthur loves passionately.' Then you would respond, 'What is Camelot?'"

"This is a game you play in Dumont?"

"Yes."

"Okay then," he said. "I believe I understand the rules."

She laughed. "Okay, the answer is, 'The woman who is crazy about King Arthur.' What is the question?"

"I am hoping the question is, 'Who is Countess Isabel?'"

"Correct!"

"Then I have one for you."

"Lay it on me, big boy."

"The kingly thing Arthur is about to tell his woman—as is his right, mind you, as kingly matter involve telling you to do that and you to do this—to do."

"What is take off the king's kingly clothes?"

"Not exactly the one I was going for, but it very much works for me, Isabel. So I will give you a correct on that one."

Isabel went to work obeying his kingly command. "You know, every once in a while there is more than one right response."

"Good. My question was, 'What is allow the king to help the countess in taking off her clothes?'"

"See, more than one right response," she said.

MARY and James walked down the hall hand in hand, both grinning. "We may be in so much trouble," Mary said.

"Did you hear a single thing shatter?"

"I did not."

"Then I believe we are safe," James said.

"Isabel would ne'er hurt me. I am certain. No matter the outcome, good or bad, she will forgive me. But King Arthur?"

"Would ne'er hurt you, Mary. Nor me."

She stared up at her giant of a future husband. "How do you know?"

"Because he is the kindest man I have e'er met. He is tough in the battle training, no question. But always, always fair to all. No matter the outcome, he will most assuredly forgive us for he will realize our good intentions."

"Then we did okay."

"We did better than okay. Last I heard they were sharing laughter."

Mary stopped James. "There is a ritual in Isabel's land where you celebrate success."

"What is it?"

"It is called a high five." She held up her palm and waited for him to follow suit. He stood looking confused.

"Hold up your hand!"

He did, and Mary smacked it, grinning. "High five!"

"What does this mean?"

"It is a sign of success. I am guessing that the two are making up as we speak."

James grinned down at his love. He held up his palm. She looked at him curiously but smacked palms with him.

"High five," she said. "What was that one for?"

"For my luck that the lady I love returns those feelings. And that I will soon be the happiest husband alive."

CHAPTER TWENTY-ONE

At the sound of the knock, Gwen glanced up from her bed to find the countess standing there, looking quite beautiful in a wine-colored gown.

In comparison, Gwen knew she most likely appeared pale and disheveled and that this bed gown was not at all flattering. "Please," she said, running her fingers through her hair, "enter."

Isabel stepped into the room and that was when Gwen realized Isabel was holding some sort of black garment in her hand. "How are you feeling this morning, Gwen?"

"I believe somewhat better," Gwen said. Which was a bit of a lie. In truth, other than a lingering tenderness in her chest, she felt just fine. However, as long as she was abed, she knew that Arthur would continue to visit her, and she might have time to change his mind.

'Twas not that she had stopped loving Lance. Truth was, she loved him desperately. But she feared the loss of her husband just as desperately.

She was being so very selfish, she knew. And deep inside she felt such shame. But since she had been so very young when Arthur had courted and then married her, she knew no other life. And fear of the unknown was a powerful thing.

"What have you there?" she asked, nodding at Isabel's hands.

"We'll visit that in a moment. I spoke with Tom this morning as we broke fast. He tells me that he sees no reason why you are not up and about by now."

"What business is it of yours?"

"Probably none. But the day-to-day running of Camelot is your business. And your servants are feeling lost without your steadying presence. They are concerned and confused. They need you, Gwen."

"You know this how?"

"During our daily recesses I hear things."

Gwen sat up further in her bed. "You have continued with the recesses without my consent?"

"You were in no shape to give consent."

"Does Arthur know about this?"

"He does. He has no objections. But the point is, your people miss you, Gwen. It would do them a world of good to see you up and about."

"Why has Arthur not voiced this opinion?"

"Because he is concerned for your health. He is not a healer. He doesn't know that, for whatever reason, you are staying abed long after you have needed to do so."

"But you do."

"Well, Tom does."

"My chest is still quite sore, and I hear I have you to thank for that."

"You're welcome."

"I did not mean that in a nice way."

"I knew that. I recognize sarcasm when I hear it."

Gwen knew she was being petty. In fact, she was aware that if not for this woman's ministrations, she might not have survived. She lowered her eyes. "I am so sorry. That was mean."

"No apologies necessary. I understand that illness tends to make people not themselves. You are a very nice woman, Gwen, with a big heart. I . . . we . . . that is Tom does not understand why you are not itching to get out of that bed and get back to the business of being queen."

"Why does this matter to you?"

"Because I hate to see your servants worry. They feel adrift without their queen's guiding hand."

"I will consider what you say. However, I would like to hear the same from Arthur's lips."

"Arthur is not going to demand that you get up. He also has his hands full preparing for the meeting of the knights. But he could certainly use your help in that matter."

Gwen nodded. "I see."

"There is also the matter of the wedding between James and Mary. Plans to be made. A menu to prepare. Tell me, is there nothing more fun than helping a bride to prepare for the most important day of her life?"

"'Tis a lot of fun," Gwen said.

"It sure is. Do you really want to miss out on that?"

Gwen cocked her head. "Tell me, Countess, why you have never married."

"I'm very picky."

"Does that mean you do not ever want to be wed?"

Isabel seemed to hesitate. "I don't rule anything out. Perhaps. Someday."

"Just waiting for the right man?"

"Something like that."

"All right, Countess, you have made your point and I have much to mull over. Now please tell me what is in your hands."

Isabel held up the black garment. "Your breeches."

Gwen nearly choked. "Breeches?"

"Yes, remember, right before you became ill, you had the seamstresses busy making breeches for the women?"

Gwen frowned. "Yes, yes, I have a vague memory of that."

"Well, these were made for you, in case you decide to join us at recess."

Rubbing her temples, Gwen asked, "Remind me again why we decided breeches for women was a good idea."

"So that they have more freedom during their morning recess. They do not have to worry about displaying more of their legs or worse while they play."

"Do you wear these breeches?"

Isabel grinned and lifted her skirts. Yes, indeed, she was sporting a pair of these things. She laid the pants at the foot of Gwen's bed. "We will be gathering in the bailey in a short while, should you decide to join us." She nodded her head and moved to leave.

"Isabel?"

She glanced over her shoulder. "Yes?"

"May I ask a favor?"

"Of course."

"Can you find Jenny and let her know I have need of her services?"

Isabel smiled. "Gladly. Welcome back, Gwen."

"Thank you."

"So?" Mary asked as the women gathered round.

Isabel shrugged. "We shall see."

"Whate'er," Madeline, one of the cooks said. "We thank you for trying."

"Thank me if it works."

"What are we doing today, mum?"

"We are playing a thing called baseball. Well, a Camelot version of baseball," she amended.

As she went to place the four small rushes around the yard, she explained, "We will divide into two teams. The teams take turns being the ones trying to score points and the ones trying to keep the other team from scoring points.

"The team trying to score points will send one player at a time to here," she said, dropping one of the rushes on the ground. "This is called home base. The player will toss a rock as far as she wants, but try to keep it from heading straight to a member of the other team, who will be scattered around the other bases, trying to defend—"

"Mum!" Mary squealed, then nodded her head toward the far side of the bailey. "The queen. She is coming."

Sure enough, Gwen came running over, holding up her skirts just enough that Isabel caught a glimpse of black beneath them.

Everyone in the bailey seemed to freeze as they watched their queen join the ladies.

They all curtsied and remained in that position, heads down.

"Please rise," Gwen said. "We have games to play. So what have I missed?"

JAMES came rushing into Arthur's working study without knocking. Arthur was about to chastise him for the unannounced interruption, but the look on his man's face stopped him. "What is it?"

"Sir, you must come see this."

"What?"

"I cannot explain. Well, I might try, but trust me, you will want to witness for yourself."

Arthur rose quickly and followed James out the door and through the great hall and out into the bailey.

He stopped short as he watched one young girl running around in a circle while others around her tossed a stone to one another and tried to chase the girl down.

There were squeals of delight and clapping and cheering. It appeared to be some sort of game Arthur had ne'er before seen.

His eyes sought out Isabel, because as certain as he was breathing was he that this was her doing. She was clapping, then cupped her hands around her mouth. "Try for third, Sarah! You can make it!"

The running girl, who was also laughing with glee, touched her foot on a mat of sorts and then kept on running as the stone was thrown all about. "What in blazes are they doing, James?"

"'Tis a game the countess calls Camelot baseball."

"Camelot baseball," Arthur repeated.

Over the last several days, he had watched as Isabel had engaged the servants in increasingly stranger and stranger play. This one, by far, was the strangest.

And yet the ladies appeared to be having such fun. "You were right, James, you could not have described this to me. It is too priceless not to see it for myself."

Without taking his eyes from the bizarre scene before him, he asked, "Is it true that our men seem to be happy with this playtime arrangement?"

"Oh, indeed, sir. They report that their wives and sweethearts seem to be in much happier moods, that they seem to have an extra skip to their steps."

"Do you see this in Mary?"

"My Mary has always had a skip to her step, but yea, I see her joy and excitement when she tells me of her day. She also reports that productivity in the kitchens, in the laundering rooms and in the sewing room has risen, as the women get back to work with a newfound vigor. I would report, sir, that this recess time appears to be a great success."

"Leave it to Isabel," Arthur said, smiling slightly. "She seems to infuse enthusiasm wherever she goes with her creativity."

He almost laughed out loud at the understatement. As much as he woke each morning, excited to get to work, to start a new day afresh, he also could not wait for night to fall, so that he could join Isabel in her quarters. And 'twas not just the lovemaking that he treasured, but also the times when they lay in each other's arms, speaking quietly of their days. He found himself more and more seeking her counsel on matters important to him. She was an avid listener, with a quick mind, grasping concepts he was certain she had never needed to confront or consider in the peaceful lands of Dumont.

Her ideas were as inspired as they were—what was that word she used? Oh, yes. Quirky. She often prefaced a sentence with, "This might sound quirky, but hear me out . . ."

More often than not, her thoughts made him laugh, but then the more he pondered, the more he would see the merit in them. Or at least slight variations. But they always, always provoked thought.

He loved that so much about her. He also loved her passion in bed sport. One touch from him in just the right place and she would immediately turn into the eager lover. He craved the moment he would get her naked, save for that blue necklace, which as far as he knew, she never, ever took off.

Her skin, so soft and creamy—

He realized suddenly that James had said something and he had not heard.

"I am sorry, what?"

"I said do you see, sir, anyone else familiar amongst the women?"

Arthur peered closer at all the others. Most were familiar, of course. He had too many servants to count, but he made it a mission to know as many by name as possible. To his way of thinking, they deserved that much, if not more, from their king, who they served so faithfully and with little complaint.

"I see many familiar faces, James. Anyone in particular you would like me to notice?"

"Look at the one in the pale yellow gown. The one chasing Mary at the moment."

Arthur glanced at the woman. And froze. The long auburn hair, the slight figure. "Gwen?"

"Indeed, my king. The queen has arisen from her sickbed."

"Oh, thank the gods," Arthur said, his voice low.

But her obvious good health was a bit too suspiciously miraculous. As he did every morning afore he headed off to exercises, this morn he had stopped by to inquire of her health. Just as the mornings before, she had appeared pale and fragile and acted as if she felt too weak to rise up and dress and go about her duties as queen. Although, as was the case day in and day out, she made attempts to lure him into her bed with her.

It was becoming increasingly difficult to mask his revulsion at the thought. When had all attraction for his wife dried to nothing but a pile of dust? He knew not. He could not lay it all on Isabel's door, as he had already begun to lose interest before Isabel's arrival. The hurt had remained, but the desire had waned before. Because as sure as he knew his own name, he knew that if he had still been passionate about Gwen, he would not have given Isabel a second glance. He was a one-woman man that way, always had been. Once his heart was engaged, he had eyes for no woman save the one who held his love and desire in her hands.

He shook his head.

On the one hand, he was relieved that Gwen had regained her good health. However, knowing she was bedridden had given him the freedom to move about as he pleased. Now that she was back on her feet, he knew that his movements would be watched much more carefully by his wife. 'Twas a conundrum. He would need to discuss it with Isabel later.

"Well, it is good to see she is better," he said. Then he looked closer. "Ye gads. She is also wearing those black leggings things that the others wear during sport."

"Mary told me this morn that Isabel was determined to lure Gwen up out of her bed and hoped that the leggings would entice her to rise up and join the staff for the recess time."

"Hmm, I wonder why?" he mumbled, not realizing he'd actually spoken aloud until James answered him.

"It seems that the servants met and discussed the problems with their queen. Since Isabel is the one that they have been turning to to find answers for questions that arose around the castle, they believed perhaps Isabel would be the logical choice to approach the queen."

"Isabel has been handling some of Gwen's duties?" Arthur asked.

"You have not noticed?"

"I must be blind," Arthur said, wanting to kick himself in the ass. "No, I did not notice, and Isabel has made not a single complaint at being forced to take over tasks that are not her concern. She is a guest at this castle, for Thor's sake."

"I do not notice the countess complaining about much," James offered. "Save perhaps whatever happened betwixt the two of you, nights ago."

Arthur rolled his eyes. "Do you know what a major fault of mine is, James?"

"No, King Arthur, I know of none."

"That I allow my most trusted men to speak their minds."

James roared with laughter. "My apologies," he said. "For speaking out of turn."

Arthur looked at him. "You appear not one whit sorry."

"I will work on my contrite expression."

Arthur clapped James on the back. "You do that. 'Twill probably take years of practice."

With one last glance toward the women, lingering longest, of course, on the one with long blond hair who was now being chased down by several of the servants, Arthur turned and headed back to his study, James's laughter still ringing in his ears. Yes, indeed, he and Isabel had much to discuss this evening. Should he be able to get her alone.

The thought that he might fail in that endeavor was truly depressing.

THERE was a time when Gwen would have thought nothing of entering Arthur's study without announcing herself, but she was acutely aware that many things had changed between them. So even though his door was open, she knocked. He glanced up from a scroll he was studying intently. The parchment appeared to be a detailed drawing of a map.

He rolled it up, set it aside and stood. "Gwen," he said, gesturing her in, "it is good to see you up and about. I trust you are feeling better."

"Very much, Arthur, thank you."

He waved her into a chair, waiting for her to be seated before he returned to his own seat. "What, do you suppose, helped . . . cure you of your ailments?"

"I am certain the countess has already informed you of our chat."

"Actually, no. I have not spoken with Isabel at all since breaking fast."

"Oh."

"Why, what has she to do with your recovery?"

Truth was truly Gwen's only choice. Arthur could always tell when Gwen was hiding something from him. He had known, almost immediately, about Lance. Oh, not that she and Lance had become . . . intimately involved, but he had known there was something amiss. "She came to see me in our . . . in my chambers this morning. We had a talk."

"Talking cured you, then? We must bottle this and sell it to our healers."

"Please, Arthur, do not make this harder than it is."

He nodded. "My apologies. That was uncalled for. Do you wish to share what transpired?"

"She . . . made me very aware that I was letting you down. I was letting Camelot and its people down by shirking my duties."

"Do you feel she overstepped her bounds?"

"Yes. I mean no." She shook her head. "She appears to be the only one brave enough to tell me some truths I needed to hear."

Arthur peered at her. "I could swear there is a veiled insult toward me in there somewhere, but as you have just recovered from a nasty poisoning, I will overlook it."

"No, no, 'twas not meant as one at all. You are trusting, Arthur. If I tell you I am still not feeling well, you will accept it to be so."

"Why the ruse, Gwen? What was there to gain?"

She stared down at her hands. "Perhaps to gain your attention."

"You did not have to feign illness, Gwen. You have but to ask."

"I am asking."

"And at this moment," he said, rising and moving to the door, closing it, "you have my undivided attention." He returned to his desk and sat. "What is on your mind?"

"You have been a wonderful husband, Arthur. Loving and

attentive, patient as I learned the ways of the crown. You have been nothing but good to me."

"I am very glad you think so."

"And I repaid that with a betrayal that I regret deeply. If I were able to turn back time—"

"'Twould have changed nothing. It was fate that you and Lance fall in love. I could no more prevent that from happening than I can prevent rain or snow."

"We could—"

"No," he interrupted, "we cannot. You are still in love with Lance, as he is with you. Desperately so, as a matter of fact. Should you deny that now I will lose what little respect I have left for you. Not to mention I will never forgive you should you shatter Lance's heart. I do not blame him. I blame you not, either." He raised his hands and shrugged. "It just happened, Gwen. But that young man means a great deal to me, and I will look very poorly upon anyone who would harm him in any way."

"So you still care about him but not your wife?"

"Gwen, if I did not care, you would be answering to a charge of treason right now. As I have said to you, too many times to count, I do not care what you and Lance do. I care only that you not be caught by any person who would have no trouble accusing you of crimes against the king. Right now there is no legal remedy here in Camelot for the predicament we find ourselves in. Although I am looking very seriously into a system they have in Dumont, where they may call for dissolution of marriage where neither man nor wife must admit to blame. I believe Countess Isabel calls it 'no-fault dissolution.'"

"You have discussed the intimate details of our situation with the countess?"

"I admit that I have."

"How dare you?"

"I dare, Guinevere, because I trust her. I trust her thoughts and opinions."

She covered her flaming cheeks. "I am so . . . mortified that you shared something so personal with a virtual stranger."

"She is no stranger. Whilst you were lying in bed, feigning illness, she has become a friend and colleague."

Gwen stared at him and the truth cut deeply. "You have fallen in love with her."

He hesitated only a moment before nodding. "That, yes, is true."

"Does she realize?"

"I have a fair feeling that she is well aware, yes."

"Does she . . . return your feelings for her?"

"I desperately hope that she does."

"How dare you . . . shame me like this? How dare she come as a welcome guest only to—"

He pounded a fist on his desk, and the fire in his eyes had her shrinking back in her chair. "I dare you to finish that thought, Gwen. I dare you to logically finish that thought."

She kept silent as he leaned forward, drilling her with his gaze. "What happened with Isabel was not planned or expected. Just as with you and Lance, it was fated to be. Would I change it if I could, as you seem to want to dismiss history? Not one chance in Hades. Other than that pesky problem that I am not free to ask her to marry me, I would not change a single thing."

In the past, tears had always melted Arthur's heart. Gwen knew they no longer had the power to move him. At least not her own tears. *I will not cry. I will not cry.*

"If not for what happened with Lance . . ."

"But it did."

"But if it did not?"

"Isabel would merely be another royal guest. Is that what you want to hear? That I would ne'er have betrayed my vows? If so, you would be right. I would most likely have looked upon her as another fresh mind to add to the mix of those who will gather here to meet and exchange ideas. But I already knew, Gwen. I already had my heart broken by you. When I saw her, I recognized that I had gotten over the heartbreak. And I felt free to want another."

"I see."

"I have no desire to hurt you, Gwen. This is not some kind of revenge. Had you not asked, I would not have said a word, as it is no one's business but mine and Isabel's. But you asked. And as you know, I value truth. And you deserve as much."

She took a breath and squared her shoulders. "I realize my next question will sound selfish and self-serving, Arthur, but I must ask. Should there come a time when we are able to accomplish this no-fault, what will happen to me? What will happen to Lance?"

"You two will be free to marry."

"But where? And how?"

"I have thought of this. If Lancelot prefers to stay in Briton, rather than return to his homeland, then I will lease land to the two of you, over which you will preside as leaders of whate'er you call it. You may start a new life together."

She swallowed, hard. "But—"

"I anticipate your next question and will not allow you to humiliate yourself by forcing you to ask. I will take care of you for the rest of your days, Gwen. I will not leave you destitute. You will always be kept in comfort. That portion of my promises to you I will keep. I have no wish to see you struggle."

"Lance will not allow us to be on your dole, Arthur."

"Should he stay as a soldier at Camelot, he will be recompensed well. He is, after all, one of my finest and most loyal." His smile was sadly cynical. "On the battlefield."

"He loves you as a father, Arthur. It tears him up inside."

"You may or may not take this as true, Gwen, but I believe that with everything in me. Did I not believe it, he would no longer be drawing breath."

Gwen rose on shaky legs. "Believe this, Arthur. I also love you."

"I believe that as well."

"For then I would also not be drawing breath."

"There is no chance I would have you harmed, Gwen. I cannot say as much for those so loyal that they would seek vengeance for their king."

She shuddered. "All right, Arthur, so what now? How do we go forward from this moment?"

"You are queen. As such, you will attend to the duties asked of you in that capacity. To all around, nothing has changed."

"Yes."

"You have always been an excellent queen, Gwen. Do not begin to fake it now."

"Yes, I understand."

"Discretion, Gwen. Discretion."

"Yes."

"And, please, no more experiments with new foods. I truly do not want a repeat of the mushrooms. Most importantly, do not ever attempt to try them in foods being served to all."

"I will not."

Arthur stood. "One last thought, Gwen, that I must insist you carry with you at all times."

"Yes?"

"Isabel saved your life. But not for her quick ministrations, we would not be having this conversation."

"I am aware."

"Whether you believe it or nay, she does truly care about you. She sympathizes with all of the twisted emotions swirling around us all. Should anything untoward happen to her, should I even see an unexplained scratch upon her person, you will see wrath as you have ne'er even imagined."

Finally the tears Gwen had been trying so desperately to blink back came to surface. "She saved my life once days ago, Arthur. She came to me this morn to attempt to save it once again. This I will ne'er forget."

"I hope you do not. As strange as this might sound to you, she would make an excellent friend and ally."

"And as strange as this may sound, Arthur, I would so very much like to make her both."

He nodded, walking her to the door. "You will not be sorry."

"I will not let on that I know of this love betwixt you."

"No need to. I shall tell her this evening. As you should tell Lance."

She nodded, then squeezed the back of his hand. "This time I shall not disappoint you."

She started to leave and then turned back. "Do any of the servants know?"

"Why ask you this?"

"So I am fully aware of who I may speak frankly in front of."

"James and Mary. They know. At least, I am presuming so." His lips tipped up in a slight grin. "They intervened in a rather amusing way when Isabel and I had a slight misunderstanding."

She nodded, although she could not believe all that had transpired as she lounged in her bed. "I am thinking it would make a good tale one day."

"It would indeed."

She waved toward his desk. "I will leave you to your planning. And I thank you, Arthur, for your honesty and your . . . compassion."

"And I thank you, as well, for your honesty this day. I wish you happiness, Gwen. I truly do."

"I know. I wish the same for you."

ARTHUR closed the door behind Gwen, because privacy was something he craved as he pondered all that had just been said.

"I will take 'The Most Happy Man in Camelot at This Moment' for a thousand, Alex," he whispered.

"Who is King Arthur?" he answered himself. "Correct!"

He shook his head, smiling, as he unrolled the parchment. "Isabel, my love, you have most certainly made me batty."

CHAPTER TWENTY-TWO

Once again, Gwen found herself outside of a door, ready to knock. It simply baffled her, the sense of humility she had learned to possess, just since the morning. This day had been trying, fun, enlightening, heartbreaking, and it was not even half over.

She heard laughter behind the door and hesitated.

"He did not!" she heard a young female voice say. "You jest."

"I kid you not. And then he attempted a kiss."

That voice she easily marked as Isabel's.

"After tossing a toad down your bodice?"

Gwen seriously doubted the two were discussing Arthur. Though he loved a good jest, a toad in a woman's bosom did not sound like his sense of fun.

"It was his way of showing affection, I suppose," Isabel said. "After all, we were eight at most."

"It sounds to me, lady, that his attempt at courting was somewhat misguided."

"You think? I thought it such a loving gesture."

The two women again broke into laughter. Gwen almost hated to ruin the mood. But more, she had hopes she would be included in the enjoyment.

She knocked.

As she feared, the laughter ceased instantly.

"Come in," Isabel called.

Gwen opened the door and stepped through. The two were seated on the floor and Isabel was doing a staining thing on Mary's toes. Half were painted a rose color.

"I am sorry to interrupt," she said.

Mary scrambled to her feet and curtsied. "Your Highness!"

"Please sit, Mary," Gwen said, "do not let me interrupt . . . whatever that is you are doing."

Isabel smiled at her. "We are experimenting with ways to make Mary the prettiest she can be on the night of her vows ceremony."

"May I join you? And please, Mary, resume what you were doing. I am quite curious of this fun."

Isabel smiled at her. "Of course you may. The more the merrier, right, Mary?"

Mary glanced nervously between them. Gwen nodded. "Sit, Mary. As a matter of fact, I was hoping you would be here. We have a wedding to plan. And I am very interested in watching and learning this practice."

Mary said, "I will sit when you do, Your Highness."

"Would you like to wager upon which of us manages to sit our backsides down first?"

Mary giggled, and Isabel laughed, which for some reason did Gwen's heart good. She had taken time to ponder all that had occurred this day, all that she had needed to face about herself, about all that she had to do to make things right.

Finally she thumped down onto the floor and waved Mary down. "Please, sit."

"May I get you anything, Your Highness?"

Gwen looked to Isabel. "Is it just me or does this 'Your Highness,' 'your Countess,' 'your whatever' tend to get old?"

Isabel looked at her, and the smile that lit her face made Gwen's heart proud. "It gets pretty tedious, indeed," Isabel agreed.

"Just Gwen, okay? At least amongst us girls. I understand the reluctance while others are around, but here, now, it is just Gwen."

Mary appeared horrified. "Oh, I could never."

Isabel rolled her eyes at Gwen. "It took me days and plenty of threats. She will give in eventually."

Gwen smiled. She was not angry at Isabel. How could she be? Arthur had been right. Her anger at his infidelity was hypocrisy at its most severe. And she loved her husband enough that after the hurt and anger came the realization that he was such a good man and deserved a woman worthy of him.

Her question to herself had been, would she take back all that had happened . . . that she had made happen . . . to save the life she lived? The answer was no. She could no more take back her love and attraction to Lance as she could reach out and bring down the moon.

"I would love some wine, Mary," she said.

"There is some right here," Mary said.

"No!" Gwen said, rising again. "I shall pour for the two of you. And for me, of course."

As she rose, Gwen witnessed the astonished glances exchanged between the two women, and smiled to herself. She was enjoying this immensely. "Please, explain to me this toe-staining thing."

"It is simply a fun thing," Isabel said. "It makes a woman's toes prettier."

"Where did this come from? Did you bring it from Dumont?"

"Actually, no, we had to experiment until we had the formula right. We colored water with flowers, then we added corn starch to make it sticky enough to adhere."

"Adhere?"

"Stick," Mary said. "So that it will dry and remain upon the nails."

Gwen returned and handed Isabel a goblet, and then held out the other to Mary.

Mary looked to Isabel who nodded. "Just this once and just a little. Just because this seems like we are having a girls' day this afternoon."

Mary smiled and accepted the goblet. "I thank you so much, Your—"

"Gwen. And as I am your queen, you must needs listen to what I ask. I ask that you call me by my given name. As you do Countess Isabel."

Isabel stared at Gwen, who smiled back at her.

Oh boy. She didn't know how Gwen had learned, but in her gut she was absolutely certain Gwen had learned.

"You know," she whispered.

Gwen sat down, a goblet in her own hand. "I do."

"But how?"

Mary's eyes darted back and forth between them, filled with worry. "I do not know of what you speak," she said, "but I swear, Isabel, that I have ne'er repeated a word of the talks between us to anyone. Save . . . oh, no! James?"

"Settle, Mary. 'Twas Arthur himself who told me," Gwen said. "He was, as always, honest to a fault."

Isabel nearly keeled over. Arthur admitted . . . she did not know what. Perhaps that they were merely lovers? That he—

"That he is in love with you, Isabel."

Mary just stared, mute. Then she said, "Mayhap I should go check on . . . something."

"Sit," Isabel and Gwen said in unison.

Gwen laughed. "Betimes honesty is overrated, do you not think so? Today it was not. 'Twas what I needed to be told. He understood that, as he seems always able to do."

"I am so, so very sorry, Gwen," Isabel managed to squeak out. "I never meant . . . it was never meant . . ."

"Sorry? For following your heart? For making a very wonderful man happy again, for the first time in many days? Do you think I fault you? Would I be here, sharing time with you if I had ill intentions or thoughts?"

It occurred to Isabel that Gwen had just recently insisted on pouring the wine. She looked down into her goblet.

Gwen watched with a smile on her face. Then she reached over and traded goblets, downing a good bit of liquid before trading back. "No, Isabel, I am not intent on poisoning you. Arthur made it clear that if he sees even a scratch upon your skin, he will make people pay. And by people, he means me. And by pay, he means with my life. As I have no desire to incur his wrath, please trust that I will ne'er, e'er harm you."

"You will not," Mary said hotly. "I will not allow it."

That was a bold move for a servant at Camelot. Alarming in fact. "Calm down, Mary. Gwen is here to discuss your wedding, is that not right, Gwen?"

"That is right. However, I would very much love to get involved with this toe-painting thing afore we get to the specifics of the menu. I have a . . . meeting this night and would very much enjoy surprising him."

Mary and Isabel exchanged glances. Finally Mary said, "Then, Your Highness, I suggest you remove your slippers."

"If you are to paint my toes, Mary, I insist you call me Gwen."

"As I have also insisted to Isabel, m'lady, only amongst us. Never, ever among others. Please do not insist so when the three of us are not alone."

Gwen shot a questioning glance at Isabel.

"Her friends, if you can actually call them that, have been shunning her out of jealousy."

"Jealousy?"

"They believe she is marrying above herself, as James is such a high-ranking soldier in Arthur's army. And though Mary has never lorded it over them, they are still envious."

Mary took a sip of wine. "Some also envy that I was assigned to look after the countess."

"Like that's been a real plumb job, eh, Mary?" Isabel teased.

"That is horrid!" Gwen said. "Oh, Mary, is there naught that I can do?"

"I believe we can shove that envy down their throats by throwing Mary and James a beautiful and unforgettable exchanging of vows."

"And that we will do. Allow them to choke on their jealousy."

Isabel raised her brows at Gwen.

"Hey!" Gwen said, holding her goblet in the air. "Have I poisoned you as yet?"

"Good point," Isabel said, toasting and taking another sip of her wine.

By the time the three of them had finished polishing their toenails, they had had interruptions from Jenny, James, Tom and Hester the Jester. Why Hester felt the need to interrupt, Isabel had no idea. They were all giggling, lying on their backs, flailing their legs in the air, trying to dry this homemade concoction.

When there was yet another knock, Isabel had just about had it. "What?" she yelled. "Good gods, it's like Grand Central Station around here."

"May I enter?"

The three looked at one another, obviously recognizing the voice. They all sat up and rearranged their skirts.

"Isabel, I need to see you, to talk to you," Arthur said. "Please allow me entrance."

"Come on in, Arthur," she said. "It is unlocked."

He opened the door and then nearly gaped as he took in at the sight of them all on the floor.

"I am sorry," he said. "I did not mean to interrupt . . . whate'er this might be. I believe I do not even want to know what this might be."

"Girly stuff," Isabel said. "We have been planning Mary's wedding."

He looked as uncomfortable as a perfectly fat and healthy chicken inside a KFC.

Gwen stood up, a little wobbly, perhaps. "Mary and I were about to take a walk to finish drying our toes, were we not, Mary?"

She held out her arm, and Mary gladly, it appeared, grabbed hold. "I believe we were, Your Highness."

Mary performed a quick curtsy as she passed by Arthur. "My king."

"Oh, please, cut it out, Mary," he said. "We are friends. Stop the groveling."

She nodded. "I apologize, King Arthur."

Arthur actually growled, but he held open the door as both Mary and Gwen ducked under his arm and, from the sound of it, ran down the hall. And then he nearly slammed it shut.

"What is happening, Isabel?"

"Mary and I were having a girlie moment, and Gwen asked to join. Why do you look so upset? Nothing wrong happened here. We were having fun."

"Gwen knows of us."

"And guess what, I know of that. She told me."

"She did?"

"Indeed. In fact, she was very accepting of the situation. So why are you upset?"

"I feared . . . well, was concerned . . ."

"Hey, I'm still here, Arthur. Gwen is not the murdering kind. You must know that. You would not have married a woman whose heart you believed to be cruel. You never would."

"I would hope not. But with you I cannot begin to take the chance."

"I love you, Arthur."

"And I, you, Isabel."

"Leg up?" Isabel asked, holding out her arm.

"What?"

"Just a saying. Meaning please help me to my feet."

He took her arm, and as he brought her up to him, he wrapped an arm around her and lifted her.

Still inches from the ground, she wrapped her arms around his neck and kissed him.

"Oh, Isabel," he said moments later. "To my dying breath, I will ne'er stop desiring your touch and your kisses." He lowered her slowly, which was his intent, as she slid down the front of his body in the most sensual way.

"Why did you, Arthur?"

"Why did I what?"

"Why did you tell Gwen?"

He brushed hair from her cheek. "She deserved the truth."

"You could have said nothing."

"That might have been an option. But what does that say about me, Isabel? Would you have me hide my love for you?"

She butted his chest with her head. "If this gets out, she and Lance could be in trouble, as all of the truth will get out. Don't you think that James would spill the truth because of his loyalty to you? There is no way he would allow you to take the blame."

"He will if I command so."

"And will you? Will you, for lack of a better term, fall on the sword?"

"No. If it comes to that, no."

"How do you know?"

"That is an easy one."

"Which is?"

"Take that one for a thousand, Isabel."

She laughed. "I will take that for a thousand, Arthur."

"The woman who Arthur, King of Camelot, has come to love so much that he will do anything to protect her from harm."

Melt. Melt. Melt. Why couldn't love come easily?

"That is a simple one," she said when she relearned the fine art of breathing. "It would be, 'Who is Arthur's beloved and besotted beagle, Pix, who follows him everywhere.'"

"Wrong, my lady, although I admit Pix would be a close second. I give you another chance."

"Pix would be a close second?"

"Lady, you would jump in front of an arrow to save Burny."

"Oh, but he is a dog like no other. Truthfully. He is a dog like no other. And I mean that in the most, 'what in hell is he, exactly,' way."

Arthur laughed and hugged her even closer. "No one knows. We do not question, we just constantly look forward to whate'er pups come about."

"He is so sweet."

"And he follows you around as if you were indeed his mother."

"I did not realize you had noticed."

"I thought I noticed every single piece of what happens around you, Isabel. Though I must admit I did not see today coming. I failed this day."

"What? In what way?"

"I ignored the obvious, while you saw it and took action."

"You mean with Gwen?"

"Yes."

"You did what any good husband would do. I just happened to talk to Tom, and then talked to Gwen."

"Which should have been my responsibility."

"You didn't fail, Arthur. How many burdens are you supposed to take on? Not that Gwen is a burden. We have been enjoying the afternoon. She has been delightful, Arthur. I don't know what exchange there was between you, but she holds no bitterness at all that I noticed. In fact, she seems more at peace than I have seen her since meeting her."

"She truly is a good woman," Arthur said. "Just so very young. I do not know what I was thinking." He kissed her again. "But no matter. I just had need to see you and make certain all was well."

"Are you relieved or saddened by your talk with Gwen?"

"Much of the former, a little of the latter."

"Understandable, Arthur."

"And then I had this burning desire to check on your welfare. Not that I believe . . . well, that is a very lame excuse. I just wanted to see you."

"Oh, Arthur," she said, brushing his hair away from his temple. Wow, it had grown so much in just days. "You have many, many issues to deal with at the moment. I should be the least of your worries."

"Worry was the pretense. Seeing you was the need."

"We will see each other later. You need to get back to what you most treasure."

He stared down at her. "Isabel, if I have not made this clear, you are what I treasure above all else."

"Camelot—"

"Is but a place. Yes, I love Camelot. But am I able to hold Camelot at night? Am I able to lie with it and share what has happened on any given day? I will, without even a moment's thought, give it up for the rest of my days if every moment of those days be spent with you."

"Oh, Arthur, I would never ask."

"Of course you would not. Another reason why I love you, Isabel. But do not ever doubt my priorities." He kissed her, and then let go. "You have not correctly questioned my answer," he said.

Isabel stood totally dazed, confused and with a heart filled with so much emotion, she didn't know what to deal with first.

"I forget the answer," she finally said.

"I will repeat. 'The woman who Arthur, King of Camelot, has come to love so much that he will do anything to protect her from harm.'" He grinned. "The first response was slightly insulting, as it was a slobbering dog. I will, however, forgive that one and allow another choice."

"Who is Countess Isabel?" she whispered.

"Oh, so correct, Isabel."

"I have one for you."

He smiled. "As you say many a time, hit me."

"The woman who refuses to allow you to give up your lands, your dream, your love just for her. The woman who is so ready to follow you into battle to keep the dream of Camelot alive."

He took her face in his hands. "The question would be, Who is the one I would hold captive afore I e'er allowed her to run into harm's way on my behalf? It will not happen, Isabel. I cannot even believe of such."

"Has it ever occurred to you that women could actually help behind the lines? Allow us to take part."

"No. I will not have women harmed. And you . . . I could not live if you were harmed. I just could not."

"And yet you expect me, or any of us, to stand by and watch you be injured, or worse?"

"I do. It is what I must do. Please, Isabel, do not make me worry about you, should it come to this. I could not do my job."

"Is it coming to this?"

He hesitated, but finally nodded. "It appears a possibility. Those not invited to the table have banded together, according to reports. We must prepare."

"Then we will."

"Isabel, no."

"I will not allow anyone to harm you without a fight. Wouldn't you do the same for me?"

"'Tis not the same."

"It is exactly the same. If you think women are incapable of doing what they must to protect their king, their castle, their life, then you are underestimating us all."

"I do not underestimate. I have need to protect. You, most of all."

"How much time do we have?" she asked.

"Isabel—"

"How much time, Arthur?"

"My best estimate with my men's information is three weeks. We believe they plan to attack when all of the knights invited to the table have gathered."

"That sounds like a pretty stupid plan to me."

"Not should there be traitors sitting amongst us."

"Do you know which?"

"I have a fair idea."

Isabel growled. "The women will not only aid, we are going to kick ass."

"Isabel."

"Yes, Arthur?"

"You excite me and drive fear into me at one and the same time."

"I hope you bring the excitement with you this evening. The fear, allow me to take care of that."

"Isabel, I am to protect you."

She thumped his arm. "Just for once, Arthur, get used to the idea that women can be very useful in taking care of their men. Just once."

"I will not allow you to go into battle, should this attack occur. Isabel, please, I cannot even stomach the possibility. I love you. Do you not ken?"

"Oh, yes, I ken. How about if I promise that none of us, not a single woman, actually enters any type of battlefield?"

He peered at her. "You have a sneaky plan, Isabel."

She offered him the falsest innocent face imaginable. "I swear, I truly swear, that we will not enter the field of battle."

"You have another plan."

"I swear, I swear we will not enter the field of battle."

"I do not know whether to laugh or shake with worry."

"I choose Laugh for one thousand, Alex."

"Isabel, I could not bear if anything happened to you. The love I have for you is . . . just so . . . I cannot even describe the feelings. I only know that should I lose you after I have just found you, I . . . I cannot imagine going on."

She chuckled as she looked up into his hard, warm, worried face. "I am not the one readying herself for battle, Arthur. How do you think I feel, knowing you are?"

"'Tis what I do."

"Oh, yes, 'tis what you do. And I am supposed to smile, pack you a lunch, send you off and say, 'Hope you're still alive by supper, Arthur. It would be such a shame to waste your favorite meal. However, Pix might enjoy it.'"

He glared at her for a moment, and then just laughed. He pulled her close. "This has been the strangest conversation I have e'er had. I love you so much."

"As you should," she said, still feeling grumpy and afraid. She'd had no idea that danger might be close at hand. He had managed to keep that little piece of information close to the vest. Or tunic. Or chain stuff. "We will not sit by, Arthur. We have ways."

"Should it come to this, I will not allow women to rush in. And most definitely not my woman."

"Women will not join in the stupid wars you men fight."

"Meaning what?"

"We are much more resourceful than you think."

"Betimes you worry me, Countess."

"I should worry you at all times."

"This is what concerns me."

"As well it should."

"May I see you tonight?" he asked.

"What is, 'The woman who wants to be with Arthur tonight more than any other on this earth.' For a thousand, Alex."

He grinned down at her. "I have yet to figure a thousand what. However, I just won them."

"For a thousand. I really, truly want to hear it from your lips."

"Who is the woman Arthur loves and desires beyond all others?"

"Oh, that is so correct. Double bonus for you."

"Tonight, then, Isabel?"

"Oh, yes, please."

As he left the room, she heard him say, "I do hope your toes have dried by now, Mary. And yours as well, Gwen."

"We must move up the date of your wedding, Mary," Isabel said, even as she was getting over total embarrassment. Good gods, they had been right outside of the door. Both, however returned as if they had heard nothing. And then the three of them looked at each other, and once again could not contain their humor. They laughed, but then sobered when she said, "The women of Camelot . . . and guests such as myself," she added, nodding to Gwen, "need to prepare to protect the men. I have a plan. Or a partial one. We need to scheme, and we need to involve all of the servants to pull it off."

She held up her hand. "Are we in?"

"I am," Mary said, joining hands.

"As am I," said Gwen, clasping both of her hands around theirs.

"Good, because, Gwen, to pull this off, I need you to put on that crown and use it for all it's worth."

"Consider it donned."

"Good. Mary, how would you like to marry James day after tomorrow?"

Mary's eyes widened. "Are you jesting?"

"No. Your dress is ready, is it not?"

"It is."

"I can take care of the feast," Isabel said. "Gwen, you have such a touch with flowers and decoration. You can make the hall lovely, I trust."

"Oh, yes."

"Excellent. Tomorrow, I fear, game time is going to be spent airing out those rushes and scrubbing the great hall. When Mary and James exchange vows, it is going to smell like spring, not like a sty."

They both nodded. "Mary, I fear you are going to have to work tomorrow. James needs a haircut, and so does Arthur."

"And Lance," Gwen said.

"And Lance. Although I must say he looks kind of cute shaggy," Isabel said.

Gwen smiled while still admiring her toes. "Yes, he does. Yet a trim could not hurt."

CHAPTER TWENTY-THREE

"M'LADY," a man said as he passed Isabel in the great hall, where she was on her knees, scrubbing the floor.

She glanced up, down, up, down, then up again. "James?"

He stopped, his face, free of hair, went a little red. "Yes, Countess."

She jumped up, pulling his burly self around to face her. "James! Oh, good gods, look at you!"

"I am not able to do that, Countess, as I am looking at you."

She laughed and wiped her brow. "Why in the world have you been hiding that handsome face behind so much . . . fur?"

"I . . . Countess, are you jesting? I feel almost disrobed."

"Holy smokes, James," Isabel said, truly shocked. Without all of that hair, he looked like a young Clooney, albeit beefier. About a foot taller. And way better. "Why have you been hiding your good looks? I mean, truly."

She was sincerely almost at a loss for words.

"I did not know I was doing such. But I appreciate it, Countess. Yet right now I feel as a newborn babe," he said, rubbing his jaw.

"Mary takes no prisoners."

"Oh, she does indeed. Right now her prisoner is the king."

She smiled. "Now I see what Mary has always seen. What a lucky bride to have such a handsome groom."

"I am the lucky one, Countess." He glanced around. "And her toes are pretty," he whispered.

"As is she."

He got a moony look on his face. "She is. I cannot thank you enough for the kindness you have shown her. She is very excited about this gown."

"She is the best kind of friend, James. I am guessing she will be that much of a friend to you, as well as your life mate."

He rubbed at his eyes. "We cannot thank you enough for your generosity."

"All I want is for the two of you to be happy. I would plant a kiss on your cheek, if I had a ladder that would help me get up there."

He surveyed the room again, and then said, "A kiss from a countess would be an honor."

He bent down and she kissed his cheek. "All good wishes, James."

"All good wishes to you and my king, Countess. I have feelings, and I know this feeling is right. You are meant for one another. As Mary and I are."

He strode away before she could utter a single word.

She shook her head and went back to scrubbing the floor. Gwen was out with several servants, all of them beating the rushes to, she hoped, a merciful death.

Although Gwen had sworn she had a formula to also relieve their miserable selves from stinking.

"Isabel!"

She nearly fell over from the shock. She looked up, and there was Arthur, clean-cut and gorgeous. "Wow," she said, standing up. "You, sir, are the most handsome king I have ever seen in my life."

"And how many kings have you seen exactly?" he asked.

None, other than Arthur of course. "Naked, you mean? That would be one."

He tried not to smile and failed miserably. "Isabel, why are you down on your hands and knees?"

"I'm cleaning. Trust me, this hall needs it badly."

"There are people to do this."

"Right. Like me. I am capable, Arthur. By the way, you look luscious."

"Do not try to distract me with words I do not ken," he said. "I want you not down on the floor."

"Too freakin' bad. I can help clean as well as anyone."

"We have people who—"

"Arthur! If I am not willing to help, what does that say about me? Do not, and I mean really, do not give me trouble for helping clean this hall."

"But there are people—"

"Do not even go there. Do you stand around as your men work out?"

"No, but—"

"Do you stand by while your men fight your battles for you?"

"No, but—"

"Then please don't be upset when I do what needs to be done. I am no better than anyone because I happened to be born into royalty." She had no idea if that was true in this alter reality, but she was going with it. "Are you any better than others because you managed to pull a sword out of a stone?"

"No, but—"

"We all bleed red, Arthur. We are the same."

"Yes, but—"

She waited, but he seemed to be stumped. "Yes, but what?"

"You missed a spot over here, Isabel."

And he walked away, into his study.

Good gods, she loved that man. She was going to kick his ass to be sure. But in the most loving way. She moved over and started scrubbing the spot she had missed.

* * *

THE wedding vows between James and Mary had Isabel almost crying. They were so true and heartfelt and Mary was a beautiful bride.

Gwen had truly outdone herself. The hall was spectacular with candles and flowers everywhere. In Isabel's day, Gwen would probably be the most successful party planner in the entire state of Oklahoma.

The results were truly breathtaking.

Isabel, obviously, had never witnessed such a ceremony. It wasn't religious, but so very spiritual.

"I do thee vow," James said.

And as his second man, Arthur stepped before them. "You will honor your wife."

"I will."

"Protect her and keep her at all costs."

"I will."

"Isabel?" he said.

She moved in front of the two and twined their hands, as was the custom.

"You will honor your husband?"

"I will."

"Protect and keep him at all costs?"

That was way off script. The wife was supposed to honor his wishes and obey his demands. But she could not have possibly choked that out of her mouth.

"She will," James chimed in before protests could begin.

"I will," Mary said.

"Excellent," Isabel said. "You are so going to live happily together." She bent and kissed Mary's cheek. "He is a lucky man, m'lady," she whispered.

Mary looked up at her and grinned. "Yes, he is."

Arthur closed the ceremony and then called for all to celebrate.

*   *   *

"WHAT in Hades was that?" Arthur asked Isabel, when he finally managed to corner her.

"What?"

"'Twas not as ceremonies go. You—"

"Went off script, yes, I know. But it was so much more truthful."

"Truthful?"

"Arthur, had you and I ever married—"

"You must mean *when* we marry."

"Okay, dream on. *When* we marry, there is no way in hell I'm promising to obey you. And there was no way I was going to ask Mary to vow to do such a thing. So I improvised."

He stared for a moment, then broke out laughing. "Oh, Isabel, you are a puzzle. And a constant delight."

"I'm taking that as a compliment. I think."

"Take it as a compliment. I think."

"Then we're good to go. Now let's go celebrate."

THE reception lasted well into the night. The food, wine and mead disappearing as fast as it was produced. To the credit of all who had to work the party, they seemed genuinely happy for Mary and James. If not, they put up a really good front. And Isabel had the feeling she knew who to thank for that.

She walked over to Gwen, who seemed to be giving Jenny a pep talk. Jenny was ringing her hands and nodding.

"Your voice is beautiful, Jenny. You will do just fine," she heard Gwen say. "Just sing it like you did this morning."

Jenny nodded a final time, then ran off.

"I must say, Lady Guinevere, your throw one hell of a party," Isabel said.

Gwen smiled at her. "*We* throw one hell of a party. I could not have done this without you."

"Or without a gazillion people helping."

Gwen laughed. "That, too."

They both looked as Jenny began singing. Oh, it was so beauti-ful. Isabel didn't know the song, but she knew a voice like no other when she heard it. All clapped at the end, as well they should have.

Wow! Impressive didn't even begin to describe it.

"She's good!"

"In many ways. She sings to me during bathing."

"Wow, lucky you!"

"Indeed."

"Speaking of which, just what did you say to the staff?" Isabel asked.

"I am certain I know not what you mean," Gwen said, swirling the wine in her goblet.

"I am certain you do."

Gwen smiled, then sipped at her wine. "I merely mentioned how thrilled I was for Mary and James, and would it not be shame-ful if others did not share in their joy this night."

Isabel nodded. "Very tactful. And effective. That was such a nice thing to do."

"'Twas the very least I could do."

"This is not the wine talking, this is me." Isabel said. "I really enjoy and admire you, Gwen. When you step up, you really step up."

Gwen's eyes welled. She glanced around. "This is not the wine talking," she said softly, "this is me. I understand, completely, why Arthur is so taken with you."

Okay, it was Isabel's turn to blink back tears. "No matter what the future holds, I hope we will always be friends, Gwen."

"That is my hope as well. Perhaps even one day pinky-finger friends."

Isabel nearly coughed up a mouthful of wine. When she finally managed to swallow, she said, "How do you like Lance's hair?"

Gwen's eyes went straight to her lover. "He does look exceed-ingly handsome, does he not?"

If you preferred the young pretty-boy types. Isabel figured that tastes differed drastically. She thought Arthur, with his rugged and oh-so-handsome good looks, was so much sexier. But at the moment she was thrilled that her idea of attractive and Gwen's were from completely different planets. "He does, indeed," she said, diplomacy being the better part of not getting her hair pulled out.

"And how about James?" she added.

"Who knew?" Gwen said.

"Mary did. She saw past all of that to his heart. But truly, he's a very attractive giant."

Gwen giggled. Then she said, "Even Mordred appears more handsome."

"He needs a few years to grow into his looks, but he really lucked out in the gene department. I look at him and see Arthur at his age."

"What did you do, Isabel?"

"What do you mean?"

"Something happened. Until recently he seemed to live to torture his father. But suddenly they are laughing and embracing. I saw them even exercising in the sword sport together just this morn. I just have this feeling that you had something to do with this transformation." She paused, sipped. "And perhaps something to do with that knee injury."

"Perhaps," Isabel said.

They glanced at each other and both started giggling. Isabel raised a fist, pinky finger out. Gwen stared for a moment, then mimicked with her own. Then they hooked up.

"This means the world to me, Isabel."

"And to me." Isabel laughed. "Is this the strangest friendship ever?"

"Very possible," Gwen said. "But rather fun, do you not think?"

"No one would ever believe it."

"Which is why it is fun."

A banging sound had them both nearly jumping out of their slippers. They looked over, and Arthur was standing on one of the long tables, getting attention by clanging a utensil against his stein.

"Please, may the happy couple step forward?" he boomed.

Isabel looked up at him and her heart nearly exploded. He was such a larger-than-life presence, so big and strong and, good gods, handsome. And he loved her. He desired her. He wanted to hold and protect her.

Maybe over time she'd be able to get him to be just a little less chauvinistic, but it really did, at this moment, strike her to the core all that he was, all he represented. He was a king, yet he was no dictator. He treated all equally. He valued every person at Camelot, treated them as family. And all here, as far as she had seen so far, adored him and admired him in return. Wonder of wonders, he loved her. She had no idea why, but then again she was not about to question it.

She could barely breathe just staring up at him.

"Please, have all of the servants come join us," he said. "They have worked so hard to make this night a success."

There was a moment of silence as Mary and James stepped up to the table and the staff filed in from all parts of the castle.

Arthur glanced around, his eyes squinting. "Well, I know that they are here, but at the moment, I cannot find them. But, James and Mary, you very likely have been too excited and busy to take note, but the queen and the countess worked as hard as all to make this night as memorable for you as is possible."

Cheers nearly broke Isabel's ear drums. She grabbed Gwen's hand and they squeezed. What a strange alliance.

James rumbled up atop the table as well, and Isabel thought all held a collective breath, wondering if there was a table on earth that could hold him. Kudos to the carpenter, this one held under his weight.

"I, too, would care to thank everyone," James said. "And I, too, thank the queen and the countess for their hard work to make my new life with my beautiful wife, Mary, start with such great joy. Our king may not ken that I saw all that you did, but I indeed was witness to it. And Mary and I cannot even begin to show our gratitude." Big, large, no, gigantic James had to wipe his eyes. "Our everlasting appreciation. Is Camelot not the greatest kingdom of all?"

Again, the cheers nearly shook the rafters. Actually, Isabel thought, did castles have rafters? Exactly what were rafters, anyway?

"And should there be a greater king to serve than Sir Arthur?"

Again, deafening cheers.

Arthur looked like he wanted to pound his stein over James's head.

"James, you are my best mate," he said, "but I fear if you do not climb down from this table, the both of us will crumble in a sea of splintered wood."

"To King Arthur!" James said, before he not so elegantly began to climb down.

"To our king!" the entire hall cheered.

"Criminey!" Arthur said. "This is about our newlywed couple! Let us keep the eye on the prize, everyone."

"What?" Gwen said.

Isabel looked down. Arthur was picking up way too many phrases she happened to blurt out at any given moment.

"Mary and James," Arthur said, "here are the door keys to your cottage. A very, very happy night for you both."

"Oh, sir, that is a wonderful gift."

"Where is the queen?" Arthur asked. "Queen Guinevere, please come forward to tell them the rest."

Gwen again squeezed Isabel's hand. "This should be you."

Isabel shook her head. "No, you are the queen, Gwen. Go!"

Gwen walked forward, and Arthur stepped down from the table to greet her. They made such a beautiful couple, Isabel was ready to shoot them both.

Gwen smiled as she took center stage, her crown glistening atop her head.

And then she said, "No, I cannot take credit for the gift that comes next. It is Isabel, Countess of Dumont, who was insistent. Please, Countess, come here to tell Mary and James."

Isabel wanted to disappear, literally and figuratively.

She shook her head. "No!"

Gwen pointed at her. "Go get her, James."

Being dragged center stage, at least a foot off the ground, was not exactly her idea of making a grand entrance. But that was exactly what James did, Mary clapping and laughing the entire time.

"My pardon, Countess," James said as he set her down. "But you have been summoned by the queen."

"I will get you for this. I don't know when, I don't know how, but I will get you," she said to Mary's new husband. "So watch your back."

"I will, Countess. I am truly shaking."

She wanted to glare at him, but how could she? "Bend down," she said.

He did and she kissed his cheek. "Happy days, James. You make her happy or you answer to me."

"Now *that* truly frightens me," he said.

"Good."

"This is ridiculous," she told the crowd. "Your king and queen are responsible, not me."

"Not true," Arthur said. "As we all pondered gifts for Mary and James, it was the countess who suggested the one the queen and I offer. So, Countess, please let them know."

Isabel turned to the couple, then she couldn't help it. She held up her pinky finger to Mary. Mary laughed and the two hooked up. And then Isabel looked at Gwen. "Your Highness?"

"You know I dislike when you call me that," Gwen said, but smiled and wrapped her little finger around theirs. "Friends!" the three said, holding their entwined fingers in the air.

They broke apart, laughing. When Isabel finally glanced up, she saw just about everyone in the hall gaping at them. Including Arthur.

Isabel ignored him and cleared her throat. "What the king and queen are too modest to admit is that their gift to Mary and James is not merely the cottage for the night. The gift is the cottage, for the two of them to live in as long as they desire."

Mary gasped. James staggered a bit. The stunned expressions on their faces were priceless. Good gods, she wished she had her camera.

Mary reached for her and Isabel held her, waiting for Mary's heaving sobs to settle.

"Mary, it isn't my gift. It is from the king and queen. You should be thanking them." She pulled the hanky from her wrist and wiped Mary's eyes. "Mary. King. Queen. Gift. From them."

Mary pulled herself together and turned to Arthur and Gwen. She tried to curtsy, but her legs were obviously a little shaky.

Arthur took her arm. "Enough of that."

"We cannot," Mary hiccuped, "thank you enough."

"You may try," Arthur said, grinning. "I will not be offended."

Isabel shot him a disgusted look, but then he pulled the big move on her. He winked. And once again she was a goner.

DEAD on her feet did not even begin to describe how Isabel was feeling.

Without Mary there to help her out of this gawdawful gown, she was in trouble.

She contemplated just dropping down in bed, gown or not, when there was a knock on her door. "Thank you, Jenny, I need so badly help out of these clothes. Come in."

And in walked Arthur. "I am not Jenny, but I will gladly help you undress."

She smiled, but it was pretty weak. "Arthur, I am so exhausted, but I will gladly accept your help out of this contraption."

"My pleasure, madam."

She turned her back to him so he could work the back laces. "This could be a problem. Jenny might show up here at any moment."

"I gave Jenny the night off."

"Jenny is Gwen's girl."

"She is. Gwen gave Jenny the night off an hour ago. Just afore Gwen and Lance disappeared."

"Oh, I am so sorry."

"For what reason are you sorry?"

"That Gwen . . . that Lance . . . that you . . . oh, hell, I'm just sorry."

He flipped her back to face him. "Why are you sorry, Isabel? Tell me."

"I guess, just that it still has to hurt at some level."

"Do you know what hurt tonight? That I was unable to

introduce you as my love and my wife. And that this pretense is killing me. That you are not my queen."

"I do not give a flying fig about being a queen, Arthur."

"Do you give a flying fig about being my wife?"

She gaped at him. "News flash. You are already married."

"Let us just pretend for a moment. If I were not already married and I asked for your hand, would you say yea or nay?"

"Are you asking me to pretend whether I'd marry you?"

"Of a sort," he said, although his expression was a wee bit wary. "If I were able to ask, would you accept, Isabel?"

"That depends."

"Upon?"

"Whether you would really want to marry a woman who is not a virgin."

He seemed to ponder. "That depends."

"On what?"

"I suppose on how much I crave that woman."

"Craving and loving are two different issues."

"Not necessarily," he said, holding up a finger. "If the craving is born from the feelings, the loving, then they are intertwined."

She hated when men made sense. They were supposed to be idiots.

"Okay," she admitted. "That is one logic point for you."

He looked mighty pleased with himself. He kissed her senseless, which was also a foul in her book. Senseless was not a good place to be when scrambled brains did not work in her favor.

Catching her breath, she said, "Arthur, this is a moot point."

"It is not. It is a simple enough question, Isabel. Will you marry me?"

She stared at him. "Are you serious? Or are we still pretending?"

"I am serious."

"Since you're already—"

"No! Today, now, we are both free to marry." He stopped. "Okay, that's a little bit of pretend since it would not exactly be today. But it can be soon. Would you agree to be my wife? Will you marry me, Isabel?"

"Yes," she whispered. "In a heartbeat."

He smiled, picked her up and twirled her around until she almost fainted. "See, was that such a hardship?"

She was still seeing stars. "Parts of it, yes."

He set her back on her feet. Isabel had to hold on to his arms for balance.

He kissed her again, then held her face. "Do you mean it, Isabel? Truly?"

She took his hands and pulled them from her head. "Arthur, please tell me what this is all about. You are not free to marry me. Not even free to ask, actually."

He grinned. "I might be. Very soon."

"How so?"

"I poured over the legal papers pertaining to this matter. I may not divorce her without cause. That cause being infidelity, which, as you know, would have serious consequences."

"Yes, I believe death would qualify as fairly serious."

"But," he said, "she may divorce me."

"On what grounds?"

"Neglect, physical abuse, infidelity and a few other horrid crimes I forget at the moment."

"You aren't guilty of any of those!" Isabel said. "Okay, maybe one, but she started it!"

"What does it matter? We can agree on whate'er she wants to claim." He stopped. "With the exception of infidelity, because I will not allow you to be involved."

"Arthur, do you hear what you're saying? You are going to allow her to accuse you of crimes you have not committed?"

He waved. "I care not what accusation she decides upon. The people who know me will realize 'tis not true. The point is that Gwen is free to dissolve our marriage with no harm to her or Lance, and I will be free to make you my wife, which, Isabel, is what I desire most in the world at the moment." He smiled. "I want to proclaim to the world that you are mine, that we are one. I no longer want the pretense of what we had to endure this eve."

"You would rather endure being labeled a wife beater?"

"I do not care! People may call me anything they want. I will be free to marry you."

Isabel didn't know whether to laugh or cry. She wrapped her arms around his neck. "Arthur, I love you so much."

He looked down at her and his smile disappeared. "I'll take Do Not Care to Hear a 'But' After That Sentence for a thousand, Alex."

Well, damn, *but* was exactly the next word on her tongue. So she rearranged the sentence.

"I don't want you taking the blame for something you didn't do, Arthur."

"If it wins me freedom to marry you, it matters not."

"It matters to me."

He shoved his hand through his hair. "Dammit, Isabel, what do we do? I do not want to hide my feelings for you. I do not want to pretend to be happy in a marriage that is a sham."

"Change the law," Isabel said softly. "You are the king, it shouldn't be that hard."

He rubbed his neck. "Harder than you think, Isabel. I cannot take out my sword and whisk it around and say, 'I have changed the laws of the land because it suits my purposes and desires.'"

"Too bad, huh?" Isabel said. "Being king is not all it's cracked up to be."

He shrugged. "I suppose I *could* do it, but 'tis not fair to the rest of the people of Camelot. What does that make me, Isabel, if I change laws to suit my own needs?"

"That would be called a dictator."

"A what?"

"An evil ruler who changes laws for his own gain."

"I do not ever care to become one of those."

"Arthur, if you were, there is no way I could possibly love you. It is the man you are that I love. We'll figure this out. We will."

If you want, Isabel, to be with your desire, find a way to make him more than your lover.

And how, Lady, do you make this true? Should I break the necklace and ask for this, too?

No, Isabel, the necklace is not for that. The tears inside will not bring what you want.

You are making no sense, Viv, and I've decided I've earned the right to call you that. So don't give me any grief. Just tell me what the hell I'm dealing with here.

Follow your heart, as I have followed mine. All things will reconcile in time.

That made plenty of sense. She banged her head to get herself back into reality. Or at least this reality.

"Tell me this, Arthur. What brought this on?" Isabel asked him

He sat down on her bed. "As I witnessed the vows betwixt James and Mary, I was envious, wishing that it was you and me in their place. Do not mistake me, I am very, very happy for those two. But I could not help but feel that it should have been us."

She sat down beside him and took his hand, intertwining their fingers. "I felt that way as well."

"It grows worse," he said, his thumb caressing her palm as he seemed to always do. And which she loved. "When I called Gwen up as my queen and wife, I nearly spoke your name."

"Oh, Arthur!"

"It was so wrong, Isabel. All upside down. It should have been you standing aside me. 'Twas you who scrubbed and directed the kitchen staff and—"

"Hold on, sport. Gwen worked her tail off, too, to pull this off in record time. Please don't discredit her part."

"No, I do not. I know that Gwen worked very hard as well. It is just that you received so little recognition for all you did. I was forced to call Gwen up to stand with me. And as much as I admire Gwen's contribution, I only know that the woman I wanted at my side, nay, the woman I wished was standing afore me exchanging those vows, was Isabel. I know it is very nasty I would feel this way, and I am ashamed. But 'tis how I feel right now, and the funny part of this is, you are the only one I feel safe admitting this to. When it is your heart that I hope to win. Stupid way of going about that, is it not?"

"Perfect way of going about that."

He glanced at her sideways. "Am I batty or are you?"

Her free hand slid up his arm. "Probably both of us." She settled farther back on the bed. "Look, I believe that what attracted us to one another was our ho—"

Whoa, she backed up on that one. Her entire life here was a lie. "Was that we could be honest about our feelings."

He was still staring down, but he grinned. "It did not hurt over-much that I thought you the most beautiful woman I had e'er laid eyes upon."

"You definitely need to get your vision checked, Arthur."

He chuckled. "My eyesight is just fine, Countess. It might have improved since you arrived."

"Flatterer."

He shook his head, still laughing softly. "Oh, Isabel, you have no idea the amount of my men that James and I have had to ward off from you."

"James and you?"

"James has my back. He knows my feelings and he anticipates what I care for. He would no more allow anyone at Camelot to try to court you than he'd allow someone to look at his Mary."

"But—"

"He believes we belong together, Isabel. Is he wrong?"

"No."

They sat together in silence for several minutes. Finally Arthur rose. "I realize how exhausted you are. I will not bother you any more tonight, beautiful lady."

"Wait!"

"Yes, love?"

"I still need help out of this freaking gown. And . . . and, it's true I'm too exhausted to even consider making love. But that doesn't mean I don't want you to hold me. Please stay."

His grin was exhausted as well, but he pulled her up and turned her around. "I will take the Two Words I Wanted to Hear from Isabel's Lips for a thousand, Alex."

"What is, 'Please stay.'"

"Correct!"

She was naked and in bed fast. It took Arthur a while longer as he was wearing what she decided was a medieval tuxedo. All decked out for the ceremony this evening. Good lord he'd looked so freaking handsome.

He climbed into the bed and held her, his body heat and delicious male scent pure heaven.

"I could get so used to this," she whispered. "I could become addicted to this."

"Isabel?"

"Yes?"

"I say it now and I will utter it with my dying breaths, I do thee vow."

Her drooping eyes shot open.

Viviane? Please, please help me. Please tell me you aren't taking Arthur from me.

No answer. Nothing. Nada.

Thanks a lot, she thought.

"I do thee vow," she whispered. But his deep breathing told her he was already sound asleep.

WHEN Isabel woke in the morning, Arthur was gone. It was a lonely, achy feeling to turn over and have the other side of her bed empty. But she shouldn't have been surprised. The man was up before dawn, worked until the breaking of fast, then straight to work out with his soldiers. Still pissed her off. Yet at the knock at her door, she was reminded she also had a to-do list a mile long today.

"Please enter."

Jenny peeked her head in the door. "'Tis me, mistress."

"Thank goodness. Tea, Jenny?"

Jenny grinned and entered, her tray full of all kinds of delicious-smelling goodies, as well as tea.

"What is this, breakfast in bed?"

"The master said you had such an exhausting evening that you might prefer to just laze a bit, mum."

"Oh, the master is wonderful."

"He truly is, mum," Jenny said.

"I am so sorry you have to pull double duty, Jenny."

"Oh, I do not mind at all. Mary has taken over my duties many times when I was . . . ill."

"Ill. Right."

Isabel drank the heavenly tea, almost moaned at the pastries and dug into delicious scrambled eggs. "This is so good," she said after a long sip of tea.

"I am so glad, Countess."

"My name is Isabel."

"Oh, I could not!"

Déjà vu.

"Would you enjoy a morning bath, Countess?"

"You know, I think I would prefer an afternoon bath today, Mistress Jenny. But thank you for asking."

Jenny giggled. She was tall and thin with really long brownish black hair. She could be a Paris runway model with a little makeup . . . and a better wardrobe.

"If I may say, Countess, Mary has had nothing but wonderful praises upon you."

"Thank you, Jenny! That is so sweet. I adore her."

"She says that you have a way of making toenails look pretty."

"It's a girl secret, but if you want me to paint your toenails, I will be happy to."

"Truly?"

"Truly. Especially if you call me Isabel."

"Oh, I could not!"

Good lord, even one at a time was tiring. She wondered if she could talk Arthur into passing a law that all servants were allowed to call people by their damn freaking names.

She smiled at runway-model Jenny. "Please go wash your feet. Scrub them and then dry them. Then come back and I will paint them for you."

Jenny's grayish eyes shined. "Thank you so much, m'lady! I will. And, oh, I forgot, Queen Guinevere would appreciate a word."

"She is welcome anytime."

And just like that, a knock on the door.

"Come on in, Gwen," Isabel called.

Except it was Mary who sailed in, her eyes glowing.

Isabel nearly jumped out of bed until she realized she was naked. So she just grabbed the top fur and wrapped it around her. "Oh, Mary, you look wonderful! I assume—"

"Isabel?" Gwen said. "May I come in?"

"Perfect timing," Isabel said.

"No! I am going to miss all of the good stuff!" Jenny said.

"Hurry," Isabel said. "We will engage in idle chitchat until you return. In fact, I'll put clothes on before you return."

Jenny raced from the room.

"Plop down on the floor, ladies, while I don a nightgown."

"I'VE promised Jenny to do her toes," Isabel said. "And she very much wants to be here for girl chat. Do either of you have a problem with that?"

Mary and Gwen both shook their heads.

"Jenny is one of the few who has never, ever turned on me," Mary said. "I trust her almost as I trust you."

"And I trust her with all things," Gwen added.

But Isabel couldn't help it. She kept looking into Mary's sparkling sapphire eyes and she fell on her side, laughing. "That good, Mary?"

"Oh, Isabel, I had no . . . It was . . . Did you guys know they have these big picklelike things?"

Gwen and Isabel looked at each other, then both fell over—Isabel again—laughing.

Jenny came running back in the room. "Oh, no! What did I miss?"

"We were discussing pickles," Gwen choked out.

"What is so funny about that?"

"I did not say pickle!" Mary said. "I said picklelike. It sort of sticks out like this, and it's kind of wrinkly and—"

"Stop!" Isabel said. "I'm going to split my spleen."

It took a while, but Gwen and Isabel finally stopped laughing, although they had to avoid looking at each other to accomplish that feat.

When Isabel finally got it together, she looked at Mary. "So?"

"I have a new found appreciation for pickles. The big ones."

They all busted up all over again, even Mary and Jenny. They were all on the floor laughing. Isabel managed to hug Mary and say, "I am so happy for you. Even though I'll never get that image out of my mind."

Mary looked at her. "Isabel, neither will I, as I will be facing it every night."

Isabel had to hold her tummy to keep it from exploding.

"Countess!"

Isabel was too busy laughing to hear.

"Countess!"

Jenny shook her shoulder. "I believe the king is speaking to you, mum."

Isabel sat up. "Your Highness?" she said, all laughter gone at the look on his face. "What may—"

"A word?"

"You may speak freely here, King Arthur."

"A private word."

She wasn't even dressed yet. But she rolled to her feet and followed him out to the hallway.

He pulled her, and not even gently, away from her door.

"What, Arthur? What is it?"

"I want you to pack and go."

"What? What did I do?"

"Camelot is soon to be under siege, and I need you safe, Isabel. I want you back, safe in Dumont."

She glared up at him. "No. I am staying and fighting with you."

"You will not. You will slip out to the west and then head north. I have already mapped your safest route with Dick."

"Oh, have you?"

"We have."

"Too damn bad. I am not leaving."

"Isabel, listen to me," he said, gripping her shoulders. "We are about to head into battle. Should we fail, we have no defense for the women."

"You dumbshit. Do you not think women can battle in our own ways? We are an asset, if you are not stupid enough to overlook us."

"Good gods, Isabel," he said, staring up at the heavens. "I do not have time for this. Do you not understand? I need you safe. Please!"

"How much time before they invade the lands of Camelot?"

"Five hours, maybe six."

"Perfect." She tried to wrench free. "Do not pull the bully tactic on me, Arthur."

"I cannot let you be harmed. Do you not see that?"

"And I refuse to lie over your dying body while you tell me 'to thee I vow.' When you say those words, we will be happy and alive."

"I want *you* alive."

"As I do you. And guess what, so does Merlin!"

"Merlin? How do you know of Merlin?"

"Do you mind if I explain that later? Right now, we have bread to bake."

She wrenched out of his arms and began running. She turned back for one moment. "By the way, I love you. Do not die, dammit. I will be really pissed off if you die."

CHAPTER TWENTY-FOUR

ISABEL did a U-turn and ran back into her room. All laughter had ceased as everyone sat still.

"We must move, ladies," she said. "Camelot is under siege, and we are going to help keep those sonofabitches from overtaking us."

"What can we do?" they all said, standing up.

"Gwen, did Lance truly lay fire to all of those poison mushrooms?"

"He did not, as Arthur warned him against fire so close to the cottage. They lay there still."

"Oh, excellent! Please, take Jenny with you as you know the way. Bring back as many as possible. The crushed ones most of all. But please try not to touch them, and if you chew on one, I will kill you before the mushroom does."

She turned around. "Mary, I need you to make wigs."

"Wigs?"

"Fake long hairpieces. Braids. That will work. You need to start with anyone who has long hair. Hell, start with me."

"Oh, Isabel! To what purpose?"

"We are going to fool those assholes. Cut my hair."

Isabel cringed as she felt the shears chop her hair up to her shoulders. "Good," she said, "now go find anyone willing to give hair for the cause."

Isabel didn't even bother to dress, so the shocked looks in the main kitchen were not a surprise.

She explained, as fast as she could, then begged as fast as she could. Every single cook went to work making breads and pastries, simply waiting for the final ingredient before placing them over the fires.

"And mead! Lots of mead. And lace it with the same mushroom as the breads. None of you drink or eat any of this. At least not after you add the mushroom mixture."

She ran to Arthur's study, but he wasn't there. So she turned and ran through the great hall, out the door and into the bailey. There were a ton of men there all geared up and ready for battle.

She looked around and might not have recognized Arthur if she hadn't seen a giant man beside him first, the two of them poring over maps.

She ran over to them. "Arthur, James, we have a plan. By the way, James, happy making-Mary-really-happy day. Anyway, I need about ten scouts to just drop crumbs and such on the way to Camelot."

Arthur took off his head armor, then picked Isabel up and *clinck-clincked* her back into the castle.

He did not look happy.

"You didn't even listen to the plan," she complained.

"You did not even listen to me. I told you, I want you gone, Isabel."

"But I can help."

"I suppose I was attempting to be nice. I should have been more clear. I am done with you. I want you out of Camelot. You no longer interest me. Be gone."

"I don't believe that for a second. You don't mean that."

"Believe what you want. I do not want you here. Gather Tom, Dick and Harry, and leave. I want you off my lands."

"You know what, tough boy? Tough shit!"

"Please go."

"No, you asshole. I am staying and I will fight for Camelot and you 'til the end. Win or lose."

"If I die, Izzy, I can no longer protect you. If you go, you are out of harm's way."

"And if you don't let us try, then we cannot even help to protect you. We have plans. Arthur, there are more ways than bloodshed. In war, deception is fully acceptable."

"What is your plan, Countess?"

Arthur whirled, Isabel still in his arms.

"Mordred, if you are behind this, there is no love strong enough to overcome how I will punish you," Arthur said.

"I swear, father, I knew naught of any of this."

Arthur nodded. "Your plan, then, is to escort the countess and her men back to Dumont."

"I'm not leaving," she said.

"What is your plan, Countess?" Mordred asked. "Unlike my father, I have learned to listen when you speak."

"We are going to spike the trails leading to Camelot with mushroom-laced foods and drink. We will drop those idiots one mouthful at a time. We might not get all of them, but we will get some. And we will definitely slow them down."

Arthur finally placed her back on the floor. "That is brilliant."

"It is," Mordred said. "You will need scouts to lay the trail of food and drink. I volunteer to head the group."

"Can we trust him, Arthur?" Isabel asked.

"You are a better judge of character than I, Isabel. And I have a bias. He is, after all, my son. What think you?"

She looked into Mordred's green eyes, so like his father's. "I believe that your son loves you. He would be proud to be part of the offensive against those who would harm you. Am I wrong, Mordred?"

"No, Countess. I would protect my father and his lands against all invaders. I know that I said otherwise afore, but 'twas only because I . . ."

"Wanted to hurt him, as you had believed all of your life that he had hurt you."

"Yes."

"And you now realize that isn't at all true."

"Yes. I am so sorry, Father."

"Please believe in me, Son."

"I do, father."

"I believe him. Okay, please round up about ten men who know those trails better than any other. Then go to the baking kitchen and gather the food and drink, and meet me back here in the great hall. There is one other part to this plan the men will probably not like so much. But it could well give you more protection, should you encounter any of these marauders."

"Yes." He turned toward the doors.

"Mordred."

He turned back. "Yes?"

"You are your father's son. No wonder he loves you as much as he does."

Mordred blinked. "I consider that the highest praise I have e'er heard. After all I have said and done—"

"You make up for it in this one great and important deed."

"Thank you, Countess. Father."

"And, Mordred. Do not, and I mean it, do *not* allow any of the men to give in to temptation and eat or drink your weapons. They are poison, pure and simple."

"Yes." He turned and broke into a run.

Arthur stared at her for a moment. "Would that I had the time to make love to you this very moment."

"Time for that after."

"I hope with all my heart that is true. There is no way I am going to change your mind about leaving, is there?"

"What is, Not a single chance in hell, Alex."

"What happened to your hair, Isabel?"

"It happily sacrificed itself for the cause."

He laid his forehead against hers. "I ne'er knew it was possible to love this desperately."

"And if you don't get back out there and continue planning, you won't know it for long."

"Yes, you are right," he said. He kissed her fiercely, right there in the great hall, for any or all to see. And she was still barefoot in her nightgown.

"Isabel?"

"Yes, Arthur?"

"With all that I am and all that I have, to thee I vow."

"Premature, but so very wonderful to hear. Now go. I have work to do."

He chuckled, shaking his head. "You love me."

"Yes, I do."

"And that is the knowledge and fortification I need to fight the battle of my life."

"No more scars, Arthur. Not a single scratch."

"I will do my best to honor that wish."

"It was not a wish. It was a demand."

"Yes, Countess," he said, grinning. "And I cannot wait to be forever at your demand."

She laughed. "Go, smartass."

"One more demand I will honor."

He kissed her one more time, then turned and strode out the door. Oh, how she wished he wasn't already wearing his armor, so she could get one more chance to ogle that incredible butt.

"I love you," he called over his shoulder.

One of his men who had just entered stopped short.

"Not you, Ashton. Her," he said, hiking a thumb over his shoulder.

The boy gaped at her.

"Ashton! Come."

Isabel laughed as she picked up her nightgown and ran up the front stairway, two steps at a time.

* * *

AMAZINGLY, by the time she returned to her chamber, Mary, Gwen and Jenny were already waiting for her.

"What now, Isabel?" Gwen asked.

It amazed her that Gwen had so quickly handed over the decision making to her. But then again, Gwen was so young and probably had never encountered war in her life. Unfortunately, Isabel had.

"Gwen, I need you and Jenny to gather the women and tell them all to don their breeches. Skirts are of no help. And then tell them to arm themselves. I don't care with what. Anything hard and capable of being thrown—"

"As in Camelot baseball?"

"Exactly, but they will need larger rocks than the small stones we used. Or hard tree limbs, swords if they happen to have access to any, anything that could be used as a weapon. Those with strong arms we will station in places where they can knock a man off his horse. Others with weapons such as swords or tree limbs we will place where they can whack the hell out of anyone who comes in reach."

"Women do not engage in battle, Isabel," Gwen said.

Isabel plopped her hands on her hips. "What, you wait for your men to die in battle, and then allow the enemy to do with you what they will? In my land, women fight. We might do it differently than men, but we do not stand by and await the outcome. Do you want to help thwart the enemy, Gwen, or do you want to cower in your chambers and hope for the best?"

"We fight," Jenny said, with a ferocity that was endearing.

"Good. Then go gather the women and tell them to dress and arm themselves appropriately. We will meet in the round-table hall and plan our strategy in, say, a half an hour or so."

She looked at Gwen. "Buck up, Queen Guinevere. Camelot is your land as well. Do you fight for this castle, or not?"

Gwen nodded. "Let us go do as she asks, Jenny."

Jenny left at a run. Gwen, not so quickly.

"The queen is a . . . a . . . What is the proper word, Isabel?" Mary asked, as her hands worked feverishly braiding hair.

"I think the word you're looking for is a wimp."

"Oh, that is a perfect word. Yes, a wimp."

"But we must give her a break. This is all unfamiliar and scary."

Mary looked up from her task. "It is not familiar to you, either, I am guessing. And yet you acted."

Isabel shrugged as she pulled off her nightgown and started to dress. "I cannot stand by and do nothing."

"The king wanted you to leave. Why did you not?"

"How did you know that?"

"Oh, I have excellent hearing. People may whisper two or more rooms away and I will hear every word. 'Tis a gift and a curse, in some cases."

"You are a wonder, Mary. What is not a wonder to me is why James loves you so much. And you, him."

"And why the king loves you," Mary said.

"You . . . overheard something?"

"Oh, please, Isabel. James and I were aware from the moment you arrived. It did not take overhearing to figure that much out. It was apparent by the way your . . . bodies interacted."

Isabel laughed as she pulled on her breeches. "In my land, Mary, we call that body language. I didn't know we were that apparent."

"'Twas apparent to us. But we said not a word to anyone, Isabel. This I swear."

"If there is anything I believe, Mary, it is that. I am a good judge of character, and I knew the moment we met that you are such a good person."

"Then I, too, am a good judge of character," Mary said. "Wear the deep green dress, Isabel. It is the least heavy of the lot and much more easy for you to move around in. And you will more easily blend in with the foliage. Twill not stand out as some of your brighter clothing might. We do not want a target on your back."

Isabel laughed. "You are a treasure beyond measure, Mary."

"I am so glad you think so." Mary looked up from her task. "I love you, Countess Isabel."

"As I do you, Mary," Isabel said, her throat choked with emotion. "This should be no way for any woman to spend her first full day of marriage to her true love."

"If he is to battle this day, it is the only way to spend it. I believe I should like more nights with the big goof."

Isabel laughed again as she managed to lace up her dress on her own. And, of course, Mary had been right. It was the least complicated dress she had, and the easiest to maneuver in. "I cannot blame that logic one bit. I hope your night was all that you dreamed."

"Oh, and more. Much more. That was one big pickle, Isabel."

Isabel almost collapsed. "Mary, you must stop making me laugh so hard." Then she stopped. "I hope he didn't hurt you."

"Oh, no, he was ever so gentle. The king gave him tips on ways to make certain he would not."

"James told you this?"

Mary just shook her head and then tapped her ear. "It appears that James was more nervous than I, last evening. The king attempted to calm him down."

Oh, Arthur. Could she love a man more? "Your vow exchange was beautiful. As were you. I don't blame James for being nervous."

"Well, 'twould seem that the advice King Arthur gave him worked, and worked well. I admit I did not ken much of what he said, but I much appreciate whate'er it was."

She stood up. "Done. I have thirty and two braids. Is that enough?"

"More than. Where did you get all of the hair, Mary?"

"I can be quite convincing when I have the need to be. Now what are we to do with them?"

"I have need of more of your hair skills, Mary. And I very much hope your convincing skills work, because I believe we are going to encounter protests like you have never encountered before."

Mary gathered up the braided hair. "Bring it on, mistress."

CHAPTER TWENTY-FIVE

ARTHUR could not believe his eyes. He stared at all of the women gathered around his round table, Isabel standing as she scratched out things upon a piece of parchment, then pointing at one and then another, and handing out what sounded very close to assignments for a battle plan.

"What goes on here?" he asked.

Isabel glanced up while most of the women, all those but Gwen, scrambled to their feet.

"Oh, sit down already," he said. "Isabel, what is this?"

"This is the round table," she said calmly, straightening. "We are planning strategy. Is that not what this table was created for?"

"For, for . . ." Oh, gods, 'twas a waste of time to argue with the woman. "Planning what strategy? First you have Mary force braids upon men's heads, and now you involve women in this fight? What will you not do, Isabel?"

"Allow any to win in their attempt to overtake Camelot. I might be mistaken, but I believe that's the goal for this day."

"And you feel it all right to involve the women?"

Isabel looked around the packed table. "Any of you who feel unwilling to join in, raise your hands. If you are at this table against your will, speak up now. You will not be punished, and you are free to go right now."

Not a single hand lifted, not even Gwen's.

"I will not allow—"

"You have no choice. Guinevere—last I heard, the Queen of Camelot—has decreed that we may help in this endeavor."

His outrage almost overruled his admiration. "This is war. This is a man's battle."

"This is a battle to preserve Camelot," Isabel said. "It is up to all of us to join in."

"You are of Dumont. You are not of Camelot. You have not authority to—"

One by one he watched as every woman at the table stood up again, this time including Gwen. And by the belligerent countenances, he was certainly aware it was not out of respect for their king. Truth be told, the allegiances had most assuredly switched to the woman from Dumont.

"I give her the authority, Arthur," Gwen said, even as she shook a little. "We are joining in, in our own ways. Every one of us at this table has a man who is heading into harm's way. We are doing our part, whether you agree or not. Isabel has plans. We are not going to do a single thing to interfere, only to, mayhap, intervene where we are able. Now go back to your plans, and leave us to ours."

And then, to his utter amazement, the women all began holding up hands, slapping them against one another and saying what he believed to be, "High five."

Too many things to take in. The most stunning was that this was the very first time Gwen had stood up and countermanded his wishes. She had, while he was not paying attention, grown a backbone. Then again, when she declared that all of the women had a dog in this fight, or a man, as it were, he knew for a certainty she was thinking of Lance, not of him. And he did not care a fig. He cared that the man Isabel was defiantly fighting for was he.

Second, that the women servants were truly and utterly defying him.

And worst of all, that Isabel not only joined in this fight to help save his lands, she had managed to form an army of females to follow her into battle for them.

He knew when he was out-womaned. "Fine," he said. "You do as you see fit. But, Isabel, if your plans involve bringing any woman into the battlefield—"

"They do not," she said. "I vow we are doing this in a way that women do best. We are smarter and sneakier than men. Not a woman will be harmed in this fight. I swear. And if we are successful, no men, either. Is that not the goal?"

"That is the goal. But, Isabel? Countess Isabel? A word?" he said, crooking his finger at her.

"I'm guessing I am going to hear more than one. And most of them will be of the swearing kind."

The women around the table laughed.

"You are right. But words we will have. Now, please."

"Shall I accompany you, Countess?" Mary said.

Oh, great, now she had people ready to attack him should he make any threatening moves or words against her. His own people. He had definitely lost control of this entire castle.

"No need, Mary," Isabel said. "Not even Excalibur at his side worries me. However, should my head roll back in here, no longer attached to the rest of my body, you may correctly assume I sadly overestimated my trust in your king."

"VERY funny," Arthur said as he dragged Isabel into his study.

"Have Mordred and his men returned yet?"

"They have."

"The mission successful?"

"He feels so. Although he could not wait to rip those braids from his head. And they were not happy about the dresses."

"It was only for added protection. Should any enemy sneak up upon them—"

"They would first believe they were dealing with helpless women, yes, I get it. You realize, of course, the irony of that ruse."

"What do you mean?"

"You are using men's beliefs of helpless females against them."

"Hey, if they're dumb enough, use whatever you have."

"We have ten men imprisoned. Those who Mordred and his men caught with that ruse."

"Cool! Now let's hope that many others are enticed to stop long enough to taste the pastries and mead."

"They are men galloping into battle."

"Well, even men galloping into battle get hungry and thirsty."

"Mordred is quite proud, Isabel. He, I am thinking, feels he has accomplished an amazing feat this day."

"He has. Good for him. Now, I have another thought."

He stared at her. "Why does this worry me?"

"Because you are so accustomed to traditional blood and guts warring that you don't get the fine art of trickery."

"And what trickery have you in mind, now?"

"Well, not trickery, perhaps, but a form of defense."

"And that would be?"

"Light a fire. A big one."

"I will not burn down Camelot, Isabel."

"No, no, I don't mean here. I mean far enough in the forest to cut off all trails leading to Camelot. Those not dumb enough to stop to take advantage of our lovely food and drink gifts will be stopped by a wall of fire. You gave me the idea when you warned Lance not to start a fire he could not contain. If you start a fire, a contained fire, blocking their way to the castle, you cut them off before they can even invade."

Arthur looked down at this woman, this utterly amazing woman. "And your plans?"

"Will not work should we leak them. Trust me, Arthur, no women will be harmed during the making of this battle."

"What?"

"Never mind, was just a joke."

"You are so strange, Isabel."

"But you love that about me."

"I am utterly perplexed by that about you."

"At least I'm not boring."

"That, Countess Isabel, is the truest of truths."

Again he kissed her, as fiercely as he had just hours ago. Then he took her hand, leading her back out of his study.

"Where are you going?" she asked.

"To start a fire. And you are going back to continue planning. That room, that table, was first meant for something completely different. But now I see so clearly that it has value so deeper than that. And, by the by, you love me, in case you needed to be reminded."

"I do, and I didn't."

She began walking back to the round table room when she heard him call, "I love you!"

And then, "Oh, for crying out loud, Frederick. I meant her, not you."

Chapter Twenty-six

THE battle, thank the gods, never happened.

Not a single sword had to be used, not a single arrow fired. In the day following the attack that failed, Arthur's men combed the trails and discovered the bodies of many men, one of them Richard of Freemont, who turned out to be a fat pig who would never turn down the thought of pastry or mead.

Isabel, Mary, Jenny and Gwen were once again gathered in Isabel's chambers, as Mary attempted to fix the hair of those she'd had to butcher.

Jenny and Gwen had supported the cause, as had Mary, who chopped her own hair to help make the braids.

"You did not hear this from me, Countess," Jenny said, "but the speaking around the castle is that the women were disappointed they did not get the opportunity to thwack a single bad man."

"We can only be happy about that. But I will thwack you if you continue to refuse to call me Isabel."

"Give it up, Jenny," Mary said as she worked on Gwen's hair. "You will not win. Isabel will wear you down."

"And I want you all to please call me Gwen."

Jenny froze. "What?" she said, looking around at them. "I have already asked this of you two. I am now asking this of Jenny. What is the problem with this?"

"You are the queen," Jenny whispered.

"Who is sitting upon the floor, having fun with women she has come to see as friends. I would like you to view me as the same."

"Mary," Isabel said. "Get that razor out of the way."

Mary sat back, the razor in the hand behind her.

Isabel leaned forward and pulled Gwen into a hug. "You are a friend, Gwen. And a very good one."

She sat back and pointed. "Now you and you. Admit you consider Gwen a great friend. After all, we have shared pickle stories. Only friends do that."

"Oh, James would just die if he knew," Mary said, and then hugged her queen. "I very much consider you a friend, my queen."

"Mary," Isabel growled.

"Gwen," Mary answered, although it was an obviously trying moment for her. "Will take some time to get used to that."

"It will just be among the pickle sisters," Isabel said.

They all fell over laughing. It took minutes for them to sit back up, although they were all holding their tummies.

"Your turn, Jenny," Isabel said. She pointed at her chest. "Isabel." She pointed at Gwen. "Gwen. Now go ahead, spit it out. Or the three of us might be forced to describe the two walnuts you can expect to find under that pickle."

Jenny stared, but then joined in the laughter. "I wish an explanation first, afore I concede."

"Oh, good gods, no, Jenny," Gwen said. "These are treasures you must find for yourself."

"Oh, a treasure hunt? I love a treasure hunt. I am very good at those."

"We must get this girl married," Isabel said. "So she may go hunting."

"Ashton wants her," Mary said, "but she has refused. At least three times, right, Jenny?"

Jenny blushed. "Yes, that is true."

"Why?" Isabel asked. "Do you not care for him? I met him just yester morning . . . in a way . . . and I must say he is a very handsome young warrior."

"It is just that I feared . . ."

"What?"

Jenny looked at Gwen. "I feared losing my position as the queen's servant."

"What?" Gwen and Isabel said at the same time. "Why would you believe this, Jenny?" Gwen finished.

"You told me so, Your Highness."

"When did I e'er say such a thing?"

"You told me that you dreaded the day that I wed, because 'twould mean you would need to find a new maid servant."

Isabel nearly choked. "You told her that?"

"No! Well, it is possible. But if I uttered such a thing, what I was thinking was that once she married, she would become a wife and would no longer want or need to be of service to me. Jenny, I never presumed you would believe I meant marriage would be the end of my need for you. If anything, I was mourning the thought of ever losing you as servant and . . . friend."

"Oh, Your Highness. I love being your servant and . . . and friend. I always have."

"It's going to take time to bring her around to the first-name-basis thing, Mary," Isabel whispered, as Jenny and Gwen held on to one another.

"As I said, she is a tough nut to crack," Mary whispered.

"A walnut?"

Isabel and Mary again fell on their sides.

"Countess," Mary said, in between giggles. "Should this keep up, my stomach will ache forever."

"Consider it good exercise for your abs. Then again, so is James."

*   *   *

"Do you really, truly want to interrupt that?" James asked Arthur, poking his finger at Isabel's door.

"If I heard correct, James, you have just been complimented on your skills beneath the furs."

James looked away, attempting, Arthur guessed, to hide a proud smile.

Arthur began stomping his boots against the floor. "I am telling you, James," he came near to shouting, "the women are in there. Possibly performing that toe-painting thing again."

James nodded. "But should we interrupt, sir?" he shouted so loud the people in the outskirts of all Briton heard him.

Arthur shook his head, leaning against the wall. When James chimed in, he did it with gusto. "We have need of their help," he said loudly. "How else will we be able to pull off tonight's celebration?"

Arthur stomped some more before waving James forward to Isabel's room.

He knocked.

"Come on in, Arthur. James."

"How did you know 'twas us?" Arthur asked, feigning innocence.

"Wild guess," she said.

He found four women sitting on the rushes as if they had just been in a solemn discussion of the merits of pickled eel.

"My apologies for the interruption, ladies. I hope that James and I did not disrupt more battle plans."

"No, of course not. We were just discussing the merits of—"

"Picked eel?"

"Not quite, but you're close. More like pickles and nuts."

And Arthur stared as the three other women bent into laughter.

Isabel waved. "They are giddy with the happiness over winning the battle. Right, ladies?"

"Correct, Countess," they all managed to choke out.

"I am so in trouble," Mary said.

"No, you are not, Mary. Is she, James?"

"Should she be?" he asked.

"Depending on how long you two were standing there listening, I would say that you are the one who may be in trouble. But knowing Mary, she is much too sweet to exact revenge."

She turned on Arthur, which was what he was so hoping to avoid. "You, on the other hand, do you really believe that fake stomping was going to fool anyone?"

"I had hopes," he said.

"Arthur, I have seen you in action. You could come upon the most acute of cats without making a sound. And yet you stomp your way here?"

"Okay, that was probably dumb."

"Probably? Please. Just say what you came here to tell us."

"We wanted to hold a celebration this eve, for the successful events yesterday."

"We wanted your help in making it as festive as possible," James added, "as we were somewhat at a loss. We have the kitchens working, but the other details?"

"A party? Jeez, why didn't you say so?" She looked around. "Ladies, I believe we have work to do." She looked back. "Please tell me we will not be subjected to more Hester the Jester jokes."

"'Twill break his heart, Isabel."

"Okay, Hester's in. But pickled eel . . ."

"Oh, the king already took care of that, lady. He banned it from the night's menu. I knew not why until this very—oof!" James rubbed his stomach. "He preferred not to offer such."

Isabel glanced at Arthur, and his heart thrummed. Gods, he wanted her. Maybe this night. Perhaps, because battle had been averted, all nights of his life.

She smiled at him, and he knew she knew his thoughts. "I have one very special request, King Arthur."

Oh, yes. She could ask for any star in the sky and he would find a way to snatch it for her. "Name it, Countess."

She looked back at the women. "Gwen, I trust you are going to make the hall beautiful once again."

Gwen rose, pulling Jenny with her. "Jenny and I will go pick the flowers right now and begin to decorate the hall."

As they went to leave, Arthur stopped Gwen. "I am proud of you, Guinevere. As is Lance. He is a lucky and happy man. And afore you begin to decorate, perhaps visit him. He is at the cottage, cleaning up after helping to put out the fires."

She looked up at him and smiled. "I am growing up, Arthur. With any hope, growing wiser. Thank the woman you love for that transformation."

"I thank her for so many things. But learning wisdom comes from within. That is all you, Gwen. Take the credit for that. Now go see Lance. I am certain that Jenny can begin cutting flowers without you."

WAS Isabel the only sane person in the room? She wasn't certain, so she asked, "Am I the only sane person in this room?"

"Trust me, love, you are most likely the least sane person in this room," Arthur said. He glanced at both James and Mary. "Anyone who considers Isabel the most crazed here, please raise your hands."

James and Mary both rose their hands.

"Mary!"

"I love you, Countess, but you are a bit . . . wild."

"Do you think I did wrong?"

"No way in Hades!" Mary said. "You were so earnest in your desire to save the king and Camelot. 'Twas something to behold. I aspire to that passion."

"But it was crazy?"

"Only because the king said it was so."

She glared at Arthur. "You, sir, are stacking the cards."

He smiled. "I have no idea what that means, but I suppose you would say so."

Isabel folded her arms over her ribs. "James?"

"With all pardons, Countess, must I choose betwixt you and my king, I must land on the side of my king. And my wife. But you and the king are so in love, it seems that siding with one is also siding with another. Am I right, wife?"

"You are so right, husband."

"Good gods, it's the pickle factor," Isabel murmured.

"I heard that, Isabel," Mary said. "And, no, it is not. It is that we care very deeply about those we treasure most. James and I truly believe you two are meant to be with one another. So stop being dumb about it, and just trust your feelings. Come, James. I believe we have some time afore we need return to work. I will be back in . . . an·hour?" she said, looking up at James. "Okay, possibly two."

Isabel and Arthur stared at one another before laughing.

If nothing else, she decided, Camelot was full of laughter.

"What is this favor, Izzy? I have high hopes that you wish to continue to practice the undressing thing."

"Oh, I've already mastered that one. No, the favor is to allow Ashton to ask for Jenny's hand tonight."

"In front of all?"

"Yes. How romantic is that?"

"Would that it could be me asking for yours. Because you have promised you would agree, yes?"

"I would absolutely say yes."

"Then I so wish it would be me tonight."

"Someday, Arthur, Someday."

Arthur shook his head, chuckling. "I have. I have lost total control over this entire realm, Isabel. And I find myself not worrying overmuch."

"You haven't. Why would you even think such a thing?"

"We have servants berating us, we have women taking up the charge. For crying out loud, Isabel, it was ideas of yours that stayed the enemy."

"Oh, please, all I did was try to think of any plan that did not involve the shedding of blood. Especially yours. That is all. It would be a mess to clean up."

"Ah, I see. Less work was your intent."

"Exactly. I'm lazy that way."

He kicked the door shut. "Mary and James say two hours?"

"I believe that was their time, yes," she said, backing away.

"Not nearly enough time, but I will take what I can get."

"Who says you get any?" Isabel asked.

"Your beautiful blue eyes, Isabel. Your eyes tell me you desire me as I desire you."

"Damn my non-lying eyes."

"Oh, no, praise those beautiful, honest eyes. Now tell me from those lips."

"I desperately desire you, Arthur," she said.

"See, we agree on so many things, Isabel," he said, then held out his arms. "A master at undressing me you say? I wish proof."

OH, yes, they were both sweaty and spent. Isabel had no idea how long they'd spent making love, but she was fairly certain their two hours were close to up.

"We should probably get dressed," she said.

"I agree," he said, "however, that does not equal with whether I want to leave your bed."

"You're good with math, are you?"

"Math?"

"Working with numbers so that, for example, you know what equals what."

"Oh, yes, you call it math?"

"What do you call it?"

"Numbers."

Isabel rolled to her back, laughing. "I love you so much."

Arthur turned on his side, grinning. "I have an example."

She turned on her side as well. "Oh, please, I can't wait."

"What would you call over one hundred men attempting to take on one much smarter woman?"

She went still. "I don't know. What?"

"Outnumbered."

She laughed. "Arthur, your men would have made toast of them."

"There we go with the toast thing again. And, yes, I agree we would have vanquished the invaders. Yet truth be told, Isabel, if not for your quick wits, Camelot blood would be staining the grounds this day. Because of your whacky plots, all of our people are alive and safe once again."

"Whacky?"

"Did I say whacky? I meant witty."

"You meant whacky."

He grimaced. "Yea, but I meant whacky in the wittiest sense of the word 'whacky.'"

Isabel smiled and traced the contours of his face until they smoothed back into contentment. "It was merely a whacky way of turning back the enemy."

"'Twas not your battle to fight."

"It was the moment it involved you. I love you. And all of the people of Camelot. This might make no sense to you, Arthur, but I have come to care for the people here in this short time. They are good and they are kind, and most importantly, they love their king. If you didn't recognize the evidence of that yesterday when the women were willing to actually stand up against you to fight *for* you, then you are woefully underestimating the love and loyalty your people have for you. They love you, Arthur. They are willing to do anything to protect and honor their king."

"I am to protect them, Isabel. Is that not my ultimate duty as king?"

"If you think so. Your second ultimate duty is to take care of them, make certain they want to protect you as their king. And so far, I think that's working."

"I sometimes doubt, and I recognize how weak I sound even admitting such a thing."

"The weak leader is the one who refuses to admit to doubts about how he runs things. The strong leader is the one who constantly questions how he can perform his duties to the betterment of all in his—or her—lands. You are the strongest, most honest and loving lord of his lands I have ever known. You do not deceive the people of Camelot, and you do not abuse them. If I were a numbering person, I would be adding those into the plus column."

He turned her on her back and looked into her eyes. "You are the best thing that has e'er happened to me, Isabel. I cannot even begin to say how much."

She smiled. "I hope that you always think so."

"I cannot imagine that ever changing."

There was a knock on her door. "Time is up, Countess," Mary called. "Do you want a bath, or no?"

Isabel scrambled out from under Arthur's arms. "Oh, yes, Mary, but please, a few minutes before you have the men bring in the water."

"Jeesh, you two," Mary said. "James and I have been married but two days, and it did not take this long."

"I will be happy to give James more tips, should you need," Arthur called, as he pulled on his leggings.

Mary giggled. "I will keep that in mind, should I need, King Arthur."

"And that," Isabel said, pulling on her robe, "is why you are a great king."

"The lovemaking tips?" he asked.

"No, the fact that Mary will probably have no problem asking you . . . should she need."

Arthur pulled his tunic over his head, then glanced around to make certain he had left nothing behind. Then he strode over to Isabel. "I love you. I wish for the day I do not have to leave your bed."

"I love you, too. I also wish for that day."

"You saved many Camelot lives yesterday, Isabel. Tonight we celebrate your success."

"No! The party tonight is for all! It was our success."

"One would think, wouldn't she? One who, perhaps, questions how to make lives better for all rather than one who presumes she already knows all."

"Arthur!"

"Tell her to get over it, Mary," he said as he left the room.

"Oh, right, good luck to me with that," Mary muttered as she entered.

"Mary!"

"Get over it. The king ordered so."

CHAPTER TWENTY-SEVEN

THE great hall, once again, looked amazing. The fire in the immense fireplace burned bright, the flowers were abundant and awesome, and the aroma in the air was truly delicious, not a single pig or chicken scent in the air.

"Is Ashton ready?" Isabel whispered to Gwen.

"As ready as any man, scared skinny at the thought," Gwen replied.

"And Jenny?"

"She knows nothing. But we had a long talk this day. She is aware that she will never lose her position, no matter the circumstances."

"Does she love him?"

"Do you love Arthur?"

Isabel stared at her.

"All right, that was not fair. I will ask an easier question. Do I love Lance?"

"I truly hope that you do. Because, Gwen, he is so in love with you."

"I do. I do not have a waking moment when I do not think of him. Nor many sleeping moments, for that matter."

"Good. He is a wonderful man. You two were meant to be together."

"Good. Now back to you and Arthur."

"You sound very much like Hester the Jester."

Gwen laughed, then sipped her wine. "That 'take my wife, please,' truly is getting old, do you not think?"

"You have no idea. I mean it, really. You have no idea."

"Now back to you and Arthur."

"How about we not go back to Arthur and me?"

"Isabel, you asked for honesty from me. I am merely asking that you are also as honest. I care for Arthur deeply. I know that I have already wounded him. I would truly hope that no other woman would scar him in that way again."

Isabel squeezed her eyes shut, then opened them again. "My honest answer is that I cannot predict the future, Gwen."

"He loves you, Isabel. Deeply. He has admitted as much to me."

"Fine," Isabel said, turning to face Gwen. "I love him. I love him more than I ever thought was possible. I would walk through fire for that man. Okay? Honest enough for you?"

It was a scene out of a really bad B movie. The music had stopped, the conversation had stopped. Everything in the freaking room had stopped. Except, apparently, Isabel's overly loud tirade.

She looked around, and the one face that stood out was Arthur's. And he was grinning.

"And *that*," she said to the entire room, "is the final line in that last play we put on in Dumont."

Nobody moved. "Okay, okay, so the play had a cheesy ending. But I didn't write it, so give me a break. Musicians? Please? Or for God's sake, where is Hester?"

"THANKS for stepping in there, homey," Isabel muttered when Arthur brought her a fresh goblet of wine.

"'Twas in a bit of shock. I did not realize that you put on plays in Dumont."

"Well, we do."

"And 'twas not a cheesy, as you say, ending to me. Sounded much more of a love story."

"Could be."

"One about a woman professing her love for a man."

"Could be."

"A woman who would walk through fire for her man."

"So you got the gist. Your point?"

"I would also walk through fire for my woman."

"And who would she be?"

"Take a wild guess. I give you two chances, and the first better not be Pix."

Her irritation sort of disappeared. Fast. "I am so sorry, Arthur," she said, finally looking up and facing him. "I never meant those words for anyone's ears but Gwen's."

"I know this. Do you know how proud and happy I am that the entire hall happened to overhear?"

"How is that possible? I could have just put both you and Gwen in jeopardy."

He shook his head. "No. We are soon to be free."

"Are you nuts?"

"I would hope those would be walnuts. I would kiss you mindlessly right now, but I made a promise to you earlier and must needs fulfill it."

And he did. He loped to the large table and jumped up on it, without using a single bench or chair.

"Ladies and gentlemen of Camelot, please have a listen."

The entire hall went eerily quiet.

"We have so many reasons to celebrate this night. We will begin with an important one. Ashton? Where be you?"

"I am here, my king," a voice came out of the crowd.

"Then get your bloody ass over here."

Arthur looked around. "Jenny, where are you?"

It just so happened Jenny was very near to Isabel. Isabel inched over. "Go with it, Jenny."

"May I have a sip of your wine, Countess?

"You mean Isabel. My name is Isabel."

"May I, Isabel, have a—"

Isabel thrust it at her. "Slug down all you want. Just remember that the word you need to pronounce correctly is 'yes.'"

Jenny did a great job of glugging. In fact, she completely drained Isabel's glass. Then she stood up tall, looking back once. "The word is?"

"Yes," Isabel said, nearly laughing.

"What is the question going to be?"

"Let it be a surprise," Isabel said, as she pushed the girl farther toward the table. "Just answer yes."

Jenny held up a thumb, "Got it, Isabel."

"WILL you exchange vows with me, Jenny? Will you agree to be my wife?"

Jenny looked back to that corner of the room to see both the countess and her queen nodding fervently.

"Yes," she said. "I want, very much, to be your wife."

Ashton stood from his bended knee. He pulled her to him and said, "Good gods, woman. What took you so long?"

"I wanted to be certain you meant it," she said.

Arthur bowed his head and chuckled, then glanced over at Isabel and Gwen, and smiled. They smiled back at him. Good gods, the women in his life. He did not know whether to feel blessed or afraid. Possibly he should feel a bit of both.

AFTER the celebration for Ashton and Jenny settled, Arthur again stood up upon the table.

"We have more to be thankful for this evening. We have peace without any Camelot blood shed." A roar from the crowd almost had Arthur wanting to cover his ears. He attempted to settle down the shouts by moving his arms up and down.

"Please, I care for my hearing and yours," he said. "A very, very low roar would be welcome. May we practice that?"

He received just as he asked.

"Excellent. Now, we had Countess Isabel to thank for much of this. Her quick thinking helped us."

"And our friends in the kitchens," Isabel yelled. "And the queen and Jenny and Mary. And all of you, willing to fight for Camelot and all it means to you."

"I was getting to that Isabel," Arthur said. "For once, just once, allow me."

"Sorry."

He shook his head. "The success yesterday came about because all of you, all of you, took part to keep Camelot safe. I am so proud of everyone and feeling so blessed that I count each and every one of you my friends. I am proud of my son, Mordred, who stepped up to a daunting challenge and succeeded beyond my wildest dreams."

Isabel looked around, finally finding Mordred standing still as a statue, staring at his father. She smiled. Their relationship was so going to be okay. Better than okay.

"When that day comes that I choose to retire from service to Camelot, I truly believe that Mordred will wear that crown well and continue the legacy that is Camelot.

"To Mordred! And to the men who willingly followed with him to carry out something of a distasteful task!" Arthur said.

"To Mordred and his men!" the people answered.

"Many more of these toasts, and there will be a hall full of lying-down drunk people," Isabel whispered to Gwen.

Gwen giggled, although her eyes roamed the hall.

Isabel didn't have to guess who Gwen was seeking out.

"He's over there, Gwen, by the entrance to the formal dining room."

Gwen looked over then nodded. "I so wish I could join him, Isabel. As I am certain you wish you could be at Arthur's side."

"I know, Gwen. I know. What a sorry pair we are, aren't we?"

"Or, depending on your thoughts, how lucky we are. We both have men who love us. There are many who cannot claim as much."

Isabel was stopped cold. "Wow, Gwen. Those are the wisest words I have heard in a long time. It truly puts things in perspective."

Gwen looked at her. "I was not born with wisdom, Isabel. But I have watched yours over the days and have tried to learn."

"Damn, I don't know about my own wisdom, Your Highness, but I can state for a fact that you are a supremely good student."

"If nothing else, Countess, you are the best model of wisdom I have e'er met."

Isabel laughed, then hugged her. "We will work this out."

"And, may I make just one more comment?" Gwen asked.

"Of course."

"You talk funny."

Isabel nearly bent over with laughter. "I know. And I thank you for trying to understand what I am saying."

"What 'I'm' saying is how you would actually pronounce it. You cut down your words in such an intriguing manner."

"Oh, Gwen, you would be head of the class."

"I will take that as a compliment, although I know not what that even means."

"Trust me, it's a compliment."

"And it is my turn, Isabel, to return the goodness in your heart. It is, as I have heard you say, a 'pay it forward' moment." She thrust her goblet of wine into Isabel's hands. "Here. Drink this. You might have need."

And while Isabel stood there, astonished, she watched Queen Guinevere push off from the wall and run to Arthur. She whispered in his ear, and he shook his head adamantly. But apparently Gwen was on a mission, and she was not to be denied. She dragged Arthur to the great table and climbed up, with his help. Then she gestured for him to join her.

Arthur looked over at Isabel with a "what the hell" expression she had no answer for. She shrugged her own confusion, then did as Gwen suggested. She took a major sip of that wine.

"All?" Gwen called out, then waited while those in the hall stopped their merriment to listen.

"I have a confession," Gwen said, "that needs to be told. You deserve the truth."

"Do not do this, Gwen," Isabel yelled, dreading what she feared Gwen's confession might be.

"That would be 'don't do this, Gwen,' to you, Isabel."

Arthur broke out laughing. "So you noticed as well?"

"We have all noticed that the countess speaks differently," said someone in the crowd. "But she speaks wisely."

"Correct, Christopher," Gwen said. "Another pouring of mead for Christopher, please."

"Gwen, what in Hades are you doing?" Arthur asked.

"Correcting a wrong," Gwen said.

"This is neither the time nor the place."

"This is the perfect time and place. For all here deserve the truth."

"Gwen, do not do this. The repercussions."

"Are something I can live . . . or die with. The lies, no."

"Good gods," Arthur said.

"Here is the truth, good people," Gwen announced. "I have been untrue to the kindest man I have e'er known. Our king."

Oh, for land fucking sakes, Isabel thought. *She feels the need to pour her heart out now?* Isabel drained Gwen's goblet, then asked for another. If there was a time to be drunk, this was it.

"I accept the consequences of this," Gwen continued. "Should you all decide to punish me, that is up to you. But I will not ever regret or rescind my love for . . . another."

Arthur planted his hand over her mouth, probably before she helped her executioners pick out just which ropes on which to hang her.

"Who is he?" several shouted. "We will hunt him and exact the punishment!"

"'Tis not treason!" Arthur yelled. "Not when I condoned that love. I knew and gave them full permission to follow their hearts. 'Tis *not* treason when your king said aye to them. I wanted, desperately, for the two to follow their hearts. Any who would lay harm to either will answer to me. How we resolve the issues will be up to us. This I demand. No harm to either. Is this understood by all?"

"Aye, King Arthur," many said.

"And while we are at admissions of truth," he began.

No, Arthur, please! Isabel thought, although she knew he and Gwen were on a truth-telling roll that was not about to end anytime soon.

Arthur glanced over at her first.

"I'll take Shut the Hell Up Right Now for a thousand, Arthur," she said.

"What is, no way, Countess?" he shouted back at her.

"Oh, good gods," she whispered.

Mary ran over to her and grabbed her hand. "'Tis for the best," she said.

"The best for whom?" Isabel asked.

"For all here. The queen had need to speak her heart. And by the by, you truly do talk funny."

"Great. And now you are turning on me as well, Mary?"

"Have you not been listening, Isabel? No one is turning on you. All are standing up for you."

"I'm sorry, Mary," Isabel said. "I just don't want the king and queen to be scorned by the people of Camelot."

"HERE is the rub, ladies and gentlemen," Arthur said, figuring he wasn't letting Gwen fall on the sword alone. He knew not what provoked her unhealthy honesty, but if she felt the need to spill to all, he was not allowing her to do it by herself. "I have also found myself deeply in love. 'Twas not meant to happen, I did not seek it out, but the fates decreed it so.

"Can you believe I have fallen for that funny-speaking woman?" he asked, pointing straight at Isabel. "'Tis true. I am desperately in love with Countess Isabel. And Queen Guinevere is in love with another. We are all happy about it. So should one of you set out to harm the queen or the countess while we work out the details to make certain the right men are with the right women, I will invoke my power as king. We have the right to certain mistakes in the past and the right to fix those mistakes to the happiness of all. Should any hold judgment against our women, take a good hard look into your very own hearts."

"Happiness to all!" James bellowed, holding up his stein. "'Tis what Camelot is about, after all."

"Happiness to all!" most, if not all, of the guests, called, also holding up their various steins and goblets in toast.

But Arthur noticed that way too many people were now looking askance at Isabel, as if she had sprung straight out of Hades. "Do not," he warned again, "cast blame against Gwen or Isabel. You do so at your own peril. For the people who know us best will be at our sides. Now please enjoy the rest of the evening," Arthur said. "And remember to tell the ones you love just how much. Often."

He jumped down and headed straight to his woman. He probably should have been prepared for the thump to his chest he received upon his arrival. He was not.

"Ow!"

"What were you thinking, Arthur?"

"Just, perhaps, some form of happiness that I was honest about my feelings for you?

"Did it even occur to you what might happen to Gwen?"

"Did you not note that 'twas Gwen who made the decision to announce her feelings first?"

"Okay, that's true. What in hell was that all about?"

"I was not standing over here talking to her. You were. How about you tell me?"

"She wanted to be truthful to the people of Camelot, is my guess," Mary said. "Do not blame Isabel, as I saw her attempt to stop the queen. Or you answer to me. Your Highness," she added with a slight curtsy. "Shall I stay, Isabel?" she asked.

"I think I can handle him," Isabel said with a grin. "But thank you, Mary."

Mary glanced back and forth between them. "Okay, I shall be right over there with that very large, very strong, very loyal man, in case you have need, Isabel." She stomped away.

"Why do I feel as if I am suddenly the bad guy, here?" Arthur said.

Isabel shook her head, laughing. "Not the bad guy, Arthur. But why, for crying out loud? You couldn't just say, 'I support Gwen, end of story.'"

"Because once she decided to say as she did, my only choice was to announce that I too am in love with another, so the people did not consider her the only one who had broken vows."

"So it was more for her protection?"

"Not more, but as much. It feels as if . . . I do not know . . . the truth will set you free?"

"Oh, boy, hate to say it, but I have a feeling that in the long run you aren't going to get the credit for that one. Damn shame."

"My pardon?"

"Never mind. At any rate, do you feel set free? Because personally I feel about a hundred sets of eyes staring daggers at me."

"Should any try to harm you, they must go through me first. I love you, Isabel. And, yes, I do feel set free. Hiding my feelings for you does not sit well. I would like to be able to let the world know my true feelings for my true love."

"Well, I'm pretty sure the Camelot world is now well aware."

He shrugged. "The ruse is over. We have no need to hide behind closed doors and in public live a lie. That does not sit well with you?"

"I could have lived with it for a while longer."

"Why?"

"Because I'm afraid for you, you big oaf. This undermines your status as king."

"I would be happy to turn the crown over to Mordred this moment if it means being free to live the rest of my days with you."

"Oh, Arthur, don't you see? That's exactly the type of thing I don't want to be responsible for. Camelot needs you. And you, whether you believe or realize it, need Camelot."

"Not as I need you, Isabel. Camelot is but land. You, you are my heart. You are . . . my everything."

She laughed, and the musical sound of it, the beauty of her, from the inside all the way to the outer beauty, had his heart pounding.

"You know, witty man," she said, "if this king thing doesn't pan out, you have a great future as a songwriter."

He grinned. "I have absolutely not one clue what that means, but I will just assume it is a good thing, and we can move on from there."

"Deal."

"Would you care to move upstairs?"

"While fifty gazillion people are watching every twitch we make? I think not."

"Later?"

"Oh, definitely. Without question." She moved closer and whispered in his ear, "In fact, your Highness, should you not appear, there will be dire consequences."

"Oh, I am frightened. I will—"

"Arthur! Arthur! Please . . . help."

He turned to see Gwen, distraught as he had ne'er seen her afore.

"What's wrong, Gwen?" Isabel asked.

"They . . . they have Lance. And they are threatening—"

"Where?"

"In the bailey."

Arthur ran. "James! Mordred!" he yelled. "I have need of you." He glanced back. "And, Isabel, you stay put," he demanded as he realized she was running right behind him and beside Gwen.

"Just try to stop me, big boy."

Good gods, he was in for the ride of a lifetime with that woman. He could not wait to enjoy the journey.

James and Mordred both caught up to him as they all left the castle and entered the bailey.

Two men were holding on to Lance as he struggled to break free.

"Leave off, Michael, David. Now! Release him."

"My lord, he has betrayed you!" Michael said. "He must be punished. It is king's law."

"Are you deaf?" Isabel yelled. "The king has told you to release him."

Arthur nearly groaned. "Isabel . . ."

"Well, you did! I heard it! Did you not hear it, Mordred?"

"I did, Countess."

"James?"

"I, too, heard it. Michael, David, should you defy your king's order, you are in much more trouble than you care to imagine."

"Betraying our king is treason," Michael shouted.

"As is defying his direct order," James said. "Do you not release this man, you are guilty of such."

That stopped them. They took their hands from Lance's arms.

"Thank you," Arthur said. "And listen to me. Listen well, my friends. I do truly appreciate your loyalty, but in this case it is misplaced. Sir Lancelot is a true and loyal soldier, committed to Camelot. Just yesterday he was willing to battle to save our land, and both of you, should you have needed his aid, he would have . . . would have . . ."

"He would have had your backs," Isabel said.

Arthur did groan this time. "Thank you, Countess. Allow me to take it from here?"

"All yours."

He heard Gwen's soft sobbing and Isabel saying, "It's okay now, Gwen. All is well. Arthur is on the case."

He nearly laughed, because he knew not what that meant, either, and by the puzzled looks both James and his son shot him, he was not alone in this. Thank goodness 'twas not just him.

"Lancelot has not betrayed me or Camelot. He merely followed his heart. With my complete acceptance. You will not, you will *not* attempt to punish him for something that I do not find a grievance against me or Camelot. Do you understand me?"

"Yes, m'lord," Michael mumbled.

"Yes, King Arthur," David said. "We but wanted to show our loyalty to our king."

"I very much appreciate that. But 'tis not necessary. Yet please understand that I care very much for the good health and well-being of Sir Lancelot, and will take very harsh measures to any who would harm him. Is that clear to one and all who are standing about listening?"

Which, as it happened, 'twas many.

"Yea," those many answered.

"The laws of Camelot are about to take a turn. I will not announce at this moment what they entail, but I assure you that neither Lance, nor Gwen, nor Isabel, nor I, for that matter, are guilty of any crime against the crown. We merely"—he shook his head, not quite certain what the correct words were, and would not you know it, Isabel chose this time to remain silent—"chose to take differing paths to happiness.

"I believe that every human deserves to choose which path, do you not think?"

"Hell, yes," Isabel said.

"And now she speaks up," he said to Mordred.

Mordred grinned. "You must admit, Father, she chooses her moments rather well."

He pulled his son to him and gave him a hug. But not for Isabel choosing moments, the rift between them might still be a relentless divide. "I fear I am never going to tame that woman," he said.

"I have high hopes you do not," Mordred said. "Life would be so dull around here."

He released Mordred, his heart full. For the newfound relationship with his son and the promise of many tomorrows with Isabel.

He raised his hands. "Then we are all now of the same mind? No harm shall befall Lance."

"Yea, my king," many said.

"Good. The drama is over. Please return to your regularly scheduled feasting. I hear there is much pickled eel to be had at the tables."

He turned, grinning, knowing he was going to pay mightily for that last jest. He could not wait.

Isabel was still holding on to Gwen, who was still crying in her arms.

"Gwen, see to Lance," he said. "I have this notion he could use your care at this moment."

At the tap on his shoulder, he turned back. Lance looked at him, his eyes still troubled. "I am so sorry, King Arthur."

"'Twas not your fault, Lance. None of this was. I am only sorry that you had to suffer the humiliation of this event. Now please, you and Gwen get out of here. Go to the cottage. Go wherever you choose. Just go and celebrate that Gwen loves you so much that she risked death to proclaim her feelings for you."

"I ne'er meant—"

"I know. Trust me, I know. And trust also that I am not unhappy. I hold not one bit of ill will. This I swear on my crown."

Lance lowered his head. "You appear very happy indeed, m'lord."

"That I am, Lance."

"You know that I pledge—"

"Yes, yes, I know. And I am grateful. Now go grab Gwen afore she has Isabel wet head to toe with her tears."

ISABEL couldn't love a man more. Not a single ounce more. She didn't know what the future held, she only knew she had never been happier in her life.

"I am so mad at you," she decided to say to Arthur as the crowd dispersed.

"Why am I so not shocked to hear that, Countess?"

"Would you like to hear why?"

"Have I a choice? If so, I choose no."

"Too bad," she said, but she couldn't help grinning.

"Now see, I expected this. What have I done now?"

"You have made it impossible not to love you."

"Does it ever, even for a moment, occur to you that you make no sense at times?"

"Oh, I've lived with that one all my life."

"So this is a bad thing. Your love for me. My love for you."

"No, that's the good thing."

"Okay, I am having you committed," he said.

"You shouldn't even know what that means. For crimes against humanity?"

"For crimes against sanity. Why, then, are you angry with me?"

"Because, m'lord, you are so wonderful, it makes my heart crazy. I have more of a cardio workout just watching you be you than I ever have on my NordicTrack."

"Once again, no sense."

"I love you so much."

"Oh, I definitely do understand that one. And I return that feeling, more than tenfold. May I ask what brought on this . . . strange conversation?"

"I admire everything about you. I love everything about you. The way you handle and care for your people, the way you want to make the world a better place, the way you believe in honesty, just everything."

He stopped her. "Are you truly weeping, Isabel?"

"May I lie?" she asked, trying desperately to get the tears under control.

"You could. But then you would be lying."

"Oh, man, your logic simply amazes me."

"What is it? Please, help me here, love. I admit I am at a loss."

"Come on, Father, she is happily in love with you. Any idiot would be able to see that."

"What he said," Isabel said.

"Thank you much for that explanation, my son. Now I understand completely."

He pulled her close, and Isabel marveled that his warmth and scent was engrained in her memory forever.

"Your warmth and scent are so much a part of me," Arthur said.

She knew—she didn't know how she knew, but she did—somehow this all was coming to an end.

Viviane, tell me what is true. Am I about to lose Arthur to you?

Merlin is happy, he is up and about. He is so grateful to you, he wants to shout.

But, what is going on, is my mission done, so that now you are willing me gone?

Trust, Isabel, trust that 'twill work for all. Remember the necklace, then you make the call.

Great. Just fucking great. She had just found love and somehow she was about to be forced to make a decision. She didn't know what, she knew only that she soon had to make a choice.

She had, as she saw it, fulfilled her part of the bargain. Okay, maybe not quite, since she'd been asked to do one thing and managed to do quite something else. But holy hell, just what had she done so wrong that the universe wanted to laugh by allowing her to love and then possibly stripping it from her? Well, at least she'd known it. She supposed that was a prize more valuable than anything. She had to thank Viviane for that.

Okay, thank you.

Merlin cannot to begin to thank you, Isabel. And I cannot thank you enough as well.

She looked up at Arthur and stroked his face. "Just know that I love you."

"I again do not understand," he said. "I believe that with all my heart. Why are you speaking as if you expect disaster to strike?"

"King Arthur!" a man called.

He turned, pulling her behind him.

"Yes? Show yourself, please."

"You killed my king, Richard, and you will pay for that crime."

"No!" Isabel screamed. "It was me. If you want revenge, take it out on me!"

"Shut up, Isabel," Arthur said. "Just this once, shut up."

She heard the arrow whizzing toward Arthur the moment it left the man's bow.

"No!" she heard Mordred say as he sailed into the air before his father and took the arrow right into his shoulder.

"James!" she screamed. "Go get that sonofabitch. And, please, beat him to a bloody pulp."

She and Arthur kneeled down over Mordred, who had a freaking arrow in his shoulder.

"No, Arthur, do not pull it out yet. It could well kill him."

"Then what? I cannot allow my son to die."

"I . . . love you, Father," Mordred said.

"I love you, son. Please do not do anything stupid like die on me."

And Isabel knew what she had to do.

"He will not die," she said. Then she spoke the words that would release the necklace. "*Lady of the Lake, this must be done for love and life for all to have won.*"

She yanked the necklace from around her neck, and then cracked it over and over until the pendant broke. She held it over his shoulder, allowing Viviane's tears to drop on his wound.

"You will not die, Mordred," she whispered as she felt life slipping away from her own body. "Your father needs you." She looked up for what she realized was the final time. "He will heal. I love you, Arthur."

"Isabel!" was the last thing she heard before she left Camelot forever.

Epilogue

Drowning was a truly sucky way to die. But Isabel was beginning to resign herself to it, as she drifted into oxygen-deprived euphoria.

Good gods, she'd had the most incredible dream during her dying process. She just wished she'd lived long enough to actually explain it.

Please, Lady, allow me my memories.

And the memories came back to her in clips. Arthur laughing, Arthur grinning, Arthur frowning and, best of all, Arthur winking.

No, wait, Arthur loving her like she had never felt loved before. The way he touched her, seemingly worshipping her. The way he became feverish with need, and those green eyes, gazing down into hers as he was inside her, making the ultimate love.

Thank you, Lady.

Would you care more to recall?

Oh, Lady, I want it all.

She found the most amazing thoughts going through her dying brain.

The way he had professed his love to her, over and over, in sometimes the kookiest ways.

She really should have gotten to know more of the people at Camelot, she decided. She'd bet just about all of them were as good and kind as James and Mary.

None as Arthur, though. The way he had laughed at her dumb jokes. It was so sweet he did that, even though he probably hadn't understood half, at least.

The way he'd accepted her stubbornness, even when any other man would have given up on her.

Oh, man, she'd loved him to the end. She hoped beyond hope that he'd known.

He knew. Isabel, he knew; he knew your love for him was true. You gave up your life to save the son, and that then your mission in Camelot was done.

Oh, well then, that was just peachy.

She didn't know what was going to happen next. She only hoped, badly, that she got to keep her memories, no matter where she was heading next.

And then something strange. It was almost like she felt banging against her SUV. She thought she felt hands grabbing her, and then an arm wrapped around her waist. It felt amazingly familiar. And that arm pulled her up, up, up, out of the water.

The next thing she knew, she was coughing and choking and spitting out water.

"Ma'am? Ma'am?"

She opened her eyes.

"Ma'am, we're here to help. Welcome back. You are going to be all right."

She was staring up into deep green eyes, eyes she had first spotted in a forest long ago and very far away. His hair was dripping, his clothing soaked.

Her hand raised to touch his face. "Arthur?" she whispered.

He sat back. "Yes, how did you know that?"

"That rescue was beyond excellent, Father. She looks okay to me." Isabel turned her head. "And he is Mordred, right?"

Mordred laughed. "I'm sorry to say, yes. How did she know, Father?"

"I have no clue, son."

"You never did, you big oaf."

Arthur just stared at her. Then he brushed her wet hair back from her cheeks.

"Oh, my lands, Father. She is the woman you dream of constantly. Your description of her . . . it matches exactly."

"There isn't a chance your name is Isabel, is there?" Arthur asked.

"As a matter of fact, it is."

"Good gods. Welcome back to the land of the living, Isabel."

"I'm glad to be here" she said. "By the way, where is here?"

"Grand Lake, in Oklahoma, ma'am"

"Isabel. My name is Isabel."

Arthur checked her neck and then lifted her into his arms. "It is very good to meet you, Isabel. Now let's get you to the hospital."

"What's wrong with Mordred's arm?" she asked, seeing that it was in a sling.

"He was foolish enough to step between me and a hunting arrow when we were hiking last weekend."

"Of course. Did you catch the idiot hunting with a bow and arrow?"

"Our friend James did," Mordred said. "Practically beat the man to a bloody pulp. It isn't even bow-hunting season."

"Of course."

"This is really uncanny. My father even dreamed one time that he'd have to perform CPR on you."

"Mordred?" Arthur said. "Can it."

"Thank you. But I really don't want to go to the hospital," Isabel said. "Thanks to you, I feel much better now."

"I'm pretty sure Mary won't allow you to walk away. Or James. They are the EMTs waiting to offer you a chauffeur-driven ambulance ride to County General."

"Of course. Where are Gwen and Lance?"

He stopped. "How could you know these names, Isabel?"

Good question. "I had this dream. This really great dream."

"I know the feeling. Gwen is likely at her shop."

"Let me guess. A florist shop?"

"My God. This is becoming beyond weird."

"And Lance?"

"And Lance is probably operating on a patient as we speak. Orthopedic surgeon."

Isabel chuckled. "Of course. He was always really good with sharp objects."

"Let's go, King Arthur," Mary called. "The woman needs treatment."

"King Arthur?"

Arthur rolled his eyes. "A very stupid name they gave me years ago when I was named chief of the fire department. They think it's funny. I find it a little irritating. But just try to stop them. I'm telling you, I have no idea when I lost control of my people."

Isabel grinned. "I've always felt that the sign of a good leader is when the people who work for him feel comfortable teasing him."

He shook his head. "This is so strange. You said something close to that to me in my dream once."

"Strange in a really cool way, though, don't you think, Father? It's like fate."

"This is going to sound like a bad pick-up line, Isabel, but I'm going to say it regardless."

"Say it."

"Have we met?" he asked, his eyes twinkling.

She grinned. "It appears we have," she said.

"I would really like to meet again so we can figure out how we know each other. As soon as you're better, maybe dinner?" Then he shook his head. "I can't believe I'm even asking. Trust me, I don't make a habit of asking women I rescue to go out with me."

"Good. Then I'm the lucky one. But a question first."

"All right."

"How do you feel about picked eel?"

He frowned. "I've never heard of it. But it sounds disgusting."

"Excellent answer. Dinner it is."

"Is she the woman of your dreams, Father?" Mordred asked.

He looked down at her. "She could very well be, son. Although I don't remember the woman in my dreams ever being quite this wet. Somehat wet once, but not this wet. Tell me, Isabel, do you believe in fate?"

"Oh, most definitely," she answered, then realizing that that little dunk in the lake took more out of her than she'd thought, she laid her head against his chest.

Yes, I believe in fate. With a little help from my friends. I can't thank you enough, Viviane.

I told you to trust, Isabel, to trust me that all would be well.

And Merlin, how is he?

I am happy to report, as well as me. And now, Isabel, move forward with your life. I am thinking that perhaps you'll make a good wife. I thank you so much for all you have done; I believe that this day, all you hold dear has won. It is time, Isabel, for us to part ways, but I leave you knowing happiness is yours for the rest of your days.

I am really going to miss you, Viviane. Thanks for the adventure.

But sadly, she got no answer.

Arthur laid her down on the ambulance gurney.

Standing on either side of it were Mary and James, and Isabel nearly started crying with happiness. "Boy, am I glad to see you guys."

"Now that's something we don't hear every day, is it, James?" Mary said as she laid a blanket over her patient.

"Sure isn't."

"What's your name, ma'am?" Mary asked, peering at her closely.

"Her name is Isabel," Arthur said.

Both Mary and James went still. "Isabel? As in the name of the woman you keep dreaming about?" Mary asked, looking at her even more intently.

It became abundantly clear that Arthur had been bothered by these dreams enough that he'd described them in some detail to his closest friends.

"We're going to try to figure that out. I'm riding in back with her."

"Honestly, I don't need to go to the hospital."

"Amuse us," James said.

They lifted her up and into the ambulance, and then Mary climbed up and locked the gurney into place.

"How are you at hair, Mary?" Isabel asked.

Mary stared down at her and then burst out laughing. "How did you know?"

"Just a hunch."

"Pretty good. I cut the hair of all of these doofuses. Why, would you like me to cut yours someday?"

"I would love it."

Mary nodded. "I think I'd like that. A lot."

She performed all kinds of vitals checking, then listened to Isabel's lungs. "How do you feel?"

"Tired, but strangely, really, really happy."

"Cheating death has a way of making people feel that way. You were damn lucky Arthur just happened to be driving by and saw you take the header."

"Lucky, yes."

"Or maybe, just maybe, it was something else," Mary speculated. "Arthur has been having these premonitions for a couple of months now. Well, he called them dreams, but . . . who knows?"

"How's our patient?" Arthur asked, climbing in and sitting on the bench.

"Lungs surprisingly clear, heart rate slightly elevated, but you tend to have that effect on damsels in distress." She opened a cabinet above her head and pulled out a blanket, tossing it to him. "She definitely needs to be checked out at the hospital, but I would bet she'll be released within an hour."

She climbed down from the back of the ambulance. "Not exactly protocol, but I see no reason not to ride up front with James. I think she's in good hands."

"Thanks, Mary," Arthur said.

Mary winked and slammed the doors.

Arthur waited a second, then smiled down at Isabel, that heart-poundingly handsome smile that she had fallen for so long ago.

He took her hand. "Seriously, how do you feel?"

"Surprisingly wonderful."

"You look surprisingly wonderful."

"I'm sure I look like a drowned rat." She glanced away, then back. "Thank you, Arthur, for saving my life."

"Thank you for surviving." He shook his head, but his gaze never wavered from hers. "Have you ever just looked at someone and you knew, somehow, you just knew?"

She didn't even need to ask, "Knew what?" She nodded. "Yes, I have. Once, a very long time ago. And then again today, when I opened my eyes on the banks of Grand Lake."

"I know it sounds crazy, Isabel, but my son was not exaggerating. I have had so many dreams about you, every day I would search for you in the crowds, in restaurants, just everywhere I went. I couldn't believe it when I pulled you out of the lake and got a good look at you. And then fear, like nothing I've felt in my entire career, took over. I was so scared that I would lose you, just when finally, finally I found you."

"Well, guess what, Arthur. I'm here, and I'm not going anywhere. Not this time."

He squeezed his eyes shut, then opened them again. "I am determined to hold you to that, Isabel. I have this overwhelming desire to make you vow to it."

"I vow."

"I'm seriously guessing it's too early to ask you to marry me."

"Not really. As long as you promise me I won't ever have to eat pickled eel."

"I swear."

"Then to thee I vow."

AND within weeks they exchanged those vows, Mary and James stood at their sides.